FAMILY FEELING

Anyone watching the two well-dressed, white-haired people touch glasses in a toast could have guessed that they might be Van Alens. You could tell they were accustomed to good living—something about the coloring, skins that had known a good deal of sun, and more, something about the way they held themselves, erect but relaxed.

When they had drunk their toast, Aaron said, "The real reason I wanted to meet you here is that I've news for you. I'm going to Europe. . . ."

Sally's eyebrows arched slightly. "It couldn't have anything to do with your visits to your old friend in the White House, President Wilson, could it?"

"As to that," Aaron replied, "I can't say, but—"

"Then I won't ask, but take me along, Aaron, please. I so would love to see England again."

"I was going to suggest it myself, but with the Lusitania sinking, I was afraid you might not want to come."

"Why not?" Sally Van Alen said archly. "We have been through rather a lot, and, you know, Van Alens aren't supposed to lose their nerve . . ."

THE VAN ALENS

BY SAMUEL A. SCHREINER, JR.

ZEBRA BOOKS
KENSINGTON PUBLISHING CORP.

ZEBRA BOOKS

are published by

KENSINGTON PUBLISHING CORP.
475 Park Avenue South
New York, N.Y. 10016

Printed in the United States of America

*For my father, the late Samuel A. Schreiner,
who passed along to me his love for the written word
and his fascination with history*

There was—and is—a very real Van Alen family that throughout history has played a prominent part in the affairs of Kinderhook and New York and Newport and, no doubt, many other places in these United States. I'm acutely aware of this since my wife, the former Doris Ann Moon, is herself descended from the Kinderhook Van Alens who were related to America's first Dutch president, Martin Van Buren. It was, in fact, my wife's relationship that inspired me to choose a Dutch family's eyes through which to view the drama of an expanding city within an expanding country, and to use the name Van Alen.

That having been said, I must assure all actual Van Alens, as well as all readers, that the Van Alens in this story, and those in its predecessor, *The Possessors and The Possessed*, are wholly a product of the author's imagination, unlike some of the other characters such as another Dutch president, Theodore Roosevelt, with whom they come in contact. Nevertheless, one of the author's greatest gratifications came when his mother-in-law, Carrie Conklin Moon, after finishing the first volume in the annals of the fictional Van Alens, said, "Why, your Sally is just like my great aunt Sarah Van Alen!"

In addition to expressing my thanks to my wife and her family for the loan of the name, I should also salute my wife's forebearance in allowing me to live so long and so intimately with the people of my imagination. For those I've taken out of history, I must again thank the cooperative staff of the Darien Library who provided much of the research material upon which I relied.

—Samuel A. Schreiner, Jr.
Darien, Conn.—April, 1981

Prelude

SALLY SCHUYLER Van Alen Brewster Hancock, the sometime Duchess of Midstone, had taken to meeting her brother Aaron regularly in the Peacock Alley of the Waldorf-Astoria Hotel down at Thirty-fourth and Fifth Avenue now that a woman, at least of her stripe, could have a cocktail and cigarette in public without causing a riot. On a particular Saturday in May, 1915, Sally pushed her way impatiently through the crowds on the avenue, ignoring the newsboys crying yet another extra about the sinking of the *Lusitania*. She had already read the gruesome details—what there was of them so far—and she could hardly wait to see what Aaron thought of it. Besides, she could use a drink.

Aaron was already there at a little table with a whiskey and soda in front of him; the stubs of half a dozen cigarettes littered his ashtray. He ground out yet another one as he rose to pull back her chair. "My God, Sally, isn't it lucky that you didn't go? What'll you have?"

"Something with gin," she said. "And give me a cigarette, will you? I'm still in kind of a daze."

"And well you might be. You got through to Charlie after you canceled out, didn't you?"

"Oh, yes. I've got his reply to my cable right here in my purse. Good show, mother, too many bloody subs about, he said. But I did very much want to see him before he went over. Can you imagine a man over forty with a family going to the front, even if he is a colonel?"

"It's the glory of the British upper classes. In war, at least, they do their share. Wonder how *we're* going to behave, because, no matter what Wilson says now, this *Lusitania* business means war."

"What I wonder is how I would have behaved if I'd been on that ship. You heard that they haven't found Alfred Vanderbilt, even his body?"

"Yes . . . This isn't my first whiskey of the day, I'm afraid. I knew Al, you know—not well but he came to me for some coaching tips when he first got into it. I read the testimony of some survivor who says she saw him help a woman into a boat and then calmly light a cigarette and stroll back along the deck. The thing is, Vanderbilt couldn't swim," Aaron said.

"God, neither can I—at my age," Sally said. "He was just going over for some kind of horse show, wasn't he?"

"So I understand. Well, something has to matter in your life, doesn't it? With Al, it was horses, though he was just getting involved with racing cars. Too bad, he was one of the nicer of the Vanderbilts. What I want to know is why you didn't go. Last I

10

heard you were all set. You didn't have a premonition or something, did you?"

"No, nothing like that. I had a reporter phone me this morning and ask the same question, and I told him that I didn't go because I can read. You probably didn't notice, but right beside the Cunard ad for the *Lusitania*'s sailing was an ad by the Imperial German Embassy in Washington—a warning that the war zone included the waters around the British Isles, that any ship flying the British flag was liable to destruction, that passengers would be traveling at their own risk. Well, from my experience, Germans usually mean what they say. . . ."

"So brother James says . . ."

"He would, wouldn't he? So you think this really means war?"

"Yes. Not right away perhaps, but if the Germans go on killing innocent people, we won't be able to tolerate it. And no matter how it ends, the war will change everything. . . . I think our kind went down with the *Lusitania*—poor Vanderbilt just stood in for the rest of us. The *Lusitania*'s sailing, bands playing and champagne flowing, in the face of all plain warnings, was almost an act of arrogance—a symbol of the feeling that the rich and powerful can escape from common destiny. Well, they can't—and didn't. All it took was one lousy torpedo."

"I might agree with you," Sally said, "but I just wish you wouldn't say 'our kind.'"

"Sally, we're different, but we are, after all, Van Alens—very different but in a sense all the same. . . . But let's have a toast to your survival. Remember how the first Sally, our grandmother,

11

used to say that survival is what really matters?"

Anyone watching these two well-dressed, white-haired people touch glasses could have guessed that they might be Van Alens. You could tell they were accustomed to good living—something about the coloring, skins that had known a good deal of sun, and more, something about the way they held themselves, erect but relaxed. Anyone could have guessed too that they were brother and sister—same long nose, same jutting jaw, same high cheekbones. If they had overheard the name, almost anyone in that room would have understood what Aaron was trying to say: for as long as there had been a Roosevelt, for longer than there had been an Astor or a Vanderbilt or a Morgan or a Carnegie or a Rockefeller or a Frick or a Belmont or a Gould, there had been a Van Alen prominent in the society and commerce of New York. But only people who knew them intimately could have understood what Sally was trying to say.

When they had drunk their toast, Aaron said, "The real reason I wanted to meet you here is that I've news for you. *I'm* going to Europe. . . ."

"It couldn't have anything to do with your visits to your old friend in the White House, President Wilson, could it?"

"As to that, I can't say, but—"

"Then I won't ask, but take me along, Aaron, please. You know how I'd love to see Charlie and Matty, and . . ."

"That's just what I was going to suggest. It would be a help to me if you did come, but I was afraid you might not want to after this—"

"Why not? Van Alens aren't supposed to lose their nerve."

"You're right," Aaron said. "Anyway, we've been through rather a lot together, haven't we, sis? So I guess we can make it one more time."

It was typical Van Alen understatement, but it called for another toast before they rose to go. No doubt people around them supposed that they were thoughtlessly celebrating some private stroke of good fortune in the midst of the unfolding disaster of the *Lusitania*'s sinking; the world never touched people who looked like *that*. It would be hard to convince anyone just looking at these handsome, smiling Van Alens that they were drinking, instead, to having made it this far through lives as peculiar and precarious as any among New York's millions, even though they did begin in a marbled mansion. . . .

Chapter 1

"*I NEVER* expected to die in a place like this,"
Sally Schuyler Van Alen told her son Peter on the
day in 1867 when they moved her up from Twenty-
second Street to the new house on Fifth Avenue.
Though covering only thirty blocks or so, the trip
itself, she felt, would hasten her end. Perhaps that
was her own fault since she'd insisted on getting up,
having young Sally dress her and letting her
grandsons carry her to the family carriage rather
than going through with her son Peter's plan to
move her, bed and all, in one of those ambulances
that doubled as hearses. "When I go out of
anywhere feet first, I don't want to know about it,"
she'd said in an effort at grim humor. But she'd been
so dizzy, in such pain with the arthritis that flared
with every movement, so confused by the noise and
bustle in the streets that she knew she'd made a
mistake. She knew, too, that she *would* die in this
great, echoing palace into which they were carrying
her.

Unlike the other members of the family, bedridden Sally had seen nothing of the Van Alen residence while it was building, and its true magnificence came to her as something of a shock. Peter, of course, had come up to her room many times during the last year or so and had proudly unrolled on her bed the plans and redrafts of plans; his wife Martha had shown her swatches of the silk that would be used for draperies and wall coverings and even some samples of the ornate ormolu that would edge the mirrors and trim the cornices; their daughter, young Sally, had raved to her about the size and splendor of the ballroom in which a hundred couples could dance at once; and James, their older son, had revealed to her, in a sort of awed pride, the rising total of the bills coming in from architects, carpenters, stone masons, roofers, plumbers, gardeners, decorators—$500,000 or more so far, a figure that exceeded the entire Van Alen fortune when she'd last been fully aware of family affairs. Only her younger grandson, Aaron, was reluctant to talk about the new place, because, like herself, he had no desire to move. The old and the young, so often together in wanting desperately to hang on to what they knew, she thought.

"The way you say that doesn't sound like you approve, mother. I was so hoping that you would," Peter said to her.

There was no use trying to tell him what she really felt, no use at all. If anybody deserved a place like this, her son Peter did after what he'd sacrificed to the making of money, and any criticism she might offer would only dampen his obvious joy in it.

"I didn't mean it that way, Peter. I meant . . . why, royalty could expire here with dignity. It's so . . . so grand."

"Yes, isn't it?" he said with no trace of false modesty. "I thought it was time that the Van Alens stopped hiding their light under a bushel. I just wish you could get around to enjoy it. But maybe you will, maybe it's the incentive you need."

Peter, dear Peter. He would never give up on her. He thought that being eighty-seven years old was a temporary illness. It was only in the last year that he'd allowed her to retire from the board of directors of Van Alen & Son and then under protest. He'd gone so far as to hold board meetings in the cramped quarters of her bedroom to accommodate her, and it was young James who had finally brought matters to a head by letting it be known that this peculiar arrangement was causing ridicule in business circles around town. Peter Schuyler Van Alen wasn't the man his brother Cornelius had been, they were saying; Cornelius would never have let a little old lady run the company. Of course, James didn't quite put it that way, but that was the message, and, of course, James protested—a little too much, she thought—that nobody loved her more than he, but the younger men of affairs in New York didn't know her and got the wrong impression. It was time anyway, particularly now that James could take her seat on the board. The way things had been going for the company in the last year had not only justified her retirement but had, apparently, justified Peter's lavish outlays on this house.

When Peter and Martha had first brought up

their plans to build on Fifth Avenue, they had gone to some lengths to make it look like some sort of an economy that they couldn't pass up. True, the opportunity had come to them through Martha's father, the Reverend Doctor James Schuyler, who leaked the news that the trustees of his Uptown Presbyterian Church might be receptive to a reasonable offer on the corner lot next to the manse since Dr. Schuyler no longer kept a horse in the stable there. The present board of trustees, or so Dr. Schuyler contended, wanted to see the land in the hands of a good Christian family, and who would be better qualified than the pastor's own daughter? Martha's sisters weren't in a position to make even a reasonable offer, and only the oldest heads in the congregation retained any memory of the slight scandal surrounding Martha's elopement with her cousin, Peter Schuyler Van Alen. In the years since, Peter had earned an enviable reputation as one of the city's few honest aldermen and as a member of the Sanitary Commission that had done so much for the boys in blue during the War, and Martha had become one of New York's most prominent hostesses and, through her work with the Philharmonic Society, art patrons. During most of this time the Van Alen family had occupied a front pew in the church, and Dr. Schuyler was as sure as a man could be sure of anything that they could have the lot for what amounted to a song. But they'd have to act fast since he was afraid that some of the newer business types coming onto the board of trustees would want to take advantage of the leaping land values along the avenue without regard to the spiritual qualifications of the purchaser. "So you see, Aunt Sally," Martha told her mother-in-law, "it's like the Lord's leading, though I know you don't believe in that. We really ought to take advantage of it. Everybody's moving uptown. Think what it will mean for Sally when she comes out, and Aaron will be near a better school . . ."

Martha had been so earnest, so innocent of irony, that Sally had forced herself to suppress a smile. It wouldn't do to remind Martha of the time she came running to Sally with a letter from her holy father disowning her for eloping with a disreputable atheistic journalist and threatening to cane Peter on sight. Martha had been so sure of herself then, and still was, that she hadn't taken the letter too seriously, and of course she had been right. Martha was one of those women who knew what she wanted and got it, not by being mean but simply by prevailing. She never thought about principles. To Martha it was only natural that the Reverend Doctor Schuyler's pride in his daughter's social prominence and in his namesake, James, would overcome his belief in all those silly biblical rules by which nobody really lived. To Martha it was only sensible that she and Peter and their children, whatever their private thoughts, should avail themselves of the respectability and exposure guaranteed by attendance at the Uptown Presbyterian Church ever since the days when Governor DeWitt Clinton had graced its sanctuary with his presence. No, Sally wouldn't smile except to herself. On the whole, Martha had been good for Peter, who like herself was too prone to doubts, too scornful of the essential hypocrisies

19

that went into the making of what people called success. If, in fact, there was anything Sally did like about this move, it was the literally concrete evidence that her son's house, casting the manse into shadow, would offer that life had a way of triumphing over dogma.

Like so many other things in their lives, the new house was clearly Martha's idea—hers or her father's—but it soon became Peter's project. Into its building had gone all the romantic urges, all the esthetic impulses he had pushed down when life seized him by the throat and turned him into a businessman instead of a poet. Outside, the house was muted—a square, Italianate building that would not compete or clash with the gothic of the church next door and St. Patrick's down the way, thereby displaying more taste than that of some of the neighbors with their turreted, gargoyled structures. Peter had a passion for marble, possibly going back to his childhood awe and admiration for the house of his uncle, Senator Peter Schuyler, the first marble house in all of New York. He couldn't afford to duplicate the senator's house on so large a scale, but he did relieve the brownstone walls with marble facings on the windows and doors and marbled the foyer and double stairway winding up three stories around a well topped by a skylight. In an expensively sentimental gesture, Peter had the marble he'd had moved from Uncle Peter's house to Twenty-second Street ripped out again and installed in the Fifth Avenue foyer. It meant extensive reconstruction before he could put the old house up for sale, but, as he argued with everybody who thought him daft, it was the least he could do in memory of a man who'd given him both his name and what was left of his goods. What Peter liked about marble was its cleanliness, its incorruptibility, its capacity to reflect light.

Marble and glass. The house was built in a square around an inner courtyard also capped by a skylight. This made it possible to have windows on both sides of the major rooms such as the ballroom that ran the whole length of one side on the ground floor and rose two stories with windows nearly as tall; it also made it possible to have double bedrooms lining a central hall on the second floor and in the servants' quarters on the third floor. What Peter wanted was light and a sense of space, and, where windows couldn't provide it, he used mirrors. He also wanted life, and the courtyard was a great, protected greenhouse in which he planted palms and other kinds of tropical vegetation to relieve the dead pall of winter in New York. This courtyard was the only feature of the house that evoked something like spontaneous approval from Sally when they carried her by it. "Oh, it reminds me of my grandmother's orangery on the manor," she said. "I always liked that, but then of course you never saw it, Peter. Maybe it's something in the blood. It makes me feel better about ending my days here. . . ."

Whatever his father thought about it, Aaron Roberts Van Alen hated to hear his grandmother talking this way. Still vivid in his memory was a death that had upset everybody, and he couldn't understand how she could even contemplate such a possibility. She had to know how special she was to him. Housebound by some trivial illness or other, he would often elect to play on the floor by the chair in which she rocked away her time. Fascinated with the "olden days," he would pump her for stories of her own childhood. Her life, as she told it, seemed to have begun when she was nine and sailing out into New York harbor on Great-Grandfather Cornelius Van Alen's sloop to watch General Washington, standing solemn and statuesque under the crimson canopy of the barge bringing him over from New Jersey. While bands played and people sang "Yankee Doodle" on surrounding vessels. She could even remember the lump in her throat and the tears in her eyes and how her father had tears in his eyes, too. "I can still feel that lump every time I think about it," she'd always say, adding, "You know, Aaron, never be ashamed of tears. They show that you care."

It was comforting advice, because at the time he'd been ashamed—or embarrassed—of his own first tears, and his father's too. On that Monday morning of April 25, 1865, he had been animated by a single happy thought—there would be no school that day or the next. He and Teedie Roosevelt could sneak away in the confusion and go over to the Hudson River where the shad should be running and try their luck or take the horse cars up to Central Park and chase butterflies for Teedie's collection or—the possibilities for making good of unexpected freedom on the days of spring were endless. It never occurred to him that, among those possibilities, would be his first experience of mourning. Aaron was not, even

22

then, so insensitive as to be unaware that something momentous and awful had happened in that distant world up there where adults moved mysteriously about their business, but he had supposed that age would exempt him from its consequences, as so far it always had. Though they told him, for instance, that he had been the most fearless and vigilant of them all in keeping watch for the "bad guys" in those terrible days and nights of the draft riots, he found their stories as impersonal and remote from reality as those he read in books. Not so this time.

Aaron had been the first one in the household to hear the cry of a newsboy in the still dark of a Saturday morning, the day before Easter. It was not only strange for a boy to be out that early but stranger still that he should be peddling papers in the quiet streets off Gramercy Park where the Van Alens lived. "Extry! Extry! Lincoln shot! President dying! Extry! Extry!" Without bothering to dress, or even to put on boots, Aaron ran down the dark stairs, paused long enough in the foyer to feel for some of the pennies his mother kept in a jar on the marble-topped table by the door to treat with occasional peddlers and ran out to buy a paper. By the time he got back, the gaslights were lit in the foyer, and his father, still in nightshirt, stood waiting by the open door. He grabbed the paper out of Aaron's hand, scanned the headlines with darting eyes, and said, softly as in prayer, "Oh, my God, my God . . ."

"What's happened, daddy? What does it mean?" Aaron asked.

"I'm not sure yet except that Mr. Lincoln was

shot . . . in a theater in Washington, by Wilkes Booth . . . he may live. . . . I've got to take this up to your mother right away." His father gave him an affectionate pat on the head, added, "You were a good boy, Aaron, to go out and get it. Now back to bed with you."

He tried to go back to bed, but it was no use. Within minutes, lights were going on all over the house. He could hear anxious voices. Hear his father telling the news to his brother James and sister Sally who'd come, curious, out into the hall. Hear his mother shouting it, as she had to now because of the old lady's deafness, to his grandmother in the next room. Hear the tap of his grandmother's cane on the marble stairway and her voice . . . "No, Martha, you and Peter go and get dressed. I'll go down and make the coffee. Don't bother the maids." If all the noise hadn't been enough to keep him awake, the aroma of brewing coffee drifting up from the basement kitchen would have done it anyway. He guessed that it would be one of those special days when they'd let him drink coffee, either because they were all too concerned about something else or thought that it was an occasion when it might do him some good like those wonderful early, early summer mornings when they would set off for Newport. So he quickly dressed and ran down. With the maids still apparently sleeping, they all gathered around the table in the kitchen. The room smelled richly, not only of coffee but of bread his grandmother had put into the oven to warm. It was ever so much cozier than the echoing dining room above with its long mahogany table that shone like dark glass and mustn't be touched, its cold chandelier that hung like dripping icicles over your head, its black haircloth chairs that scratched your legs. They did let him have coffee, nearly whitened with milk, but none of the brandy his father poured from a bottle he'd brought down from the sideboard in the dining room into his own cup and those of his mother and grandmother, saying, "I think we may need this in the next hours."

Even before they'd finished eating, new extras were on the street with the news that the President had died, and what had started out as a special day was ruined. Fearful that the assassination might touch off rioting, his father decreed that he and Sally and his mother and grandmother would stay in the house. Aaron sulked in his room, considering it unfair that his Saturday plans could be upset by such a distant and incomprehensible event. Although it was a matter of family knowledge and pride that his father had almost joined Mr. Lincoln's cabinet, Aaron at his age couldn't understand how anything happening so far away as Washington could have any bearing on whether he could go across the backyards of two blocks here in New York to play with his friend, Teedie. Worse, his father ordered the carriage brought down from the livery stable and took his brother James, who was seventeen, with him to go out and see how things were at the office and the factory over in New Jersey. He wouldn't have eaten lunch if his grandmother hadn't come into his room, tray trembling in her hand, and said, "A boy your age gets hungry no matter what. I know how you feel, but you'll get over it." Often in those years, Aaron thought that his grandmother was the only person in the house who ever did know how he felt, and in appreciation he gave up sulking long enough to ask her to sit down and tell him what she knew about Mr. Lincoln while he ate.

"Not much," she said. "I have to admit that, after seeing General Washington, I didn't think Mr. Lincoln looked the part of a president. And the one time I met him his feet hurt. It was the night he made his first speech in New York, and we were all walking away from the hall and he was limping. I asked him if he was lame, and he said, no, his new boots were too tight. They always talk about great men having feet of clay, but they never mention that they might have tender feet. Well, I should have known better since my cousin, Matty Van Buren, was president, too, and he was as human as they come. You know you're related to a president, don't you, Aaron?"

Of course he knew it. How could he not? Over the mantlepiece in the dining room, just across from where he always sat, hung a portrait of a baldpated man with curled side whiskers who was referred to as "our cousin, the President, you know" whenever new guests were present. What he couldn't quite appreciate was that the man, stiffly formal in a black coat and white collar so high and tight that his chins rolled over it, had ever been really alive, much less human. "Did his feet hurt, too, grandma?"

"No, oh, no. Cousin Matty was always very careful about his clothes—too careful, some said. You see, he was a small man, little taller than me,

26

which is why I'm always telling James not to worry if he doesn't gain more height," his grandmother said. "Perhaps because he was so small, Cousin Matty was rather vain. They say when he left the White House they found in his private rooms a little oval rug set in front of a mirror and worn nearly through from his pacing on it while he tried on clothes and practiced his bows and gestures. . . . Ah, well, great men can rise above their feet, Aaron. Whether his feet hurt or not, Mr. Lincoln will always be remembered as the Great Emancipator for his freeing of the slaves. Few men in history have done more in their time. . . ."

In some ways, Sunday was worse than Saturday. Instead of erupting in riot, the city lay still—and stunned. Except, that is, for the churches. Their bells tolled and tolled, and a shocked people jammed into their pews and spilled over into the streets. The whole Van Alen family, except for grandma, who for some reason, possibly her health, never had gone to church as long as Aaron could remember, squeezed into their regular front seats in the uptown Presbyterian Church. Because his grandfather, the Reverend Doctor James Schuyler, was the church's minister, Aaron was reasonably well disciplined to endure the discomfort and boredom of divine services. There was a legitimate element of pride involved in maintaining a pose of solemn decorum beyond his years since, as his mother explained, "all eyes are upon the minister's family." When he was much younger, he used to have the creepy sensation that he could actually *feel* those eyes on him, and the back of his neck would prickle. Once he told his sister Sally about this and she said, "Silly, if they're looking at anyone, they're looking at *me*." Sally was very vain, he thought, and, after what his grandmother told him, he now guessed that her vanity must have been inherited from their cousin, President Van Buren, but still the thought that she might be right made him feel more comfortable. His mother had devised a kind of game to, in her words, "kill two birds with one stone," because, according to his mother, his father "worked so hard all week" that he had a tendency to slip into snoring slumber along about the second point of Grandfather Schuyler's sermon. So Aaron was stationed next to his father in the pew and given "secret orders" by his mother to stay alert and attentive and to nudge his father at the first sign of flagging interest. Aaron played the game seriously, but he doubted that the orders were all that secret, because his father would wink at him and smile when he was nudged and then shoot an unreadable look in his mother's direction. Something about the situation would make him feel closer to his father than anything else that ever happened during the week, and he would come all over warm and think for a while that going to church was fun. But this Sunday was different, as he knew right away when his father kneeled right there in front of the pew the way Aaron thought that only Catholics did, and buried his face in his hands.

Aaron could hear a kind of rustling through the church, and when he looked around he saw that a lot of other people were following his father's example. He kneeled, too, and shut his eyes and soon the choir began singing, softly at first and then louder and louder, "Mine eyes have seen the glory of the coming of the Lord; he has trampled out the vineyards where the grapes of wrath are stored. . . ." By the time the choir had finished, chills were making goose flesh of his skin. After the "Amen," everybody got back into their seats, and his grandfather who had been kneeling, too, rose and stepped up to the pulpit. For a long time Aaron's image of God was a lot like the figure of his grandfather in the pulpit—tall and handsome with a crown of white, wavy hair and possessed of a melodious voice, but curiously disembodied by the black robes he wore. The figure had very little to do with the very human grandfather who always carried candy in his pockets to reward good little boys and girls, much to the annoyance of his mother, who thought that candy was bad for the teeth, and who was always being teased for his piety by his father and Grandmother Van Alen, just as if he were an ordinary fellow. Now his grandfather stood there, looking as solemn as God, and waiting for the shuffling and rustling and coughing to die away.

"My friends, my sorrowing friends," he said at last. "This is a sad day for the world, a sad day for the nation, a sad day for New York, a sad day for all of us—and sadder yet for some of us. When I observed how the tragic event of Friday, of Good Friday, had moved so many of you, perhaps beyond your own will, to a kneeling display of humility in prayer unknown to this sanctuary, I was seized with an inspiration. . . ." Aaron couldn't be sure, but he thought that his grandfather was looking right at his father, that their eyes were locked in some kind of strange personal exchange. "I have decided to keep this sanctuary open all this day for a vigil of prayer for our country, and I invite any and all of you to remain here with me in prayer for as long as God grants us the stamina to seek his solace. . . ." It was then that Aaron knew that it would be a bad day, because, from the glances his parents exchanged, they would be staying. And there would be no game to play. His father was so tense and alert that he could almost feel the vibrations.

Since it was, after all, Easter, they all stood up and sang with the choir, "Jesus Christ is risen today. Hallelujah!" And then his grandfather began to preach, and he decided that he might as well listen since there would be a long, long time to pass during that prayer vigil.

"Yes, Hallelujah, Christ is risen!" his grandfather began. "My friends, my flock, I cannot out of a heavy heart pretend to deliver to you the joyous Easter message I had prepared for this day. Yet I cannot help but wonder if our despair is any greater than that of those disciples who also saw their leader slain and cannot help but hope that we, too, will somehow this day discover that the stone has been rolled away from the sepulchre.

"I do not think it blasphemous to equate the event in Washington with that in Jerusalem. The fact that our President was assassinated on the very day, Good Friday, that we have fixed as the day of Christ's agony on the cross is a coincidence too remarkable to leave any doubt in the minds of those of us who believe that God directs the affairs of man—indeed, that they are predestined—and that this is a sign given unto us. Not only is there a parallel in terms of timing between these untimely deaths, but there is a parallel in terms of personality, for they were both good men, and in terms of purpose, for they both sought to teach love even toward our enemies, and in terms of prophecy, for the history of prophets among us is that their words fall upon ears so deaf that we put them to death.

"It is this last point to which I wish, with great difficulty, to address myself. All those of you who have known me during my long ministry in this church cannot but be aware that my views with regard to slavery were, as I can see most clearly in the light of this tragic event, at best limited. I held that the institution by my reading of scripture was ordained of God. It is no excuse, no absolution, for me to say that my convictions were shared by many of my fellow ministers at the south as well as many of you now sitting before me in this sanctuary. Nor is it an excuse, nor an absolution, for me to say that, when conflict broke out, I raised my voice on behalf of the Union cause, for I was moved in great part by the practical considerations of ministering to a congregation whose sons and brothers would be called, many against their will, to give their lives for that cause. I, like those who sat in judgment upon Christ, saw only the divisiveness, disruption, destitution and danger that a new testament of freedom would bring to our society. And I, like the smug elders of Jerusalem, saw in the instrument of that testament only a crude, poor, uneducated, irreligious man from the provinces. Yes, I was deaf to the prophecy, and scornful of the prophet, and, as such, I stand here as convicted in this hour as Mr. Booth, for whose soul we pray.

"I cannot therefore now ask any of you to do more in the light of this new Good Friday's judgment upon us than to search your own souls, as I have mine. But I do pray that this will be a new Easter, too, that out of Mr. Lincoln's death will come a national rebirth, that, as he himself so eloquently proclaimed at Gettysburg, 'the nation shall, under God, have a new birth of freedom, and that government of the people, by the people, for the people, shall not perish from the earth.' Let us pray . . ."

Like the choir's singing, his grandfather's voice, rising from almost a whisper when he spoke of his own guilt to an exultant shout when he intoned Lincoln's words, caused Aaron to shiver and pimple. But the prayer went on, and on. Almost nobody left the church, and when his grandfather's voice, or ability to summon words, gave out, he asked them all to pray silently. It was terribly hard not to fidget, especially when you had to piss. He wondered whether it was right to have to piss when you were supposed to be praying, and the more he tried to forget about it, the worse it got. It became a positive pain. He was terrified he'd let go and embarrass himself as he had once in his first year at school. Then the master had made him exhibit his wet pants to the class and had delivered a lecture on not being a baby, and he had hated school ever since. This would be worse, of course, because there were girls in church. But at least he knew what to pray about:

"Oh, God, don't let it happen, don't let it happen." And his prayer was answered when his father leaned over and whispered, "I have to relieve myself. Do you and James want to go with me?" There was something comforting in learning that, big as they were, his father and brothers were almost as badly off as he was and something educational in realizing that the word "relieve" which he'd always thought grownups used so they wouldn't have to say a bad word like "piss" was, in fact, a most accurate description of the function.

Aaron felt so relieved that he was emboldened to make a try for freedom. "Don't you think grandma will be worried about what's happened to us, daddy?" he said. "I'll run home and tell her."

"If anybody goes, I'll go," James said. "You're too little. . . ."

"No, I'm not. I go all the way to the park. . . ."

"You wouldn't if mother knew . . ."

"Boys, boys," Peter Van Alen said. "We're all going back in there and pray. For once I think your Grandfather Schuyler is doing the right thing, and we're going to support him. It's nice of you to think about her, but your Grandmother Van Alen isn't the kind to fuss over our being gone a few hours."

Somehow that Sunday passed, but life did not return to normal in the next week, as Aaron had thought that it would. There was nothing but Lincoln, Lincoln, Lincoln in all the papers, not only in New York but everywhere in the country. At dinner one night, his father read a letter from some old cousin way out in Chicago named Francis Livingston, who owned a paper there: ". . . and only

33

you, Peter, can know what this means to me, can understand that it is not by way of boasting that I claim Lincoln as my own creation—and yours, too, for the part you played in bringing him to speak at Cooper Union in New York. My only consolation, as yours must be, is in the astonishing expressions of genuine love from the people. We at the paper have been so deluged with letters, mostly in verse, that we can't run any of them. One of my reporters in an idle hour went through this mail and counted more than a hundred verses beginning, 'Toll, toll, ye mourning bells' or 'Mourn, mourn, ye tolling bells.' As something of a poet once yourself, you'll appreciate that this could be amusing were it not for the terrible occasion. . . ." Aaron was happy to see that his father did smile at this, the first sign that people might get back to thinking about something else. But all they did in school was talk about Lincoln, and the master made them each memorize the whole Gettysburg address and the last lines of his inaugural speech in March, which went: "With malice toward none, with charity for all, with firmness in the right as God gives us to see the right, let us strive to finish the work we are in, to bind up the nation's wounds, to care for him who shall have borne the battle and for his widow and orphan, to do all which may achieve and cherish a just and lasting peace among ourselves, and with all nations."

When the news came through that Lincoln's funeral train would pause in New York on Monday and Tuesday, the whole city started draping itself in black. His sister Sally, who was ten and considered herself very grownup, got all excited and made a big rosette out of black silk to hang on their door. She had to get Grandmother Van Alen to help her with it, and it was one of the first times Aaron ever heard his grandmother say anything sad: "I can remember doing something like this when I was just your age, Sally. We were decorating your Great-Grandfather Van Alen's house over on Broadway, but it was a gay celebration for Washington's inaugural, and I made stars of candles to hang in thirteen windows. Oh, where have we come since then?"

All this was beginning to oppress Aaron until news that school would be dismissed for the days that the funeral procession passed through New York lifted his spirits. On that Monday morning when he awoke early, full of plans having nothing to do with death, he was surprised and crushed when his father knocked, came into his room and said, "Get up and get dressed in your black Sunday suit, Aaron. I'm taking you with me to City Hall to see the President. . . ."

He couldn't help himself. "Aw, daddy . . ."

His father came over, sat on the bed and touseled his head. "I know, I know," he said. "You were hoping to run off and go fishing with Teedie or something, weren't you? I don't blame you, son. This can't mean much to you now, but it will for the rest of your life. If I didn't take you with me, there would come a day when you'd blame me for it. Few people in history can say that they've looked upon a true martyr."

They went together, the whole family, except for grandmother, who had to walk with a cane and couldn't stand in lines. By the time they reached

35

City Hall Park, all New York seemed to be there; people milling around spilled out of the park and on down Broadway. His mother was upset at the sight. "I should think, Peter, with your connections, you could have arranged for a private viewing," she said. "We'd be all afternoon getting through this."

"I didn't want a private viewing, Martha," his father said. "I wanted the children to experience what it's like when a whole people mourn."

"Well, goodness knows what they might catch in a crowd like this. . . ."

"If you don't like it, take Sally and go home. The boys and I will wait it out."

It was one of the few times Aaron wished that he had been a girl, because his mother did take Sally's hand and turn away. His father made him feel better, though, when he said, "Well, boys, you see why they call women the weaker sex?"

Actually, there were as many women as men in the crowd—lots of them quite old, too, bent and shuffling along, dressed in little more than rags with shawls or kerchiefs over their heads instead of the smart straw hats trimmed with black lace that his mother and Sally wore. Most of the men were dressed in rough corduroy or denim or uniforms, and he and his father and brother in their black broadcloth sort of stood out, especially with his father's shiny top hat. Aaron was a little embarrassed when he heard a man say, "Would you look at the swells?" as they eased their way into line. The only thing that really interested Aaron was looking at the soldiers, and he got James, who knew all about such things, to explain to him their ranks and

regiments from their uniforms and insignia. Sometimes either James or his father knew what battles
they'd probably been in, and he tried to imagine
what it would be like to be in a battle. You really
couldn't tell anything about what they'd seen or
done by looking at their faces. No matter how hard
you stared. Even that game got boring by the time
they reached the hall—and then it happened. By
stretching and peering around the tall people in
front of him, he could just see the lights of tapers,
the white satin lining of an open coffin lid, the heads
and uniform caps of rigid guards. A shiver like what
he'd felt in church ran up his spine, because it was at
that moment that he knew what was really going to
happen to him: he was going to see a dead person for
the first time in his life.

Just before they reached the coffin, a woman in
front of them kneeled by it and did something
strange with her hands in front of her chest. "It's
the Catholic way of praying—she's crossing herself.
But I think we should kneel too," his father
explained. Just then, though, the woman got up and
started to bend over the coffin. The guards who
looked more like statues than men came quickly to
life, grabbed her and pulled her away. She cried out,
"I just wanted to kiss him. I wanted to thank him for
saving my boy." The guards pushed the woman
along and then snapped back to attention, as Aaron
and his father and brother kneeled quickly before
the coffin. Then his father lifted Aaron up so that he
could see inside.

He didn't know whether he was more fascinated
or frightened. The face, framed in satin, was just like

37

the face he'd seen in many pictures except that the skin was as cold and white and shiny as candle wax. Though the eyes were closed, and there seemed to be a little smile on the lips, Mr. Lincoln didn't look a bit like a person sleeping. Everybody lied when they said death was sleep. It was something else. There was no sign of where the bullet had torn into his head, but looking at him, Aaron suddenly remembered what his grandmother had said about Mr. Lincoln's feet hurting and wondered how much more that tearing in his brain had hurt and was filled with the sadness that had unconsciously been building and building in him for a week. He started to cry, to shake with his crying, and his father's arms tightened around him. He looked up into his father's face and saw tears running down from his eyes and glistening like drops of dew on his mustache. His father kissed him for the first time in years, the wet mustache wetting his own cheek, and kept carrying him as they moved along.

Just as they got out of the door, they could hear a man behind them actually chuckling as he said, "Well, Paddy, I'm satisfied—the son-of-a-bitch *is* dead. How's for a drink to celebrate? I'm dyin' of the thirst." Aaron could see his father's face flush, the muscles tighten in his cheek. He turned to the man and said, "You damn animal, I could kill you." But before his father could put him down and do anything, the man was running off with his friend and saying loud enough for everyone around them to hear, "Get a load of that swell! He don't have to worry about a nigger taking *his* job. . . ."

At least the incident got them over crying and

gave them something safe to talk about on the way home. His father apologized for losing his temper. "I don't want you boys to get the idea that fists and curses are a way to settle anything. I . . . well, I just wasn't myself. I'm rather glad your mother wasn't along after all to see me lose my head," he said.

If Mr. Lincoln's death could make everybody feel like that, how much worse would it be when his grandmother, who was always here, died? Now he knew why his grandmother hadn't wanted to move into this house any more than he had; there was something scary about getting away from everything and everybody you knew. No amount of fancy decoration could make up for that.

Left to himself, Peter might have created a house more to his son's liking—a house as austere as truth, a kind of Greek temple with central heating. But he felt obliged to yield to his wife Martha's feminine instinct for warmth and color in matters of furnishing and decoration, which accounted for the ormolu trim, the gold silk draperies, the Oriental rugs that were scattered like soft jewels around the polished parquet floors. He made a concession too to the masculine taste of the day by having one of the receiving parlors off the main foyer done up like a downtown club in dark paneling and soft leather, a secure hideaway for the inevitable after-dinner brandy and cigars and profanity. Altogether, though, the house was so unlike those his architects had been asked to create for his fellow rich that Peter found it necessary—and a pleasure, he had to admit—to spend a good part of every day with them or the workmen on the job to make sure of getting what he wanted. It was a blessing under the circumstances that James was so willing and able to take over at the office—and a somewhat humbling surprise that the business was doing better than ever under his son's supervision.

Of course, it was the times. In this year of 1867, anything having to do with railroads couldn't help making money. They said that the crews—some 20,000 men in all—of the Union Pacific pushing west, and the Central Pacific pushing east, were laying track at the astonishing rate of five miles a day, and it wouldn't be long before trains could run the whole way from New York to San Francisco. Crafty old Commodore Vanderbilt had finally got control of the New York Central and was in something close to warfare with Jay Gould's Erie, a happy circumstance for suppliers of locomotives and other equipment like Van Alen & Son. Not by nature a businessman, Peter wasn't entirely comforted by the reassurance of friends and colleagues to whom he confessed his shortcomings. "Don't worry," they'd say, "with the Van Alen name and product you can't miss." So far, this was proving true and whenever he *would* worry about the bills piling up for the house James, who took care of the books, would reassure him. "Don't give it a thought, dad," he'd say. "I'm sure the deal with the cars will go through and then we'll be able to declare a dividend that will more than cover whatever you can spend."

Good as it looked on paper, that deal about the cars made Peter uneasy, though he wasn't exactly sure why. It was brought to them by his cousin, John Charles Smith, Jr., whom Peter had retained as special counsel to the company against everyone else's advice, precisely because of Charlie's contacts with the railroad people and the politicians who worked hand and glove with them. If, said Charlie, Van Alen would think about building sleeping and parlor cars in addition to locomotives, he was sure that he could get them a very favorable contract from the Erie. Everybody knew that the equipment on the Erie, known around Wall Street as the "Scarlet Woman of the Railroads," was in terrible shape, and, now that they were fighting Vanderbilt, they'd have to do something to convince stockholders and the public that they were sound. What better than ordering rolling stock from the firm with the best name in the business, Van Alen & Son? Of course, the kind of big contract Charlie had in mind might mean putting Gould or Tweed on the Van Alen board—Fisk was out of the question with the Van Alen reputation to think about—but would that be so bad? Gould knew more about Wall Street than anybody in America, and, with his political power in New York, Tweed could be useful in more ways than one.

"Wouldn't this get us in trouble with Vanderbilt?" Peter asked. "He's our oldest and best customer. And you're forgetting Sophie, Charlie. She's our biggest stockholder, and the commodore, after all, is her grandfather, though you'd hardly know it from the attention he gives her."

"Hell, it's a free country, isn't it?" Charlie said. "The Erie needs cars, and the Central doesn't. It's as simple as that. If he were in your shoes, old Vanderbilt would be the first to jump at something like this. Anyway, maybe you could get your mother to talk to him. They're still friends, aren't they?"

Charlie was plausible, had always been plausible, even when he'd scrounged thousands of dollars in commissions from the government for providing rotten shipping during the war and brought Van Alen & Son under such sharp congressional scrutiny that Peter had been forced to give up his work with the Sanitary Commission to try to save the firm's good name and keep it in war production. He'd eased Charlie off the board then for the sake of appearances but had retained his counsel for just this sort of thing, and it was not becoming for him to protest too much when young James, new on the board and eager for expansion, and the others voted at once to go along with Charlie. Peter wished that he hadn't let his mother resign, or that he'd been able to persuade his niece, Sophie Vanderbilt Van Alen, to take her place. Women, he'd found, often had an instinct, not so much for business as for people, that could be saving in a situation like this. Peter himself didn't really know any of the people over at Erie, but any person in New York would have to keep his head under the covers not to be aware of "Colonel" Fisk, a fat and vulgar man who flashed his mistress as boldly in the faces of respectable people as the diamond in his cravat, or Tweed, the Tammany tiger. He doubted that Sally or Sophie would want any involvement with them. Still, as his fellow directors argued, business was business, and was the commodore, with his tricky ways, any different?

In the four years since all those circumstances had forced him to take over the operation of Van Alen & Son, Peter had increasingly come to feel like a sailor overboard in shark-infested waters. Almost daily he became aware of the snap and flash of the circling predators' sharp teeth, like those of the old commodore, gobbling down more money in the last three years than in all of the sixty years he'd fooled around with ships. Peter could barely imagine his having the nerve to pull the kind of stunt the commodore had got away with in acquiring the New York Central. To be sure there was nothing illegal about it and perhaps nothing immoral either unless you put public service ahead of private gain, as Peter had tried to do through all his years as a journalist and politician. A shark troubled by that sort of thinking would worry about hurting its victims and starve to death. What the commodore had done was to order his Hudson River Line, the only rail service between New York and Albany, to stop just short of the Hudson River Bridge at Albany. Passengers were left to fend for themselves, to get out and walk with their baggage in all weathers, and freight coming in from the west on the New York Central was left to rust or rot. The situation was so intolerable that the commodore was summoned before the Legislature at Albany, where he blandly produced an old law, passed by that same Legislature on behalf of the Central, that prevented the Hudson River Line from crossing the river. So far, the commodore seemed to have a legitimate grievance, but his subsequent testimony made Peter inclined to agree with his fellow directors that dealing with the commodore, in spite of his mother's curious friendship with the old pirate, wouldn't be very different from dealing with Gould & Co.

"Why didn't you run your trains *to* the river?" a legislator inquired.

"I was not there," said the commodore.

"But what did you do when you heard of it?"

"I did not do anything."

"Why not? Where were you?"

"I was at home, gentlemen, playing a rubber of whist, and I never allow anything to interfere with me when I am playing that game. It requires, as you know, undivided attention."

Charlie Smith supported the commodore's testimony because he was frequently one of the players in the almost nightly game going on at the commodore's old house at 10 Washington Square. Some might have put this down to the eccentricity of a seventy-three-year-old man, but the commodore's adamant refusal to do anything about the situation caused Central stock to drop to a point where he felt it prudent to buy in—and now the road was being run by Vanderbilt-appointed directors, like his son Billy. Once the giant of shipping in America, Vanderbilt had become by that one brazen lunge the giant of railroading. But Charlie, knowing him so well, offered the Van Alen board some inside information.

"I think the old boy's going around the bend, I really do," he said. "You know he's messing around with those Claflin sisters who are teaching him clairvoyance or something like that and trying to get

44

him interested in women's rights. Can you imagine old Vanderbilt giving a damn about women except for . . . well, you know what. Anyway, I wouldn't put all my money on him against Gould. Now there's a man with a head on his shoulders, thinks of nothing night or day but how to make money. Quite a fellow, doesn't smoke or drink or hell around. Well, it's your decision . . ."

In the end Peter voted with his son and the other directors to go ahead with the cars if Charlie could work out a satisfactory deal. There was no reason why Van Alen & Son couldn't build good cars, no matter who bought them, and the money would at least make possible his dream of a house. Except when he was a young man trying to write poetry, Peter had never known any pursuit quite as gratifying as this building, and he could almost go along with Martha's feeling that they'd been led into it by the hand of God, or providence. To see an image in the mind gradually take shape in solid masonry was what he imagined an artist might feel in creating a canvas or sculpture. That it had a function, that it would be a home—their home—made it all the more exciting. Ostentation, he told himself, was not his purpose, but he did think that there was some merit in making a suitable showing for a family like the Van Alens who'd been in New York since before the Revolution to match that of all these parvenus from the west who'd had lucky strikes in gold or oil or stocks and that of old Jacob Astor's children who seemed intent on spending the money he'd left as fast as he'd made it. There had been a time when Peter had scorned money, but he'd found himself so out of step with the rest of New York, including the people he loved most, like his mother and his wife Martha, that he decided if you were fortunate enough to have money, at least spend it in good taste and in the interests of those you loved. Martha desperately wanted to float with the social tide uptown, and he loved Martha more than he could express in any other way than to try to fulfill her desires.

He'd been a little disappointed—but not really surprised—at his mother's disinterest, bordering on disapproval, whenever he talked to her about the house. It was, though, a natural reaction for a person of her age who hadn't been out of her bed for a couple of years and who kept talking about dying as the only adventure left to her. It was typical of her, commonsensical and to the point, but Peter saw no reason why, if she really tried, she couldn't get back on her feet and live to be a hundred or more. He deeply hoped that if she liked it as much as he hoped she would, the new house might just give her a new lease on life. At least he'd been sure that here, in these new surroundings, she wouldn't be haunted by any ghosts from the past; there'd be no dark corners where they could hide. But what was that about an orangery?

When they had Sally tucked into bed again, Peter lingered. Close as he'd been to her in so many ways, he'd never been able to get his mother to talk much about her life on the Schuyler manor up near Kinderhook. All he really knew was that there had been some serious trouble with her father over her relationship with her cousin George Van Alen and

46

hat, at something like sixteen, she'd been banished
from the manor—rescued, rather, by George's
father, the first Cornelius Van Alen—and brought
to New York as George's reluctant wife. Peter had
taken her back to the manor once to have a look at
her parents' graves, but even then she hadn't said
much, claiming, "It's all ancient history." He'd got
the impression that the purpose of the trip for her
was to satisfy herself that the past was, indeed,
buried. But could the past ever be buried? Not if you
judged by her instinctive reaction to the sight of the
courtyard. Maybe this was a time when she'd talk. "I
never even heard about an orangery, mother. It
wasn't there when we went up."

"Torn down when the tenants rioted, I heard. Too
bad—it was the only cheerful part of that place,"
Sally said.

"Tell me about it—"

"Not now, Peter, not now; I'm too tired. Besides,
you ought to be helping get your things moved in.
And you ought to be with Martha. It's really *her* day,
you know. Now go. Please, go."

"All right, mother, but when you're feeling better I want you to tell me more about the manor before—"

"Yes, I know, before I die. Well, if you haven't
learned it yet, Peter, you will learn that a person
ought to die with some secrets. So go along. . . ."

Going toward Martha's room, Peter shook his
head: his mother was always amazing him. Of
course, *he* had secrets, like that business with
Amelia Downing, that he wanted to take with him to
his grave, but . . . well a man of fifty-five ought to

know that his mother might too, but you never really thought of your mother that way. Oh, he knew that his mother had been through a lot with her drunken husband and was proud of the fact that she'd done things other women didn't dare, like learning from her brother, his Uncle Peter, to ride and sail and shoot and helping Uncle Aaron save his ship, the *Cathay*, from fire, and piloting, for God's sake, Vanderbilt's steamship back in the twenties to outfox the law and the monopoly. But secrets? He would have to pry again and again before . . . well, he didn't really like to think about that, even if she seemed to. What he was thinking about was that, now that the Van Alens were properly housed, he ought to shine up his rusty pen and compose a history of the family which, in a real way, would be a history of New York itself. If he did that he'd have to know all he could about Sally Schuyler Van Alen, who'd been the backbone of the Van Alen family for seven decades.

Peter found Martha in her white and gold bedroom, which was in a state of total disarray—colorful mounds of silk and cotton dresses piled on every available piece of furniture, boxes scattered around the floor. One of the little Irish maids was "yes ma'aming" and scurrying to carry out Martha's orders to put this here, that there.

"Well, we're here," Peter said, and Martha, kicking boxes aside, came over and put her arms around him. "Yes," she said, kissing him over and over, "and it's lovelier than I'd ever imagined it would be, thanks to you."

"Well, I'd do it all over again for a reward like

48

this. But it was really your idea—yours and your father's."

"And your work of art," Martha said. "Have you been to your room yet? They tell me Patrick has it all straightened out already. Come on, let's see. . . ."

This business about the bedrooms was one thing Peter distinctly did not like about his new house. Martha contended that as long as they were building a big house they should each have a bedroom, as most of the civilized people their age did. It wasn't that she felt any differently about him, but he would have to admit that it would be more convenient when he came in late from the club or a meeting— the sort of convenience they could afford now. They wouldn't be far away from each other. Leading him through the connecting bath and dressing rooms, she said, "See, it only takes a minute." A minute, twenty or so feet; however measured, this separation would, Peter worried, put a time and distance between them that had never existed before. Though at forty Martha was, if possible, more beautiful to him than she'd been as a bride of twenty-one, rounder, softer, warmer, he was worried that he might not be so for her. People, particularly Amelia Downing, were always telling him that age had conferred distinction on him. Maybe. Though white, his hair and mustache were still thick and curly; his lean frame was still erect; the lines gathering permanently around his eyes and mouth reflected a generally benign disposition. Distinction was not, however, the stuff of passion, and Martha's desire for separate rooms seemed to him a signal that passion was not an important concern in her future. *That* could be a problem. . . .

When they stood in his room, looking about, Martha clapped her hands and said, "Isn't it just perfect?"

It was, in comparison to hers, neat. Patrick had put everything away, even lined the shelves built into the wall over his bed with books that he'd presumably want to read for company at night. Despite his preference for order and light, Martha wanted his room to be "masculine," and she had prevailed. Except for the one with the bookcase, which he did not appreciate, the walls were wainscotted in dark mahogany; there was a mahogany armoire—at least he'd managed to get its doors mirrored—so huge that either he or Patrick would have to use a stool to reach the top drawers with his cuff links and tie pins; the leather chaise and chair were bought in the same lot from Sloane's as the furnishings for the men's reception parlor. The place smelled of new wood, leather and furniture polish, and all it needed, according to Martha, was a whiff of tobacco smoke to make it exactly what she'd always imagined his very own room would be. Peter, with a half-smile, got out his pipe and puffed it into life while Martha fussed with the deep red draperies that matched the cover on the bed. The pipe also gave him an excuse for not showing more enthusiasm, but she had enough for them both.

"Oh, Peter, don't you love it? We're going to make this the happiest home there ever was, aren't we? I hope the children love it too."

"I'm sure they do, though Aaron seems a little doubtful—"

"He's a little boy, he thinks the world's coming to an end because he has to leave Teedie Roosevelt, but Cousin Theodore tells me that they're looking for a place uptown too, so it will all work out. . . . Well, now that *you're* settled, what are you going to do with the rest of the day?"

Peter went over and put his arms around her. "You know what I'd like to do . . ."

"Peter, please. This is no time to . . ."

"Any time is time for love, Martha."

She took his hand and squeezed it. "We have tonight, Peter," she said, and then actually giggled. "Are you going to come to see me—or am I going to come to see you?"

A good question, Peter thought, as the rest of the day wore away. It would probably be a question hanging between them for the rest of their years. But it wasn't to be answered that night. When they sat down to dinner in the windowed dining room, softly lighted by the many-candled chandelier above the table—though there were gas jets on the walls for emergencies or big parties, Martha had decided that candlelight was more elegant for dining—they all felt silly grand. "I hope those people out there are looking at us and—" young Sally said. Peter jumped on her. "Sally, that isn't the right attitude."

"Sally's just vain," Aaron said. "Grandmother said so. She said Sally takes after our cousin, the President."

"Now, Aaron, you shouldn't talk that way about Mr. Van Buren," Martha said, and trying to keep it light, added, "He might hear you." She was referring to the portrait of former President Martin

51

Van Buren which they'd brought up from Twenty-second Street and hung over the mantel of the new dining room.

"Well, grandmother says so," Aaron repeated.

"Grandmother's a fine woman, but she's very old and out of touch with the way young girls think these days," Martha said. "Sally was just trying to say how proud she is of our new house. I hope all of you are."

"*I'm* not," Aaron said, "and I don't think grandmother is either."

"Now, Aaron, if you talk this way you'll hurt your father and—" Martha was interrupted by a maid who came running in from the parlor side of the dining room. White-faced and nearly incoherent, she nevertheless managed to get out the message that the old lady upstairs had "taken a turn."

Peter ran up the marbled stairs two at time. He was relieved to see from her eyes that his mother was still alive; in fact, she looked much the same as she had for a long time now. Always small, she'd shrunk to the point where Peter thought of her as almost a doll. Her skin was like aged china, slightly tea-colored and crazed, but her black eyes were still clear as the eyes of a child, and in them now was a look he couldn't read—fear? surprise? awe? He only knew that she was in some kind of terrible trouble when he asked, "What is it, mother?" and she couldn't speak. She pointed to her throat and made gagging sounds. Oh, my God, why had he let her have her way, why hadn't he *made* her come up on a bed? He took her hands, they were already cold. "I'll

52

send for the doctor, mother," he said, but her cold hands, surprisingly strong, gripped his and she shook her head. He could sense the others behind him, crowding the doorway. He motioned them away, but his mother again shook her head and gestured for them to come in. He could hear Martha whispering, "Aaron, run and get your Grandfather Schuyler."

"Why do we want him?" Peter asked. "If she doesn't want a doctor, she certainly doesn't want him."

"How do you know? They've had their differences but I think they still like each other. Anyway, when I was praying that you'd come home safe during the draft riots, your mother told me there were times when it's worth trying *anything*. Didn't you, Aunt Sally?"

Surprisingly to Peter, his mother nodded slightly, but he didn't think there was much comprehension in her staring eyes. Well, it was no time for argument, and Aaron had already gone, and there didn't seem to be anything else to do. "I still think we ought to get a doctor," he said to Martha. This time there *was* comprehension in his mother's eyes, a pleading, as she clutched him again, and again shook her head. Her eyes were moving from face to face like a camera lens.

Behind those eyes, her mind was busy too. It had just come on her, this choking. It wasn't so bad if she didn't swallow or speak, but she knew it was growing, whatever it was, and that she soon would no longer be able to breathe and that no power on earth could help her. There was the pain too in her chest, and, cold as she was, she was clammy damp with sweat. She was most certainly dying and most certainly afraid and yet curiously more afraid to fight. She wished it didn't have to happen just now, on the day they were all so excited and happy about moving into this house. She wished that she hadn't said those tasteless things about dying. She wished . . .

What would become of them all? It was the only thing she really wanted to know and the only reason why she hoped now, against all rational conviction, that there would be a knowing afterlife. She was pretty sure of Peter and Martha unless they let money go to their heads as Martha might have done with this house. But Peter was basically sound, sane, a good man, and Martha was more intelligent than she sometimes let on, and they loved each other, or seemed to, which as Sally knew more than most, was all anybody could ask out of life. And James. She was pretty sure of James too. Though only nineteen years old he was, like old Cornelius and her own son, young Cornelius, already a man in the way of business, but he had inherited a grace that they lacked from his mother's side of the family. He was short like her own Cornelius but chunky, fleshy and blessed with that smile of his grandfather, the Reverend Doctor James Schuyler, that made you almost like him even when he was damning sinners whose only fault was being born Catholic or Jewish. Yes, she could picture James—cocksure successful, like his mother unhampered by doubts or abstract principles. She was less sure of Sally. The child was vain for a twelve-year-old, as she herself had been vain, thinking herself special somehow. Young Sally had reason: she'd been endowed with all the Dutch blonde beauty that ran through both sides of the family and the kind of inquiring, skeptical mind girls weren't supposed to have. What young Sally was lacking yet was a heart, and old Sally knew all too well the pain of acquiring a heart. And Aaron. *Where was Aaron?* Could it be a mercy God granted her that this Aaron had the same sea-gray eyes, the same blond hair, the same determined chin as that other Aaron, her old love for whom he was named? No, it was simply nature, blood, at work. But would this Aaron also be fearless and dedicated and capable of a surpassing love? It was hard to tell at nine, but he did show some signs of it, and it was her deepest regret that she couldn't linger to see this Aaron grow. *Where was he?* She had one last thing to do.

When Aaron came in with his grandfather on his heels, Sally ignored the preacher and motioned Aaron to her side. With great difficulty, she pointed with her eyes and one feeble hand toward her bedside table. Everybody tried to guess what was on her mind, and Aaron began picking things up. First her medicines and then a book, because lately he'd often been asked to read to her. She kept shaking her head until he had in his hand the little jade dragon that had sat by her bed for all the years he could remember, and then she nodded. "You want *me* to have it, grandma?" Aaron asked, and she nodded again.

Somewhat impatient to get on with his work, Dr. Schuyler pushed the others aside and knelt by the bed. He'd seen more people die than the average doctor, and he knew that there was no use praying for any miracle in this case, other than salvation. He took Sally's cold wrist and felt for the pulse; he couldn't find it but the covers still rose and fell with her effort to breathe. "Aunt Sally," he said, "I'm sure the grace of God will be with you. . . . Let us pray. . . . Dear Lord Jesus, forgiver of all sins, take unto thy soft bosom the soul that departs this flesh and comfort those who mourn her passing. . . . In the name of the Father, the Son, and the Holy Ghost."

Dr. Schuyler knew that she was dead before the rest of them. The covers on the level of his eye had stopped moving. Her eyes were so wide open and deep black that you could almost fall into them. Practiced in death scenes, Dr. Schuyler signaled the end by reaching up and thumbing the lids over those eyes. Even he, believing in resurrection, found it unnerving to look into eyes when the light of living had gone out.

Van Alens and Schuyler weren't the sobbing sort, but there was a certain amount of throat clearing and furtive dabbing at the eyes. When Dr. Schuyler got back to his feet, he said, "Well, she lived a good long life, Peter. I meant what I said just now." For once Peter had no doubts about his father-in-law's sincerity. "I hope I can go like that—I didn't even know she'd stopped breathing," Martha said. James and young Sally, possibly because they hadn't yet learned to be Van Alens or Schuylers, fled from the room. Aaron suddenly realized that his hand hurt, his knuckles were white from clutching the dragon in his fist. Opening his fingers and looking at the soft green object lying cool against his palm, he said, "She gave it to *me*. . . ."

Chapter 2

CHARITY WAS not likely to be the ruling virtue
of a beautiful seventeen-year-old girl about to make
her debut into society at what everybody predicted
would be the New York social event of 1872. So
Sally Schuyler Van Alen's reaction to the news that
her Cousin Sophie would be moving into the room
left vacant over the years since her grandmother's
death might have been expected. "What if somebody *sees* her?" she asked.

The news came, as did most news in the Van Alen
household, at the dinner table, because it was the
only affair of the day at which everybody had to be
present. Sally's comment caused her mother Martha
to suspend a forkload of food in midair. "Sally,
that's really not very nice—"

"I can't help it. She's so . . . so ugly and so . . . so
queer. Will she be eating with us and everything?"

Though accustomed to frank statements from this
daughter, who was normally the delight of his eye
and heart, Peter Van Alen was exasperated; this

time she'd gone too far. "Yes, she'll be eating with us and *everything*, whatever she wants to do," he said. "And I expect you, Sally, and all the rest of you to make her welcome. It's the least we can do for her, and it's taken me five years to argue her into making this move. I should think you'd have some compassion for what your Cousin Sophie went through."

Back in '63, Sally had been too young, only eight, to comprehend much about Sophie's ordeal. But Sophie had been badly burned trying unsuccessfully to rescue her father, Uncle Cornelius, from the fire that the draft rioters had set in their house on Lafayette Place. What Sally hadn't been told then, because she was so young, or still, because everybody was trying to forget it, was that the burning had been a terrible mistake: the rioters had mistaken Cornelius Van Alen's house for his brother's—Peter, Sally's father, whose political support for Abraham Lincoln in Democratic New York had earned him the nickname "Nigger-loving Pete." Since they'd never seen much of her Uncle Cornelius or Sophie, except in church, Sally's chief emotion at the time had been disappointment that her uncle's death had canceled out their plans to move to Washington, where her father was supposed to become a cabinet officer or something for Mr. Lincoln. As for Sophie, she'd hidden herself away in the St. Nicholas Hotel on Broadway, the same hotel where another relative Sally could do without, her father's cousin Amelia Downing, lived. Once or twice, Sally had been taken under protest to visit Cousin Sophie and had spent most of the time

59

sitting as far away as possible and trying not to see the awful scars on Sophie's face when occasionally the heavy veil she always wore slipped. People said that Sophie hadn't left her room for nine years, having her meals sent up from the hotel kitchen. She read a lot and crocheted helter-skelter patterns of flowers into handkerchiefs and scarves she sent out as birthday and Christmas presents. Sally had a whole drawer full of them which she guessed she'd have to use now if Sophie were in the house.

"Yes, and don't forget that Sophie owns the controlling stock in the business," her brother James was telling her. What a stuffed shirt James was, always thinking about business. No wonder he was still a bachelor at twenty-four.

"Well, I *like* Cousin Sophie," Aaron said. What a little brat Aaron was, forever contradicting her and trying to get on the good side of their parents. The smile Martha bestowed on her younger son didn't escape Sally.

"You might also remember, Sally, that your Cousin Sophie *is* a Vanderbilt, which could be of some importance to you this year," Martha said.

Now Peter was exasperated with his wife. In the years since they'd moved into this Fifth Avenue house, her head seemed to have been filled with social plans. He had to admit that her social aspirations and skills had been attributes back in the days when he was making his way in politics, means to a worthy end. But now social success seemed to have become an end in itself for her. It certainly didn't help him much in business, since Martha wasn't at all interested in getting to know most of the people he was doing business with, like Gould and Sage and Carnegie and Rockefeller. Who ever heard of their families? Who indeed? On the other hand, Martha was always positioning for invitations from one of the Astors even though, as rent collectors, they had no use for railway engines and cars, and even though Peter's memory of how old Jacob had foreclosed on his mother's property up on the manor was alive and bitter. When he'd complain Martha would ask sweetly, reasonably, "Should the sins of the father be visited on the sons?" It was a distortion of the scripture she'd absorbed at her father's knee, but still a question Peter hesitated to answer affirmatively. As for the Vanderbilts, the old commodore had, as Charlie Smith predicted, gone around the bend, what with marrying that young Frankie before *his* Sophie was cold in her grave and setting that Woodhull woman and her sister, Tennessee Claflin, up in the brokerage business. Young Cornelius Vanderbilt was a man to be avoided in the streets—if he didn't hit you up for a fiver he'd try to persuade you to join him in his round of bars and brothels. But William was running the New York Central very well, and it did make some sense to be on good terms. Not that it would help Sophie much. Old Cornelius had very little use for his own daughters, let alone a granddaughter whom he evidently dreaded to look upon as much as most other people did.

"It doesn't matter that Sophie's a Vanderbilt or that she owns a good deal of our stock," Peter said. "What matters is that she's a human being in *need* of us, and maybe we're in need of her too. Having

61

Sophie around could remind us that life doesn't always turn out the way we think it should, even when one has money . . ."

Peter, Martha decided, was getting preachy, and she'd had enough of that from her father. She pushed back from the table. "Come along, Sally. Lucy Smith's coming over this evening, and we have to get busy with the lists."

They found Lucy, another cousin of her father's whom Sally had always thought ought to be kept in a closet, already at work in front of a card table in the ladies' receiving parlor just off the dining room. In the months they'd been working on the lists, Sally had come to have a grudging respect for Cousin Lucy, despite her resemblance to an ill-clad horse. It had seemed easy enough to pick out four hundred or so names—they figured that, what with the old people, only half would be dancing at any time—until you got right down to who wouldn't be seen in the same house with whom, whose family had skeletons rattling too loudly in their closets, which families had eligible sons, and the like. Making up proper social lists was Lucy Smith's whole function in life. She'd done it for her mother, daughter of Lady Lydia Wentworth Van Alen, daughter in turn of Sir Robert Wentworth and social queen of New York in those confusing days of the Revolution and after, and she'd done it for Martha Roosevelt Schuyler Van Alen, Sally's own mother. Lucy, it seemed, knew everything about everybody, and her knowledge made her an implacable tyrant who could not be moved by argument or tears. Sally had tried tears when Lucy drew a very firm line through the Freemans, whose daughter was one of her best chums at Miss Ogden's school. "In all my years I've never seen the name Freeman on any list. Shouldn't be surprised if they're Jewish," Lucy said. "But Mr. Belmont's Jewish, isn't he?" Sally argued. "*Was*, I'd say; he married a Perry," Lucy said. Before Sally could answer, Lucy held up her hand. Tonight Lucy had a surprise for them.

"I ran into Amelia at Stewart's today," she said, "and she told me that she'd heard from one of her brothers in England—I don't know which one, I never could keep those Downing boys apart—and he said that a young friend of the family, the Duke of Midstone, is coming over here just about the time of your ball. It seems he's temporarily embarrassed for funds, so he'll be staying with Amelia. Now *there's* somebody you ought to invite."

"Is there a Duchess?" Sally asked.

"Oh, no, he's unmarried, as I understand. I don't know how old he is, but he must be thirty or so if he's a friend of the Downing children. Let's see, Amelia's over sixty, and so her brothers are older than that."

"I wonder why Amelia didn't come right to me with the news?" Martha asked.

"It probably didn't cross her mind," Lucy said. "You know what Amelia thinks of debutante balls. She says they remind her of the slave auctions where they used to put young girls up on the block for the highest bidder. Well, I suppose we'll have to add Amelia to the list too."

"Yes, of course, we can't invite the Duke without inviting Amelia if he's staying with her," Martha said.

"*Mother* . . ."

"Now, Sally, I've gone along with you about not inviting Amelia just because I do know how she feels about these things. But if you want a Duke at your party—you do want a Duke, don't you? . . ." and Sally nodded. "Well, there's no other way to do it properly. I know we haven't seen much of her lately, but Amelia still is one of your father's and my oldest friends . . . well, more than a friend, a cousin."

Sally did know that, and it puzzled her. If Cousin Sophie was something like a dark secret in Sally's mind, Cousin Amelia Downing was a public shame. There wasn't a woman's suffrage meeting in New York that didn't find Cousin Amelia right up there on the platform with Mrs. Stanton and Miss Anthony and the others. Her name was always getting in the papers, and because she was so huge, the cartoonists took off on her, the last one picturing her as a billowing pillow smothering a little man. It was just impossible to believe her father when he said that Cousin Amelia had once been handsome, like a Greek statue. Now she was mixed up with *Woodhull & Claflin's Weekly* that the Claflin sisters were putting out with all that money they'd made in the stock market, and it was said that Cousin Amelia herself had written that shocking editorial advocating free love. Well, it was possible, because she was forever saying the most outrageous things. Though it was too raw to get into the papers, it got around town fast enough the time that an enraged male heckler got up and said, "If the good Lord wanted women to vote, he'd have given them . . . uh . . . dinguses," and Cousin Amelia snapped back, "If the good Lord had wanted men to rule the world, he'd have given them these," and she took hold of her breasts. Sally was just glad that Amelia's name was Downing instead of Van Alen. That way nobody she knew connected them, and Sally couldn't understand what her distinguished father and beautiful, ladylike mother could ever have had in common with that woman.

There was one relative, though, that Sally would have liked to have at her party if he hadn't died—Cousin Charlie, Lucy's brother—John Charles Smith, Jr. There was a whiff of scandal about Cousin Charlie too, as rich as the cigar smoke that always trailed him, and she knew that her Grandmother Van Alen hadn't liked him—in fact, he hadn't been allowed in the house until after she died—but Cousin Charlie was even handsomer than her own father, and he knew how to make a girl feel as pretty as she hoped she was. For Sally, there was a touch of glamor about the kind of things Cousin Charlie was said to be mixed up with, and he was full of inside gossip about what you read in the papers. He'd actually dined in Josie Mansfield's house with Colonel Fisk before another of Josie's lovers shot the colonel, and Cousin Charlie would have to admit that Josie was "some looker with that hour-glass figure" and would add with a wink that he might have suffered a little lead poisoning himself if he'd been younger. Cousin Charlie rode on Colonel Fisk's yacht with President Grant, too, and it was really his undoing. Whatever happened on that yacht, Cousin Charlie and the colonel and Mr. Gould got the idea that the President wouldn't put any government gold on the market and started trying to buy up all there was in the banks. Though she hadn't understood it very well, being only fourteen in '69, Sally could remember Cousin Charlie trying to argue her father and brother James into joining him in buying gold, and it had seemed to her a pretty exciting thing to do. But it was good they didn't because, on what people were still calling "Black Friday," the President did release gold and the prices fell so fast that Cousin Charlie and a lot of other men were ruined. They said the pressure of men trying to buy and sell in the Gold Room on Wall Street was so great that Cousin Charlie might have suffocated, but the doctor was sure that he'd died of a heart attack. Cousin Charlie had sold all his stock and mortgaged his house to buy gold and had left his family without a cent, but the Smith girls had married well enough that nobody worried. She'd felt like crying when she'd heard about Cousin Charlie's death and had been surprised to hear her father say, "It's good Charlie died the way he did before he could find out that Gould was selling and making a fortune, instead of buying the way he was supposed to be doing, in the last half-hour before news came through from Washington. Charlie might have added murder to his other sins." Too bad, though. Sally thought she'd have been rather proud of the building Cousin Charlie was always talking about putting up at his alma mater, Columbia College, with his name on it.

What Sally couldn't know about, because her father was old-fashioned when it came to sharing business problems with the women of the house, was that even now he was having no end of trouble as a result of Cousin Charlie's sins, if they could be called that. In this year of 1872 when it seemed impossible that even Diogenes could find an honest man in either business or government, the sharks in the waters through which Peter was trying to swim were biting off even larger chunks of flesh from whatever prey they could reach. Now that the figures were coming to light, it seemed most appropriate that spikes of gold and silver had been used to join the tracks of the Union Pacific and Central Pacific at Promontory Point, Utah, in '69. Peter—at least the poet and politician in him—had seen the event at the time as one of man's greatest feats, throwing a thin ribbon of steel clear across the rivers and endless plains and over the enormous mountains of a great, wild continent. Peter, the businessman, could now see that it was one of man's greatest steals. The directors of Union Pacific had contracted with themselves for the construction work, paying out $94 million, $50 million more than the estimates, and putting the booty into Crédit Mobilier, which passed out shares of its soaring stock to members of Congress, and even Vice President Colfax to ensure that no embarrassing questions were asked. The smell of the deal was so great and so close to the White House that Peter's old friend and employer, Horace Greeley, had consented to run this year against Grant as the candidate for both the new Liberal Republican Party and the Democratic Party. Peter doubted that Greeley would have much luck since, as he well knew, the business community was solidly behind Grant, and the little general remained an authentic hero to the powerful Grand Army of the Republic.

Against that background, Van Alen & Son's embarrassing involvement with Charlie's old chum, "Boss" Tweed, and the Erie Ring could almost be seen as doing business as usual. As a matter of fact, when it turned out that electing William Marcy Tweed to the Van Alen & Son board was a necessary part of Charlie's deal for a large order of cars from Erie, it was certainly the lesser of two evils, the other alternative being Jim Fisk—and quite possibly a boon. Back then, it was possible for almost anybody who didn't know how he really operated to call Tweed a statesman. State Senator, Grand Sachem of Tammany Hall, chairman of the city's Department of Public Works, director of the Erie Railroad and numerous other companies, Tweed had come a long way from the shop on Pearl Street, where he'd made chairs like those gilt ones that Charlie Smith had in his foyer at Gramercy Park. Big, bald, bearded, genial, Tweed was known for handing money out of his own pockets to widows and orphans in need and for getting things done. A number of Peter's acquaintances, like John Jacob Astor II, went out of their way to congratulate him on getting Tweed on his board. Peter wasn't entirely clear why Tweed, busy as he was, would want to take on another directorship even though it did give him a right to acquire some of the closely held Van Alen stock. Tweed's motives became more apparent when a few months after he joined the board the water leases that Van Alen & Son had been seeking from the city to expand its warehouse and dock facilities on the Hudson came through at stunningly low prices, and the stock jumped five points. Peter, of course, was suspicious, but Charlie Smith, a lawyer by profession, was very soothing. "Nothing illegal, Peter, I can assure you. Hell, you ought to know from being in politics yourself, it's just a matter of somebody at City Hall shoving the papers along. You're in good company. Ask Goelet and Astor and Delano and a few others how they got their leases."

Charlie's explanation was certainly believable; nobody had more influence at City Hall than Tweed. The mayor, A. Oakey Hall, "elegant Oakey," was his hand-picked candidate, and Richard B. Connolly, the comptroller, and Peter B. Sweeny, Chairman of Parks, were fellow Tammany tigers. So the embarrassment of having Tweed as a colleague did not really set in until after Charlie died, until, in fact, a year or so ago, when *The New York Times* began breaking the stories of what they called the "Tweed Ring's" thefts from city contracts—$8,000,000 on the new County Courthouse alone, they said—and when Theodore's brother, Bob Roosevelt, came around to ask Peter to serve on the citizens' Committee of Seventy to look into the frauds. "Some of us have long memories, Peter," Bob Roosevelt said, "and we recall when you were alderman and known as 'Unbuyable Peter.' We need somebody like you with the kind of knowledge of city government and that kind of reputation. And don't forget, we're going to have to put up some lily-white candidates to replace those thieves. Now that your son James is helping in the business, you might be interested. . . ."

He might have been, might well have been. Peter had no stomach for business as it was being done these days. He would still, he was sure, have been in politics, or perhaps back with Greeley on the *Tribune,* if it hadn't been for Charlie Smith's getting the family firm such a black name in Washington with his shipping deal, if it hadn't been for his brother Cornelius' awful death, which had been meant for him. . . . Why hadn't he got rid of Charlie entirely, as his mother had argued he should? He'd never liked the fellow, never trusted him, but he'd considered himself fairly clever in keeping Charlie on since Charlie knew too much about the business, about the family, and it was better to have him with you, where you could see him, than against you, where you couldn't. Well, his conscience would pay for that. If not for Charlie he might not be in this mess with Tweed. And, face it, if not for the business Charlie had brought in, he might not be sitting in this grand house, in this soft leather chair. The brandy he was sharing with Bob Roosevelt tasted bitter as he said, "I'm sorry, Bob, I guess you didn't know that Tweed's a member of Van Alen and Son's board of directors. Of course, we can—and will—force his resignation in the light of these disclosures, but for your sake it wouldn't look right for me to serve with you, would it?"

"No, I suppose it wouldn't," Roosevelt agreed. "I'm sorry too, Peter." Roosevelt, Peter noted with some dismay, didn't even finish his drink.

Only an indictment finally got Tweed off the Van
Alen board, but it was far from the end of the
troubles Charlie had bequeathed him with the Erie
connection. If Tweed had been looting the city,
Gould had been as systematically looting the Erie.
Although furnishing the Erie with sleeping and
parlor cars had been good business on paper, it was
in large part just that, and Fisk's inglorious death
along with Tweed's indictment was causing in this
year of 1872 more concern than usual about what
the Mephistopheles of Wall Street was up to with
Erie stock.

One early spring night when Peter was at dinner
with the family and Amelia and the Duke of
Something—Peter thought that British titles were
about as silly as the people who usually bore them,
and this young man seemed no exception—Patrick,
the butler, came in with the card of an unexpected
visitor.

When Peter looked at it, he decided that the Duke
of Something might be useful after all. "Your
Grace—isn't it?"

"Ah, yes, but I wish all of you would use my
Christian name. Perry, you know."

Perry. It suited him. He was handsome, but in a
delicate way, small-boned, fine-featured, blue-eyed,
blond, with skin that tinted with involuntary
blushes and a laugh-giggle that tended to escape into
the upper register. Amelia had brought him over to
introduce him in advance of the ball, but perhaps
wisely she hadn't stopped talking long enough for
him to open his mouth. He was, however, devouring

71

Sally with his eyes, and Peter was a bit annoyed that his usually spritely daughter seemed stricken mute with awe. Good that the fellow was much too old for her, thirty-five or so to judge from some remarks he'd dropped, and, he was sure, too foppish.

"Well, then, Perry, do you know a Mr. Gordon Green of London? Says here he represents Southwick, Ltd. Bankers, I gather."

"Oh, yes. Not well, mind you. But Southwick are my own bankers," the Duke said. "I hope he isn't pursuing me for an overdraft. . . ."

Meant to be a joke no doubt, but in poor taste, Peter thought. Gentlemen didn't reveal their financial affairs, especially in front of ladies. Peter stood up. "Excuse me," he said, "we'll soon see."

Patrick had ushered Mr. Green into the men's reception room, where Peter found him pacing back and forth. White-haired, heavy-set, dressed in black, he looked as solid as a British banker should. When he took Peter's outstretched hand, he couldn't apologize enough. "So sorry to break in on you at dinner, Mr. Van Alen. Really should have sent my card around, but I'm just over this day from London on urgent business and—"

"It wouldn't have anything to do with the Duke of—what is it?—Midstone?—would it? He's in the dining room now. I'll just get him," Peter said.

"Oh, no. His Grace here? Well, well. Mind you the Duke is sometimes careless with his checks, but oh, no. This has to do with the Erie Railroad. I've been appointed to represent a number of London investors, and we are . . . well, concerned . . . at the way the stock's been wobbling on the market. I

72

didn't know where to start. So I came right to you, though we haven't had the pleasure of meeting, because I noted that Van Alen and Son is listed among the Erie shareholders, and your firm has the soundest of reputations in London."

Green was simultaneously the bearer of both bad news and good. His very presence indicated a worrisome concern in London that, carried too far, could render the Van Alen holdings in Erie worthless. London, and to an extent Amsterdam and Paris, were the principal sources of the capital needed to feed America's galloping business enterprises. But Green's good news was that, in London, the Van Alen name was still good. He'd been afraid that the Tweed business had left Van Alen & Son as badly scarred, in the public eye, as poor Sophie, rustling around in her veils in the room just above them, a room she'd refused to leave despite all entreaties ever since she'd moved into the house.

"Yes, we do hold some Erie stock, Mr. Green, but I don't know how we can be of help to you beyond offering the company of misery—"

"What I propose, am authorized to propose, is that we organize a party of like-minded shareholders and confront Mr. Gould in person. I'm certain that if we could get the true information we'd find grounds for a stockholders' suit. I thought you might join me and might know some others here in the city who would be interested," Green said.

"Let me get my son, James."

James was enthusiastic. "If we get enough stockholders together, Gould would have to listen to us. I know half a dozen men I could approach right now, and Mr. Green's interests are great. We don't have anything to lose and everything to gain, dad."

Peter was skeptical. "We have time to lose—and plenty of legal fees. Gould has bought the legislature and the courts before, and he may well do it again. After the fight he put up with Vanderbilt, he won't give in to some disgruntled stockholders. We need to think this over—"

"Respectfully, I disagree with you, sir," Green said. "I've had a long voyage to give it thought, and my feeling is that surprise might be our best weapon. Mr. Gould doesn't yet know I'm in town, though I'm sure he soon will. I don't think tomorrow morning would be too soon to move. What do you think, young man?"

"I agree with Mr. Green, dad. I could go out right now and get some recruits. If we find what I think we're going to find, we might be able to force Gould to resign—and *then* the stock would go through the ceiling. As it is, he'll keep passing dividends and keep those printing presses in the basement of the Opera House grinding until we're all holding worthless paper. Besides, this is bound to make the papers, and it would take whatever bad smell is left over from the Tweed business out of people's nostrils."

This last argument was more convincing to Peter than the thought that they could best Gould at a dirty game he'd been playing better than anybody else in the city for a dozen years. One of Peter's "shortcomings" as a businessman was that he simply couldn't come to grips with the fact that the fluctuation of stocks by a point or two either way had anything whatever to do with what a man could honestly call business. He could understand making locomotives and cars, or putting out a newspaper, or baking rolls and selling your product for enough to live on and a little more, but, as it had been to his mother before him, making money from manipulating money or the markets in which it was traded *was* unreal, without foundation in supplying true human needs and, therefore, somehow wrong if not immoral. James was afflicted with no such thoughts, or qualms, which probably accounted for the welcome spurt in dividends since he'd involved himself in the business. But Peter could also understand that being out there trying to restore some honesty to the market place might make men like Bob Roosevelt and his friends who'd been rather cool to him lately come around again. So Peter agreed, and James hurried out into the night in search of help.

By ten the next morning a group of a dozen men, looking, Peter thought, in their business suits like pallbearers at a friend's funeral, gathered in front of Pike's Grand Opera Palace at Twenty-third and Eighth Avenue, the improbable headquarters of the Erie Railroad. Fisk had bought the place and moved Erie's offices into its second floor so that he could keep an eye simultaneously on his railroading and theatrical enterprises or, as some said, on the scantily clad girls he might surprise in the dressing-room hallways. Others claimed that Fisk, canny beneath his clowning exterior, thought that the noise of the orchestras and choruses rehearsing onstage would drown out the rumble of the printing presses down below when they were turning out worthless Erie securities in time of need, such as when Commodore Vanderbilt tried to buy up control—a futile gesture that cost him millions. Another device not common to opera houses was a vault running through several stories in which these unvaluables, as well as some presumably real treasures, could be stored. What people couldn't understand was why Jay Gould, known to have no fleshly vices or interests, went along with Fisk on using this preposterous place as an office. Could it be that the man did have a sense of humor, though he never smiled?

It was the first time that Peter, or any of the assembled stockholders, had ever entered the building. "Looks just about right for the Scarlet Woman of the Railroads, doesn't it?" one of them said. The remark broke a tension that had been growing in view of their serious purpose, and they all laughed. It was apt: the lobby was paved with enough marble to have covered Peter's whole house, and was dripping with cut-glass pendants of enormous gas chandeliers; the grand staircase leading up to the Erie offices was trimmed with balustrades of gold. And the suite in which they did find Mr. Gould was even more appropriate to the lair of a scarlet woman than the lobby. With its drapes and hangings of silk, it was a decorator's dream of an Oriental harem. It seemed most inappropriate to the man who, because of his small stature, looked a little like a curious turtle peeking over the shell of his large desk.

Peter, who had never seen Gould before, was

impressed with his icy calm in the face of an unexpected invasion. There was no color, no twitch of a muscle to be seen in that part of his face not covered by his full black beard and mustache, no sign of fear or even of surprise in his hooded eyes. He was young, only thirty-six, but looked curiously ageless, as if he'd been born with the full powers of fifty. Perhaps he had. He'd been a farm boy, Peter knew, from up in Roxbury, but brilliant and impatient in school, he'd gone to work as a surveyor at sixteen, honing his keen mind on mathematics; by twenty-three when he moved into New York, he'd already been in and out of numerous enterprises, leaving behind the picked bones of old and honorable businessmen who'd trusted him with their capital. He was both feared and admired and, as a person, almost totally unknown. His voice when he spoke at last, was a soft monotone. "You gentlemen wish to see me? I wasn't aware of an appointment."

Green nominated himself as spokesman. "We have no appointment, Mr. Gould. I'm Green of Southwick, and I represent your British shareholders. You probably know Van Alen here and his son, and Wilson there, and the others. We're here to see your books."

"You'll have an annual statement shortly," Gould said. "Good day, gentlemen."

"We demand those books now!" Green insisted and, turning to James Van Alen, said, "Come with me, young man. We'll find them. The rest of you entertain Mr. Gould with our suspicions."

Silence fell in the room, a silence so deep that

they could hear faint strains of music from the stage where a rehearsal was evidently in progress, could hear angry voices from an outer office where Green and James were confronting the clerks. Looking from one to the other of them with apparent unconcern, Gould did an odd thing. He picked up a piece of paper from his desk and began shredding it into little pieces with his fingers. Peter tried to think of something to say but realized then that he'd been thrust into this so suddenly that there'd been no time for homework. He knew relatively little about Erie affairs. Gould's attitude warned against making ill-informed or rash statements. The embarrassed silence continued until Green and James came back into the room, arms full of books and brushing off a furious clerk plucking at their elbows. "I couldn't help it, Mr. Gould," he was saying. "That young man pinned my arms before I could—"

Gould simply waved the clerk away. Green plunked himself on a pink satin couch, and with James looking over his shoulder and pointing to this and that, ran through the books. "Lord!" he said. "These don't bear study. It's worse than I feared. On the face of it, there are no visible assets against some sixty-four million dollars in securities you've been printing, Mr. Gould. Why, if word of this gets out of this room, none of us could sell a certificate for the value of the paper. I can tell you right now, Mr. Gould, that my people are prepared to sue—and I'm sure these gentlemen will go along with us, unless—"

"Unless what, Mr. Green?"

"Unless you resign and make restitution, if you

have anything to make restitution with."

"That's just the point, isn't it, Mr. Green? If I'm ruined, what good would a suit do you? But, gentlemen, now that you've come to me, I have a proposition. Mr. Fisk, as you may know, was in charge of operating the railroad, and, since his death I've found I have no interest in that aspect of the business. But I have fought long and hard to keep it out of the clutch of the monopolist Vanderbilt, and I have, if I may say so, a feeling for it. I would be loath to see Erie smeared with a suit—or to relinquish all interest in its affairs. So I *will* resign as president provided I can increase my Erie holdings. I'll pledge this opera house which, as you can see, is a valuable asset and six million dollars' worth of securities in other enterprises which I have right here in this vault . . ." Gould turned, sweeping with his elbow the small pile of paper he'd been picking apart onto the rug like a scattering of ashes, and pulled aside a silken curtain to reveal the face of the famous vault. ". . . against an option to buy two hundred thousand Erie shares at the going rate of thirty dollars. *That*, gentlemen, should demonstrate both my faith and self-sacrificing interest in this enterprise. Does that satisfy you?"

Even Green was stunned beyond immediate speech. As easy as that, and yet there must be a trick to it. Finally Green said, "I think we ought to go out in the hall and talk this over." But the stockholder, Wilson, said, "Why? I think Mr. Gould's offer is very fair. I'm for taking it. Just the news that he's resigned will jump the stock before the day is out." There was a general chorus of consent, and Gould said, "Then good day, gentlemen. My attorneys will be calling upon yours." The papers did break the story of Gould's resignation—James Van Alen saw to that—calling it the Erie Revolution. In the next few days, a bull movement, fed by a number of the brokers who fronted for Gould, lifted the stock to $75, when it suddenly staggered under the impact of a mysterious 200,000 shares for sale. By the time the dust cleared, Mr. Gould was no longer a stockholder of the railroad, but his sentimental regrets, if any, had been assuaged by a $9,000,000 cash profit. Even that seemed fair enough until the lawyers for the stockholders discovered that Gould's supposed $6,000,000 in pledged securities were actually worth only $200,000. They'd been had once again, but they could only grind their teeth.

Talking about it with his son James, Peter said, "It's clear now that we should have persisted and forced him to the wall, put the railroad into bankruptcy if necessary. Letting men get away with making millions for themselves out of railroads that are supposed to serve the public, letting them actually kill the public the way the Erie's been doing with its wrecks, is worse than any sin your grandfather preaches against."

"You can't mean that, dad. That's what the market's all about, and ninety percent of the men in business in New York, *including* most of grandfather's congregation, would be damned. Actually, I sold *our* stocks at sixty . . . I was going to tell you about it, but you've been so busy with the plans for Sally's ball and the cottage at Newport that . . . well . . . you don't have to worry about going ahead with all those things now . . ."

Peter looked hard at his son. The young man responded with that wide, disarming smile he'd inherited from his Grandfather Schuyler; he was obviously expecting a pat on the back, or perhaps even a hug. Apparently it had never occurred to James that the honorable course might have been to stick with the other stockholders, to suffer, as they deserved to, while they took responsibility for straightening out the mess that Gould had left behind him. Misreading his father's look, James rushed on, "I know I should have consulted you, dad, but Mr. Howland from our broker's office called and there wasn't much time since he'd heard from a friend that Gould was starting to sell and I figured that on our twenty-five thousand shares we'd be making seven hundred fifty thousand over what we were carrying on our books which ought to be enough to raise the dividend to fifteen percent this year when I know you need it so much . . . I guess the rumor was false and I should have waited like Mr. Gould or been smart enough to pick up some more shares before I told the press, but everything was happening so fast. I'm sorry, dad."

Peter put a hand on his son's shoulder. "Don't be sorry, James. As you saw it, you did well." And added to himself, it's I who haven't done so well by you . . .

At approximately the same time that Peter and James were discussing the Gould coup in the Van Alen & Son offices just off Wall Street, Perry Goodenough, by the grace of God and the crown and the early death of his father, the Duke of Midstone, was ringing the bell beside the wrought-iron-and-glass doorway to the Van Alen mansion on Fifth Avenue. If the Duke could have read Peter Van Alen's thought that he hadn't done well by any of his children, he would have laughed ironically. It was *his* father who hadn't done well by him. Nothing was crueler than to leave a man a duke without the funds to live like a duke. The old gaffer hadn't even known that there was no money because he'd been content to live down in that drafty stonepile at Midstone like some ruddy farmer. But that wasn't Perry's style. A man of his birth ought at least to have a proper London town house, not to mention a few horses capable of a go at Ascot, together with enough left over to take care of very special friends. He couldn't say that he'd come over to the colonies deliberately in search of cash, but he'd be a fool to pass up the opportunity that this innocent little Van Alen girl was virtually thrusting on him.

After that first dinner with the family the Duke had gone around to Gordon Green's hotel and managed to pry a few facts and figures out of the old banker. Mind you, according to Green, the Van Alens weren't millionaires in the class of the Astors or Vanderbilts, but they had a tidy little firm. If he personally could get his hands on any of their stock, he would. And then there was talk that old Mrs. Van Alen, as shrewd a lady as had ever lived in New York, had left a few acres of land and buildings down on the East Side that she'd picked up for a song after the great fire thirty-five years ago and that must be bringing in a small fortune in rents from all these

82

immigrants. And, of course, the present Mrs. Martha Van Alen was related to the Roosevelts who'd been successful merchants and good borrowers from Southwick for longer than he, Green, had been with the firm. "To sum it up, your Grace, the Van Alens are just about as sound a family as you'll find in all of New York," Green said. "Between you and me, I'd always rather do business with the old Dutch than these shifty fellows from nowhere like that Gould. By George, did we best him! I've no doubt it was the Van Alens being there, though they didn't say much, that let him know the jig was up." Poor old Green was on the high seas again before everybody in New York, including the Duke, knew that Gould had gnawed Erie to the bone. Still, he hadn't been wrong about the old Dutch; the Duke wormed out of his hostess, Amelia Downing, a Van Alen stockholder, the good news that young James Van Alen had bit off a pretty good chunk of flesh himself.

Inspirited by the banker's endorsement and the glitter he'd seen with his own eyes, the Duke had begun what for him would be a trying and tiresome campaign to capture the princess before her debut would make her publicly available. He'd sensed that a frontal assault on the Van Alen citadel was doomed to failure. The girl and her mother had seemed duly impressed with his title and name-dropping line of chatter, but the frosty father and bored brothers had not. It had been, however, quite evident that the father doted on the girl and would probably do anything to make her happy. So the key to the treasury was the girl herself; he had to make sure of her, one way or another, before he asked for her hand and demanded the dowry a Duke deserved.

The campaign got under way when a little inquiry revealed that the girl was in the habit of riding in Central Park on fine spring mornings. Though he loathed exercising of any kind and rising before noon, the Duke commenced dragging himself out of bed, taking the horsecars up to the park and renting a nag from a livery. It took a couple of mornings of this distressing activity before he finally encountered her, seemingly by happy chance. It wasn't the most appropriate moment, since the only horse he could get that day was not only knock-kneed but noisomely flatulent, making difficult the impression he wished to create of ducal grandeur. Actually, it turned out to be a lucky break. "It's a disgrace that your Grace should have to ride such a horse," Miss Van Alen said. "We've another horse in our stable, a lively little mare, that doesn't get enough exercise because nobody in the family rides but me. Come, we'll get her." After that, they met by design rather than accident, and, apart from acquiring a saddle sore or two, the Duke was finding his morning forays rewarding.

For one thing, it wasn't long before he was certain that, if he had to go through something like this at all, Sally Van Alen was the perfect prize. He had an appreciation for beauty, even in women, and she was, or would be, a beauty. Thin and tall for a girl, though he understood American girls tended to be tall, she had appropriately gold-colored hair which she piled in a high pompadour, rosy Dutch coloring that he could imagine covered the flesh unseen as well as seen, high cheek bones, and a noble, aquiline nose such as those in the portraits that stared down from the walls of Midstone and the other great estates of England. She attributed this feature to her great-grandmother, who'd been known as Lady Lydia before she married the first Van Alen anyone had ever heard of because her father had been knighted before the Revolution. "So I'm some kind of royalty, aren't I, your Grace?" And he replied, "Not precisely, but it'll do to have you call me Perry—if I may call you Sally."

Besides her looks, she possessed another quality he prized: total innocence. Only seventeen, she'd led a sheltered life, and he could count on her not seeing through him until it didn't matter. Though there were times when she showed flashes of irreverent wit—"See that man there . . . no, the old one in the phaeton with the four-in-hand who's about to wipe us out if we don't get off the track— that's Commodore Vanderbilt, and I think he should have stuck to the sea from the way he handles horses"—and steely nerve, as when she nearly killed him by leading him over jumps that only a professional should have tried. Generally, though, she was a goose of a girl with a head full of fluff about balls and baubles and boys. Her mother, who had the look of an ambitious woman, had quite obviously, and no doubt properly, been raising her to make a suitable match and had, in the process, imparted a protective sense of social values that some called snobbery. His title brought this wall around her down like a blast from Joshua's trumpet, and his age and presumed experience made her trusting to a degree that was nearly touching.

The first time he'd kissed her was when they'd just come in from a ride, and she was boasting about beating him back to the stables. Like a doting uncle, he said, right there in front of the grooms, "You jolly well deserve a kiss for that—and I think I'll just give you one." She seemed to take it in the same mood, actually holding her face up to his, but he realized he must not let her off with an avuncular peck. He put his hand to the small of her back and pulled her close to him, and he let his lips linger long enough to feel hers move with life. Might as well find out how hard it was going to be now. She did squirm away and lead him out to the sidewalk: "I suppose I should have slapped you or something—doing that right in front of the grooms."

"It was perfectly innocent until . . . well, I was carried away," he said. "D'you know, I've fallen head over heels for you. Now that we're engaged, may I call?"

"Engaged?"

"Yes, well, rather. In England when a man and woman kiss . . ."

"But . . . but, I—"

"Come now. You liked it, didn't you?"

She blushed, tucked her chin down, stared at her feet.

"Well, then, let me call and make an honest woman of you. How do you think I'd be received?"

"Mother'd be pleased, I think. She's going around telling how we're having a real Duke at our ball. I don't know about father."

"What about the most important person—you?"

86

"I . . . I guess . . . I think I'd like that. I'm tired of making up stories about why my rides are getting longer and longer. But I never thought—"

"I was just teasing, half teasing. But I do love you, you know, and I want to make you my duchess. You've given me the impression these mornings, particularly this morning, that you wouldn't find that too bad a fate. Am I right? Be honest."

She nodded and blushed again, and he kissed her again, right there on the street. "Now the whole world knows about us," he said. "I'll be calling soon."

So here he was, and nobody was answering his ring. He persisted; somebody had to be home in an establishment like this. Finally, the door opened a crack, then a little wider. She was standing there herself, all that hair cascading like a golden waterfall over the shoulders of a blue silk Chinese robe, embroidered in the same shade of gold, that she'd evidently pulled hastily over some flimsy undergarments. "Oh, it's you," she said. "I'm sorry, I was having a nap. I didn't hear the bell at all but Cousin Sophie screamed at me." She didn't invite him in, and he talked, just to keep the door open.

"Where's your man—Patrick, isn't it?"

"Out. All the servants have Thursday afternoon off. There's really nobody here, . . . you'll have to come back another day—"

"But you're here . . ."

"But I'm not . . . I mean I'm not decent."

"Oh, you are, you are. Compared to the girls at Niblo's, you're a Chinese nun, if they have nuns in China."

That brought a little laugh from her, and he went on. "Let me in . . . please. I've walked all the way up here from the hotel, and at the least I do need to rest a bit."

"Well . . ." And she opened the door.

This was true luck, as if God himself were blessing his plans. In mulling it all over he'd come to the conclusion that the surest way to get this girl would be to compromise her before he had to deal with her parents. A kiss in the streets wasn't enough. It must be the *actual* thing. It disgusted him, but it had to be done. The only question was where and when. Could this be the place and time? He rather appreciated that opportunity had come upon him so unexpectedly; sheer excitement and surprise might be enough to make him function this once. He only needed this once.

"Where's this Cousin Sophie? Maybe she'd receive me," he said.

"Up in her room. She never leaves her room."

"Oh, what you call a skeleton in the closet," he said, making a little circle around his temple with his finger. "Every English great house has one."

"Oh, no, nothing like that. She was badly burned, and, well . . ."

"Oh, I'm sorry." His roaming eyes had picked out the glass doors under the marble arms of the stairway leading to the courtyard garden. "What a lovely garden. I didn't see that when we were here at night. Can't we go out there and just sit a minute? It must be warm enough, protected from the wind."

"I've got to get something on . . ."

"Why? We'll really be just a minute, long enough

for me to catch my breath. And we are engaged, aren't we? Come, show me your garden."

In the middle of the garden, shielded from the windows of the house by a lush planting of palm and fern, was a fountain, the water pouring from an urn held in the arms of a finely sculptured but unmistakably naked nymph. "Well, I didn't know you had such statuary in New York," the Duke said.

Sally giggled and blushed. "Somebody said she was modeled from me."

"I can believe she could have been."

"Actually, a friend of my father's brought it from Italy. My grandfather—he's a preacher, you know— was shocked and said he never thought he'd live to see a thing like that in the home of a daughter of his, but my father just laughed and said that the kind of people he let into the heart of his home wouldn't take a prurient interest, whatever that is, in a true work of art."

"Well, my interest isn't prurient, and I'm glad you don't know what that means. I've been to Italy, you know, and I've never seen anything more perfect. This whole place is lovely . . ."

Around the fountain was a circular marble bench, and around that a small apron of real turf. Spring sunshine streamed down from the skylight, striking fire from Sally's flow of hair. The Duke sank down on the bench and pulled her down beside him. ". . . and you are, too, do you know that? The way that robe touches up the blue of your eyes, and that sun gilds your hair . . . Oh, lord, since the other day I've dreamt of nothing but your kisses, but we never had a proper one. Here, let me show you—"

"I shouldn't . . ." She had her face turned away from him, but he took her chin and turned it back and pressed his lips firmly against hers.

Now began the part he didn't like, but he'd have to force himself through it. He could only hope that he'd be ready if it worked, ready enough, at least, since in her innocence she wouldn't know the difference. If he could only get her to . . . well, no, not yet anyway; she couldn't be *that* innocent. While they kissed, he stroked her hair, letting his hand finally fall and casually cup a soft breast. Through the thin silk, he could feel a nipple rise and knew enough to be aware that he was exciting her.

She broke away. "No, Perry . . . no, I'm afraid—"

"Afraid of what? We're alone, and, as I've pointed out, we're engaged. In England when you're engaged you make love to . . . to be sure."

"We're supposed to wait till we're married . . ."

"Isn't that silly? We *will* be married soon enough, once your father knows . . . well, he'd do anything to make you happy. You do want to be my duchess, don't you?"

"I . . . I'm not sure . . ."

"Well, you see, my little goose, we have to make sure, don't we?"

He managed to get her in his arms again, start kissing her again. Now he was bolder. His hand slipped through the loose fold of her kimono, under the strap of her chemise or whatever she was wearing, encountering warm flesh, the stiff nipple. His tongue played along her lips until they opened.

She was shivering slightly. Heedless of ripping cloth, he pressed his hand down from her breast, along the ripples of Dutch-pink flesh, down into the damp melt. When he let her up for breath from his smothering kiss, she said again, "No, please Perry, no . . ." But that most sensitive part of her opened its soft and slippery lips to his busy fingers, and he closed her mouth with another kiss, rolling her gently down onto the soft grass.

She did start to resist then, wriggle under him, lock her legs. "We shouldn't, it's a sin, my grandfather says . . ."

He could force her now, would if he had to. It would be better, far better, to get her to yield, to leave her with guilt that would keep her from making ugly accusations. Still caressing her where he could feel the rush of desire that would surely soon weaken her will, he played on her ignorance, innocence. "Oh, darling, darling, you know so little of the world. If it were a sin, heaven would be empty. And you know nothing of men. You'd be heartless to stop me now. I'm in agony, ecstasy. Feel me . . ."

Thank the good lord his cock was hard, hard enough so that when he took her hand and put it on it she could know that something was *happening*. "If you make me stop, I don't know what I'd do. You've heard of men killing themselves for love—"

"Perry, you wouldn't . . ."

"Yes, indeed I *would*."

Now. He freed his half-sprung member. If she could wait, he couldn't; he might lose what he had. Easing her legs apart, he murmured, "It will only take seconds darling, and remember how much I love you." His time prediction was right. She was virgin tight, and he could barely force the tip of a cock shriveling fast into that damp. But he did manage, and the deed was soon done. And she, of course, was not hurt enough to scream or do anything silly. She was just lying there looking up at the skylight with tears coming from the corners of her eyes.

Time now to be tender. "Ah, thank you, thank you, my precious darling. You are even more beautiful than that nymph, and I know now that I can always love you. Can you love me?"

"I . . . yes, I think so. But I can't help it—I feel so . . . so wicked."

"Don't darling, *don't*. Remember, we're engaged. I'll speak to your father in the morning—"

"It isn't that, Perry. It's . . . well, I couldn't really help myself. I felt funny all over and wanted to . . . but nothing happened. I still feel funny . . ."

"That's just the way it feels to be in love," he said. "And something did happen, I can assure you. Of course, it will get better with time and when we can be in our own bed."

"Oh, will it, Perry? I hope it will. And you really won't think me wicked?"

"I think you're an angel."

He was covering her up, covering himself, when they heard a rustle in the palms. What? No wind could ever penetrate this sheltered place. And then they both saw a black figure, trailing veils, disappear through the glass doors into the house and fly like a bat up the stairs.

"Oh, my God, Cousin Sophie!" Sally said. "She must have seen *everything*. What's going to happen now—?"

"What could happen? By tomorrow everybody in the family at least will know that you're going to be my wife, my duchess. So even if she talks—"

"But I feel so indecent. Oh, God, Perry, hold me . . ."

He did hold her and wipe the tears that were flowing again, but his own mind was singing. Luck upon luck. There was no way that she could back out now, and there was no way that the stuffed-shirt businessman Peter Van Ålen could refuse to talk generous terms. He might have a little trouble explaining it to Algie when he brought her back to England, but then Algie liked to eat well and had a fondness for the track, and he could indulge him now. Would it be too much to think that he'd just pulled off a reconquest of America? Not really, though he'd bet that some of the London gossip columnists would come up with a thought like that when they saw him living like a duke should live.

Chapter 3

ON A Saturday morning in the fall of 1876 Aaron Roberts Van Alen was trying to keep breakfast on his churning stomach and concentrate on a particularly turgid passage of Greek when "Tommy" Woodrow Wilson from down the hall came into his rooms. "Would you look at the private varnish out there? Somebody important's come down to see the game," Wilson said.

Aaron jumped to the window. In his present state, any diversion might help. Aaron's rooms were on the third floor of Witherspoon Hall, overlooking the spur that the Pennsylvania Railroad had built off its main New York-Philadelphia line to service the small town of Princeton, New Jersey, and the equally small college of the same name. Parked on the tracks, where it had evidently been deposited during the night, was a railway car which was, indeed, a most splendid piece of private varnish. Its high-gloss sides and gilt trim glowed in the already wintry November sunlight, and the leaded arches topping its windows looked to be set with precious stones instead of stained glass.

"Oh, my God, it's my father," Aaron said.

"Oh, I didn't know . . ."

"Why should you? Anyway, father's in the business, you know, and he uses that thing for advertising."

It wasn't strictly true. Something had happened to his father three or four years ago—he thought it had to do with the famous Erie Revolution, but he wasn't sure—and he'd practically turned the business over to older brother James. With time on his hands, his father had started to travel, and he'd had this car specially built at the Van Alen works so that he could take his wife along in comfort. There was, for instance, a small piano, custom-made by Steinway to fit into one of the parlor bulkheads, because aside from her social affairs, music was Martha's passion. There was a galley so that they could take along the cook from either Fifth Avenue or Newport, whichever place wasn't in use at the time, and bunks for the cook, Patrick, and Martha's favorite maid, Eileen, blessed be her name. There was a dining salon, a double-bedded stateroom for Peter and Martha and two guest accommodations with upper and lower berths and, of course, a bath. Aaron's only comfort in the sight before his eyes was the thought that he might be able to get into that bath after the game instead of shivering in the cold line waiting for a crack at one of the tin tubs under the gymnasium. Some said it was the fanciest bit of private varnish yet turned out, as befitted the carriage of the maker's nominal president, and in a way Peter did use it for business, so Aaron wasn't really lying. Peter had taken Andrew Carnegie out to Pittsburgh as a guest when they were closing a deal to buy Carnegie's steel, and just this summer he had loaned it to President Grant to bring Dom Pedro II, emperor of Brazil, up from Washington to Philadelphia for the opening of the Centennial Exhibition, thereby getting more mention in the press than the new refrigerator car on display in Machinery Hall. Here in Princeton Aaron saw no reason to emphasize the luxury of his life, particularly with a man like Tommy Wilson who was the son of a Virginia preacher and presumably in circumstances that were no more than comfortable, if that.

Staring as if transfixed at the car, Aaron said, "God, how I wish you hadn't got me into this, Tommy. It was bad enough before, but now . . . I suppose he brought grandfather and all the rest with him."

"Good," Wilson said. "Your father's an alumnus, and your grandfather too, isn't he? I was hoping that some important and . . . uh . . . financially comfortable alumni would get interested in football."

"So that's why you trapped me?"

"No, oh, no, I didn't really know. I wanted you because you're as good as I knew you'd be. I was watching you at practice the other day, and you're faster than anyone on the field—and stronger too, I'd judge by the way you hauled that brute Brewster down. He must outweigh you by fifty pounds."

"Yeah—and you don't know how it hurts to have two hundred pounds fall on top of you," Aaron said.

"I have a vivid imagination. I only wish that I

weren't all thumbs when it comes to handlnig the ball or I'd be out there with you."

"We need you where you are," Aaron said, and he almost meant it.

Though he didn't play—and probably just as well since he was tall and thin and a little delicate-looking—Wilson, as secretary, was responsible for managing the team, including recruiting. As soon as he and Aaron had moved into Witherspoon, practically next door to each other, Wilson had started working on him. The summer before, Aaron had won the matches in the new game of lawn tennis at Newport's Casino, and his athletic reputation had preceded him to Princeton. "Anyone who can play lawn tennis ought to be able to play football," Wilson had argued out of total ignorance, since only a comparative handful of people who were privileged to use the Casino or the Staten Island Cricket Club had ever seen, let alone played, tennis. It was the talk of New York back in '74 when Mary Outer-bridge, of all people, was held up at customs coming in from Bermuda, because the Finian lunkhead who found a net and some rackets in her luggage thought that they were meant for some nefarious purpose. But it was a far cry, as Wilson would have known if he'd seen it, from running around on soft grass in flannels and a blazer and patting a ball back and forth across a net to butting your way back and forth on ground already iron-hard from frost in padded knickers and vests and those ridiculous tiger-striped jerseys. You could get hurt in football. Did get hurt, Aaron thought.

The only reason Aaron had consented to play,

other than to placate Wilson, who as a sophomore and a member of the new campus newspaper, *The Princetonian*, deserved being placated, was that he had long ago learned to endure being hurt in his bouts with Teedie Roosevelt. One of the things Aaron hadn't liked about being Teedie's best friend when they were little was those awful asthma attacks; they were terrible to watch and, worse, always ruining their plans. So Aaron was only too willing to go along when Teedie, or maybe his father, decided on a body-building campaign. He kept Teedie company working out with weights and bars in the little gym Cousin Theodore installed in the old Twentieth Street house, and he put on the gloves with him, giving, he hoped, as much as he took. It was probably a good thing that Teedie had gone up to Harvard, because they'd surely be in competition on the same campus. When Aaron had written Teedie about going out for football, Teedie had replied, "Bully for you, Aaron. And I quake for our Harvards if you're on the field."

Just now, though, Aaron was quaking for himself. Today's game would be the first game of the first regular intercollegiate series in history, and much attention would be paid to it by the press. Ever since the very first game between Princeton and nearby Rutgers in '69, football had been a sometime, catch-as-catch-can event. Yale and Harvard and Columbia were playing it too, but any one of them would be lucky to have a game a season, since the faculties frowned on it and nobody could seem to agree on the rules. This year, though, they were all using the style some Yalie had brought over from his school days in Rugby in England, so you could run with the ball as well as kick it, a dubious improvement for Aaron, who as the fastest man on the team was most frequently the runner. When you had the ball, the opposing team not only tried to tackle you by anything they could grab above the waist but piled on you when you were down to squeeze the ball right out of your arms or, as it often seemed, cripple you beyond running again. Bad enough to be out there in front of strangers, like as not fumbling or getting the wind knocked out of him or a black eye when he was crushed in a pile, but with his family watching him? He hoped to God that his mother hadn't come along. He knew that she couldn't take seeing "her handsome boy" subjected to such punishment.

Well, no use wondering any longer. "I'd better go see what the governor's up to, Tommy. Meet you at the field," Aaron said, and started out.

The sight of his father's private car had multiplied the butterflies infesting Aaron's stomach, and he decided on a detour by way of the South Campus, or the Cloaca Maxima, as the more scholarly students called the vile-smelling latrines that served the needs of five hundred young men. At least they were solid this year, made of white-washed brick instead of the wood planking that was always being ripped away to fuel bonfires, but constipation was still said to be the besetting ailment of more sensitive undergraduates. Better to be empty when hurt, Aaron thought, delivering breakfast in several different directions. He was surprised to find the mighty Brewster, veteran of three seasons, doubled over in similar agony. "You too?" he asked.

Brewster clapped him on the back a bit harder than necessary and said, "Best thing for you, Aaron. Happens to me before every game, but you get over it."

It was some consolation but not enough to keep him from feeling shaky when he approached that palace on wheels that his father had christened *Cathay* after Great-Grandfather Cornelius Van Alen's China trader that his own namesake, Aaron Roberts, had captained. Grandfather Schuyler *had* been brought along. He was sitting alone on the observation platform, in his wheelchair and wrapped in blankets. Shortly after his wife had died in '73 he'd had a stroke right in the pulpit and been forced to resign after fifty years as pastor of the Uptown Presbyterian Church. They'd moved him into their own house, into the room next to Sophie's, but Dr. Schuyler wasn't about to stay in his room as Sophie did. So a ramp had been laid along one side of the marble staircase to make it possible to wheel him up and down. The Fifth Avenue house had been built too soon for elevators, but fortunately his father had installed one in the Newport cottage more out of fascination with the gadget than any foresight that it would be needed. Aaron could remember his father taking him down to the opening of the Equitable Building at Pine and Cedar Streets in '70, because it had the first elevator of any office building in the city. "I want you to remember this, son," his father told him as they rode up and down, up and down, "it's going to change the face of this city more than anything I've seen in my lifetime. There will be no limit to how high we can build." Anyway, his grandfather had to be eighty if he was a day, and Aaron had to admire his guts: Schuylers, it seemed, didn't give up on this life even when, like his grandfather, they believed that there was a better one coming.

"How are you, grandfather?" Aaron asked.

"Tolerable. Tolerable. They wanted to leave me home, but I wouldn't let them. Haven't been back here in ten years. That the Witherspoon where you're living?"

Dr. Schuyler gestured toward the five-story pile of stone with its arched windows and fussy cupolas rising above them.

"That's it, grandfather."

"Huh! Looks more a luxury hotel than a proper dormitory. Should have stuck to the old colonial style of Nassau and Reunion. Too much money around these days, if you ask me. We came to college to study, not to loll around—or play games either. What *is* this football?"

"You'll have to see it to understand it, grandfather. But it's being organized by Tommy Wilson—Thomas Woodrow Wilson, to give him his full name. I think you know his father, Dr. Joseph Wilson."

"Ah, I do, I do. One of the great Presbyterians of the South. It was men like Wilson who made it impossible for me to think that God was only on our side during the war. Fellows like that Greeley—God rest his soul—called me a Copperhead for it. It's a mercy *he* wasn't elected. He'd probably have gone crazy and died in the White House instead of up there in Westchester or wherever it was. Grant's

101

been bad enough . . ."

"Yes. Well, grandfather, you'll have to meet Tommy. He's always defending the southern cause. Who came with you?"

"Your father and Sally."

"Sally? I didn't know she was home."

"Came just last week—without the boy. Something fishy about it, I don't know."

"James and mother?"

"James doesn't care a whit for Princeton, and he works Saturdays just like your Uncle Cornelius used to. Good boy, James. Your mother couldn't stand to see you play a rough game."

That last about his mother was the best news since he'd first seen the car. Patting his grandfather on the shoulder, Aaron went inside. He hadn't seen Sally for four years; the one time his parents went to England to see her and their grandchild, Charles, it had been thought unwise to take him out of school. And when Sally had been around, his interest in anything female had been at a very low ebb. He'd considered her mostly a nuisance and a scold. Whenever he and Teedie would be up to any mischief, she'd tell on them; whenever she had her friends around she'd shoo him away, not that he cared what girls did or talked about. In those growing-up years, four years was an ocean of time and the other sex a foreign country. He had to admit, though, that catching a duke, even though the fellow seemed a little sissy to him, had finally aroused in him some admiration for his sister. After the announcement at her coming-out ball, which, thank God, he hadn't been forced to attend, the

102

papers were full of it, and some of the glory shown round about him too when he went to school. . . .

Aaron had been little more than a curious spectator during that hectic time between the ball and the summer wedding. Something had been going on that Aaron could sense more than see. Everybody was tense and edgy. Conversations were interrupted when he came into a room. Either his mother or Sally was often in tears which wasn't his idea of how people ought to feel about a wedding, and his father retreated into that grim silence with which he always displayed fury. Only the Duke seemed happy, and he did do something for which Aaron liked him: he spent a lot of time up visiting with Cousin Sophie. Aaron did know, largely because it was impossible not to hear his grandfather's pulpit voice from any corner of the house, that the Reverend Doctor Schuyler objected so strongly to "a girl of her age just running off like this with a perfect stranger" that he refused to go up to Newport to perform the ceremony. Martha had tried to explain to her father that the reason for the haste was the Duke's long-planned sailing to England, but the old preacher sniffed suspiciously. "He could return in due time, couldn't he? Or can't he afford it? Shouldn't wonder but what Peter's settled a pretty penny on him." *That* was something young ears weren't supposed to hear about, and his mother quickly shushed her father up. But, although he didn't yet know the amount, Aaron had to guess it was a lot from his father's attitude and from the way James acted glum throughout the whole affair and from a remark James dropped to him when they were

103

watching the couple leave: "Well, Aaron, there goes a big hunk of our inheritance." That leaving, by the way, was the only keen part of the wedding for Aaron, and it made him wonder whether he hadn't underestimated his sister. Even though the cottage was far from finished then, they'd decided to hold the ceremony and reception at Newport since most of their guests would be there anyway, and Sally had come up with the idea that they'd leave the party by sea. It took some doing. Sally got one of the Vanderbilt girls to persuade her father to lend them his yacht, and the Duke cabled some old boy in London who knew the Cunards to arrange for their liner taking them to Liverpool to sail by way of Newport and heave-to long enough to take them aboard from the yacht. So Aaron's last memory of his sister was seeing her, all dressed up in a brown silk suit and a hat like a flower bed, standing in the launch that would take her to the yacht right from their own dock and tossing flowers to her brides-maids with one hand and sipping champagne with the other. It was a considerable show, no question. . . .

Aaron was now very interested in things female, thanks to Eileen of blessed name, and he increasingly wished he had a sister about to give him some advice. Sometimes he'd thought of writing a letter to Sally, but her letters to the family were either so gooey about that baby Charles or so brittle and bright with chitchat about going down to Lord Somebody's country estate for a weekend or seeing Prince Edward at Ascot with so-and-so or bathing in the Mediterranean where some French woman went into the sea with nothing on at all that he didn't think she was likely to be interested in a little brother's problems.

As far as he was concerned he might as well have not had a sister at all, and yet here she suddenly was. She and his father were still sitting at breakfast in the mirrored salon. He didn't know what he'd expected, but he was surprised to see that marriage and motherhood hadn't changed her at all; she was still slim and girlish-looking and—yes—beautiful. She went well with the gilt trimmings of the *Cathay*. But when she stood up to kiss him, he decided that he'd grown a lot or she'd shrunk, because he found himself looking down on her and feeling oddly that the years that had made her always his big sister had been wiped out. But evidently not for her. "What do you think of this, Aaron? I came all the way from England so that I could see my little brat of a brother clobbered by those toughs from Rutgers. I wouldn't have missed it for the world."

"I can see you haven't changed," he said. "I thought marriage might improve you."

"Now you two . . ." Peter Van Alen said. "How are you, Aaron?"

"Fine, father," he said, shaking Peter's hand. "This *is* a surprise."

"Yes, well. I've been reading in the papers about this football business, even though you haven't communicated much about it, and I thought it would be a good excuse to have a look at the old campus and see how you're getting along. You know

I haven't even seen Witherspoon or Dodd yet."

"Wait till you see South Campus—it's all brick now."

"But I'll bet it doesn't smell any better."

They laughed together, easing that slight tension that seemed to be present lately in every meeting between father and son. "I can't wait," Peter said. "I'm just going to roll your grandfather over there for a look and leave you two alone. You haven't seen each other for a long time, and Sally's caught us up on the news."

When Peter left them, Sally seemed different, no longer the teasing sister. "Father's a brick, isn't he?" she said. "I mean he's so . . . understanding to leave us alone. Why do you think mother didn't come?"

"Well, grandfather said that she didn't want to see me roughed up."

"Rubbish! She doesn't know enough about football to anticipate that, but I do. I saw it at Rugby, so I cooked that up for grandfather. What mother is is prostrate. Simply prostrate about me . . ."

"How? I mean why?"

"I'll tell you, little one. I didn't come home a duchess with outriders and trumpeters heralding my passage. I came home with my tail between my legs."

"What do you mean?"

"Well, it's a long story, dear brother. Do you want to hear it?"

"Sure, I guess so."

"Good. God, Aaron, I've got to talk to *somebody*. No matter what they've been through, mother and father are shockable, so they don't know the half of it. I only told them I've left the Duke and won't go back under any circumstances. I said he beat me. And James . . . I've never been able to talk to brother James about *anything* that matters, have you?"

"No, but—"

"Why you, little brother? I know I used to tease and torment you, but I've always thought you had some of the same stuff in you that I seem to have. I was even more sure of it from the way mother was always fussing about you in her letters, like about the time you took your boat out when hurricane warnings were flying and the time you got drunk at the Belmont wedding. And then I came back and heard about Eileen . . ."

Aaron was furious with himself for blushing. "What about Eileen?"

"Oh, didn't you know? Mother fired her on the spot, about a month ago, when she said she was pregnant by you. Mother said no son of hers would be involved in such a sordid thing—"

"Lord!" Aaron's face was hot, and his empty stomach was churning again.

"Stop blushing, Aaron. You don't have to be embarrassed in front of me. I'm just glad you're learning somewhere, and I'm delighted you're *normal.*"

"But the poor girl—"

"Poor girl, my foot! From what the other servants say it could be any one of a dozen men. And don't worry about her. Father took care of her, so just take my advice and *never* bring it up with them. And let her go, Aaron, let her go. There will be other

Eileens, I guarantee you."

Aaron was breathing a *little* easier . . . this was
what he needed to hear from a sister. He'd never had
any delusions about loving Eileen, but the other was
pure joy. It was like the greatest game ever invented,
and she seemed to enjoy it too. In fact she'd asked
for it. All the previous summer he'd kept bumping
into her, as it seemed by accident, in out-of-the-way
corners of that rambling Newport cottage. Awkward
and full of apologetic giggles, she'd duck out of the
way but never without managing to brush against
him, touch him, and once he was sure, almost sure,
that her hand had somewhat lingeringly grazed his
cock, which jumped like a spring in a box. He'd
thought that she'd tittered, but then she was always
tittering. After that she'd really haunted his
thoughts, thoughts he'd tried to swim away, or play
away on the courts, or sail away in the little catboat
his father had given him for a seventeenth-birthday
present.

Then one long afternoon when a threatening
storm kept him to the house and everybody else was
out and there was absolutely nothing else to occupy
his mind, he'd gone really looking for her and had
found her in her room. Thinking he'd heard a
"Come in" in reply to his knock, he'd opened the
door and had been rooted right to the floor by the
shock of what he saw. She'd been lying on her bed,
fanning against the heat and wearing nothing but a
thin chemise that had ridden up to her hips and
exposed all those black furred private parts he'd
only dreamed about. Frightened and fascinated at
the same time, he'd just stared and stared, and she'd

fanned and fanned, making no effort to cover herself. "And aren't you going to stop staring and come to me?" she finally said. "Sure and it's taken you long enough to get the message." He might still have turned and run off if she hadn't jumped up, taken him by the hand and literally wrestled him down onto the bed, where she was all over him, giving him no more time for thought. They'd spent what was left of the summer playing together like shameless puppies wherever and whenever they could meet without detection . . . it had been a wonder he could win any tennis matches. He might not have had any illusions that it was love, but he had been looking forward to Christmas vacation and now he could see that she'd just been setting a trap for him. Well, he'd have to deal with his disillusion about that later. Anyway, God bless his innocent mother, and his understanding sister.

"But what about *you*, Sally? What's all this about you?"

"As I said, it's a long story . . . but first I'm going to have a cigarette . . ." He'd never known a woman who smoked, but then he realized that he'd never known a woman like his sister was turning out to be. He watched in a kind of awe as she rummaged a pack out of her purse, lit a cigarette and took a deep drag. ". . . and a sherry, too. Father ought to keep some strong waters on this rolling bordello . . ." Aaron laughed, shocked again to hear such a word from his sister, but it was so right. ". . . I know it's early in the day, but I got used to what they call 'elevenses' in that *fawncy* life I was leading, which I'm going to tell you all about. So be a good brother and see if you

109

can find something."

Aaron went back to the galley, where Patrick, polishing glasses, produced a bottle of the best Spanish sherry. When he brought it back Sally poured a glass for both of them and shoved her pack of cigarettes toward him. "Join me—or don't athletes have vices?"

"I suppose I couldn't feel any worse. I was throwing up a minute before I saw you."

"Bad as that?"

"Just first-game nerves . . ."

"Well, you might throw up again when you hear my story. So go easy on that stuff if you're not used to it . . ."

But as she talked he was too fascinated to feel sick, and the sherry did seem to settle his stomach, and for a long while he completely forgot that he was likely to be hurt before the day was over. . . .

Some people who weren't honest with themselves might have called it a sort of rape, but looking back Sally knew that she'd wanted it. The damnable thing was that she hadn't got what she wanted, and she'd tried every way short of outright indecency to get the Duke to do it again, but he'd argued that once was enough to let them know that they loved each other and that it would be immoral to do it again until after they were married. Dangerous, too. What would people think if a baby came too soon? What a laugh! Aaron knew, didn't he, that little Charlie was "premature." Anyway, the Duke was too seasick, or pretended to be, on the passage over to be interested in that sort of thing, and by the time they reached England she'd passed her period twice, and there was no question in the mind of the old London doctor the Duke had rushed her to right off the boat that she was pregnant. Well, she'd never seen anybody in her life as happy as the Duke. Can't let a bloodline as blue as his run out, don't you know? Can't be too careful. Best wait it out down at Midstone where there were trusted family retainers to look after her. And none of *that*, either. They'd have separate bedrooms so he wouldn't be tempted. It would be hard on him, but . . .

Hard on *him?* If Aaron could believe it, she'd rather have had her baby in the Tombs than at Midstone. It looked a little like a Gothic cathedral without the spire and was just about as spooky. Dark? Even if there was sun shining, which wasn't very often, those tiny leaded panes wouldn't let any of it in. They'd never heard of gas lights, so you had to go around with a candle that was always blowing out in the drafts. Half the time she was scared to death in the dark. And cold? They'd never heard of central heating either, and their fussy little coal fires wouldn't warm your behind if you sat on them. And they hadn't heard of bathrooms, so you were always shivery jumping in and out of water that was tepid by the time they lugged it from the kitchen to the tub they set up in your room. And they actually had chamber pots under the beds like the ones grandmother used to tell us about. Even if they'd heard of modern conveniences, they couldn't have afforded them, as she soon learned. Some of those lovable old retainers hadn't been paid in years, and instead of looking after her, they looked *at* her as if they wanted to kill her.

111

When her father's first check came in . . . Aaron knew about the checks, didn't he? Probably not too much, even she'd been taken in by their sweet father's story that they were just a little wedding present for his favorite daughter. When she learned of the amounts later, she would have been shocked but by then she was beyond shock . . . Well, when that first one came in she pleaded with the Duke to start fixing things up at Midstone, but he used it to rent a flat in London, where he had to go constantly on "business." She was so dumb then that she thought that there might be some kind of business to being a duke. Still, she was upset when he left her alone there with those creepy servants and spent most of the week and some weekends too in London. Even though they weren't sleeping together the Duke was at least somebody to talk to and ride with . . . Could Aaron believe it, she was so dumb then too that it never occurred to her that riding was worse than *that* for the condition she was in, and yet the Duke did encourage her to ride. Oh, God, how stupid innocent she was . . . Well, she got so lonely and miserable in the middle of one of those awful dull weeks that she just got on a train and went up to London to find the flat and surprise the Duke. And, God, Aaron, what a surprise. She could still close her eyes and see it all like a horrible dream that won't go away . . .

It was around midday, she thought, when she got there, and she thought the Duke might be out so she found the old man in charge of the building and told him she was the Duchess and got him to let her into the flat. The drawing room was a mess, clothes all over the place, glasses and bottles on the table. There didn't seem to be anybody home, so she started down a passageway. A bedroom door was open, and she looked in, and there they were—the Duke and another man stark naked on the bed and so . . . so engaged that they hadn't even heard her . . .

Aaron's flesh was crawling with revulsion, and curiosity. He'd heard vaguely of such things but couldn't imagine them in detail. "Engaged in what?" he blurted out.

This time Sally blushed. "I shouldn't . . . I . . . Oh, Aaron it was in his mouth . . ."

She rushed on with the story. She'd screamed, she thought. She'd certainly fainted. She came to with the Duke bending over her, wiping her face with a cold towel. When he saw that she was conscious, all he said was, "Well, now you know." She got up and ran out of there as fast as she could in her condition and took the next train back to Midstone because she didn't know where else to go. She cried all the way back and all that night, and she couldn't think of a sensible thing to do. She was in her eighth or ninth month then, and going back to America was out of the question even if she dared to. Maybe Aaron didn't know, but their father had absolutely refused to let her marry the Duke until the Duke persuaded Cousin Sophie to talk to him— she did tell Aaron, didn't she, that Sophie had seen them there in the garden—and then their father had gone into that grim act of his and had really not spoken to her more than he had to. As far as she knew, their mother hadn't been aware of any of this, still wasn't and it would kill her to know. And then there was the baby. She really wanted that baby. So there wasn't anything to do right away but kind of shrivel up inside whenever she thought about the Duke and wondered what the rest of her life would be like.

The Duke came down the next weekend, acting as if nothing important had happened. When she got him alone she called him every bad name she could think of, but he just kept smiling until she'd blown off her steam, then said that she was an innocent little goose who didn't understand that this sort of thing happened with the best of people. Especially the best of people. The man she'd found him with was, after all, Algie, Lord of Something-or-Other. He and Algie had been lovers since they'd gone down to Oxford together, so she couldn't accuse him of being a rounder or anything like that. She was, after all, a duchess and would soon be mother of a viscount with any luck, and she'd better learn to behave like one. People in their circles put family first and learned to overlook peccadillos like this as long as everybody was discreet. Once the baby was out of the way she could have her own kind of lover if her Presbyterian conscience would let her. Now that her father's money was coming in—did she know that it was a hundred thousand pounds over the next ten years and would probably be more once they had a grandchild?—they could go anywhere, do anything, no holds barred. Now was that so bad to look forward to? For his part, he was just glad that he didn't have to pretend anymore, but he did wish that she'd *knock* next time.

Aaron would have to understand that she was only eighteen then and all alone in England and about to have a baby and too ashamed of what she knew, had seen, to talk about it with anybody. So she just went along with the Duke, living from day to day until the baby came and really saved her life. That baby was one reason that she'd never, ever envy a man. Oh, it was hard having him, but you forgot about that almost as soon as it was over. Aaron wouldn't understand, no man *could* understand, what it was like with that little warm body nuzzled up to you, sucking from you. You had feelings all over . . . well, she was happy for six months or more until the baby was weaned. She was the most important person in somebody's life, in nearly everybody's life. All the Duke's distant relatives came trooping down to Midstone to oh-and-ah over the heir and give her presents, and as Aaron knew, her own parents made instant plans to cross the Atlantic and cabled her a present of a thousand pounds which, thank God, she'd had sense enough to put away or she wouldn't be here now. Even the Duke, puffed with pride, went out of his way to be nice to her. He actually spent some of their father's money on her, outfitting her with gowns to fit her restored shape, buying her a new horse, giving her a diamond pendant big enough to use as a weapon. So she decided to really try being a duchess, especially after their parents came and she could see how proud they were of that grandchild and how generous—you know father, Aaron, so it wouldn't surprise you that, after one look around Midstone, he marched the Duke down to a plumbing contractor and arranged to pay for having pipes and W.C.'s and bathtubs put through the whole place at lord knows what cost.

The Duke went his way, and she went hers, which she found wasn't at all uncommon in their set. With the baby out of the way, she started riding to the hounds and met some nice people. They all knew about the Duke, it seemed, and they felt sorry for her. They began to include her, with or without the Duke, in their house parties even as far away as the south of France, and she began having what she thought was the kind of good time she'd expected when she grew up. She didn't take a lover until the baby was old enough to leave safely with his nanny, but then she had one after the other—well not that many, three actually. But, oh Aaron, it wasn't really fun. It seemed safer if they were married too, complaining about wives who were cold or ugly, and almost . . . well . . . good because weren't she and her lovers helping each other in a difficult situation? Still, she didn't get much more out of it than she had that first time with the Duke. It's difficult for women, Aaron. Maybe she *did* have a Presbyterian conscience. Maybe all those sermons of their grandfather she'd had to sit through had rubbed off. She'd even tried to tell herself that she wasn't any worse than the sainted Dr. Henry Ward Beecher, who went back to his pulpit at Plymouth Church after it was pretty well proved he'd committed adultery with his best friend's wife, but she'd always hear her grandfather thundering, "Beecher isn't a Presbyterian. I knew he'd come to no good preaching all that mush about love instead of

116

original sin and damnation." And her poor lovers. They were afraid to . . . well, with everybody knowing about the Duke, it would be an intolerable scandal for her to have another baby. And gradually she realized that what she wanted *was* another baby but not enough ever, ever to sleep again with the Duke even if he wanted to, which she very much doubted. So she decided that she'd just have to leave him, and she told him so.

He was furious. She'd never seen him furious before and she was frightened. In fact, one of the things that had made life more or less tolerable was that when she did have to be with the Duke, which wasn't often, he was always in good humor. He had everything he'd ever wanted—plenty of money, a perfect cover in her for his own private arrangements, an heir—and he was enjoying life. But when she told him, he turned purple—literally purple, Aaron—and his voice shot up into a high register like a woman's scream.

"You'll never leave me, you . . . you little whore," he said. "If you try to I'll ruin you . . . or . . . or kill you."

She tried to appeal to his better instincts, if he had any. "It's for our child, Perry. You're no fit father, and you know it, and if things go on this way I'll become an unfit mother—"

"Become? Become? You already are. If you try to take my son I'll have you in court and bring out your filthy adulteries. I'll divorce *you*, and you'll never see your precious baby again. And don't think you have anything on me. You've no witnesses but yourself, and you'll never get any, and they'll say it's all in your filthy little mind. I haven't had other women. I've been faithful to you—"

"We'll see about that—"

"Oh, no, we won't. I'll ruin you, I tell you. You're a sillier goose than I thought if you think I care what happens to you. I want that money, and I'm not going to lose it. I'd . . . I'd . . . I'd kill you first. Believe me . . ."

She was furious now too. "You wouldn't have the guts—"

And then he hit her—not really hit her but slapped her across the face like a girl would. Hard, though, and there was a look on his face that made her realize that he could kill her. Not with his hands, he wasn't strong enough. But poison? There were all those old retainers she still didn't trust. "Just wasted away, poor girl." Or a gun? He had a whole rack of them behind glass, and only he had the key. "A shooting accident, poor girl." Nobody had ever hit her before. Nobody had ever looked at her like that before. She panicked. Feeling cornered, she hit back—not really hit but brought her knee up into his groin the way somebody had told her to do if a man ever tried to . . . well, he doubled right over screaming, and she ran all the way to the Midstone station. She was lucky in her timing. There was a train up to London in a few minutes, and it got there in time for her to get to the bank and get the thousand pounds she'd been keeping for the baby. She took the next train to Liverpool and bribed an American captain to take her aboard under an assumed name and hide her until he sailed in case the Duke tried to follow her. She didn't know yet whether he had. She still felt terrible about leaving little Charlie, but she knew that he'd at least be safe . . . the Duke had such a stake in him . . . until this was all straightened out . . .

Wasn't it a mess? An unholy mess? Couldn't Aaron understand now why she couldn't tell anybody, anybody but him, but why she had to tell *somebody*. She was glad that the Duke had hit her, because she hadn't had to really lie to their father. He was a real brick about it, Aaron. He said he'd never condemn a daughter of his, or any woman, to life with a wife beater and got his attorneys on it right away. It will probably cost the poor man another fortune to get a decent divorce and some rights for Charlie to be with us. But he hasn't complained once. In fact, he's almost seemed happy. "I always did think the fellow a bounder," he said, "and it's good to have my little girl back again." So did Aaron see why she couldn't really tell him, ever, and why she'd deny to her last breath whatever the Duke might say about her, though he'll probably be greedy enough to keep his mouth shut if negotiations go his way, and they probably will. Wife beating is no grounds for divorce, so it will have to be put on her—desertion, she gathered. Of course, Aaron could see why their mother was prostrate, because news of the divorce at least will get into the papers, and everybody'll know that her little girl didn't have the stuff in her to be a duchess after all. Their mother thinks it's the absolute end of the world, and she could be right as far as Sally was concerned. "Oh, Aaron, do you think that any decent man could ever want me, after . . . ?"

119

Aaron didn't know what to think. He was stupefied, shocked. It was a heavy load for a seventeen-year-old who had himself just discovered that lust could be both an alluring adventure and a painful trap. And this was his own sister, a nice girl, a girl who'd grown up in the protection of those marbled walls on Fifth Avenue, a girl who'd had every lesson in grace and manners available, a girl confirmed in her own grandfather's rock-hard faith, a girl who was as close to a princess as America could produce. He was stunned. He couldn't get over looking at her, staring almost, because none of this damage showed. Like gold, her beauty didn't corrode. But she was also crying, soundlessly, the tears beginning to make little rivulets in the makeup she'd taken to wearing.

He had to say something. "Sally, it's not your fault. He's a . . . damn swine!"

"No good, Aaron. Remember how Grandmother Van Alen used to say that it does no good to lay the blame on other people—you can't change them, you can only change yourself. I didn't know what she was talking about, but I know now. Oh, God, I wish she were still alive. I think she might have understood. I . . . I just feel that nobody can love me, or even ought to . . .'"

Aaron was deeply moved. Here was this big sister who'd been so domineering and cuttingly sure of herself pleading with him for some understanding, support. He acted instinctively, put his arms around her. "Sally, I . . . I love you. I'm sure it will turn out all right. You'll see."

"*Thank* you, Aaron. I guess you're going to have

to be a big brother now.... Oh, oh, here comes father, I can see him through the window. I guess I'd better run and repair the damage to my face. Father would notice I've been crying and wonder why . . . Oh, and Aaron, I didn't mean that about seeing you clobbered. Go out and win that game for me. I need something, somebody, to be proud of. . . ."

Aaron went into the game with a lot more to fight for than the honor of Old Nassau. He could see his sister and father along the sidelines, flanking his grandfather in the wheelchair and talking to Tommy Wilson, who would probably stick to them like a mustard plaster, explaining the finer points of the game and charming them with his southern accent. Wilson was in need of funds for more balls and pads and cleated shoes, and he had a politician's instinct for where to get them. He could see, too, that Wilson had been bowled over, reduced to a stammer, by his sister's looks when he'd introduced them, which might be part of an answer to her question. So, in fact, had Brewster. "Who's the doll?" Brewster had wanted to know. Aaron had passed it off with, "Oh, just my married sister" without bothering to make introductions, since he was sure that Brewster wasn't Sally's type. But if he'd learned nothing else from his sister's astonishing confession, he'd learned that you couldn't tell what was going on inside a woman by the way she looked. It made them more interesting to him—and more frightening. For instance, it had never crossed his mind that Eileen, now of cursed name, had had anything more on her mind than the fun she seemed to get out of their

121

encounters. The little witch. He'd thought that it was his cock she yearned for, as she kept telling him, but it was only his father's money. Was he really so different, when he thought about it, from Sally? Yes, he'd try to be her big brother, because she needed one, just like he needed a sister. The way to start was to win this one for her. He felt a little like a knight in those old tales who rode out to joust, with a lady's favor tied to his lance . . .

Princeton won the toss and elected to receive, and just before they went onto the field Brewster came up with a Topper of an idea. Instead of going out to block they'd all surround the fellow who caught the ball, all fourteen of them, and form a wedge, locking arms. Then they'd drive like an arrow right through the scattered Rutgers forces. If nothing else it would probably surprise and scare them enough to be good for one touchdown or get them close enough to kick a goal. Because he was fastest on his feet and better than most with the running drop kick, Aaron was stationed back in the center where he was most likely to get under any respectable kick. The Rutgers line was coming forward, and his empty stomach collapsed and rose right up into his throat. No time to worry about it. The ball was up there, spinning in a long arc. Eye on the ball, eye on the ball. Nothing else. The ball would have been easier to catch a year or so ago when they were still using a sphere instead of this Rugby oval. The damned thing could jiggle right out of your arms if you didn't take it just right. Under it, under it. Now?

Aaron caught the ball, jammed it into where his stomach ought to have been and started running. As promised, his fourteen teammates grouped around him in a kind of wedge and ran with him. It slowed him down, but the first, confused Rutgers men just bounced off the human walls they encountered. The strategy was working. Then one huge opponent with a brighter mind than you'd expect to find behind such an ugly face simply threw his whole weight and strength into a block of the man leading the Princeton triangle. Aaron's linked teammates started stumbling and falling over each other in a writhing pile. An instinct for saving his own neck rather than thought now prompted Aaron . . . He ran right over the backs of his own teammates, scoring them with his cleats and hardly hearing their howls. In a second he was out in front alone with only two defenders between him and the goal. All he had to do now was run, run and dodge, and he was good at both. Fear evaporated. He was no longer aware of his stomach, of his body really. He was a burning brain. Lead them this way, then reverse. More, more, a little more. Now cut, cut, cut. One lumbering giant charged harmlessly by in the wrong direction. You can outrun the other if you angle. Run, run, run. He was over! The Rutgers man, pounding and puffing behind him, said, "I'll get you the next time, you little squirt." His own teammates were around him, forgetting their scratches and pounding him on the back. "Atta tiger!" People on the sidelines were clapping and yelling, and he was sure he could hear Sally's voice above the rest.

But the game had just begun, and the men of Rutgers were mad. They were also fast learners. When, with a running drop kick, Aaron sent the ball spiraling over the goal line, the Rutgers team ran back and formed their own wedge around the man who caught it. Speed was not Aaron's ally this time. He was well ahead of the Princeton pack. Fear solidified again, making him acutely aware of his vulnerable body. Why hadn't he held back? Nobody would blame the kicker for that. Too late now. Well, what had worked once could work again. He threw his body across the knees of the man at the point, trying to roll and take the blow on his back. Not fast enough. The knee caught him in that tender stomach. Not heavy enough, either. He went down, and they charged right over him like a troop of spike-shod horses. He couldn't breathe, and the pain in his solar plexus was like a hot poker. He was a ball of agony. Instant death would be a mercy. Wilson was bending over him, dabbing at him with a wet towel and asking in worried tones, "You all right, Aaron? You all right?" Miraculously, breath came back and with it the hope of life. He hurt all over, but he nodded at Wilson, who asked, "Want me to get somebody else to play for you?"

He'd never wanted anything more in his life. Why was he saying, "No, no, just got the wind knocked out of me." Had his brains been knocked out too? When he got shakily to his feet there were more cheers, more friendly slaps from teammates. Aaron Van Alen was a real tiger. Brewster had broken through the wedge, faltering from Aaron's attack, and brought down the ball carrier, so Princeton was still ahead on Aaron's touchdown. Back to the game, which for Aaron became a teeth-grinding ordeal. With surprise gone, neither team tried the wedge again and went back to the familiar style of scrimmage—a thudding, grunting, cursing melée. Carrying the ball over and over again, Aaron found himself at the bottom of one bruising pileup after another. He already hurt so much that more hurt didn't matter. Inching each other back and forth, the teams wore away the afternoon. Once Rutgers got off a kick that missed by inches; once Aaron thought he'd broken loose again on a run, only to be caught from behind and ridden down with an elbow vise around his neck, and a voice saying, "Told you I'd get you, squirt." He could feel the man's fist hammer into his kidneys, but as the others piled on, Aaron used the quick jab he'd learned in the ring to remind his tackler that size wasn't everything. He was learning survival in a hard school. When the game ended with his score still standing, he was hoisted on shoulders and paraded around the field. He was glad that he'd stuck it. What was a little hurting to a hero? . . .

In need of hot water to soothe his bruises and food more palatable than they were served in Mrs. Wright's boarding house to appease his hunger, Aaron took Wilson back with him to the *Cathay*. Dinner was a form of celebration. First there were toasts to him and then to all the tigers. Peter wrote out a check for Wilson to use in buying equipment, and Sally kept saying over and over how proud she was of her little brother. Only Grandfather Schuyler, who had no wine to make him merry, grumbled. "Don't see how a game like that is going to do anything to make better ministers."

"Oh, grandfather, not all the boys in Princeton

125

are going to be ministers," Sally said.

"They were in my day."

"But father didn't go into the ministry, and I'll bet even Mr. Wilson here has other ideas. Don't you, Mr. Wilson?"

"Yes, I'd thought of teaching."

"And you certainly can't imagine Aaron as a preacher, can you, grandfather?"

"I don't know, I don't know. I've hoped. Runs in the blood, you know—on his mother's side. . . . I thought maybe the influence here in Princeton . . . seems I was wrong . . ."

There was a catch in the old man's voice, a note of wistfulness that brought on a brief, embarrassed silence. It had, of course never crossed Aaron's mind to follow in his grandfather's footsteps. All the church he'd been forced to attend had been a bore, although it was standing him in good stead now since he could doze through the compulsory religion courses and endure with fortitude the compulsory chapel services. He'd also been sensitive to the fact that his two favorite people in all the world, his Grandmother Van Alen and his father, had, despite efforts to conceal it in front of the children, shown a tongue-in-cheek attitude toward Grandfather Schuyler's sometimes pompous piety. Once in a while it would break out into open argument, and Grandfather Schuyler would shrug and say, "A prophet is not without honor except in his own home." So could the old man even have hoped, as he said, that Aaron would become a minister? The mere fact that he did made Aaron feel curiously uncomfortable about his sins of the summer, which evidently didn't show on him any more than Sally's did on her. He exchanged looks with his sister who made him feel better again by giving him a very definite wink. But it was Wilson who got him off the hook.

"I can assure you, Dr. Schuyler, that the influence here hasn't changed, football or no. Why Dr. McCosh, our president—"

"McCosh? McCosh? Didn't I hear that he believes in that fellow Darwin's godless theory that men come from monkeys? How a man of God could take *that* view is beyond me. I don't know . . ."

"I think Dr. McCosh may just mean that we should keep open minds, Dr. Schuyler," Wilson said. "But let me, if I may, tell you a story . . . Last year when I was rooming at Mrs. Wright's the fellow across the hall became ill with a fever. It was touch and go for a while. He went into delirium and then became unconscious. Since we have no nurse or infirmary, as you know, I was doing what I could for the poor chap with cold compresses when Dr. McCosh looked in. He kept shaking his head and finally asked, 'Is he a Christian?' I said, 'I think he's an Episcopalian, Dr. McCosh.' Well, the good doctor grabbed my hand and said, 'Down on your knees with me, Wilson, while we pray for his soul.'"

Grandfather Schuyler laughed loudest and longest, and when they were walking back to Witherspoon together, Aaron said, "Thanks for getting me out of that thing with grandfather, Tommy. I could no more be a minister than I could fly. But . . . well, he *is* my grandfather and—"

"Sure, look here, I grew up in a manse, you know, and have more preachers than horse thieves hanging from my family tree. One thing I've learned is that nothing works as well with them as a preacher joke, though that thing actually did happen with Jimmy McCosh."

"You know, what you ought to be is a politician, Tommy. Have you ever thought of that?"

They'd paused by silent, mutual consent on the open stone porch of Witherspoon, reluctant to see a day of glory end. Above them the ebony bowl of sky was sieved by stars. It was a time for long thoughts, and Wilson turned serious. "Hmm. I don't know. But what about you, Aaron? I could agree that you're not cut out for the ministry. If nothing else, you have too much trouble with Greek. But what do you want to do with your life?"

What, indeed? Aaron was ashamed to admit that he'd never given the matter much thought. He'd grown up with the tacit understanding—of the family—that he would follow his brother James into the firm. He had no real interest in the business, but it was a way to justify his existence while he did what he really wanted to do. Which was what? Find another Eileen? Sure. Win some more tennis matches? Maybe that too. Get hold of a real boat and see what he could do with it? Yes . . . But none of those things was an answer to Wilson's question. Did he have any kind of an answer? Aaron had originally come down to Princeton to appease his father. James, who'd dropped out of Columbia after a few months to go to work, argued that a college education would do him more harm than good in business, but his father had insisted. "I'm not sure Aaron wants to go into the business, and I don't think he is either. What he needs is some time to himself. My mother insisted on that for me, and I've always been grateful." Aaron hadn't liked the insolence in his brother's reply: "But, dad, you'll have to admit it didn't do you any good as a businessman." His father, however, had taken it in stride: "I learned, James, that there is a good deal more to this life than business. I'm sorry you missed that opportunity, James, but I am grateful for your help in the business . . ."

So Aaron had come to Princeton, and he was beginning to think that what his father had wanted for him was happening right now—it was to be exposed to important, difficult questions rather than to discover pat, over-simplified answers.

So having no true answer, he fell back on, "I guess I want to beat Columbia next week."

Wilson understood. "Atta go, tiger."

Lying in bed that night, hurting all over but proud of it, Aaron still wrestled a while with Wilson's question and then decided to go along with a text of his grandfather's—"Sufficient unto the day is the evil thereof." Only in this case, it was the good. Tomorrow, he knew, the *Princetonian* and the New York papers would be full of his exploits, and at least nobody could get away with calling Van Alen a spoiled rich kid. He could take it, and he could give it, and beating Columbia didn't sound like such a silly answer after all. No Van Alen in all history, as far as he knew, had ever been an athlete, unless you could count the tales his grandmother used to tell about her father-in-law Cornelius' sailing exploits on the Hudson River. But even those were by way of making more money through faster service. For Aaron, sport, like the poetry his father used to write at Princeton, had no earthly use. It was a pure testing of man's spirit against keen competition and within acknowledged rules. Scoring a point, making a goal he guessed provided some of the same satisfaction as catching the right words to turn a prosaic thought into a thing of beauty, a song in rhythm and rime. There was a kind of ecstasy in risking yourself for no other gain than glory, an ecstasy he'd heard veterans of the war try and fail to put into words and, having tasted it, he wanted more. He rather thought that Sally might understand and appreciate his ambition, and he drifted off to sleep in the warm blanket of that thought.

Chapter 4

IT WAS by the grace of God that he'd just come in from an after-theater supper at Delmonico's and was still very much awake and fully dressed when the damned thing started ringing. He'd agreed with his father that having a telephone in the house was "an infernal nuisance . . . a gentleman would take the trouble to conduct his business in person." But his mother had finally insisted on it because so many of her friends were beginning to use it to make their social arrangements. Ordinarily it was Patrick's duty to answer the phone's imperious summons, but in the dead of night like this the sound wouldn't reach up to the servants' quarters. Father ought to have some kind of extension put up there, although in the year or so since they'd had the contraption it had never rung outside of civilized hours. So Aaron rushed down to answer the ring with a feeling of as much apprehension as annoyance.

It was Sally, and her voice sounded as if it were coming from across the Atlantic instead of from the manse next door. "Oh, Aaron, thank God it's you! I'm in trouble. Can you come right away?"

"Trouble? What kind of trouble?"

"I can't talk . . . but come . . . And be careful— he's roaming around downstairs."

"Who? Who's roaming around?"

"Bud . . . oh . . . oh, Aaron . . ."

A click, and then silence. Lord, what now? When he hung the receiver on its hook and turned away, he saw out of the corner of his eye a figure on the stairs. It was his father, who'd evidently heard the ringing too. He was descending with that odd, one-step-at-a-time shuffle he'd been using ever since his heart attack. For all the seeming gentleness in him, Peter Van Alen was turning out to be another stubborn Dutchman when it came to taking care of himself. He refused to use the wheelchair and ramps they'd fixed for Grandfather Schuyler. "You can bring it out for my eightieth birthday—but not before." Well, this was only 1881, and that was nearly a dozen years away, and looking at his father now Aaron was afraid that he'd never live to use that chair. The attack had not only put a shuffle into his steps but a stoop in his shoulders, as if he felt that a wounded heart could beat easier in a concave chest. Since he'd just gotten up from bed, his mane of white hair was tousled, his chin white-stubbled, his eyes blinking against the light. In that moment Aaron knew for certain that whatever his chronological age, his father was an old man, and he was aware of the blessing of providence that had allowed him to reach the phone first.

Peter stopped halfway down the stairs. "Oh, it's

you, Aaron . . . what is it, and at this time of night?"

"Just a friend of mine, dad—phoning from Delmonico's. They want me to come back to the party—"

"This hour? Why, it's going on two."

"I know, I know, dad. But you see they've managed to snag this girl I've been wanting to meet from the revue at Pastor's and—"

"Aaron, you know what your mother thinks about girls like that—"

"From what Cousin Amelia tells me, I'm just a chip off the old block, dad. Isn't that right?"

"Well . . . your head won't be fit for business in the morning—"

"Don't worry, dad. James understands. I think he'd rather have me hung over than sticking my nose into things around the office."

"Not from what he tells me. James says you're spoiled by college and all that football business—a bad example to all the other hard-working young men."

"Look, dad, I've got to hurry or that girl will get away."

"Aaron—"

"Dad, I am over twenty-one. Now go back to bed and don't *worry*."

In a way he hated to leave his father like that, leave him to fret over the fact that his younger son seemed both frivolous and insubordinate. But better that, far better, than to give him the slightest suspicion that Sally was in some kind of serious trouble. Whether all that fuss and bad publicity over Sally's divorce—DUCHESS DESERTS DUKE AND SON . . .

GLAMOUR WEDDING OF '72 ENDS IN DIVORCE . . . HINTS OF OTHER MEN IN NEW YORK BELLE'S LIFE . . . DUCHESS BUYS BABY RIGHTS; SETTLEMENT SAID TO BE HALF A MILLION— hastened his father's heart attack would be hard to know for sure, but Aaron all his life had been aware of, and jealous too, of his father's doting love for Sally. God, how fortunate that the old man didn't know what really had gone on in that marriage.

On the other hand, it might have made him a little more understanding about Sally's choice of Bud Brewster. What the very hell could have happened? Whatever it was, this wouldn't be the first time that Aaron had discovered that his father's hunches about people were sound. But, my God, what could have been more dramatic public redemption than for the notorious ex-duchess to walk down the aisle with the city's most promising young minister? Only the father of the bride hadn't seen it that way, and only somebody who knew that father as well as Aaron was getting to know him could have detected it. Though he publicly held his peace, Peter marched through the ceremonies with somewhat of the same grimness he'd exhibited during the affair with the Duke, and once Aaron had walked in on the end of a talk between his parents and overheard his mother say "For heaven's sake, Peter, the way you act a person would think that *nobody's* good enough for Sally. I think she's most fortunate—we're all fortunate—to get our good name back after that scandal. For her sake, try to smile, won't you? . . ."

It was probably just some sort of spat, though it wasn't like Sally to sound an alarm over nothing. If his father had answered that phone, heard that faint

134

and scared voice, he might have just keeled over, considering how he felt about Sally—and about Bud Brewster.

Yes, until Aaron found out what was going on, let his father's concern be for him. There was a great possibility, in fact, that for all of his fussing his father might go off to bed more amused than concerned. In the year or so since he'd been home from college, Aaron, in search of himself and via research into his father, had taken to having long talks with both Cousin Sophie and Cousin Amelia, two ladies who for different reasons were easily flattered into garrulousness by the attentions of a handsome young man. Out of it was emerging a picture of a father so unlike the sweet but reserved man he'd always known that Aaron was more than a little intrigued. In Cousin Sophie's family, Peter Schuyler Van Alen, her father's younger brother, had been held to be a scandalous character, "something like those Communists who believe in free love and giving everybody's money to the poor." Not that she agreed, mind you, but "where there's smoke, there's fire, isn't there?" Cousin Amelia talked of an idealist, a sensitive poet and crusading editor, a lover of the theater, or at least of women of the theater. There was something in her eyes and manner when Amelia talked about his father that gave Aaron the impression she was holding more back than she was telling, that . . . well, it just couldn't be imagined that there might have been such a thing between this formidable giant of an old lady and his fastidious father. The lines of the cousins' testimony crossed, however, on the point that, before his marriage, Peter Schuyler Van Alen had been somewhat of a disgrace in the eyes of the Dutch traders and puritanical preachers who made up so much of the rest of the family. All this made it clearer to Aaron why, behind the expected fatherly noises Peter made when he got into some kind of trouble, he'd often detected the light of a suppressed smile in those sea-gray eyes so like his own.

And so as he raced across the few feet of sidewalk separating the Van Alen mansion from the manse, Aaron wasn't really worried that his supposed dissipation at Delmonico's would keep the old man up for very long.

Shuffling back up the stairs toward his room, Peter was certain that there'd be no more sleep for him that night. One of his mother's favorite sayings popped into his head. Whenever anything would happen in the night she'd jokingly quote Shakespeare, "Macbeth doth murder sleep." During her last years, as he recalled, she was using that line more and more, and he found his own increasing difficulties in sleeping as frightening a sign of age as his heart attack. It might be easier to get through the nights if he could just roll over in bed and take Martha in his arms as he'd done in those years when they'd lived down on Twenty-second Street. He hated to think about the numbers of times since they'd moved into this mansion that he'd walked through the dressing rooms and just caught himself before he knocked on her door. She always said that she "slept like a baby," so what right had he to turn himself into her sleep-murdering Macbeth? . . .

This night he'd even tiptoed by her doorway to the hall for fear she might wake up and want to know about the phone call. She'd be furious with him for letting Aaron go out. After that thing with the servant girl Eileen, Martha had been very afraid that Aaron might get mixed up with some fortune-hunting female. Not that she thought for a moment that he was guilty; you know what the other servants said about the girl, and he was so young and innocent and . . . well, a son of hers would have better taste. But there wasn't *anything*, from what she'd heard, that these young women today, particularly the ones in the theater, wouldn't do to trap someone as rich and handsome as her Aaron. Peter often wondered what mechanism was working in Martha's head that allowed her to forget, while she was saying such things, that he himself had been the subject of newspaper notoriety when he'd been beaten to a pulp by some Bowery boys while escorting a young lady of the theater to what he'd profoundly hoped would be a "fate worse than death." He really marveled at her ability to live in the present, and plan for the future, as if the past were irrelevant, or had never happened. His mother had had much of the same ability, he recalled, and perhaps that's why she and Martha had liked each other. Could it be something female, a kind of natural survival mechanism that in its most primitive form let them forget the pain of childbirth to go on bearing children? He didn't know and probably never would.

Which was another thing about getting old, or

feeling old . . . you began to realize how many things you'd *never* know for sure. He did know, though, that whatever Aaron was up to wasn't worth much worry. He could never let on for the sake of peace with Martha that he was as sure that Aaron was at least one of Eileen's lovers, as she was sure he wasn't, nor could he let on that, having looked the saucy girl over, he found it hard to blame his son. Aaron had always been full of what people called hell, but so, he guessed, had he. Another way of putting it was that Aaron, as he'd demonstrated out there on the football field, was willing to take risks with life, and in that way Aaron reminded Peter especially of his mother. If he believed in such things, Peter might attribute it to some magical property from that little dragon that Aaron kept always at his bedside, as old Sally had done before him. "Rub it before every game, brings luck," Aaron had once mumbled in embarrassment when his father had found him fondling it.

Thoughts of the dragon prompted Peter to get down the heavy ledger in which he'd been slowly inscribing his account of the Schuyler-Van Alen families. Since he couldn't sleep, he might as well work. Where was he? Oh, yes . . . "During my youth, there was often in our house a sea captain by the name of Aaron Roberts, whom we called Uncle Aaron. . . ." He hastily scanned the paragraphs he'd so far composed about Captain Roberts, a somewhat enigmatic character who for him represented more of a boyhood dream of life's possibilities than a real person. No mention of the dragon. How could he have forgotten that when it meant so much to his mother? Well, he'd insert it. Let's see . . . "At some point in time Uncle Aaron brought from China a little jade dragon which he presented to my mother . . ."

Peter put down his pen. He felt too fretful to concentrate on writing. Even though the specific mission didn't worry him, Aaron's going out like this into the night had aroused a kind of shapeless dread about all his children. Sally? Silly to worry about her. Nothing could be wrong with Sally, who was snug in bed in the manse next door, no doubt dreaming sweet dreams about the baby she'd have before long. He'd probably been wrong about Brewster. When he faced himself honestly in the middle of the night, Peter had to admit that he was often as intolerant of the pious as they were of him. Brewster had reminded him too much of his father-in-law, the Reverend Doctor Schuyler, on whose narrow-minded preachings against sins of the flesh he still blamed the fact that at this moment he wasn't cuddled up to Martha's comforting body. Yet over the years he'd come to a grudging admiration for old Dr. Schuyler's honest, if irrational, consistency of thought and the rugged physical courage he'd shown up until the moment of his death. Both of them, out of mutual love for Martha, had learned at least to tolerate each other, and in that toleration had developed a kind of affection. He'd never forget how he'd felt when Dr. Schuyler, on his death bed, had reached out to him and said, "Peter, I was wrong those many years ago. You've been good to my little girl and for that God will bless you." Maybe tolerance of each other's sins and stupidities was the

139

key to the kind of love families should provide, and maybe working on his own tolerance for Brewster would let him feel as good about Sally as she seemed to feel about herself . . .

But James. Odd that, of them all, it was James who troubled him most. Convene any panel of outside observers of the Van Alen family, and they'd unanimously elect James Schuyler Van Alen the perfect son. He had, at the age of nineteen, voluntarily dropped out of college and entered the family business in which he had proved so adept that, at twenty-four, he'd virtually taken it over, freeing his father to pursue a leisurely life which was made more secure each year by the shrewd expansion and investment of Van Alen & Son. Not only had James transformed the company from a relatively small manufacturer of locomotives and steam engines into an enterprise producing virtually every kind of rolling stock—sleepers, oil tankers, refrigerator cars—for the nation's expanding railroads, but through his business and social associations he had engineered stock exchanges that made Van Alen & Son a holder in, and himself a director of, such other solvent enterprises as the Standard Oil Trust, Carnegie Steel Corporation, Western Union and Manhattan Elevated Railroad. Though he so obviously profited from James' dedication to business, this trait in his son reminded Peter unpleasantly of his older brother Cornelius, and yet . . .

There was a certain charm to James, a kind of saving grace that Cornelius had lacked. People who had truly long memories thought that James might be more of a throwback to the first Cornelius Van

Alen than to his uncle Cornelius. It was certainly physically true James was fat Dutch, like old Cornelius, like his Roosevelt relatives on the other side. Fat and exuberant with a beaming smile and booming voice. Yes, James Schuyler Van Alen *enjoyed* doing business, and he made no bones about it. Unlike his uncle Cornelius or a sour old trader like Daniel Drew or a silent schemer like this John Rockefeller, James at least did not confuse business with righteousness. He was as religious in church attendance as any of them—another mark of the perfect son—but in the market he was working for Van Alen and not the Lord. Peter liked James for that and thought that the young man might have inherited a little of his own skeptical honesty about human motivation after all.

If James enjoyed making money, he seemed to enjoy spending it too, and in this way he was more like his mother Martha than anybody else. James had been a most supportive son to her, arguing away his grandmother's and father's doubts when she'd first wanted to build the Fifth Avenue house and then the Newport cottage, and when she wanted to put on ever more lavish entertainments to compete with *the* Mrs. Astor. It had also been James who'd proposed building that gleaming piece of private varnish, the *Cathay*, which Peter had to admit that he enjoyed. "Dad, it's good for business to make a bit of a splash," James would argue, but it had turned out to be good for something else too. After waiting out most of his twenties with an almost disturbing lack of interest in the opposite sex, James had come up with the hand of Anne Schermerhorn—in the opinion of old Lucy Smith, who ought to know, the biggest fish in the social sea; her family had been both comfortable and prominent as long, or longer, than the Van Alens. Though Peter thought Anne rather mousey—she even looked a little like a mouse with her slightly protruding teeth and that nervous twitch to her nose—Martha had been so pleased that she'd insisted on their building a house for the couple further up Fifth Avenue as a wedding present. Martha's argument—"Thanks to your Uncle Peter's money, we didn't exactly start out in a shack, or do you forget?"—and his own passion for building overcame Peter's initial reluctance at lavishing so much money on one of the children, though it was less actually than they'd spent on Sally's disaster with the duke. He didn't make the place quite a match for their own—a bit smaller, fine hardwoods instead of marble, a touch more Gothic than Renaissance. Now Anne and James were busy filling it with a son flatteringly named Peter Schuyler Van Alen II and another child on the way. Yes, a perfect son. Or so it seemed.

Quite a few people would stop Peter on the streets and compliment him on James, but the most surprising gesture of that sort had come from old Commodore Vanderbilt just before his death. That had been back in '76–'77, and Peter had been ashamed of his former profession when the newspapers mounted that ghoulish, round-the-clock guard outside the commodore's Washington Square house for the six months that he battled to keep his old heart from giving out. New York Central stock would fluctuate wildly with every rumor a reporter could buy or beg out of a backstairs maid or a nurse or a visiting family member. Despite the fact that they harbored an apparently forgotten granddaughter of the commodore in their house, in the ghostly presence of his niece Sophie, Peter's instinct was to stay away from Washington Square. He hadn't seen the old man in person since the war, and he doubted that the dying railroad magnate would be much like the crusty sailor his mother had befriended. All the excitement of the deathwatch was, of course, owing to the newspaper reports that Commodore Vanderbilt would leave behind him more than $100,000,-000, the largest private fortune ever amassed in the history of mankind, beside which the Astor forty million was peanuts. Since the bulk of this money had accrued to the commodore in the hectic post-war years when Peter hadn't known him well, he had every good reason to suspect a change in character. But—and it was one of those "buts" that always cropped up in Peter's mind when he thought of his first son—James, with an eye on all that money, had persuaded Sophie that she had an obligation to say goodbye to her departing grandfather and Peter that he had an obligation to conduct this timid recluse on what for her would be a perilous journey into the world. James would do it himself, you understand, except that the commodore didn't know him from Adam, and of course it would take precious hours away from his business. Truth to tell, and a bit disturbing to his own self-esteem, Peter was so curious that he bought James' logic rather easily.

On the wintry day in December '76—it must have been less than a month before the old man died—

that Peter and Sophie went down to Washington Square, Peter developed a new respect for his niece. "I don't know why I let James argue me into this," she said. "He thinks I have something coming to me, but I don't. I'm going to tell grandfather that I don't want a red cent of his money because *my* father took care of me very well, thank you." And that's just what Sophie told the commodore, whispering through her veils as she stood by his bed. But she added, "I know you've never given a rap about me, but I just came down here to let you know that at least one of your descendants isn't eager to see you die."

The commodore came as near to laughing as he could in his condition. "By damn, girl, I like that," he said. "Well, just so's you know, I ain't really forgot you. I give most of those daughters of mine, wailing away out there in the halls, two hundred and fifty thousand dollars in sound bonds of the Lake Shore and Michigan Southern Railroad Company, and I put you down for the same in memory of your mother. If I'd have known the kind of girl you are, it might have been more, but I ain't going to die if I have my way about it, so I still might be able to make a change. Now, you get out of here, girl, and let me have a word with your uncle."

The commodore's reference to the wailing women had nearly made Peter laugh. When they'd arrived at the house, they'd had to wait in a parlor with half a dozen of the commodore's eight daughters. To pass the time, these aging ladies, one nearly as old as Peter, were singing, "Nearer My God to Thee" and other lugubrious hymns. Young Cornelius, swaying

144

slightly under his load of drink, kept pacing back and forth, cracking his knuckles and saying from time to time, "Shut up. For God's sake, shut up." The ladies hadn't been in a charitable mood. One of them had humphed at Sophie, "Where have you been hiding yourself all these years? It's a little late to come around here now. He'll never see you. He won't let *us* get near him, so why you?" They'd been, Peter noted, properly astonished when the attendant who'd taken the name Van Alen up to the sickroom returned with an invitation to visit.

When Sophie had gone, the commodore said to Peter, "Can't help it. Can't stand to look at her with all them scars. But, by damn, she's got spirit. Takes after your mother. Now *there* was one hell of a woman. Always wished she was younger, or I was older. How's that younker of yours?"

"Who—Aaron?" Since the commodore was something of a sportsman with his horses, it was always possible that he'd been reading about Aaron's exploits on the football field.

"No, no. Ain't never heard that name. The one running the business. James, ain't it?"

"He's fine, commodore. Doing well."

"So I've heard. Takes after your mother too, don't he? Wished I had one like him. William's steady enough, but he ain't got the flair like your James. And you've seen all them worthless pups downstairs. Guess I'll have to leave it all to William and hope for the best. Now if George had lived . . ."

The commodore shut his eyes, and Peter thought that he saw tears trickling from the corners. George Vanderbilt had been one of the few rich young New

145

Yorkers who had scorned buying his way out of the draft during the war and had paid the ultimate price.

"I don't want to tire you, commodore," he said. "I know that Sophie will be grateful for your thinking of her—"

Just then the doctor came in, and Peter started to leave. "No, wait," the commodore ordered.

The doctor sat down on the bed, took a pulse reading, peered into the old man's eyes and mouth, then said, "Nurse tells me you're having trouble keeping anything on the stomach. I've ordered up some champagne . . ."

"Won't soddy water do?" the commodore asked. "Damned sight cheaper."

"Well," said the doctor, winking at Peter, "you can try it. Wouldn't want your mind troubled by the cost."

On his way out the doctor whispered to Peter, "Tough old bird. Those people down there may be in for a long wait yet."

For all of his spending on horses and some said women too, and of course on sometimes ruinous competition in the stock market, the commodore's frugality was legendary. Peter could remember his mother's shocked account of how she'd plucked the poor girl who became Sophie's mother out of the slums where the commodore had stashed his large family while he was saving his stake. While other successful businessmen, like Peter himself, were building new mansions on Fifth Avenue, the commodore lived contentedly on in this modest square brick house he'd acquired back in '45. From the looks of it, he'd probably occupied the slightly tarnished brass bed in which he was dying for all of his eighty-three years.

"Didn't want you to go until I'd warned you," the commodore said. "Don't you and Sophie say a damned word about what I told you. Nobody else but Judge Rapallo—my lawyer, you know—knows my business. Don't know what made me tell you 'cepting I felt sorry for that girl. If she is grateful, she'll be the only one. All them hymn-singing women down there ain't interested in saving my soul. They want what they think's their fair share of what I got. So does that drunk Neel. There's going to be hell to pay when I go—if I go."

Whether the commodore's reading of James' character was accurate or not, his prophecy certainly was. One of the disappointed daughters along with young Cornelius went into court to contest the will, creating a family circus for the public. It was charged, among other things, that the old commodore's mind had wandered under the influence of the Claflin sisters and another lady spiritualist; that William and the commodore's young wife, Frank—despite the fact that her $500,000 share in five-percent U.S. bonds was part of a prenuptial agreement—had conspired to poison the old man's mind against the other children, notably Cornelius, who'd been followed to dens of iniquity by detectives; that the commodore's bump—a phrenological term—of accumulative greed was so large as to distort the function of his brain. William, sitting on his hundred million, remained impassive throughout, though in the end he peeled off a few of those dollars to placate siblings. Not enough, apparently, for Cornelius, who killed himself. Peter often wondered what the commodore would have thought of it all. Whatever public dignity the world's richest man had attained was stripped from him in court. Ex-Mayor Oakey Hall, not a very creditable witness in view of having had his hand caught in the public till, testified that the huge $100,000 statue of the commodore at St. John's freight terminal which was supposed to have been erected by public subscription in honor of the city's great benefactor had, in fact, been secretly paid for out of Vanderbilt's own pocket. This was supposed to show that the bump of vanity on the commodore's head was also outsize and therefore unbalancing in relation to such other bumps as those of charity or familial affection.

The last few years had made Peter wonder whether the commodore's unfavorable comparison between his William and James was correct. From what James told him, the New York Central was so prospering under Williams' tight-fisted control that it was paying out between sixteen and twenty percent on capital and had thereby increased that hundred million by some fifty percent. Totally unlike his flamboyant father, William was homely, timid, methodical—a behind-the-scenes man. It was said that he set spies on his workers to make sure they kept their hours and that he read every single voucher, haggling over nickels and dimes. Once he refused to pay a restaurant's bill for a lunch sent into his office because it included coffee he hadn't ordered. But William was not without arrogance to match his father's. He'd got the railroad and himself

148

into a good deal of hot water about a year ago when a reporter asked how the public would get along when the New York Central canceled an extra-fare mail train to Chicago. "The public be damned," said William. "I am working for my stockholders. If the public want the train, why don't they pay for it?" Normally William kept his foot out of his mouth by leaving such matters up to his front man, voluble Chauncey Depew, a lawyer earning a reputation as one of America's best public speakers and New York's most public-spirited citizens. That Depew was worth whatever money Vanderbilt paid him became evident when the papers quoted New York's Republican boss, Roscoe Conkling, who said, "Chauncey Depew? Oh, you mean the man that Vanderbilt sends to Albany every winter to say 'haw' and 'gee' to his cattle in the legislature."

In his own smiling way son James could be as arrogant and contemptuous of public servants as William Vanderbilt. When Peter would argue with him, referring to his own unblemished public career and evoking the sacred memory of Cousin Matty Van Buren whose personal integrity, as distinguished from his political wiliness, had never been questioned, James would say, "Dad, you're living in the past. There hasn't been an honest politician since Lincoln was shot. There isn't a franchise in the country that hasn't been bought, and there isn't a businessman in this city who wouldn't starve if he didn't play the game. Besides, making money's what this country's all about, isn't it? Look how everybody's thriving. Why do you think we've got these millions pouring in here from Europe? They

149

all know it's the land of opportunity because a man who's willing to work hard and is smart enough to use the system can get his. I know how you feel, dad, but these are different times from yours . . ."

Were they really? Peter could still recall with bitterness how he'd been maneuvered off the board of aldermen by Tweed with the help, he suspected, of his own cousin, Charlie Smith, to make way for the Vanderbilt interests to grab the franchise for the Broadway street rail line. The difference wasn't in the times but in the position in which he found himself. Once he'd been committed for what he still felt were all the right reasons to take over the business; he'd been forced, step by step, to march with the others, and he couldn't really fault James for being in the parade too. In the night like this when he was brought face to face with himself, he knew that he no longer had such a great moral leg to stand on, and felt that he had somehow perhaps failed James.

But he no longer knew a soul in New York—now that Greeley was dead and he'd broken off with his old friends like Walt Whitman—who wouldn't literally laugh at his fears. He had, after all, "James, the perfect son." Some of that flair the old commodore talked about was evident in the way that James was working the other side of politics. Just recently, for instance, the names of James and his wife had been prominent on the published list of notables invited to the first White House dinner given by the new president, Chester Arthur. "It isn't that I'm famous or anything, dad," James said. "It's just that Chester—I mean the President—is the

150

kind of man who returns favors."

Indeed. James had introduced Roscoe Conkling to a number of his business friends whose generous contributions had created the war chest with which Conkling was able to thrust his friend Arthur on the Republican convention as candidate for vice president. There had to have been a good deal of money in that chest—Arthur was not easy to sell. He'd been fired from his post as Collector of Customs in New York by Republican President Hayes for depredations in that office that could no longer be concealed. But—"the public be damned"—Arthur had powerful friends where they counted, among the city's politicians and businessmen. He'd used his office to reward loyal Republicans with undemanding jobs and had at least overlooked some of the ways by which businesses avoided those onerous duties that cut into their profits. Peter didn't know whether James had ever slipped anything by—and didn't want to know for the sake of what was left of his conscience—but he did know that James rather admired the deft handling of the Phelps, Dodge and Company case. When it was charged that the company had eluded a million dollars in import duties on zinc and lead by having those metals cast into crude statues of Diana, Venus and the like and declared works of art which would later be melted down, a settlement of $271,017.23 was accepted; Collector Arthur unabashedly took $21,906.01 in fees.

At the time of Arthur's nomination James had resorted to his old "times have changed" argument with his father. This time he was closer to being right. In the days when Cousin Matty Van Buren ascended to the presidency, the vice president was held to have a virtual lien on the White House. These days he was expected to keep his mouth shut except when gaveling down an unruly Senate and to depart in peace with any change of administration. His service to the party was to heal old wounds, as in Arthur's case. A "stalwart"—one of those Republicans who wanted to see Grant returned to the White House because Hayes had been soft on the South— Arthur was meant to keep the Grant supporters in line behind Garfield. The strategy worked as far as the election was concerned, but even the politicians who were supposed to be sensitive to such things had underestimated the war's residue of hatred. The man who shot President Garfield in the Washington station this July and put Arthur into the White House had shouted in triumph, "I'm a stalwart! Now Arthur is President!" James had been shocked when it had happened but not, in Peter's view, enough. "It can't help but be good for business—and good for New York," Peter's son had said.

Peter guessed that what troubled him about his son was that James was out there swimming with the sharks . . . was a shark. Though a creature beautiful to behold in its efficiency, a shark was hard to love unless, he supposed, you were another shark. James loved them all. He had an almost religious reverence for the Rockefeller brothers who'd just moved into Peter's neighborhood and were setting up Standard Oil offices in Pearl Street . . . "Think of it, dad," James said, "they've got all the oil in the whole *world* under their thumbs. Of course I've got to go along with the railroads and give them a kickback on tankers, but the thing is that it's steady money. None of this cutthroat competition, and you know for sure where your next dollar is coming from."

Then there was that ugly young banker with the big nose, J. P. Morgan, who, according to James, had saved William Vanderbilt's hide back in '79 by unloading 350,000 New York Central shares in England and keeping the price up on the exchange here. James was so impressed that he'd shifted the Van Alen accounts to Drexel, Morgan & Co. Peter had thoughts of protesting, but on what grounds? That Morgan had bought his way out of the draft in the war? Well, so had most of the other men now in control of major businesses, like Andy Carnegie. That Morgan had bought 5,000 defective carbines for $3.50 a gun, sold them to General Fremont for $22 each, then sued the government when it refused to pay after men began shooting off their own thumbs with the guns and won a $58,175 judgment? Well, thanks to Charlie Smith, Van Alen & Son had also profited from commissions on defective ships. Anyway, Peter was afraid that James would only admire Morgan's ingenuity and gall if he brought all that up, a logical fear in view of James' attitude about Jay Gould.

Gould had used the money he milked from the Erie to acquire even more miles of rails in the west and up along the side of Manhattan and to secure the Western Union monopoly. His raiding methods were so ruthless that most of the other sharks feared him—and now *he* feared *them*. Even James Keene, the silver fox of Wall Street, was caught short on the

153

Western Union deal when Gould was buying instead of selling as he'd promised. Keene was so enraged that he and Major Selover had picked little Gould up and pitched him down a barbershop well in Exchange Street a few months ago, and ever since there had been guards pacing in front of the Gould house down the avenue, and Peter understood that Lyndhurst, the estate Gould had just bought up near Tarrytown, was virtually an armed fortress. But none of that seemed to bother James.

"Look, dad, I don't like Gould, but you can ride his coattails into a pretty good thing if you're smart enough to see where he's going," James once explained. "My method's simple. I read Gould's sheet, the *World*. As an old newspaperman you ought to agree that a paper's editorials reflect the owner's interest. So when the *World* started attacking Western Union as a monopoly that was unfair to Gould's American Union, while at the same time the bears were clawing down its stock, I figured that Gould was secretly buying and went with him. So now we're sitting on a *real* monopoly. Same thing with the Manhattan Elevated Railroad. The *World* came down hard on its management last spring, and the stock went from fifty-seven to twenty-nine, at which point I started buying. Well, you've seen what happened. Gould turned up with a controlling interest and the stock's up to forty-three. What's that old saying grandmother was always coming up with, dad—'If you can't lick them, join them'?"

James, the perfect son. Because of the shrewd way he was playing his cards all the Van Alens were getting richer by the hour, it seemed. If Peter's conscience rebelled at the game, he could throw in his cards, but that was about all he could do. Though nominally patriarch of the Van Alen clan, Peter didn't hold controlling shares in the venture. They were in Sophie's hands as her father's inheritor. Peter knew that Sophie hadn't been overly in love with her cold and calculating father during his life; Cornelius had been difficult even for his mother to love, and much of the time Peter had actually hated him. Since that terrible fire, however, Sophie had begun to enshrine her father. The stocks he'd left her in an enterprise to which he'd devoted more love than he had to her became her sole interest in a life otherwise circumscribed by her disfigurement. Getting richer was to her a kind of revenge on fate, and James understood that. Like Aaron but for different reasons, James would spend long hours with her, discussing details of business, and she would reward him with her highest compliment: "James, you're so like my father—but nicer." In extremis, Peter might be able to rally all the other stockholders, Sophie's share being only about thirty percent, as he'd once done in a battle with his brother, but at that time Martha and Amelia and his mother had been with him. Martha could not care less about the business now, and for her James *was* the perfect son; Amelia was older now and in need of whatever her stock brought in to live and to support her causes; his mother's stock had been left in trust to the grandchildren, as had her real estate, with only the income going to him and Martha for life. Any outside stockholder Peter approached would consider him crazy to suggest that the smart young James might be unethical in giving them such large returns on their investment—"Why, I see him passing the plate in the Uptown Presbyterian Church every Sunday." It had, in fact, been only an appeal to their wartime patriotism that had enabled Peter to get the other stockholders behind him and against Cornelius in the wake of the shipping scandal. There was no war on now, no war at all, unless it was between the have's and have-not's, and Peter had been enlisted in the ranks of the have's by the accident of birth.

Pacing his room and finding a measure of comfort in the sight of lights glowing dimly in the manse— Brewster was probably working on his sermon for Sunday—Peter decided that this uneasiness about James, about them all, was plain silly, a pretension to some abstract idealism. That he'd personally done no evil, as far as he knew, in the pursuit of private gain and that he'd occasionally even sacrificed his own interests in some quixotic effort to right a perceived wrong *should* be enough to let him lie down now and sleep well. He was aware that everybody in his family, and most of his casual acquaintances, considered him to be a good man, and maybe he was. All of his mental sweats ended up in a single question: who was he to find fault with anyone else? It was this questioning of his own motives, this acknowledgment of his own compromises with life as he found it that accounted for what some called decency and tolerance and others called irresolution in him. Did the gray of his eyes have something to do with his always seeing gray where other people saw black and white?

He paused at the window and looked down again at those comforting lights in the manse and then up at the steeple of the church on the other side, a darker blur against a dark sky. He thought of all those hours he'd spent sitting down there under that steeple placating Martha and pretending by his presence to be Christian. He just wasn't up to the plain demands Christ put on His followers. Sell all you have and give it to the poor, for one. Give up your family and follow me, for another. He doubted that any of his fellow pew sitters were either. In fact, a *true* Christian would be so disreputable and disruptive to society that he wouldn't be allowed in the doors. Lately, though, since his heart attack, he'd found himself wishing that he could find some assurance in mumbling the right phrase, going through the right motions. So many others could or had—his brother Cornelius, his father-in-law, his wife Martha, his son James, his son-in-law Bud. It had to be a good feeling not only to know that you were right but to know where you were going when your heart gave out—a feeling quite unlike staring into the dark, as he was now. Eyes roaming over the rooftops of the city, he was reminded of something he really did believe in, of those lines Whitman had first shared with him . . .

> . . . but as I pass O Manhattan, your frequent and swift
>   flash of eyes, offering me love,
> Offering response to my own—these repay me,
> Lovers, continual lovers, only repay me.

To hell with it, he thought, and strode purposefully through the dressing rooms and bath connecting his room with Martha's. He rapped on the door, and the sound, so unusual lately, evidently frightened her. "Peter! Is it you, Peter? What is it? What's happened?"

"Nothing, I just wanted to visit you."

"At this hour? Are you ill?"

"No, not at all. I'd like to come into bed with you—"

"Oh, Peter, you know I need my sleep tonight. I have to look right for that charity luncheon at Sherry's tomorrow—"

"I'll just hold you. I—"

"Now, Peter Van Alen, I know you too well. I don't think we should with your heart—"

"To *hell* with my heart."

"Peter; we're mature people. We have responsibilities. You check with the doctor first and then—"

"All right, damn it. I just needed you *now* . . ."

"Peter, it isn't that I don't love you. I love you too much to . . . well, you know that, don't you?"

Back in his own room, he noticed that the lights were out in the manse as he got into a cold bed. He hoped for Bud's sake that Sally wasn't as sensible as her mother. And he hoped for Aaron's sake that that actress would prove more pliable than a number he'd known. He thought for perhaps the thousandth time of that season of passion when he and Amelia Downing had been unrestrained lovers and decided that he had no reason to feel sorry for himself. And yet . . . *Lovers, continual lovers, only repay me.*

Sally knew that she shouldn't have called home as soon as she'd done it. Suppose it had been her father, or worse her mother, who'd answered instead of Aaron? What could she have said then? The fact that she'd called at all without thinking showed how desperate she was. And why had she asked Aaron to come over? What could he do that wouldn't make matters worse? She'd made her own bed and she had to lie in it, as old Sally, her grandmother, used to say. Except she was so terribly afraid. Bud was clearly mad, in the crazy sense of the word, or he'd never have done what he did to her. It wasn't much help to know that he was probably praying down there, because men out of their minds got strange answers to prayer. It was too often people who thought that they were in touch with God who took it into their own hands to rid the world of evil. And she was evil, evil, evil. Hadn't Bud told her so?

With everything that was in her, Sally had yearned to make this marriage work, and she had really thought that it was working until a few minutes ago. For her, it had not been a love match in the storybook sense. She'd been through too much to believe in stories. More out of instinct than reason she'd been looking for a man who would have all the qualities that the Duke lacked—youth, strength, virility and a total disinterest in money. They weren't easy to find. As soon as news of her divorce began appearing in the papers the bolder young men in her social set began finding excuses to call on the Van Alen house. Opportunistic men without the proper credentials would manage to encounter her in public places—at the Philharmonic Society, in an art gallery, when she was riding in the park. For a while there she'd been afraid to go out without an escort. Though most of them tried to disguise it, all of these men revealed either a leering interest in an "experienced" woman or a greedy interest in all that money that was likely to be hers.

Howard Ernest (Bud) Brewster was different. She'd actually first taken notice of him at that football game in Princeton when he'd knocked down all those Rutgers men who'd trampled over her brother. Later in the season, after a Columbia game, Aaron had brought him home. Though he was a few years older than Aaron, nearly her age, Bud had seemed younger than both of them and totally unsophisticated. He was a huge bear of a boy who filled their large rooms with his presence and voice. The son of a minister somewhere out near Pittsburgh, he showed exuberant awe at the size of the mansion. He actually whistled and said, "Boy, oh boy, Aaron, I didn't know you were *this* rich!"

Aaron said, "Oh, we're not that rich. There are lots of bigger houses right here on the Avenue. Anyway, money isn't everything. It won't get a football across the goal line."

But Bud just kept shaking his head in wonder. "Man, oh man, would I ever like to live in a place like this, but I guess I never will . . ."

"Why not? Half our neighbors started without a dime."

"Well, I'm going to be a preacher like my daddy, and daddy says people keep their preachers poor to keep them humble."

Sally thought that Aaron had been as surprised as she by this announcement. From everything he'd told her, Bud didn't sound like the ministerial type. Aside from exhibiting ferocity on the playing field Bud was known as one of the college's chief mischief makers. True, he did keep out of the tavern, but otherwise he was always giving the faculty head-aches. As a freshman, Bud had been the first in his class to climb the Nassau Hall belltower in the dead of night and steal the clapper; as a sophomore, Bud had so terrorized freshmen in the cane sprees that one timid youth from a prestigious Princeton family withdrew from college; as a junior, Bud had organized a bonfire in which a number of classroom desks had been consumed and a professor of Greek burned in effigy for flunking the best pitcher of the baseball team out of school; as a senior . . . well, the year wasn't half over yet. Still, Bud's announced intention of becoming a minister was a dash of cold water against the small flame his so obvious manliness had kindled in her. Growing up a minister's granddaughter, she'd been put through more than enough deadening church services, heard more than enough ranting against fleshly sins that she'd found, in most cases, pleasurable. A preacher's wife? No, thank you.

What none of them could have known that first night was that Bud *would* do a lot of living in a place like theirs during the next few years—in their place, to be exact. If Bud's announcement startled her and Aaron, it was a kind of trumpet blast to their grandfather, the Reverend Doctor James Schuyler. The old man didn't literally leap out of his wheelchair and start marching, but he showed more life than he had for quite a while. Here was a young man of his grandson's generation, a fellow Princetonian at that, to whom he could truly relate. Within days he'd fixed it up with his successor at Uptown Presbyterian Church that Bud would act as a kind of unpaid assistant during his seminary years, a most convenient arrangement since Bud could occupy one of the many spare bedrooms in the Van Alen house when he was in New York on weekends. Bud rapidly became the grandson that old Doctor Schuyler wished he'd had, and Sally would have to admit that it was nice to see her grandfather's last year warmed and eased by the young man's attentions. Bud not only listened respectfully to the older man's theological discourses but used his physical strength to shove him around in the chair and lift him in and out of bed during the final months. By the time Dr. Schuyler died, Bud was a fixture in the Van Alen house, something like a poor relation. For a long time nobody, least of all Sally, ever foresaw any deeper relationship between Sally, with her cigarettes and sherry, her notoriety and sophisticated friends, and the impecunious seminary student whose thundering sermons against sin were already attracting so much attention that the senior minister was said to be considering early retirement.

When did something happen—and why? Sally often pondered these questions without coming up with very exact answers. Whatever her own feelings, she'd been thoroughly aware of Bud's. Like a good minister-to-be, like a good surrogate brother, he made no overt sexual advances. But while he could control his hands, he could not control his

162

eyes, or the desire in them. They had no special engagements or trysts, but no amount of scriptural study could quite control Bud's animal spirits, and he let them loose by joining her riding and skating outings in Central Park. His fearlessness and natural athletic ability made him more than her match: he'd take jumps she'd never dare, and he'd waltz her across the ice into a delightful dizzy haze. He began working on her vices. When keeping up with him left her breathless as too often it did, he taunted her into quitting smoking. Wine might be all right because it was mentioned in the Bible, but did she really need it? He'd bet her a dollar she didn't have the will to give it up. Pride made her win that bet. While there was, to her, a rather annoying tone of moral superiority in his teasing, there was also a note that, alone of the men she was meeting, Bud really cared about her, really thought her capable of being something other than her public image of a frivolous, somewhat tarnished, belle. And his bump of morality made him, oddly, one of the most supportive people around her during the public scandal of the divorce. She'd told him only what she'd told her parents—that the Duke had beaten her. He'd been enraged. "By God, if I'd been there you'd be a widow instead of a divorcée. As far as I'm concerned, you *are* a widow, because a man who would strike a woman *ought* to be dead."

When, a year ago now, the senior pastor *did* retire and Bud was called to the pulpit of the Uptown Presbyterian Church, he finally forced the issue . . . They'd been skating, and he suggested that they walk home instead of taking a horsecar. It was a

163

brisk, bright Saturday afternoon. Snow had fallen during the night before, whitewashing the city's dirty streets, and people had switched their rattling carriages for silent sleighs with bells that tinkled a merry warning of their passage. It was the sort of day that made her feel Christmasy, full of hope and anticipation. Apparently Bud did too; before they'd walked more than a few steps he said, "Sally, I want you to marry me."

She laughed, her voice another bell. "Oh, Bud, you can't mean that. You know as well as I do that I'm not your sort. What would your congregation say if their pastor married a gay divorcée?"

"I've . . . well, I've already sounded out some of the elders and deacons. They were a bit surprised but . . . well, they said that you are after all Dr. Schuyler's granddaughter and—".

"I'm not sure I like *that*. In the first place, it's rather presumptuous of you, and in the second place I don't think those old goats have any right to pass judgment on me. What if they'd said no?"

"I'd have asked you anyway. Sally, I love you, you must know that by now. You're the only girl I've ever loved, or ever could—"

"And you're very naive to say that. I thought that I loved the Duke once. How do I know you just don't love my money? That's all he loved."

"Are you comparing me with that . . . that—?"

"Careful—you're a minister." She laughed.

"Yes, I am, and you know money means nothing to me. I don't even know if you have any after that settlement."

"Oh, but I do. Even if father disowned me, my

164

grandmother set me up with a trust fund. It might be hard on your self-esteem, having me richer than you. I don't intend ever to live like a churchmouse, and people would say you're a kept man."

"I don't care what people say. I love you, and that's all that matters."

"All? Have you ever . . . ever had a woman?"

He blushed and shook his head.

A virgin! Sally found the thought of his purity intriguing. At the very least, this wouldn't be another sordid adventure. She tried to ease his embarrassment. "Well, I just asked because I think that has a lot to do with your love for me. Not that it isn't flattering, but . . . well . . . that sort of thing might wear off and then we'd be left with serious problems."

"Such as?"

"Such as I'm not even sure I'm a Christian, and I don't know whether I could take your work seriously. I'm a lot like my father in this, and you've seen how he'd tease grandfather."

"Sally, Sally, don't talk nonsense. You were baptized, weren't you? I've seen these last months how you can turn your back on bad habits, and I know the stuff you're made of. I think you were just so badly hurt that you blamed God for it, but you'll change when you have a man who loves you and can give you the only thing you really want."

"What's that?"

"Another child . . ."

If she'd had to pick a moment when she crossed the line, that was it. She was touched by Bud's sensitivity because she'd never talked much about her child; it was too painful. Under the terms of the expensive agreement she was allowed to spend a month a year with little Charlie—but only in England. The Duke had been afraid that once they got hold of his son in the States they'd find a way, legal or otherwise, to hold onto him. As far as she was concerned the Duke's fear was not groundless, but she'd been forced to give in to avoid a public airing of charges and countercharges of adultery and other indecencies. So once a year, usually in summer, she went back to Midstone which the Duke vacated, also by terms of the agreement, to visit with her son. It was an all too short, too emotional time, and she would come back with an empty yearning for a child she could be with always. Yes, it was the promise of a child, the promise she'd felt in the air suddenly defined, that made her say yes, hoping that some sort of love for Bud might come later.

Her mother, who saw in Bud much of her own father and whose socially turned mind detected at once what such a union would do to reestablish her daughter's reputation, was nearly as delighted as she'd been over the capture of a duke. James, already a trustee of the church and nervous about what a sister he considered somewhat "unbalanced" could do to the Van Alen public image of probity that he'd found so useful in business, was equally enthusiastic. But those whose judgments she most trusted were disturbingly cool. "I guess Bud's all right, but, just between us, I used to think he was too much of a tiger when he got all riled up," Aaron had said, "though maybe the seminary's changed him. What I really wonder is how you're going to swallow

166

all that religion, sis." Her father invited her to a long, closed-door discussion in his study, one of the few they'd ever had in their lives. There was considerable embarrassment on both sides, but he managed to convey his message. In essence, it was that he had nothing against religion, which seemed to do a lot of good for some people, but in his experience the pious could be relentless to those who didn't share their beliefs and . . . well . . . dull. Was she sure that, after the life she'd had in England, which judging from her letters had had at least some good and exciting moments, or in view of the life she could lead here with another kind of man, she wanted to immerse herself in a manse with all that implied? Bud was, in fact, a lot like her Grandfather Schuyler had been in his early days—physically handsome and vital but with a mind set in concrete.

And then he came right out with something that had only been intriguingly hinted at all her life: "One of the things I've come to appreciate about your mother is that she has what *my* mother used to call a good forgetery for bad scenes. Your Grandfather Schuyler, you know, so bitterly opposed her marriage to me—I was a journalist in those days hanging around with what he thought were disreputable poets like Poe and dangerous radicals like Greeley and I hadn't darkened a church door for years—that she had to elope with me. It got into all the papers and was something of a scandal, partly because we were married by a Negro minister at a time when blacks were even lower than the Irish in the esteem of proper New Yorkers. Anyway, your grandfather virtually disowned your mother and threatened to cane me on sight. He softened up a bit when, thanks largely to your mother's efforts, I became respectable—and a lot more when your brother James came along. For your mother's sake, your grandfather and I worked out a modus vivendi, so to speak, but I can't say that I ever really liked him or forgave him for the unnecessary anguish his fit of righteous rage caused. But then I'm not enough of a Christian to be good on forgiveness, as your mother seems to be. So I'm still leery about fellows like your Bud who judge people on the basis of some sort of received truth rather than out of human sympathy. I could be wrong in Bud's case, but I feel I ought to alert you . . ."

Another person who came up with a surprising revelation was Cousin Amelia Downing. As a result of her shattering experience with the Duke, Sally no longer found Amelia's ranting against the injustices men inflicted on women embarrassing. Amelia now made a good deal of sense. So after her return from England she'd begun visiting Amelia, and they were soon sharing brandy and confidences. Amelia's frank and sometimes vulgar tongue that had also been an embarrassment to a young and innocent debutante now became an invitation to similar talk from her. She finally told Amelia the awful truth about the Duke that she'd only shared with Aaron. "God forgive me, Sally, for my part in ever getting you into *that*," Amelia said. "I never did like him with his mincing ways, but he was thrust on me by my relatives, who've become more British than the British when it comes to titles. Well, now maybe you can understand why I've been happy getting along without a husband, and you might think about that too." It seemed then that it was the mere fact of her getting married again that distressed Amelia when she told her about Bud, but there was more.

"I . . . I want another baby, and I . . . well, I need a man, if you know what I mean . . ."

"Oh, I know what you mean," Amelia said. "You probably don't think this fat old carcass ever knew that kind of need, or pleasure from having it satisfied. But I wasn't all that bad-looking once, and I had a lover who . . . well, it was so wonderful it's lasted me a lifetime."

"Really? Who?"

"Now, honey, you know better than to ask a question like that. I hate anybody, man or woman, who kisses and tells."

"I'm sorry, I guess what I meant was what happened to him? Why didn't you marry him?"

"One of the reasons was that I was verging on being too old to have children, and he deserved to have children, and thank God he did. I loved him enough that I wanted that for him. But the real reason is that I wasn't about to play second fiddle to any man and eventually that would have made him unhappy. But I still know what wanting a man can be like, and I guess I can understand you. What I can't understand is why, for God's sake, a preacher. He probably won't be any good at *that*."

"Why not? You've seen him, Amelia, and you'd have to agree he's a real man. I just wish you could have seen him on the football field—"

"You can't tell much from looking, but I guess

you ought to know that now from your experience with the Duke. Have you had any lovers? . . . Well, I shouldn't ask, and don't tell me. But from the way you talk I'd doubt they were much good either . . . I'm just wishing for you what I've had, and I'm afraid from what I know of preachers that they think sex is only for producing babies. . . ."

There'd been many times when Sally had wished that she could go back to Amelia and tell her that she must have known the wrong preachers, but she couldn't. Right up until the wedding, Bud had retained his gentlemanly control, allowing himself only a few kisses and an occasional embrace. She'd liked the feeling of being in his arms—it was a lot like being enfolded by a large and gentle bear. Compared to him, she was no longer a tall girl, and she could let herself for the first time feel nicely weak and feminine. It might have been a mistake to spend their first night in the atmosphere of the manse, but they couldn't get the boat to Newport, where they were to have the cottage all to themselves, until the next morning. She'd seen that he was embarrassed about exactly what to do when they were finally alone together and had tactfully suggested that he'd find her in bed, once he'd changed into his nightshirt. The light had been dim, only a reflection off the white ceiling of the gas lamp in the street, but not so dim that she couldn't detect that he was ready for her. Then had come the first surprise, or shock. He'd insisted that she get out of bed and onto her knees and pray with him. "Done this every night ever since I was a little kid," he said, and then intoned in a voice shaky with excitement a prayer for God's blessing on "This union and its issue." After that he took her without preliminaries, as if he were charging the Rutgers line. His enormous member came searingly up into her delicate, dry passage and then exploded in an instant. He hadn't been unkind, letting out the intensity of his love for her now that he'd claimed her and begging reassurance out of her experience that it was "all right." Allowing for his inexperience, she'd given that assurance, cuddling his head to her breast and saying, "It's fine, Bud . . . wonderful . . ." She'd had to console herself then with the thought that he was unmistakably a man and that it might get better.

In some ways, it did. Once he'd learned some control, he had, at her suggestion, allowed for a little kissing and stroking between prayer and performance, enough at least to let nature ready her—but for what? Instant, sighing satisfaction would drop Bud immediately into deep sleep while she would lie awake trying to deal with the tension brought on by frustrated feelings in her body over which she had no control. It had been that way with the Duke the first time, and in one or two of those fast and furtive grapplings with lovers; it had been easier to tolerate when she felt nothing at all but discomfort, as on her wedding night. She'd wanted to talk to Bud about all this, but the fact of performing his marital duty—confirmed and blessed by the first signs of her pregnancy—had not corrupted Bud's innocence: sex, like elimination, was necessary and relieving but not a fit subject for discussion between man and woman. His gratitude to her, amounting to adoration, and his gift of a child within her womb would apparently have to be enough, and on the whole she'd decided that it wasn't such a bad bargain. After all, he'd bestowed upon her something else—respectability. As Mrs. Brewster, wife of the dynamic young minister pulling them in at Uptown Presbyterian, she had higher standing with the right circles in New York than she'd ever had as the Duchess of Midstone. It was a bother not being able ever to have a cigarette or a drink (except on almost secret trysts with Cousin Amelia), but the deference paid her by sniffing social snobs who'd shunned anything as dangerous as a divorcée made it all seem, on balance, worth the while.

Sally had not burdened Bud with any unnecessary detail about her life in England. She doubted that, in his innocence, he could ever understand how little the affairs she'd fallen into out of frustration and despair meant to her. Time and her new life were doing such wonders in lightening the load of guilt she'd been carrying that, like her mother, she was finding it possible to forget the past or look on it as some crazy dream from which she'd awakened. Which was why she hadn't been devastated when this past summer difficulties with her pregnancy kept her from going to England to see Charlie. She wasn't anxious to arouse old memories in the midst of her effort to build a new marriage; in another year she'd probably feel differently. Then came the letter from the Duke's solicitors. It seemed that a fine-print clause in the agreement required that she avail herself of her visiting privileges some time during any calendar year or lose them forever. She was furious with her father's lawyers for letting this clause pass, but they assured her that she'd agreed to it at the time, thinking a year's separation from her baby more than she'd ever endure anyway. So she arranged to go to England for the month of December when Charlie, now in school, would be on holiday.

Bud wanted to go with her. How could they be separated on their first Christmas? She was in no condition to travel alone; what if something happened to *their* baby? He'd always wanted to see England. She wouldn't hear of it. Christmas was the busiest time on the church calendar and it wouldn't be fair to the congregation for him to be away. She was such a seasoned traveler that she'd manage, and the doctor assured her that she was carrying the baby so well now that there would be no danger. It wasn't a question of seeing England but freezing in that dreary Midstone. What she couldn't tell him was that she was a different person in England. Whenever she arrived, the old fox-hunting crowd, including some of her lovers, rallied around, and she pretended at least to be the same adventurous girl they'd known. She hadn't jumped into bed with anybody on these parental visits, but she hadn't seen any reason to isolate herself in Midstone with Charlie, like some nanny hired for the summer. In truth, she wanted Charlie to think of the mother he so seldom saw as a glamorous and popular figure who brought excitement into his life, and so she'd make of Midstone a month's carnival of children's parties with ponies and balloons and house parties with hunts and dances and feasts. Her reward came in letters from Charlie, now that he could write, that were touchingly full of memories of these good times and pleadings for her return. Once she'd accepted the fact of it, she was glad that she had been forced to make this trip; Charlie didn't deserve to be deserted in her own selfish interests. But the thought of introducing Bud into this society where her transgressions were so commonly known and accepted that a slip of the tongue could occur at any moment—or worse, chancing his meeting the Duke, who'd delight in revealing her past, especially to a man of the cloth—was too frightening. He just couldn't go.

Until tonight she'd thought that Bud had accepted her arguments. She was in her nightdress, sitting in front of her mirror and putting her hair up for bed when Bud, who'd been to a late meeting of the church's session, came in. He was still fully dressed, and in the mirror she could see him pull the gold watch his father had given him at their wedding out of his vest pocket. "Past midnight," he said. "Boy, that was a long one but I finally got the elders to agree to hire a temporary replacement for me so I can go to England with you over Christmas."

She put down her brush and turned to face him; he was beaming like a schoolboy presenting a good report card. "I thought we had that settled," she said.

"Oh, I knew you were just being brave for me, so you wouldn't disrupt my work," he said. "But you mean more to me than my work, and I've been praying over it. The other day my Bible just fell open to that passage in Ruth where it says, 'Whither thou goest, I go.' It was plain as day the answer to my prayers, so I went right down and bought a ticket on your boat and argued the session into it tonight. They didn't like it much but when I told them about my prayers and—"

"Bud, you just *can't* go."

"Why? Why, darling? It's all set now, and I *am* going. I thought you'd be as happy as I am."

"Oh, God, Bud . . ."

She started to cry. She so seldom used tears that they were usually effective. Rational argument no longer seemed possible. He came over, kneeled by her, took the brush from her hand and held her hands with his. "What *is* the matter, darling? Are you afraid that Charlie won't like me? Or do you think your snooty English friends would look down on a preacher from Pittsburgh?"

His earnest face, working with emotion, was a blur through her tears. Knowing his strength and temper, knowing how he worshiped her, she felt that he'd be a loaded gun by her side in England. The slightest slur on her character might trigger him into violent action. Intuition deserted her in this crisis and she decided that, if he went he'd have to know. And wouldn't all their future years together be better without a secret between them?

"Bud, things . . . things happened to me in England . . ."

"Things? What sort of things? Do you mean the Duke beating you? He doesn't come near you, does he? I thought the law kept him away. Anyway, I'll be there to protect you—"

"It isn't the Duke, Bud. It's . . . well, it's . . . I

had a lover—"

A blow to his solar plexus might have hurt him less. He actually fell back from her, then scrambled to his feet, towering over her. "You *what?*"

"It wasn't anything special. I . . . I was so shocked and lonely that . . . It doesn't *mean* anything to me now, it didn't really then—"

"Doesn't *mean* anything to you? You committed adultery and it doesn't *mean* anything to you? No wonder the Duke could hold you up for so much money. By God, Sally, why didn't you tell me this before we were married?"

"Because I didn't think you'd understand, and I was right."

"Yes, you were," he said, and grabbed a hank of her hair, painfully yanked her face up toward his. "Look at me, Sally. Who is this man? You go back to him, don't you? That's why you don't want me along."

"*No.* There's no special man. I didn't love—"

"You mean there were others?" He jerked harder on his fistful of hair, and the hurt turned her from contrition to anger.

"Yes, there were others," she said coldly, "but none since I've known you and never again. I'm telling you this because I just didn't want you to get upset if you heard anything about me in England—"

"Oh, my God and my God, it's worse than I thought," he said. "I'm married to . . . to nothing but a prostitute, an evil whore. Evil, evil, evil . . . how in God's name could you do this to me—?"

He was shaking her head with her hair and the pain made her cry out. "Let me *go.* Bud, you're *hurting* me—"

Instead he pulled her to her feet, began tearing her nightdress off with his free hand. The comforting bear had turned into a terrifying beast. "How did they do it to you? . . . like this? . . . like *this*? . . . Were they better than me?"

He was dragging her down by the hair onto the bed. She would have fought him except for the child inside her. "The baby—"

"The baby . . . the baby . . . how do I know it's *my* baby?"

He covered her, spread her, stabbed her again and again until his fury escaped with his juices. And then the bear started to cry, to shake, to pray . . . "Oh, God . . . oh, Jesus, my Lord . . . deliver me from this evil . . ."

She was sobbing herself and could have offered up the same prayer. Without a word he left her, slamming the door behind him, clattering down the stairs. Even as she phoned for help she could hear his heavy footfalls going back and forth, back and forth in the parlor below, hear his voice but not the words he spoke. What would happen when Aaron arrived? Bud was too big for him and might kill him if he tried to protect her. She'd have to stop what she'd started. She put a robe over her swollen body and started down the stairs. But she was too late. Aaron was coming through the door, turning into the parlor. She could hear his voice . . . "What's going on here, Bud? Sally just called and—"

Bud's laugh was crazy. "Oh, nothing, nothing at all. I just found out that your sister's an evil little whore and I showed her how a man treats a whore—"

She heard a smack and a crash, and she rushed to the parlor door. Aaron was standing in the middle of the room in a boxer's stance. Bud, rubbing his jaw, was lying where he'd fallen backward over a stool. "Stop it, both of you *stop* it . . ."

Over his shoulder Aaron said, "Stay out of this, Sally . . ."

Up on his feet again Bud rushed and got his huge arms around Aaron. They struggled for a minute, and then Bud picked Aaron up and threw him. Aaron's body crashed against a whatnot in the corner and a shower of China figurines popped and cracked against the walls and floor. Sally watched, transfixed by a kind of horrible fascination and an instinctive fear for what might happen to her unborn child if she got between them. Aaron was up in seconds, moving toward a hard-breathing Bud in a boxer's crouch. Bud lunged. Aaron ducked and sent a right cross to Bud's jaw that spun his big body like a top. Bud reeled and fell clear over the top of a settee. He lay sprawled, and still.

"You've killed him," Sally said.

Kneeling beside Bud's body and feeling the pulse, Aaron shook his head. "Just knocked him out. Broke my hand, I think. He'll come to soon enough, so get something on and come home with me. You can tell me about it later . . ."

Numbly, she did as he told her.

Chapter 5

AT PRECISELY 9 A.M. of a crisp fall morning in 1883, Aaron Van Alen handed his wife Mary up to the high driver's box of a coach parked in front of the Hotel Brunswick on Madison Square and then climbed up beside her. He was suffering from some of that same nausea of excitement that had afflicted him before those football games in Princeton. It could, of course, have something to do with the fact that he'd just spent an hour in the cavernous stables on Twenty-seventh Street back of the hotel picking and matching the team of four horses he wanted to use for the start. To some of his fellow Coaching Club members the reek of manure, urine and sweat that permeated the stables was sweeter than perfume, but it tended to turn Aaron's stomach. Repugnant as he'd found it, the effort had paid off in a team almost perfectly matched as to size and color, coats gleaming in the pale sunlight like polished mahogany. The horses were properly nervous too, snorting little puffs of mist into the air from quivering nostrils, stamping their hooves, twitching their muscular rumps as if in anticipation of the touch of his whip. No matter how often he'd made the drive, and particularly on this morning. Aaron was as keyed up as the horses, and he knew that it was this dry-mouthed tension, more than the manure, that accounted for his queasiness.

Mary seemed to understand how he was feeling, keeping blessedly quiet while he fiddled with the reins to see that they were running properly through the tackle to the bits in the mouths of the lead horses and evenly adjusted in his driving hand. Mary was well aware of the upsetting excitement that usually preceded any precise and daring performance, a sensation as stimulating and addictive as that produced by a drug despite the overtones of nausea. When he'd tried to describe it to her once she'd said, "I know. I always felt the same way just before the curtain went up." But Mary's presence in itself was one of the reasons, only one, that this drive had him more on edge than usual. Except for the club's annual parade down Fifth Avenue, which was a docile line-of-march for the purpose of showing off their equipages and horses and, of course, the ladies' new bonnets, he'd never wanted her along on the grounds that she'd interfere with his concentration to the detriment of his paying passengers and the interests of his partner in ownership of the drag, his brother-in-law Pierce Hancock. If you didn't take this business of coaching seriously, you didn't belong in the club, and he and Pierce, alternating at the reins, had maintained the best schedule of the lot with the result that the twelve seats on top of their drag were always full. Sixty dollars for a day's work involving an expensive coach, twenty-four highly bred horses and the Lord knew how many grooms at the changing stations was a laughable and losing proposition to somebody like his brother James, but then James had the soul of a merchant instead of an athlete. The only risks James ever took were in the market, on paper and not in the body. At the Knickerbocker Club, where the Coaching Club met, it was widely held that James was not really a gentleman; a gentleman never counted costs.

In any case Mary had, by throwing a fine Irish tantrum, overcome his better judgment for another reason that made this trip special: the whole coach had been hired by theatrical friends of Lily Langtry, who'd made her dazzling New York debut the season before in *As You Like It* at the Fifth Avenue Theater and was returning for another engagement. It had been thought that a coaching party was the proper way of welcoming Mrs. Langtry, who offstage moved in England's highest social circles—indeed, she was known to be a very close companion of the amorous Prince Edward—and coaching was *the* sport of British aristocracy. The choice of the *Tally-ho*, the Hancock-Van Alen drag, by the Langtry party was a natural not only because of its fine record but because its regular run to the Ardsley Club on the Hudson, where a sumptuous luncheon would be waiting, and return to the Brunswick by 6 P.M. on the dot would give Mrs. Langtry ample time to get to the theater. Still star-struck, Mary had wanted to come along as soon as she'd heard who was going to be in the party.

"You just *can't* keep me from meeting *her*," she'd said. "Besides, I wouldn't dare trust my husband near a woman with a reputation like that."

"Mary, you've got to understand that a man with four in hand and a schedule to keep can't even think about something like that—"

"Well, I don't care. *I'm* going."

"What about the opera? You'll be blown apart up there on the box with me, and you won't have an hour to change."

"Oh, damn the opera. I dread that, and you know it. At least going coaching and meeting Mrs. Langtry will keep my mind off that. I swear, Aaron Van Alen, if you don't take me, I'll hang onto your horses' bridles and scream to the heavens that my husband is unfaithful."

Aaron had laughed. "Knowing you, I almost believe that. All right, come along, but just remember that this is going to be more like an athletic contest than a social event for me, and there'll be no idle chitchat."

Aaron did have to concede that Mary had made a good point about keeping her mind off their evening's engagement. The grand opening of the magnificent new Metropolitan Opera House on Broadway would be a social event of far more importance than even the Vanderbilt ball that had filled the papers last March. As a longtime patron of the Philharmonic his mother had of course taken a prominent box for the season, and she'd invited them, along with James and Anne and Sally and Pierce, to join her on this special occasion. Even though the invitation was a peace offering that must have cost his mother considerable anguish, he had been all for turning it down for pride's sake and had been quite surprised, but secretly pleased, when Mary had said, "Why shouldn't we go? You know I was planning to be at the opening of the opera, though not quite this way, and aren't I as much of a Van Alen as anybody now?" It wasn't any desire to hear the music, he knew, that prompted Mary's acceptance. The closest she'd come to grand opera in all of her twenty-one years was kicking her legs and flashing her derriere in Offenbach's cancan chorus line, a performance that had inspired one of Martha Van Alen's more acid reactions: "I just don't see how you can marry a woman who's shown the whole world *everything* she's got." Sitting through an opera in the company of assembled Van Alens would be an ordeal for Mary, a tense time when she'd be playing a new role before thousands of eyes without anything in the way of proper preparation.

Still, Aaron had to admire her courage, and he'd been hoping that she would have sense enough to devote considerable effort to strengthening what he considered to be her unassailable asset—her beauty. From his point of view Mary O'Donnell Van Alen was the one woman in New York, Lily Langtry not excepted, who could outshine any other woman in any company. He had no doubt that every social watcher from the orchestra to the topmost balcony would be asking, "Who's that lovely creature?" or that every man in the audience with the slightest excuse to do so would be dropping by the Van Alen box for a closer look. But, as he always kept telling her, she'd look beautiful in a gunnysack, and perhaps the air and excitement of the outing would do more for her than any amount of time in front of a dressing table. Fretting alone all day could leave her with that worry frown that sometimes ran deep as a scar between her eyes and stole away her insouciant Irish charm.

Right now she was stopping people in the streets. Men on their way to work were pausing, looking over their shoulders, bumping into each other; some even tipped their hats. Mary probably thought that they were staring at the drag, but Aaron knew better: a coach in front of the Brunswick was a daily sight. Aaron couldn't blame these men, was, in fact, proud that his wife attracted such attention. She was dressed in a smart gray wool suit trimmed in dark velour to match her hat, and the fit of the jacket revealed the soft curve of her bosom and her tiny waist. The tang in the air turned her cheeks to ripe-apple red, and the sun imparted a sheen to her blue-black hair. But her eyes—blue jewels encased in the black velvet of their lashes and brows—were what stopped a man, for there was clearly mischief in those eyes. Yes, she'd be a sensation at the opera tonight.

Aaron's red-coated guard blew three loud blasts on his long brass horn, and the Langtry party that had been lingering over breakfast in the hotel came scurrying out. It was well known that the *Tally-ho* departed on time, with or without its paying guests. There was only the briefest flurry of introductions during which Aaron noted that Mrs. Langtry, in the full bloom of her thirties, was as attractive offstage as on, a rather rare discovery in his experience. He also noted with some amusement that Mrs. Langtry, the only woman in her party except for her maid, who would be tucked away inside, seemed by her manner to find Mary an unpleasant surprise. "I'd thought to ride up with you, sir," she said. Aaron gave Mary a warning nudge and replied, "And so you shall, madam. I'm sure Mrs. Van Alen wouldn't mind joining the gentlemen." Mrs. Langtry, still eyeing Mary, had second thoughts: "No, I'll be perfectly all right back here." Aaron winked at his wife who positively glowed with what she knew to be a kind of triumph, and as his guard jumped to the postillion box and sounded another long note, he touched the lead horses with his whip and called out, "Tally-ho!"

They were off, heading up the crowded canyon of Fifth Avenue at as fast a trot as he dared. As usual Aaron forgot about his stomach in the intense concentration of action. All four reins in one hand and whip in the other, he kept his coach moving in and around traffic, eyes alert for the thoughtless pedestrian who might step out in front of him, for the horse that might spook as they passed. His own horses, blinkered against confusion and trained to respond to the slightest tug on the reins, could be shot like an arrow through any gap that opened in front of him. Abruptly the near-wheel horse was breaking from a trot to a gallop—if the rest followed him it could be runaway panic. Slow the leader; it sometimes worked. It did. Beside him Mary let out a little shriek, "Watch that man!" He'd seen him, but there was no time to stop. Go around outside that dray and in front of that oncoming horsecar. The frightened car driver was jangling his bell in fury, but Aaron had made it. His passengers were whooping with excitement, and Lily, who'd forgotten her peeve, was shouting louder than the rest.

On they went, past hotels and store fronts, past the slab-sided Croton reservoir at Forty-second Street into the chateau country of the very rich. Eyes front and busy, Aaron would hardly have known where he was except for the voice of the guard who'd been trained to sing out the sights. It was mostly a litany of names, a roster of American royalty in this century when men of business were enthroning themselves in palaces—"the Vanderbilt residence" . . . "the Gould residence" . . . "the Goelet residence" . . . "the Ryan residence" . . . "the Vanderbilt residence" . . . "the Astor residence" . . . "the Rockefeller residence" . . . "the Van Alen residence" (here Aaron always touched his hat in sardonic salute, hoping one or another of his relatives who considered his coaching a wasteful pastime would be watching) . . . "the Vanderbilt-Webb residence" . . . "the Vanderbilt-Twombly residence" . . . "the Whitney residence" . . . "the Astor residence" . . . "the Harkness residence" . . . "the Hancock residence" (here Aaron would always look for Sally, who sometimes leaned out a window and called out, "Atta tiger!" But she wasn't in evidence today—too bad, she'd have enjoyed the sight of Mrs. Langtry jumping up and down like a schoolgirl) . . . "the Huntington residence." . . . Here and there the litany resolved into a kind of organ swell: "On your right, St. Patrick's Cathedral" . . . "on your left, St. Thomas'

Church" . . . "on your left, the Metropolitan Museum."

When he heard this last, Aaron knew that he was coming close to his first stage and began reining in. Everything depended on how fast the grooms made a change of horses. He was due at Ardsley at 11:30, and a few minutes of fumbling at any of the six stages could mean pressing the horses beyond the twelve-mile-an-hour gait that he'd found close to the outer point of safety with a topheavy, swaying coach—or an unthinkable failure to meet his schedule. Today, fortunately, the grooms were on their toes. Aaron jumped down and clocked them with his watch as they unharnessed his puffing, sweating team and backed four matched grays into the traces. Less than five minutes. Good. "Hup! Giddup! Tally-ho." Another blast from the horn, and they were away again. Now there was little traffic, few buildings to be seen but the squatters' shanties across from the north end of the park. Soon they were coursing through a fiery wonderland of red and orange autumn foliage. Mrs. Langtry had never seen anything like it and could hardly find words to express her amazement and delight. "No wonder you call your country America the beautiful," she said.

Somebody had thought to bring along a jug of wine which was passing among the passengers. A singer in the group struck up, "Hail, hail, the gang's all here, what the hell do we care . . ." Everybody joined in, including Aaron, taking the song's rhythm from the steady sway of the coach as the horses settled into a cruising trot. Mary stopped singing long enough to whisper to Aaron, "Oh, I *love* it! Thank you for bringing me along."

Aaron reached over and squeezed her knee affectionately. "What I love is you," he said, "and mother will too. You'll see."

"Why did you have to remind me of that? I'd almost forgotten . . ."

"Don't *worry*," Aaron said. "You saw how Mrs. Langtry looked at you. You'll have them all in the aisles. Anyway, as the song says, what the hell do we care now? . . ."

Aaron wished that he were as confident of the outcome of tonight's engagement as he tried to sound—and was perhaps more in need than Mary of the distraction that running the rig would provide for the next eight hours. He hadn't really expected to encounter such bitter opposition from his mother—and, to a lesser extent, the other members of his family—when he had announced his intention of marrying Mary O'Donnell. Among the comments that still rubbed raw on his nerves was one from that daffy, doddering Cousin Lucy Smith, the fount of all social gospel, who'd huffed, "Well, this will be the first time that a Van Alen has married shanty Irish." His mother had rung every change on the how-could-you-do-this-to-me theme. James had put in, "If Aaron would pay more attention to his business and social obligations than his pleasures, he'd find a more suitable mate, as I did. At the very least, we've got to keep this out of the papers." Sally's more gentle thrust had gone deeper than all the rest: "Aaron, are you *sure?* Remember that girl

Eileen? This may sound snobbish, but I've *finally* found out the hard way that it's better to marry into your own class." Only his father, pretty much out of things since his second heart attack—or stroke, the doctors weren't sure—had turned him into a kind of near-vegetable of a man waiting to wither away, had said, "Well, well. Marrying that Irish dancer, eh? Guess your mother's upset, and she's pretty smart about these things. But I don't know. You'd have had a Jewish mother if I hadn't listened to *my* family when I first fell in love . . . and . . . well, I sometimes have regrets, not that I don't love your mother . . . I just don't know . . . but well, God bless you, son . . ."

None of them knew Mary, or they would never have spoken about her like that, he was certain. Their ignorance, though, was his fault. He'd conducted his courtship in secret, as far as the family was concerned, out of some sort of instinct. He'd guessed that they'd suspect him of enjoying only a dalliance with Mary and would be insulted, and insulting in turn, if he were so indiscreet as to bring her home. The only one of them who knew anything about Mary at all was Pierce Hancock, and his attitude was infuriatingly plain: from time to time he'd wink at Aaron behind the backs of the others and ask, "How's your friend with the cute bottom?" Aaron was honest enough to acknowledge to himself that his own interest in Mary had been far from pure at the beginning, and so he couldn't fault his family with an entirely clear conscience. . . .

He'd met Mary O'Donnell at the bachelor party at Sherry's before his sister Sally's wedding to Pierce

Hancock. He'd been in a glum mood that night, a mood that wouldn't yield to any number of after-dinner brandies and raw wedding-night jokes. Though Pierce, as a fellow member of the Knickerbocker and Coaching clubs and co-owner of the drag, was a friend of sorts, Aaron was as uncertain of him as a brother-in-law as he'd been of Bud Brewster. Sally's taste in men was baffling. It had been just barely possible to understand her falling for a muscle man like Brewster after her terrible time with the Duke—but a lightweight like Pierce? And so soon?

After that night he'd rescued her, Sally had never gone back to the manse. Aaron had apparently knocked some sort of Christianity into Brewster, because he had taken himself off to a coaching job in some little college in Ohio and had let Peter Van Alen's lawyers arrange a quiet divorce on the grounds of desertion. He'd left behind a letter to the church elders in which he'd explained that, after a year or so in the pulpit, he'd discovered that his first love was football and that he was perfectly in accord with his wife's decision not to leave her New York home and follow him into a new and uncertain career. Really pretty decent, as even Sally had agreed, saying, "Makes me feel a little better about carrying his child."

Well, you'd think twice burned, twice shy. Not Sally. She'd gone to England that December to see her son and had returned a duchess again in everything but name. As soon as her child was delivered—a little girl named Martha Van Alen Brewster but called Matty to differentiate her from her grandmother—Sally was off to the social races, first in Newport and then in the city. The fastest horse on that rack was Pierce Hancock, who himself had just been through a highly publicized divorce in which he had been charged with adultery. Tall, gangling, red-headed, Pierce had popping blue eyes, a bristling mustache and an Adam's apple that bobbed like a fishing float when he swallowed the champagne on which he seemed to thrive. Blessed with unassailable wealth, Pierce had caused himself to be ejected from Yale by harboring a girl in his rooms and had since done nothing whatever to earn a living. He was, however, completely serious about two endeavors, both of which cost him more money every year than most men made. One was maintaining the most perfect coaching schedule on either side of the Alantic with *Tally-ho*. To that end Pierce would spend winter weeks and months shivering his way around the snowy farmlands of Maine to select the teams they'd need next season, and bargaining like a Yankee for a good price; he'd be punch proud when he'd sell the horses off in New York for a profit at the end of the coaching year, a profit that didn't meet half his costs. His other serious venture was running his steam yacht, *Pride of the Sea*, a vessel just a hair smaller than Gould's *Atlanta* or Morgan's *Corsair*, as a time-beating luxury ferry between New York and Newport for the convenience of commuting friends who were willing to pay his fares. Since these again weren't enough to cover his costs, his reward consisted in being generally called "Captain," not only by his social friends but by toughs around the waterfronts

191

where his skill was admired. Pierce had for years been "one of the crowd," to be seen regularly at balls in the city and on the casino courts at Newport, where he and Aaron kept trading off winning the singles championship. Considering his nearly comic looks, Pierce's attraction for women was thought to lie in his ability to keep them in luxury, an ability for which Sally had no apparent need.

Aaron had never been satisfied with Sally's attempt to explain her desire to marry Pierce almost before the ink had dried on her divorce decree. "Matty needs a father" was very nearly irresponsible in view of the fact that Sally knew as well as he did that Pierce seldom hung his hat at home and had never shown the slightest interest in his own children by his first wife. "Well, damn it, he's fun, and I haven't had any of that in a long, long time" made a little more sense, but was marriage really for having fun? Once she'd quoted St. Paul via their Grandfather Schuyler: "It's better to marry than to burn"; yet hadn't she been burned twice in marriage? Finally, he'd wormed out of her what was probably the best reason she'd ever given: "Well, all right, I don't love Pierce in the schoolgirl sense of the term. I spent all that on the Duke. And I don't think Pierce is really in love with me either. But we've known each other since we were so high, and I don't think either of us will find any unpleasant surprises, the way we've done before. Did you know his wife was so frigid that . . . ? Well, anyway, and most important, we don't need each other's money, and we both know the same people and pretty much like to do the same things, and . . . well . . . I sometimes think he's the boy I should have married in the first place. He's one of us. Now don't call me a snob. It's just that I'm tired of looking for something better just because it's different. He told me that he launched on a life of lechery to get over his devastation at the announcement of my engagement. You have to like somebody who would come up with an excuse like that. The thing is that, if I wait around too long, somebody else will catch him *for* his money . . ."

This time it was to be a very small and quiet wedding in the Van Alen home, performed by a judge and with no attendants and no guests but family. While Martha Van Alen rather admired her daughter's ability to latch onto someone as socially suitable as Pierce Hancock after all she'd been through, she was still too much of a minister's daughter and too conscious of the proprieties not to think that any sacred or public ceremony would be a travesty. Still, Pierce's clubmates couldn't let the occasion go by without using it as an excuse for a party; and hence the bachelor dinner. One of them had prepared an elaborate surprise, hiring the entire cancan chorus and their orchestra to appear at the party after the show. In need of any distraction, Aaron welcomed their arrival. The music was a gay romp he'd always liked, and the kicking, tail-flipping girls were uniformly enticing with their long, smooth-stockinged legs and saucy, frilled behinds. It was announced that the girls would break up after the dance and join the guests at their tables for "refreshments" and understood, of course, that the guest of honor would have preference. Aaron studied the girls, then nudged Pierce, who was sitting next to him. "Since you're marrying my sister tomorrow, there isn't any future in this for you, but there might be for me," he said. "Consider that little dark one on the left end. She's got the cutest rear of the lot . . ."

Which was how he met Mary. When she came to their table she seated her trim posterior on the edge of her chair, ordered ice water instead of champagne and talked and talked and talked. She ignored Aaron entirely and fixed her blue-eyed attention on Pierce, who was more than a little drunk. When Pierce made a passing reference to coaching, she started asking him question after question, as if it were the most fascinating subject in the world. Pierce, of course, lapped it up. There was nothing he'd rather do than talk endlessly and boringly about the fine points of judging horses and all the tricks you used to out-Yankee a Yankee in buying them and how you trained and matched them. Out of the corner of his eye Aaron could see a few other girls climbing into laps and an occasional couple disappearing through the doors. Oh, God, when would he learn that you couldn't tell what a woman was like from her looks? But what looks! While Mary chattered on to Pierce, he found himself actually more fascinated by her eyes than her figure. There was intelligence in them and, yes, mischief. In the glances she occasionally gave him he could read her amusement at Pierce's gullibility and his own frustration. Was it a subtle tease? If so, it was surely working.

Finally he broke in. "This poor man is getting married in the morning, and he needs his sleep," he said. "May *I* take you home, Miss O'Donnell?"

"Oh, no," she said. "I can manage."

"I doubt that there are many cars running this time of night, and you wouldn't be safe in the streets in a costume like that. Please let me escort you. You've done us all a favor by coming here . . ."

She looked him over appraisingly and shrugged. "Well, all right. I do have to get up early in the morning."

"In the theater? I thought—"

"I help my father in his saloon."

"Oh, I see."

Outside, they climbed into one of the hacks that were always waiting in front of Sherry's for the late trade. Aaron knew from experience that nothing that happened between a man and woman in the dark cavern of the cab would surprise or shock these cynical drivers, but he took the precaution of slipping this one a folded ten-dollar bill. The address Mary gave was familiar to Aaron—a dreary section of the West Side near the Van Alen & Son warehouse and docks. As the carriage rattled off, Aaron casually draped an arm across the seat above her shoulders. Mary moved toward the door, sat forward and started talking again. Her talk was cooling.

"You said your name was Van Alen, didn't you? So you must own the docks where my brother Hugh works."

"It's my brother really."

"Oh, well, that's good. Hugh doesn't think much of the wages he pays and the way he drives the men. Hugh's starting a union, and he says he's going to make the Van Alens pay through the nose before he's through. . . . Isn't it funny that we should meet like this? . . . Hugh will probably be up when we get home, so you'd better just let me slip out. He's usually drinking, and . . . well, I wouldn't want to see any arguments. . . . Do you work for the company, Mr. Van Alen?"

"I go to the office now and then. But let's not talk about business. Let's talk about you—and how beautiful you are . . ."

He moved a little closer to her, and she put a hand on the door. "Another inch, and I'll jump," she said.

He laughed, sighed, sat back in his own corner. "You would, wouldn't you? All right, let's talk about you and what you're up to. Do you really want to be a dancer?"

"Oh, yes. It's the only thing a girl like me can do to get ahead. I'm not going to slop beer all my life—not me. I'm taking ballet lessons, and when the new opera opens I'll be ready."

"I've got to admire your ambition, but aren't there . . . well, you know, other nights like this?"

Now *she* laughed. "Sure there are, but I know how to handle them, don't I?"

"Too well," he said. "But I'm beginning to *like* you. Couldn't we see each other again?"

"Oh, you wouldn't find much in common with me. I'm really just a working girl, and I've no time for . . . for this sort of thing."

"Please?"

"Well . . . all right, suit yourself. I . . . I rather do like you too. I guess it's because you've been more of a gentleman than most I have to deal with.

But I'm warning you right now. I'm a good Irish-Catholic girl, if you know what that means, and I have four big brothers who are stevedores and they're going to see that I stay that way . . ."

Their meetings over the next months were more frantic than furtive. She kept a schedule, he soon discovered, that would cause one of his best coach horses to drop in the traces. She'd work in the saloon, a beer-smelling place called simply O'Donnell's which covered the ground floor of the building where the family lived, until the stevedores crowding in for their noontime dram went back to work; then she'd go down to a barnlike loft above a music store on lower Broadway for ballet lessons and practice; then she'd go uptown to the theater. Sometimes he was able to buy her a quick bite between engagements; more often he just trotted along beside her, trying to talk in the jostling crowds. He spent hours in that dim and dusty loft watching her painfully bend at the bars or tremblingly toe her way through difficult steps, and spent so many more hours in the theater that he came to hate Offenbach's shallow, showy music. As an athlete he admired her dedication and stamina; as a man he was totally entranced with her sinewy, supple body. But it was her elusiveness that most intrigued him. Though she made it plain that she liked his company and attentions—she was the only girl in the chorus who got flowers at curtain call night after night by reason of a standing order he'd placed—she literally dodged so much as a peck on the cheek; an occasional holding of hands was all the familiarity she'd allow. Her reason for keeping him

197

at arm's length was hard to fault for its flattery: "I don't trust myself with you, Aaron, and, like I said, I'm a good Catholic girl."

Although he was too engaged in his pursuit to analyze his feelings at the time, Aaron later realized that Mary O'Donnell was maybe the first thing in life he hadn't been able to have for the asking. The rich had to invent challenges for themselves, and in moments of introspection Aaron knew that this at least partly accounted for his involvement in sports, where neither his inherited wealth nor his looks were any guarantee of success. In romantic matters, however, these gifts had proved so potent that Aaron was more often the pursued than the pursuer. In his own circles he was considered a prize catch, and the efforts of his mother's friends to deliver up their daughters to him, body and soul, would have been more enjoyable if it weren't for the humiliating vulnerability of the girls themselves. He'd taken to dodging as many social affairs as he decently could and to seeking occasional release of his animal spirits with women who, short of being outright whores, had nothing to lose in trading their favors for what he could offer them in the way of amusement or some bauble. He'd selected a lapel pin, a small diamond set in gold, as a birthday present for Mary, but she'd turned it down. "If my father or brothers saw me wearing a thing like that," she'd said, "they'd know I'd lost my virtue for sure and kill me—or you . . ." So Mary became a challenge that he hadn't had to invent, and his every thought and effort were devoted to winning her.

When he began seriously talking marriage, their

encounters generally turned into arguments. She had a million of them, all of which would have made perfect sense to his family and friends and all of which boiled down to the fact that, though they inhabited the same city, they lived in different worlds. She'd barely had enough schooling to learn to read and write and add up bar bills. She was a good Catholic who'd never leave the church; if they did find a priest who'd marry them, their children would have to be raised Catholics. She'd never ridden a horse, been in a sailboat, seen a tennis court, played a hand of cards or a game of croquet, danced at a ball. She'd never been north of Central Park, west of the Hudson, south of the Battery and wouldn't have been as far east as Brooklyn if she hadn't been among the crowds of the curious who'd gone down to see President Arthur and Governor Cleveland open the Brooklyn Bridge and then walk across. She'd never been inside a grand house like his on Fifth Avenue except to help out washing dishes in one of the kitchens when her father was down on his luck. What would his family think if he married a girl like her? He knew very well, didn't he? It might be different when she was a star and had money of her own, but he'd have to wait a long time for that, and she doubted that he would. Worse, what would her own family think? Her father and brothers really hated the owners like the Van Alens, and she wouldn't vouch for what they'd do if they even knew that she was seeing him like this.

Most of her arguments were hard to counter with reason, and he usually fell back on protestations of love. Only one presented no problem: he'd join her church; he might as well stay away from that as his own. The last, however, offered opportunity for action, and the longer this affair wore on, the more Aaron suffered from that familiar pre-action tension. "Why don't we find out?" he asked. "Why don't you take me home?"

"Why don't you take *me* home?"

"We'll get to that later. First things first. I think it's time to let your family know that you *are* seeing me and that my intentions are, as they say, strictly honorable. Let's go now—tonight."

It was after the theater and they were walking toward her home just to prolong their time together. They'd taken to parting a few blocks from O'Donnell's, in the shadows of the Van Alen warehouse where he'd stand and watch her splash through the pools of light from the gas lamps with a melancholy feeling that each time she was disappearing forever. This night he'd discover her world, but she was adamant, "No. Not now. It's the wrong time, the worst time. I'm *sure* they've been drinking tonight since it's Saturday. If you must come, come tomorrow—after mass. We all go to mass, they're sober then. But in the name of all the saints, don't let them get you into an argument."

It was a bad night, not unlike the night before his first big football game. In the morning Aaron dressed so that there would be nothing but the quality of cloth in his black suit and the mirror shine that Patrick applied every Saturday to his Sunday boots to distinguish him from a working man dressed for church. He took the horsecars as far as he could and then walked. The saloon was closed for the morning so as not to tempt any good Catholic to miss services; access to the family living quarters was by way of a rickety staircase on the side of the building. For a man in his condition the climbing of those stairs couldn't account for the way his heart was beating. Mary, who must have heard him, came out to hold the door open. She said nothing beyond hello, but the look on her face mirrored his own anxiety.

He walked into a dim, stuffy room that seemed to steam from the heat generated by outsized human bodies. Though there were only five men there, they were so massive, so sweaty-uncomfortable in their Sunday suits and collars that they dwarfed the space. The four brothers were standing stiffly around a lumpy chair in which the father sat. Aaron had a quick and crazy vision in which he saw himself entering a dark cave in those remote times of the Celtic tribes to confront an aging king guarded by warriors all dressed in black pelts. "This is Aaron Van Alen," Mary announced tonelessly, "and he asked permission to speak with you, father."

Frank O'Donnell reached for a pair of crutches leaning against his chair and heaved himself, grunting, to his feet. His heavy features were like a carving in gray granite, matching the color of his wild bush of hair. Upright, he was nearly as tall as his sons. Even sagging on crutches his body showed traces of the power that had made him, according to Mary, the fastest hod man on the Croton reservoir job before he'd fallen from a scaffolding and been crippled. He'd saved just enough, the Holy Mother be praised, to rent the saloon downstairs or they'd all have starved. O'Donnell did not hold out his hand or even say hello. He got himself over to where Aaron stood, looked down on him and said, "I consented to y'r comin' only to tell you to stay the hell away from my daughter. Her mother, the saints preserve her, would turn over in her grave if she knowed that a Fifth Avenue swell was trifling with her little girl."

It was probably only an illusion that Aaron thought he heard growling coming from the mastiff-like young men in the background. He dropped the hand that he'd held out and said, "I came to tell you, *sir*, that I am *not*, as you say, trifling with your daughter. I happen to love her and want to marry her."

"Huh! I'll have no daughter of mine marryin' a Protestant—"

"I've promised Mary I'd convert. I think a Christian is a Christian."

"And what would your fancy folks think of my Mary?"

"That she's good and beautiful and—"

"If you think that you're too young to know a damned thing about life. They'd cut her up in little pieces. Oh, I can't blame you for losing your head over Mary. You're not the first. We've dissuaded quite a few, ain't we, boys?"

He was *sure* he heard a growl, but it was only the voice of one of the sons, the youngest by his looks. He was about Aaron's age and as handsome as Mary was pretty, with the same coloring, the same blue-black hair and brows which in him made Aaron think of the black Irish. It had to be Hugh, because he was saying, "Bad enough if you weren't a Van Alen. I've had more of your stinking wages and long hours than a man can stand, and I'm starting a union. Did Mary tell you that? It's going to be fighting we are before long."

"I don't have much to do with that end of the business. I'm more what you'd call a salesman . . ."

"But you're a Van Alen, and it's me, me and the rest of us, paying with our sweat for that fancy coach you drive. No sister of mine's going to become a Van Alen except over my dead body."

Mary cut in. "You see, Aaron, it's hopeless. You'd better leave now . . ."

And then she saved the day. She started to cry. Almost instinctively, Aaron for the very first time put his arms around her. Her father, swaying in his crutches, said, "Stop that now, stop that. You're like your mother was. Can't have your way, you start blubbering. Can't stand it."

The boys stirred uneasily and one of them said, "Aw, c'mon now, Mary . . ."

It was apparent that these hulking fellows who could probably crush a man's skull with pleasure were unnerved by a woman's tears, especially their little sister's. Aaron decided to play on it. "There, you see, you've made her as unhappy as I am. I have a proposition for you, Mr. O'Donnell. Let me come courting Mary properly here in her home for a month, and we'll all get to know each other. If it doesn't work out, I give you my word that I'll never see her again. Is that all right with you, Mary?"

Mary still couldn't speak for crying, but she nodded her agreement. Her father, scratching away at his chin, said, "Well, if it's your wish, Mary . . . what about it, boys?"

Hugh, their self-appointed spokesman, said, "Okay, Van Alen, but no funny business with Mary, hear? And don't think your comin' around here'll change my mind about giving your brother what he's got coming to him. . . ."

From then on, Aaron spent a month of stifling summer Sundays calling on Mary and pressing his suit. Since the O'Donnell living quarters mostly smelled of cooked cabbage and the smoke from cheap cigars, they spent nice days wandering the waterfront, often as far down as the Battery, and bad ones sitting at a back table in the bar which was open afternoons to let the men of the neighborhood cut their morning's dose of religion with a drop of the good stuff. Aaron liked the mood of the bar. The men, enjoying their one day off, were usually cheerful, trading friendly insults and outrageous lies. When once in a while an argument over a horserace or prizefight resulted in a chair-shattering brawl, it was carried off in the spirit of good fun, and Aaron, as acknowledged beau to the daughter of the house, was exempt. Still, it was fighting that turned out to be Aaron's lucky break. He'd soon discovered that one of Mary's brothers, Jack, had aspirations in the ring, which was to him what the theater was to Mary—a way up and out. Watching Jack in an impromptu scuffle in the bar, Aaron realized that the fellow knew next to nothing about boxing, so he offered to give him lessons and spar with him. Aaron's knowledge and his ability to stand up to a much bigger man—indeed, cut him up at will—so impressed the O'Donnell men that even Hugh finally told Mary, "Your beau's all right after all. Just wish he wasn't a damn Van Alen . . ."

Another bit of Aaron's youthful training came in handy during his courtship. The local parish priest was almost as impressed with the knowledge of things biblical he'd picked up from his grandfather as the brothers were with his boxing skill. Admitting him to the true church would be no problem at all, at all, as long as he acknowledged that the Pope was Christ's vicar on earth. At the time, at least, this presented no difficulty to Aaron, for whom religion was mostly a ritual, a ritual actually more mysterious and impressive in the Latinized Catholic service than in the Protestant version. For Mary, his acceptance of the church, and his acceptance by the priest, were proofs of the sincerity and sanctity of his love. The next Sunday he brought a dazzling diamond at Tiffany's and she let him slip it on her finger. She let him kiss her too, and hold her close, and then she kissed him back so hard that their teeth ground together. Aaron could feel that tense, trained body quivering under his hands and was certain that all her rigid control would explode in passion when the right time came.

It was also fortunate for Aaron that this courtship was taking place in the summer when his own family was at Newport. It made it easier to make excuses about not introducing Mary to them—his father wasn't feeling well; he, Aaron, had to stay in town to mind the store while James was on vacation; she, Mary, wanted to finish the run of her show—didn't she?—and a single day off wasn't time enough to go all the way up there and back. This last was an item of contention between them. He'd wanted her to give up all this dancing business as soon as he slipped the ring on her finger, but she'd wanted to keep on until they were married. Actually, Aaron did steal up to Newport for a couple of weekdays, telling Mary he'd be over in New Jersey inspecting the factory, and had got the shocking reaction to his marriage plans. Mary was already so sensitive to the situation that, if he brought her up there she'd know instinctively what they were thinking, no matter how politely they lied. Then he'd surely lose her; Mary would run away out of pride. The only thing to do was to marry her at once and rely on the Van Alen kind of pride to make the best of it.

It took all of Aaron's powers of persuasion to get Mary to agree. He was in love and he didn't give a damn what his family thught. Why should she? . . . She was a woman, and families meant more to women, she told him. Besides, how could he risk cutting himself off from his family when he— they—depended on them for a living? If they didn't like her, she wanted to know about it now . . . Oh, they'd love her, just as he did, but they were a bit stuffy about things like the theater and the church and . . . The Irish? . . . Oh, not that—his father was very unprejudiced, he'd almost married a Jewish girl.

In the end it was nature that turned the trick. Their embraces had been getting increasingly warmer, a warmth that he knew was mutually felt. In the midst of one of them, he confessed his inability to control himself any longer, pleaded with her not to go on teasing and tormenting him, argued that, deep down, she felt as he did, and they stood on the brink of sin. If they got married while there was still some summer left, he'd take her up to Newport as his bride and they'd have the most beautiful honeymoon she could ever imagine. He had a new boat, a Burgess sloop, that had been lying idle at her mooring, and they'd turn her into a private love barge and gunkhole from harbor to harbor all along the coast. Could she imagine anything closer to heaven—alone together, just them and the sea and the sun, and able to make love all the time?

Somewhat reluctantly, she surrendered, and a date was set for early August. Aaron had pretty much agreed with James that the wedding should be a quiet affair, but it soon became apparent that the marriage of a daughter of an O'Donnell to the son of a Van Alen would not take place without fanfare, either in the neighborhood or the city as a whole. The press, ever on the lookout for Cinderella stories, jumped on it: SALOONKEEPER'S DAUGHTER TO WED RICH PLAYBOY, headlined one sheet. AARON VAN ALEN, NOTED ATHLETE AND BUSINESSMAN, MARRIES DANCER, said a kinder one. To the O'Donnells, it was the most important family affair since Katy O'Donnell's funeral, and it would have been unthinkable not to invite the Van Alen family to participate. Though he dreaded the outcome, Aaron couldn't prevent notes in Mary's misspelled handwriting from going out to Newport without arousing undue suspicion about his family's attitudes on the part of the proud O'Donnell men. Martha Van Alen's rather chill reply was that, due to the precarious state of Mr.

Peter Schuyler Van Alen's health, Mr. Van Alen could not make the trip and that she, as his wife, felt obliged to remain at his side. Mrs. James Van Alen simply declined without excuse, which as Aaron learned later, was about all she could do; James, as a Presbyterian elder, absolutely refused to set foot inside a Catholic church. Only Sally, God bless her, accepted on behalf of the Hancocks, although, as it turned out, she would have done them a favor by staying away.

"Captain" Hancock decided that the occasion called for a special voyage of the *Pride of the Sea*. He brought her around up the Hudson and tied up at the Van Alen docks, appearing at the church in a uniform that, but for the lack of insignia, would have done honor to an admiral. As soon as she saw the neighborhood and rather shabbily dressed crowd on hand—virtually all of Frank O'Donnell's patrons and the boys' fellow workers had turned out for the big event—Sally knew that arriving in a yacht was, to put it mildly, in bad taste. Catching Aaron just before the service, she said, "My God, I'm *sorry*. I told Pierce we oughtn't to do this, but you know Pierce. . . . Well, good luck, little brother—you'll need it. I must say, though, I caught a peek of your bride out in the vestibule and she's ravishing. Can't wait to meet her." That meeting took place at the reception, which was held, inevitably, in the saloon. Guests hadn't been invited; they just came and were, in a couple of cases, actually hanging from the rafters. Irish whiskey, served neat in tumblers, was on the house, and it wasn't long before Captain Hancock with his champagne palate was so happy drunk that he had a generous inspiration. Climbing up on a table and roaring to make himself heard, he said, "C'mon, you all. Let's have a party on my yacht."

Hugh O'Donnell, just as drunk, jumped up beside him. "You hear that? He wants us to have a pa—ah—ty on his ya—ah—aht. Ain't this a grand party right here, boys? We don't need your damned yacht, mister."

Pierce pulled himself erect, took a tug at his admiral's hat and said, "Sir, I'll not have you insult my vessel. I only meant to offer you and your friends some fine champagne—"

"Well, I'll not have you insultin' my father's hospitality," said Hugh, "and—"

Only the many hands crowded around the table kept Hancock from breaking his head on the floor as he went down. Women screamed and Aaron plunged into the melee to rescue his brother-in-law. When Sally took her slightly battered husband off his hands outside, she said, "He did have it coming to him, but I'm sorry to have spoiled your party, Aaron. You've certainly shaken the family up, I'll say that. I just hope like the devil you can handle it."

At that moment Aaron blessed his new saints that as a result of the cool response to the invitations he'd scrapped the idea of a Newport honeymoon and booked passage on a steamer to Bermuda instead. Which didn't turn out to be such a good idea either, since Mary was so appallingly seasick that he had to wait nearly a week before he could relieve her of her virginity. But when it did happen, it was worth everything he'd done to bring it about. Her primness had been a mask for her essential earthiness. By the time they got back to New York he really didn't give a damn what anybody thought about her or their marriage. He'd found, he was sure, that rarest of women—a wife who was a mistress too.

One game he'd played with her had to do with where they would live. It would be a fine house, but it would be his wedding present to her and so it would have to be a surprise—presents were no fun if they weren't surprises. There was more point to his game than she might have suspected; until the very last moment he himself hadn't known what to do about living arrangements. Under the circumstances there had been no question of his marriage being blessed with the gift of a house, as had his brother James'. Nor had he had the temerity even to suggest such a thing. As it developed, his father had sent him a check for $5,000 with the explanation that, since the senior Van Alens didn't know the lady, they had no idea of her taste in silverware or china or any of those things that might make more appropriate gifts than money. James and Anne had sent a Chinese vase that looked suspiciously like one Aaron had seen for years in their foyer; Sally and Pierce, relying no doubt on Aaron's sense of humor, had brought with them on the yacht a set of somewhat chipped gilt chairs that were supposedly made by the infamous hand of Boss Tweed before he got into politics and had descended to Sally from Uncle Charlie Smith via Cousin Lucy Smith as a gift at her next to last wedding. So, as to housing, Aaron was left to his own resources, which, all appearances to the contrary, weren't all that great.

Aaron drew a decent salary from Van Alen & Son which, as long as he was living at home, was more than enough to cover his coaching and sailing and romantic investments. In addition he had a certain amount, mostly in real estate, in trust from his grandmother Van Alen which would be his when his parents died, as would presumably be a share of their much larger estate. He was more wealthy in prospect than in the present, but his own pride would not allow him to treat his wife, especially in view of the family attitude about her, with much less favor than had been bestowed on James'. He discovered that the bankers were willing, within reason, to lend him enough money against his inheritance and any property he might buy to get a quite decent place. But where? Building on Fifth Avenue itself was unfortunately out of the question for *any* Van Alen by the time Aaron needed a home; the competition for available land all the way up to the park, not to mention the competition to put up a structure of equal magnitude and magnificence to neighboring mansions, was limiting the site to people whose millions couldn't be counted, and in any case the process of building would take too long for Aaron's purposes. So he started looking just off the Avenue where there were many respectable brownstone residences in which people of equal standing and probably more sense than those on the Avenue lived. The Roosevelts were at 6 West Fifty-seventh, for instance, and what Aaron understood to be the *real* Mr. Rockefeller, John D., was content with a place on West Fifty-fourth instead of making a splash on the Avenue like his brother, William.

It was, in fact, Teedie's brother Elliott who finally solved Aaron's problem. In recent years Aaron had been seeing more of Elliott than Teedie, who was either up in Albany making loud noises in the legislature or out west somewhere playing cowboy on a ranch. Elliott, however, was often to be found in the clubs Aaron frequented—too often, some thought. A very sociable fellow. Elliott wouldn't turn down a drink with anybody, with the result that he picked up gossip the way a black wool suit gathered lint. Knowing that Aaron was looking for a house, Elliott caught the chatter of a clubmate who wanted to sell out just down the block from the Roosevelt home and take his family to the continent for an extended stay. Within hours after Elliott had relayed the tip, Aaron had bought the house and furnishings. It was to this house, staffed by a Negro couple whom Aaron had engaged instead of the usual Irish help out of sensitivity to his wife's background, that he brought Mary from the Bermuda boat. Possibly he had made a mistake in pointing out the James Van Alen place and the Hancock house on their way up the Avenue, because her first reaction to what he considered a handsome home in comparison to the rooms above O'Donnell's saloon was surprising, and faintly disturbing. "Oh, Aaron, it's nice, but isn't it a little small? . . . Oh, well, I guess we can move when we have a baby, can't we?" Her first act of housekeeping was a surprise too. She discharged the Negroes and hired two Irish girls. "I can't help it, but those people scare me," she explained, "and daddy always said they're keeping bread out of good Irish mouths."

Aaron didn't argue with her; he only wanted her to be happy and compliant in bed. He himself was supremely happy. After years of catch-as-catch-can affairs, each day of coming home to a willing woman was a precious gift. He'd always thought that Teedie Roosevelt was rather silly for the way he raved about his Alice, but now he was beginning to think that Teedie had been way ahead of him in discovering this kind of bliss. It was hard to know since, despite their long friendship, they never talked about things like that; when it came to sex Teedie was something of a prude and—Aaron had no doubt—a virgin on his wedding night. Until he experienced the excitement of a real woman's passion himself, Aaron had rather supposed that Teedie's head was turned by having *any* woman. Be that as it may, it was Alice Roosevelt, as sweet as she looked, who so far had been seeing to Mary's happiness. If it hadn't been for her, Mary might have found the atmosphere in the upper regions near Fifth Avenue chilly, even in September.

The James Van Alens and the Hancocks, back from Newport, did make duty calls, which were dutifully returned. The elevation and twitch to Anne's mousey little nose as she tried to make conversation with Mary was to be expected, but Aaron was upset to detect a wariness between Sally and Mary, as if they were somehow rivals. "Your sister tries to be nice to me, but I don't think she really approves," Mary said, and Sally said, "She is beautiful, Aaron. Dangerous is more like it from the way Pierce looks at her, but I guess I have to wonder what you find to talk about." By contrast, the

213

Roosevelts were warm and hospitable. Teedie was quite frank. "Bully for you, Aaron," he said. "She's lovely, and since I've been in politics I've come to have great respect for the Irish. They're already running this city, and they'll be running the country before long." Mary was often in the Roosevelt home—with Teedie away so much, a house of women. Besides Alice, there was Mrs. Roosevelt, ailing and forgetful but graced with southern charm, and Teedie's unmarried sister Bamie and, of course, baby Alice. Playing with the baby, as pretty a thing as her mother, gave Mary a yearning for a baby of her own, a yearning that Aaron was happy to cooperate in gratifying.

In addition to keeping Mary amused and bolstering a confidence that might otherwise have been shattered, her association with the Roosevelt women was drawing Aaron back into the orbit of his old friend. When the Van Alens and Roosevelts visited together, Teedie, restless as always, would sit a few moments with the ladies or perhaps romp on the floor with the baby, and then say, "Come on, Aaron, let's leave the women to their chatter and look in at the club." The club Roosevelt had in mind wasn't the Knickerbocker or Century but the local Republican club, where the habitués, though they ran more to German than Irish seemed interchangeable with the men Aaron had come to know in O'Donnell's saloon. Incongruous in these surroundings, what with his expensive dinner clothes and falsetto voice ringing with long Harvard "a"'s, Roosevelt nevertheless got along well with the crowd exchanging banter and probing with hard

214

questions to learn their real problems. One night, though, a man made the mistake of saying, "Don't listen to that sissy." Roosevelt calmly floored him with that right cross Aaron had found so dangerous. Going home, he asked, "Do you still fight, Aaron?"

"Matter of fact, I'm teaching my brother-in-law Jack to box," Aaron said.

"Bully for you," Teedie said, clapping him on the back. "I wish I could get you interested in politics. We need men who will fight for the right things."

Another night Roosevelt dramatically demonstrated what he meant by "the right things." Instead of walking to the club, he surprised Aaron by hiring a hack. "Get in. I want to show you something." He gave the driver an address on the lower East Side.

"Begging your pardon, governor, but I don't want to go into a place like that this time of night," the driver said.

"If you're that much of a coward, you can drop us on Broadway and we'll walk," Roosevelt said.

The man was that much of a coward, and they walked for blocks through streets that Aaron was surprised to find choked with people, though it was going on toward midnight. It still being summer and hot, men in shirtsleeves and a few women among them sat fanning themselves on stoops. Pushcarts, mostly manned by black-bearded Jews crying their wares in a variety of tongues, clogged the roadway. If English was spoken here, Aaron heard little of it except for one taunting remark—"Would you look at them swells!" Walking purposefully, Roosevelt seemed oblivious to their surroundings until they passed an alleyway where a group of small children, eyes glistening like those of cornered animals in a shaft of light from the street, huddled together. Roosevelt paused and pointed to them. "Sleep there, poor devils."

At an aged brick house that had probably once been a prosperous merchant's home, Roosevelt pushed by the people on the steps and led Aaron into the hallway and up the stairs. The smell of human waste was so powerful that Aaron almost gagged, and Roosevelt sniffing loudly, said, "That's right—no plumbing. Eighty people live in this building." On the second landing, Roosevelt knocked and entered a room that was dark except for a single lamp in the middle of a table where two men, stripped to dirty underwear, sat rolling cigars. In the shadows, on beds that took up most of the rest of the room, were the lumps of women and children trying to sleep. "Good evening, Mr. Rakosky," Roosevelt said. "Do you remember me? I'm Representative Roosevelt, and I just came to tell you that the bill I introduced in Albany on your behalf ought to be passed soon." In an aside to Aaron, he explained, "These men are on piece work. I knew they'd be up, because they work until they drop. The prices they get paid ought to make every man who lights up after dinner at your Knickerbocker Club ashamed." The men were voluble, though nearly incomprehensible, in their thanks. When they were outside again, Roosevelt asked, "Do you have any idea who owns that building, Aaron?"

"Why should I?"

"Oh, I just thought you might," Roosevelt said. "When I started to work on a bill to help those poor fellows, I looked up the land records. It's part of the Van Alen trust . . ."

Aaron came home that night so quiet that Mary thought he was sick until she prodded him into telling her all about it. She surprised him again. "I don't think you should worry so much about it, Aaron. If those people want to come over here, they have to take what they can get. We Irish did, and I don't want you getting mixed up in politics like Mr. Roosevelt. Why, that poor Alice is almost a widow. I don't want to be a widow yet, Aaron. What I want to do is go to bed and make a baby."

Going to bed with Mary made it easier then to forget what he'd seen. Besides, what could he really do about it? He wasn't a trustee, and those who were, like James, would probably say, "Well, those people have to live somewhere. If we sold the buildings, somebody else would gouge them for even more rents. We can't help it if they choose to live the way they do. We didn't *ask* them to come over here." Besides, living with Mary and getting to know to some extent her brothers and their friends, was making him wonder whether Teedie Roosevelt wasn't wasting his time and missing the point, barging around and trying to right every wrong with some kind of law. If they didn't like things as they found them, the O'Donnells either tried to get up and out, like Mary and Jack, or fight, like Hugh. They had even less use for the suffering poor than the inhabitants of the mansions on Fifth Avenue. This was the land of unlimited opportunity for those who had the gumption to go after what they wanted. It was this knowledge, this feeling, that was causing

immigrants by the thousands to file through the old
Castle Garden at the Battery, and wasn't it really this
that that huge statue a fellow named Bartholdi was
making in France would celebrate? Aaron thought it
very fitting that a Jewish girl named Emma Lazarus,
rather than some proud patroon, had been inspired
by the news of the statue's creation to write:

> . . . Give me your tired, your poor,
> Your huddled masses yearning to breathe free,
> The wretched refuse of your teeming shore—
> Send these, the homeless, tempest-tossed to me,
> I lift my lamp beside the golden door!

The golden door. You could read it any way you
wanted to, but Aaron would guess that, for most
people, it meant a chance to improve themselves
that didn't exist anywhere else on earth. To make
money and enjoy it. You had to be very careful when
you thought about tampering with a society in
which this was so obviously possible for just about
anybody. The having of money was as natural to
Aaron, or for that matter Teedie Roosevelt, as
breathing, and the temptation was to be scornful, or
shocked, by the ruthless means other men used to
get it—and to pity those who didn't. In Aaron's
view, neither attitude was quite fitting for a person
in his position. The first was self-righteous, and the
second supercilious. In his college days when he'd
been briefly seized by a fit of moral indignation over
the injustices of the world, Aaron had threatened to
move out of the family's Fifth Avenue mansion and
renounce his heritage. His father, recognizing the

symptoms, had known what treatment to apply.

"Good for you, Aaron," he'd said. "You've caught moral fever, and it's as natural at your age as discovering that women are interesting. I had a bad case of it too, so bad that it nearly got me killed when the poor I thought I was befriending beat me up for insulting them with a patronizing editorial in my paper. I think it was about then that I decided that I couldn't help being born to wealth any more than I could help being born with gray eyes, and that I'd stop *apologizing* for it. You're facing the same thing. If you walk out on your heritage, all you accomplish is to leave it in other hands. When it does come to you in due time, you can give it all away if that will cure your fever, but by then I doubt you'll feel that way. Human beings have a way of adapting to the circumstances they find themselves in." His father had sighed and added, "I don't *honestly* know whether I hope you'll get over this or not. I can tell you, though, from my experience, that finding the right woman will have a lot to do with it. Women have an instinct for survival that some men seem to lack—and a practicality. Like a bird, a woman'll feather her nest as well as she can to protect her own fledglings, and maybe that's the natural order of life."

Aaron's fever hadn't quite subsided. He'd kept his mind off it by inventing all those challenges on the readily accessible football field or coaching course. Now, as his father had predicted, it was at least being cooled some by a woman's hand. He was, in truth, so busy being a husband, so concerned with making Mary as happy as she was making him, that nothing else much mattered . . . which was why tonight's evening at the opera was an event of such importance. Aaron knew from hints that Sally had dropped that his mother's lingering at Newport until the unavoidable day of the opera's opening had more to do with her distress over his marriage than the reason she gave—"The sea air's so good for your father." She'd also used his father's health as a pretext for not inviting them up. The whole performance was close to being a deliberate snub, and Mary was bright enough to recognize it as such. It infuriated Aaron and at the same time dismayed him, for, almost unconsciously, he'd spent a lifetime seeking the favor of this imperious and glamorous woman who was his mother. Up until now he'd succeeded. As the youngest of her children he'd been somewhat of a pet. Though she'd clucked in a motherly way over his supposed misdemeanors and dangerous athletic feats, she'd also boasted about them to others. And she'd taken a very feminine, and often embarrassing, delight in his physical attractiveness, forever hugging him until he got too big for that sort of thing, and saying, "And how's my handsome boy today?" It was this pride in him, this form of love, that accounted for her reaction to Mary. It was a plain case of dashed hopes. In the heat of his own amorous feelings, Aaron was convinced that his mother's behavior was silly, inexcusable; once she knew Mary she'd change her mind. He'd probably have to thank the Roosevelt cousins' favorable reports on Mary for tonight's invitation. While it didn't rank with the teas or dinners she should have given for her new daughter-in-law,

Martha's invitation to the opera was a slight crack in the marble facade she'd erected, and Mary's spunk in accepting it gave promise of driving a wedge through that crack.

The coaching trip was a perfect overture to the opera. At lunch and without even trying, Mary more than held her own with Mrs. Langtry in terms of male admiration. Even the star melted a little when she learned that Mary had reversed her own course, going from the theater into society rather than from society into the theater. "I think you're going in the wrong direction, my dear, but then if you're like me it's probably the challenge you find exciting," Mrs. Langtry told her. By the time they returned at exactly six, Mary had taken on a glow that came as much from confidence as the fresh fall air. Though they barely had time to change their clothes, Mary was so radiant when she came down the stairs that Aaron let out a whoop. "You'll really knock them dead in the aisles," he said. She was wearing a pink silk dress that she'd had made for the occasion from a Paris design, the very first ever she hadn't picked off a rack or sewn with her own hand. Her taste was perfect. The lace trimming the elbows and high collar and drape like a shawl across the swell of her breasts suggested modesty and restraint, and she wore around her neck and on her arm only the matching strands of pearl and bracelet that he'd given her just before their wedding. Her black hair was braided, turned around her head like the crown she deserved and held with a pin whose white pearl head shone like a drop of purity. He hurried her into her cape and into a waiting hack. It wouldn't do to be late—he wanted to march her into that box before the house lights went down.

All the others were in their seats when they arrived. There was one small and rather unpleasant surprise. Evidently his father hadn't felt up to coming after the trip down from Newport, and his mother had asked Cousin Amelia Downing at the last minute to take his place. Though normally Aaron enjoyed the uninhibited old lady just because you never knew what she'd say or do, he didn't want this moment made more difficult for Mary by some outrageous happening. There'd been enough on his mind during his courtship and marriage so that he hadn't gone out of his way to see Amelia, or his other peculiar cousin, Sophie, who'd moved into James' house in a disapproving huff when Sally had left Brewster to come home and have her baby, and he hadn't bothered to tell Mary about them. Bad enough that she had to face up to the Van Alens who could afford to be proud without having to cope with Van Alens who could afford also to be eccentric. Pride was something Mary could well understand; eccentricity was, he suspected, a luxury she'd not considered. . . .

Martha Roosevelt Schuyler Van Alen acted like a queen. When Aaron and Mary entered the box, she turned and beckoned them forward with a nod. Tiaraed and draped with diamonds, she flashed fire with every movement. Diamonds, the purest and hardest gems that earth can deliver, transcended, it occurred to Aaron, evanescent human vanity. Were it not so, he might have been embarrassed by his mother's glitter in comparison to his wife's soft radiance. And Aaron would have to say this for his mother: only someone who knew her as well as he did could have detected the tightness of her lips, the slight strain in her voice when, holding out a diamond-encrusted hand to Mary, she said, "My dear, I'm *so* sorry that Mr. Van Alen's health has prevented our meeting earlier. You *are* as lovely as I've been told you were . . . ."

Mary shot the first arrow, and whether it lodged in the heart or not would take time to determine. She didn't, Aaron noted with thanks, do anything stupid like curtseying. She took his mother's outstretched hand and said, "I'm sorry, too, Mrs. Van Alen, but . . . well, may I call you mother?"

At this point, Amelia couldn't contain herself. "Of course you can call her mother," she said. "I could kill this husband of yours for not bringing you over to meet me earlier. You're an absolute jewel. I'm Cousin Amelia—Amelia Downing—Mrs. Van Alen, and I'm delighted to make your acquaintance. I suspect you're what this family has needed for a long time . . ."

Aaron was grateful for the fact that the lights finally started to dim, and his mother said, "Shush. We mustn't upset the conductor with our talk."

In whispered greetings as they took their seats, Sally was brief, and kind: "Wherever did you get that dress, Mary? It's stunning . . ."

Pierce, who'd obviuosly anesthetized himself against the boredom of sitting through a whole opera, was indiscreet: "I hope none of those killer brothers of yours are waiting in the wings . . ."

On the whole it hadn't gone too badly, Aaron thought as he sat back with Mary at his side—holding his hand, actually—and listened to the first solemn strains of the orchestral introduction to Gounod's *Faust*. The management had made a fine choice of an opera for this occasion when much of the audience came to be seen rather than to hear. There had been, he knew, talk of putting on *Parsifal* as a kind of memorial to Wagner, who'd died earlier this year, but it would most certainly have induced either fidgeting or snoring in the jammed patrons' boxes. From what he'd heard of Wagner's music Aaron went along with the fellow who said it consisted of divine seconds and dull hours. Something like Mozart's *Marriage of Figaro* would have been lively enough but too sophisticated. *Faust*, with its easily understood story of the devil at work and its rapturous melodies, was just right.

Whatever else happened, Aaron was determined to let himself enjoy the music. His love of music was a part of his life that he hadn't yet shared with Mary or anybody else but his mother. The feelings music aroused in him were, like the art itself, wordless and therefore almost impossible to communicate to others. They'd been with him for as long as he could remember, and he owed them to his mother. In the earliest scene of his life that he could recapture he was curled up around the warm body of the family's spaniel in his "secret lair"—the dark cave under the old square Steinway grand in the house on Twenty-second Street. While he watched his mother's silk-slippered feet work the pedals, chords of a Beethoven sonata poured down on him like soft rain and drenched him. He had thought that his mother didn't know that he was there, and she had had the wisdom to pretend that she didn't. For quite a while—until he was six or so and began to discover the outside world where a love for music was considered sissy by his peers—it was a favorite game between him and his mother. To what was now his regret, he bowed to the judgment of his peers and resisted his mother's later efforts to teach him to play. Unlike James and Sally, who regarded it as dreadful duty, he did, however, genuinely enjoy all the concerts that their mother, as a member of the Philharmonic Society, dragged them to. In those growing-up years, Sally would accuse him of trying to be a "mother's pet" when, and if, he expressed any enthusiasm, and so he gradually learned to make music a secret, private thing. Nobody, even Mary beside him and holding his hand, could have detected that Aaron Van Alen, slouched in his seat in a pose of elegant indifference, was transported.

Aaron let himself slide with the music, let himself descend into the meditations of a lonely, aging Faust, let his spirits rise again at the sound of the happy girls singing in the streets, let his romantic imagination soar as Faust's pact with Mephistoph- eles evoked a melodic promise of youth and love. The first act, for him, ended all too soon, and the rising lights and instant buzz of conversation as the audience turned eagerly to the real business of the evening jarred him as would a commotion in the night ending a dream. "You like it?" he asked Mary, not risking more.

She was honest. "I don't know. I don't understand French."

"Probably nobody else here does either. It's the music . . ."

"I wonder when I would have come on, if—"

"In the last act—that's when they have the ballet. Well, we have visitors."

As Aaron had anticipated, the Van Alen box with its three striking women—Martha, Sally, and Mary—and its well-connected matron Anne became an interact mecca. Happily, the Roosevelts were the first to arrive. Though Teedie was in Albany, Alice was accompanied by Cousin James, down from Hyde Park without Sarah, who felt that she couldn't leave her Franklin, who was little more than a year old, for so long a time. Elliott, too, was without a wife who'd just had a daughter, Eleanor. In the warm presence of the Roosevelts, Mary was included naturally in the conversation, and the proliferation of Roosevelts led to some friendly teasing about when Mary would provide the world with another Van Alen. Which allowed Aaron to lay to rest any suspicions, if there were any, about his wife's virtue: "Well, now, give us time. Mary's a good Catholic girl who doesn't believe in *premature* babies." He thought that Sally was slaughtering him with her eyes, but never mind: you had to seize opportunity when it came along.

By the end of the second act, James' business friends were also paying their respects. As a sort of outside man for the firm, Aaron knew most of them too, and he did find a subject for ready conversation

226

with Colonel Oliver Payne, the treasurer of Rockefeller's Standard Oil, whose steel barque, *Aphrodite*,
more than three hundred feet long, was by far the
finest yacht in America. By showing enough
interest, Aaron managed to wangle an invitation
aboard for the following summer if "you'll promise
to bring along your beautiful bride." Another
Standard Oil man, Henry Rogers, brought with him
the most fascinating of their visitors, a big, shaggy
man with a Missouri twang named Samuel Clemens,
whose writing under the pen name of Mark Twain
was making him the most famous author in the
country. Having laughed his way through *The
Gilded Age*, which he took to be an attack on the
greed and pomposity of both businessmen and
politicians, Aaron was surprised to see Twain in the
friendly company of a man like Rogers. He was even
more surprised that the author seemed more eager
to discuss with the other men the value of stocks in
various ventures than literature. Aaron tried to tell
Twain how much he'd liked his book, but Twain
brushed his compliments aside with, "What I wish
you'd tell me is how I could put some of my profits
into Van Alen stock. My friend Rogers here tells me
it's sounder than Standard Oil."

At the end of the third act the Van Alen box drew
all eyes away from the great golden curtains hiding
the stage. General and Mrs. Grant and their son,
Ulysses, Jr., and his family made a public pilgrimage
to the throne of Mrs. Peter Van Alen. Martha and
Peter, who'd met the general during Peter's wartime
service in Washington, had been among the first to
call at the Grant brownstone at 3 East Sixty-sixth

Street back in '80 and welcome the ex-President to New York, and Grant was forever grateful. Conversation with the Grants, too, was all about the market. The general had thrown what little was left to him after his White House service into the private banking firm of Grant & Ward which his son had formed with Ferdinand Ward, "the Napoleon of Wall Street." Now the partners were said to be worth $15,000,000, and the general, who'd nearly starved as a storekeeper before the war, couldn't quite get over being rich. The "miracle of the market," he called it, and in a way it was an even more satisfying reward for his services than had been his triumphal trip around the world before he settled in New York.

None of the male visitors to the box failed to pay special attention to the youngest and prettiest of the ladies, Mary, as Aaron noticed with satisfaction, and he hoped that his mother was noticing it as well. Mary held herself proud and displayed her native intelligence, as she had on that first meeting with Pierce, by pretending to be fascinated with dull talk of stocks and bonds. The men who hadn't met Mary before all went out of their way to congratulate Aaron, and General Grant provided a climax to the little drama going on in the box by telling Martha, "You must be proud of your new daughter-in-law, Mrs. Van Alen. As Mrs. Grant and I were saying to each other when we saw her come in this evening, we didn't set eyes on a lovelier lady in all of our travels." If Martha's "Thank you, general" seemed lacking in enthusiasm to an anxious Aaron, her look of new appraisal in Mary's direction held possibilities. He was certain by the arrival of the last act that his Mary, performing as well as any singer on the stage, had made a mark his mother couldn't ignore.

Plunging from the complicated and seemingly trivial social drama running on between acts into the simple but universal Faustian fable of good and evil, lust and divine forgiveness, would have been impossible for Aaron if not for the music. In that last act, shifting from Walpurgis Night revels to a stark battle for the soul of the ravished Marguerite in a jail cell, Gounod managed, in Aaron's opinion, to ring every emotional change that music could provide. He knew that critics, favoring the more fashionable dissonances and dark harmonies of Wagner, were beginning to call Gounod's work trite and overly romantic. Well, maybe he was romantic too, but Aaron could feel his flesh crawl, his hair rise, as Marguerite intoned her triumphant prayer to heaven against Faust's anguished cries and the devil's sour mutterings in the background. Listening then to the last angelic chorus was, like listening to Handel's *Messiah*, as close as Aaron could ever come to having a religious experience. There was no use in analyzing it. It was just there—a hope of heaven in glorious sound.

Whether others felt this way or not, the grandeur of the occasion called for rising applause, which rolled in waves of sound over the lip of the stage. Coming slowly back to earth, Aaron again asked Mary, "Well, did you like it?"

"Oh, yes—especially the ballet. I could just imagine myself out there if—"

"If you hadn't married me. Are you sorry?"

"Oh, no . . . Aaron, do you think your mother likes me?"

"Well, it's short acquaintance, but I can assure you that after this she'll have to pay attention to you. Do you like *her?*"

"I . . . I don't know. I guess she frightens me."

"Frightens you? She's only a poor parson's daughter. I doubt my grandfather ever made more cash money than your father makes out of his saloon. If it hadn't been for the house the church let them use—"

"Oh, you don't understand. Your mother's been a rich man's wife for a long, long time, and . . . well, you people are different, all of you. I didn't know half of what anybody was saying tonight. I wonder if I'll ever feel like I belong."

"Nobody would have known by the way you acted. Don't worry, you will—you *do*—belong. *Anywhere.*"

The house lights came on, and though the applause continued, Martha Van Alen rose and swept by them, leaving as always just in time to reach her carriage before the crowds made it difficult. In passing she paused long enough to say to Mary, "I haven't seen your house and I'm told it's very nice. Would tomorrow be convenient?"

"Yes, of course . . . uh . . . mother . . ."

"Shall we say four—for tea? Perhaps I can persuade Mr. Van Alen to come with me since it isn't that far. Good night."

Aaron squeezed Mary's hand. "Well," he said, "I'm *sure* you're a Van Alen now, for better or for worse."

On the way home, Aaron, out of exuberance, began singing aloud Marguerite's prayer:

"Anges purs! anges radieux!
Portez mon âme au sein des cieux!"

Mary, suddenly relaxed from a long day in the air and an evening of tension, rested comfortably against him with her head on his chest. "Aaron," she said, "what do those words mean?"

"She's asking the angels to take her soul to heaven."

"Poor girl. I think I'm already there."

Aaron stopped singing, held her closer and pressed his lips against an exposed patch of silky skin at the nape of her neck. She shivered a little at the touch of his lips, and Aaron knew that they'd both soon be in the only kind of heaven he truly cared about.

Chapter 6

IT WASN'T really a sad funeral. The choir sang triumphal hymns like "Onward Christian Soldiers" and "Faith of Our Fathers," and the new minister who didn't know Peter Schuyler Van Alen very well delivered a vague eulogy about "this most Christian of gentlemen who had so obviously found favor in the eyes of the Lord." Shaking hands with members of the family as they came out of church, people were moved to make such comments as "Well, he had a good, long life, didn't he?" or, more intimately, "It's a blessing he's out of his misery, isn't it?"

Both were true in part. In this year of 1886 the deceased was in his seventy-fifth year, and his last years had been shadowed by a series of heart attacks and strokes. Since his death could have come as no surprise to any member of the family, it was also no surprise that his widow held up so well at the services. Some malicious mourners even insinuated to equally malicious friends that the social-minded

Martha Van Alen was busier counting the house than praying for her husband's soul. It wasn't considered in the best of taste that the daughter—who's she married to *now;* somebody named Hancock, isn't it?—was heard sniffling in the quieter moments, nor quite manly that young Aaron was seen repeatedly daubing at his eyes and blowing his nose. James, though he'd been closest to his father in the business, was more like his mother; he got through the proceedings with the kind of dry-eyed dignity and restraint that people expected of the Van Alens.

Family watchers were struck, too, by the proud self-control exhibited by the young Van Alen ladies, particularly that pretty wife of Aaron's—"Black is so becoming to her with that black hair, isn't it?" It was a bit of a shock when she kneeled and crossed herself right here in a Presbyterian church, but then it was nothing like her performance at the Roosevelt funeral a couple of years back when she'd sobbed so loudly that her husband had had to lead her out of the church. Well, everybody knew that the Irish were emotional about death, with their drunken wakes and all that, so her behavior now must be a sign that she was becoming a real Van Alen. You really had to hand it to the Dutch—look at Teddy Roosevelt over there. That Roosevelt funeral *was* a sad affair, what with them burying Teddy's wife and mother on the same day, just as they'd died on the same day in the same house on Fifty-seventh Street. Typhoid, they said, took off old Mrs. Roosevelt—well, not so old, only fifty—and Bright's disease carried away Alice in only her twenty-third year. It

233

was almost spooky, happening as it did in the worst February fog New York had ever known, so bad that Teddy couldn't get back from Albany in time. Even Elliott, who was not given to morbid fancies, was heard to say, "There's a curse on this house," and Teddy must have agreed. He sold it off and left his little girl with his sister Bamie up on Madison Avenue and disappeared out west. Anybody would have understood if he never came back, yet there he was, sitting in this very church with the woman everybody said he'd marry soon, Edith Carrow, and flashing those teeth of his like a jack-o'-lantern since this wasn't a sad funeral. Good thing, though, that Teddy lost out in the race for mayor last month, probably because that single taxing fellow Henry George stole the workingmen's vote from him; a businessman could trust what a Tammany fellow like Hewitt would do, but young Roosevelt had never met a payroll, and riding about shooting bears wasn't any way to learn how to run a city. If it weren't for the way he'd come back after that tragedy, you might doubt that Roosevelt was really Dutch.

In their carriage on the way to the cemetery, Mary Van Alen offered Aaron an apology of sorts for what might have seemed her indifference: "I never really got to know him well. I just wish now that I had."

Aaron said, "Yes, too bad he was sick so often. I guess this is a blessing, as everybody says, but I can't help how I feel . . ."

"I know. I know how it was when my mother died. What do you suppose is going to happen now?"

"What do you mean?"

"Well, at the . . . you know, at the meeting this afternoon . . ."

"Oh, that. I really don't care but I wouldn't be surprised if James got it all—except for grandmother's trust, that is."

"Why? You're as much a son as James, aren't you?"

"Please, Mary, I don't want to talk about it . . ."

She fell back into silence and let Aaron, in turn, fall back into the mood that had brought tears to his eyes during the services. He thought that his sadness came from the fact that he, too, had never really known his father well enough. Born when father Peter Van Alen was already forty-six, Aaron had grown up to see his father as a gentling, graying man, conservative in dress and habit, tolerant to the point of seeming to be tentative in opinion. True, faded newspaper clippings of poems his father had written, family tales about his work as a young, crusading editor and his romantic elopement, letters from President Lincoln about his work with the Sanitary Commission, provided intriguing glimpses of a younger, different kind of man, of a stranger Aaron thought he might have liked if he could ever have gotten to know him. But for too many years Aaron was too busy being young, too content to take the father he did know for granted to seek out that stranger, and when he did he was too late.

Whether it was failing health or a philosophy of life, his father, like his grandmother Van Alen before him, turned away probing questions with comments like, "That's all ancient history. It's what's happening now that counts." And once, when Aaron had pushed for more detail about that passing and fascinating reference to some Jewish girl, his father had said, "As your grandmother told *me*, people ought to die with some secrets." Still, Aaron had gone on hoping that some time might come, perhaps in one of those death-bed scenes, when his father would really open up, but there'd been no such scene. Like William Vanderbilt almost exactly a year ago, his father had simply risen from his chair and fallen dead on the floor, taking whatever secrets he might have had with him. It was, as everybody kept saying, the way to go.

Aaron wasn't so sure. He'd wanted, if not revelation, at least some last word, some blessing from his father, like the jade dragon his grandmother had given him. For fear of being thought odd, he'd never told a soul, especially Mary, that every time he fondled that dragon, he felt a kind of strength flowing into him. There'd been a little argument with Mary about keeping it there on the bedside table. "I don't care if it is jade, dragons are so . . . so ugly," she'd said, wanting in its place one of the china dogs she was collecting and displaying on the étagère in the drawing room. Why dogs? Her answer to his rather idle query had been one of those things about Mary that kept surfacing. "I always wanted a dog but my mother said we couldn't afford to feed it, and I'd look at ladies walking their dogs and think that that's what it was like to be wealthy. I'd want a real one now, Aaron, if it weren't for the baby coming." But Aaron had been firm about the dragon, the surest sign of its importance to him since he'd given in to Mary on nearly everything else, including looking into getting a bigger house on the avenue, now that they had two children.

Although his father had left no dragons, there had been one special moment of hope for revelation on that night his father died. Aaron had been summoned by his mother to the Van Alen mansion, a summons that might not have come to him if it weren't for the fact that James and Sally were hard to reach at the Schermerhorn ball, an event that he and Mary had had to decline because she was still nursing the infant Francis. After he'd done what he could to soothe his mother and help Patrick carry his father's body—surprisingly light, as if a great deal of substance had departed with the spirit—up to his bedroom to await the ministrations of the undertaker, Aaron had spotted an open ledger in his father's handwriting on the desk. It was something called "The Van Alen Story" by Peter Schuyler Van Alen, and Aaron had scooped it up and taken it home, thinking that, at last, he'd know everything. All that night he'd sat up reading through the volume and suffering profound disappointment. The entries were sparse, wooden, nothing but dates and places and names with little or no indication of the passions that might swirl around them.

"My mother, Sarah (otherwise known as Sally) Schuyler Van Alen enjoyed a tranquil childhood on the Schuyler manor overlooking the Hudson River near Kinderhook, N.Y.," the story began. "The most exciting event of her youth was a journey to New York where she witnessed the inaugural of George Washington and where she met her cousin, George Van Alen, who, whilst she was still in her

237

early teens, persuaded her to enter into a secret marriage that was displeasing to her father, Jacob Schuyler. This displeasure arose, as the writer was given to understand, from both political and personal reasons. Mrs. Van Alen, known as Lady Lydia, was the daughter of Sir Robert Wentworth who had been knighted for his services to the crown as a leading tea merchant of New York, and during the Revolution she maintained her residence in lower Broadway in which she harbored British officers. Her husband, Cornelius Van Alen, was held to have supplied with his river sloops the British garrison of New York at considerable profit to himself. Jacob Schuyler, a patroon with extensive land holdings, was an outspoken patriot and, at considerable cost to himself, was a major supplier of the Continental forces. Thus there existed, despite the familial relationship, a deep difference of views between the Schuyler and Van Alen families. The personal matter had to do with the character of George Van Alen, who was what was then known as a 'man about town' and who remained so with the result that he became a victim of spirits. Nevertheless, Cornelius Van Alen claimed my mother, his sister's daughter, as his daughter-in-law and brought her to New York in 1796 in his then famous sloop, *Lady Lydia*. My mother gave birth to Evelina, who died in infancy, a son Cornelius and, subsequently, this writer. In the course of these years she became closely associated with the affairs of Van Alen & Son, an association she maintained to the benefit of both the firm and the family until the year of her death. She was, however, permanently estranged from the Schuyler family with the exception of her half-brother, the late Senator Peter Schuyler, for whom this writer is named, and her nephew, the Reverend Doctor James Schuyler, son of her other half-brother, Jacobus Schuyler, who was the father of this writer's beloved wife Martha. . . .

Dull and familiar stuff. Aaron started jumping through it searching, naturally, for references to himself. The first had to do with the Captain Roberts for whom he'd been named, and it raised more questions than it answered. Only a few sentences, one of them relating that the dragon had been a gift from the captain to his grandmother. A gift seemed understandable enough in view of the fact that the captain was in the Van Alen employ, but it certainly didn't explain why, as he'd always been told, his grandmother had proposed his name. The only hint of a reason was his father's statement that Captain Roberts had been known to them as "Uncle Aaron," a familiarity not accorded a mere employee. Aaron's eyes raced on. In the process he got the impression of a certain majesty to the journal. At appropriate points in the bare family chronicle his father had paused to record what he evidently regarded as significant developments in the city and country— the triumph of steam on the rivers and seas, the opening of the Erie Canal, the piping in of Croton water, the installation of baths and water closets, the building of railroads, the lighting of gas lamps, the laying of tracks for horsecars, the erection of new and ever larger buildings, the invention of the telegraph and elevator. The last of these entries, recorded on September 5, 1882, read: "Yesterday

Mr. Edison's power station on Pearl Street went into operation. Driven by steam, it lights 60 buildings with 400 incandescent lamps. Electricity will change our world more than any other new development I have seen in my lifetime." Reading this, Aaron was reminded of what his mother had reported about his father's last moments. "You know, Aaron, just before he . . . just before it happened . . . he was talking about taking all the gas lines out of this house and replacing them with electric wires the way Mr. Morgan's done," she said. "It was so like your father—always looking forward."

It was also so like his father to make the births and marriages and deaths of Van Alens seem insignificant compared to developments in the world around them. Surprisingly, politics was very little mentioned except in relation to Cousin Martin Van Buren, who belonged in the journal as a distant relation by marriage—his mother had been a Mrs. Van Alen before marrying Abraham Van Buren. But a key to his father's political thinking—rather, his slighting of politics despite his own political career as a New York alderman—lay in one entry: "In the election of 1840, Mr. Van Buren was defeated by General Harrison. It was thought by the writer at that time that General Harrison would bring the country to ruin and, even more so, when the general died, leaving our fate in the hands of an unknown Mr. Tyler. That no great disaster befell us may be evidence that the generally held notion that this nation is blessed by providence is true or, more likely, it may be evidence of the naivety of this writer, who has since learned through hard experience the limitations of political activity in significantly influencing the course of human existence." As for his own importance, Aaron rated only a mention of his birth and a later reference with one of his father's few touches of sardonic humor: "Aaron Roberts Van Alen graduated this year from Princeton College with honors in football." The writing ended before Mary's existence could have been known or noted by his father. Aaron tossed the journal aside. Peter Schuyler Van Alen's secrets were still safe.

Nevertheless, there was one secret that his father couldn't take with him—the extent and division of his wealth. This would be revealed this afternoon, right after the funeral luncheon in his mother's house, and he guessed that he couldn't blame Mary for her curiosity, however indelicate it might seem. Even the press was hounding them; New Yorkers took as much interest and delight in reading about the wills of the wealthy as in the results of horseraces or the extravagance of costumes at society balls. Perhaps it had something to do with an instinct in the public that the ever larger estates confirmed America's potential for producing unlimited riches. And, in a way, they did. The $200,000,000 William Vanderbilt left was astounding even to his neighbors, the Van Alens; in eight short years he had doubled the value of the holdings his father had taken some seventy years to amass. Aaron, of course, should not have been surprised. He'd watched with interest as the two brownstone Vanderbilt palaces rose on Fifth Avenue at Fifty-first and Fifty-second streets, one for William himself and the other for two of his daughters. He'd gone so far as to cite details of their construction— sixty stoneworkers alone, six hundred artisans imported from Europe to decorate the interior—to prove to Mary that building anything respectable on Fifth Avenue was beyond their dreams. She'd been nearly convinced when they'd been invited to a reception in the William Vanderbilt house and she'd seen with her own eyes the huge dining room with its carved gold oak wainscotting and its ceiling paneled with original oil paintings of hunting scenes and the equally large drawing room with walls hung in pale red velvet, embossed with flowers and butterflies and set with crystal and precious stones. "The whole Van Alen fortune couldn't buy that," he'd said to her on their way home, and she'd agreed, "I'm sure you're right. I just don't know much about money."

Lack of knowledge did not, in Mary's case, mean lack of interest. Her constant and vocal interest in the monetary value of things was a small irritation to Aaron, but he curbed his temptation to temper by reminding himself that it was he, not she, who'd chosen to ignore the fact that they came from such different worlds. It was chilling, too, to hear her refer wistfully to "when you get your inheritance" on those rare occasions when he felt obliged to deny her something on the grounds that they couldn't afford it. It was as if she wished for the death of his father, then clinging stubbornly to life, or his mother, at just sixty a perfect example of Schuyler vigor. He doubted that that was Mary's meaning, but now that his father *had* died he couldn't doubt the strength of her hope that the news for them this afternoon would be good. He'd like to think so too, but he had to caution her. After all, and especially in old Dutch families like his, the claims of the older and favored sons were almost invariably recognized at death, regardless of relationships in life. Take the Vanderbilts: the old commodore had left nearly everything to William, who, in turn, had divided half his estate between his favorite sons, William K. and Cornelius, and sprinkled the rest like a fine golden rain on the heads of his other six children. It shouldn't matter when there was enough, for even the most neglected Vanderbilts could not be called poor in any sense. Yet it did. Whether from injured feelings or out of pure greed, families would mercilessly tear themselves apart in public, as the commodore's children had done, in wrangles over money. Pray to God, Aaron thought as the carriage turned into the cemetery gates, that that won't happen to us.

"Oh, look! Now why did they have to come?" Mary said.

Standing by the grave site and looking more like a matched team of professional pallbearers than Van Alen relatives were the four O'Donnell brothers. "Maybe they think there's going to be a good wake," Aaron said.

"That's not nice, Aaron. I *told* them they didn't have to come. Oh, God, Aaron, you don't suppose they're here to start trouble?"

"I doubt it. I just think they want to see a Van Alen buried for a change."

"Aaron, don't be so bitter . . ."

"It's hard not to after what happened," he said.

She took his hand and squeezed it as they approached the little group gathering around the grave. "I know. Now you go and be with your mother, and let me take care of them."

Watching his wife's small, slim figure march resolutely up to that line of hulking men, Aaron marveled again at nature's ability to bring forth such different creatures from the same source. It was nervy of the brothers to show up like this, but then the O'Donnells were never lacking in nerve. It was ominous, too, and he could see his brother James casting glances of alarm and displeasure in their direction. No wonder; he didn't feel easy himself. It was only when he saw them start moving off, evidently at Mary's command or beseeching, that he could concentrate on the minister's benedictive reading—"ashes to ashes, dust to dust"—and forget for this while last summer's awful events. . . .

Nobody knew better than Aaron that the general strike in Chicago in that May of 1886 for an eight-hour day, a cooperative venture of the Knights of Labor and other unions, was the event for which his brother-in-law Hugh O'Donnell had been waiting, though he saw Hugh rarely. Mary resisted more than he making occasional duty calls at the old saloon on the West Side. "I can't seem to find anything to say to them anymore, and they're always so angry about something." Aaron didn't have that problem. He was still interested in Jack's ring career, which seemed to be prospering with his tutelage, and he was beginning to pay more attention to Hugh's rantings, owing to his experiences with Teddy—he had to keep remembering not to call him Teedie anymore—Roosevelt. Hugh was gradually persuading his fellow workers to sign on with the new American Federation of Labor being organized by Samuel Gompers, a little East Side cigar maker with a head that looked like a bullet and was just about as dangerous, who had persuaded Roosevelt to put through that law prohibiting the manufacture of cigars in tenement houses. It was well for Aaron's peace of mind, when talking with Teddy or Hugh, that he was unaware of the part the Van Alen Trust, fearing loss of rents, played in bringing the law before the State Supreme Court where it was declared unconstitutional on the grounds that it deprived owners of the right to profit from their property, and, as the court said, "It cannot be perceived how the cigar maker is to be improved in his health or his morals by forcing him from his home and its hallowed associations and beneficent influences to ply his trade elsewhere." From his own visit with Teddy to what Gompers called a "sweat shop," Aaron could certainly perceive it, even if the court couldn't, and he began to understand why fighting men like Hugh had given up on their political leaders and were looking to their own resources to correct injustices. "I'm telling you, warning you, Aaron, and you'd best warn that brother of yours," Hugh would say, leaning close across the table and fixing him with those sky-blue eyes so like Mary's, "that when the time is ripe, Van Alen and Son will do no business except on our terms."

Shortly after news of the Chicago strike came through, Aaron and Mary were making a visit to the saloon when Hugh jumped up on a table and began haranguing the men. "You've heard what they're doin' in Chicago, haven't you? Well, what are we waitin' for here in New York? Are we a bunch of cowards? Are we going to sit idly by and watch others fight our battles? I say *no*. The time has come to stop talkin' and start fightin'. Let's join our Chicago brothers. Let's not load one more piece of Van Alen machinery until we're doin' it in an eight-hour day. What do you say, lads? Are you with me?" Amply fortified with what had once been Dutch courage but was now being appropriated by the Irish, the men responded with a resounding affirmative, and Hugh went on, "Now, you all know we've got a Van Alen right here—me brother-in-law Aaron. He's not a bad sort—you've seen him with his fists—but he can't help bein' who he is. But you go tell that brother of yours, Aaron, that he might as well not go to work tomorrow, or any day, until he sits down with us and talks turkey, 'cause nothin's going to move on or off his docks. Ain't I right, boys?" Shouts of "Right! Right!" and "You tell'im, Aaron!" rang through the room. Hugh called for a glass of whiskey, lifted it high. "All *right*, boys, let's have a drink to tomorrow—and the eight-hour day!"

Aaron did feel obliged to warn James. After he got Mary safely home he strolled over to James Van Alen's Gothic house on the Avenue. A tangle of carriages standing in front of the cathedral-like door reminded him that James and Anne would be having one of their Sunday night suppers. He and Mary were never invited, a mercy from his point of view since the guests were invariably business acquaintances and their wives, and the unwavering routine was a heavy repast of terrapin and canvasbacks, followed by business talk among the men in the dining room as the brandy was passed, and domestic chitchat among the women taking their tea in the drawing room. There was no mingling; before the men could join the ladies, James would take out his watch, consult it and say, "Well, tomorrow's a work day—another day, another dollar, eh, gentlemen?" Guests who didn't get the hint weren't invited back. It seemed odd that Mary who, because of her youth and background would presumably find these events duller than he would, felt slighted. "I wonder why they never ask us? I just know it's because they don't like me—at least Anne doesn't," she said one Sunday night when they passed and saw the carriages. "Don't be silly. They never ask the Hancocks either," Aaron tried to reassure her. "But that's different," Mary argued. "You know that Anne and probably your brother, too, don't approve of Sally because of her divorces, and then Pierce drinks too much." She had something there.

This mission was too important to be put off by a party; it would take only minutes in any case. Aaron sent in his card with the butler and said he'd just wait in the hallway. A gloomy cavern paneled in dark mahogany, the hallway was blessed with only one patch of color—an oil painting Aaron hadn't seen before. It must be one of the art works that James had begun collecting at the suggestion of his banker, Mr. Morgan. Inspecting it, Aaron had to smile. It was obviously by an Italian hand, and it depicted a pale and willowy madonna clutching a chubby infant to her breast while a cloud formation of cherubim and seraphim swirled around their heads. Though not to his taste, Aaron could recognize that the artist had achieved a certain beauty, particularly in his handling of the flesh tints, but what amused him was the irony of an exultation of the Virgin hung on the dark walls of this most Protestant house. He was hardly aware of James' coming up behind him until he heard his brother's cheery voice.

"Fine piece, isn't it? Just picked it up this week. Cost me three thousand dollars not counting the dealer's commission, but even J. P. agrees it ought to be worth twice that in a few years. He came to dinner tonight just to see it. Won't you join us? We're just having brandy."

"No. No, thanks. I just dropped by for a minute, James, to tell you I've been over at O'Donnell's and Hugh is calling a strike on our docks tomorrow morning."

James, mellowed by good food and drink and his banker's approval of his acquisition, let out that whinnying Roosevelt laugh. "Come now, Aaron, it's Sunday, and you just heard Irish whiskey talking," he said. "When those fellows sober up they'll be at work all right. Most of them can't afford to lose an hour's wages. They've been talking strike for years now and—"

"It may be different this time. They're all fired up by what's happening in Chicago, and Hugh—"

"That reminds me, Aaron," James said, "I think

248

it's time we fired that troublemaker. I've been holding off on your account, but he's going too far. This business with the American Federation of Labor *could* be serious."

"I don't know. Hugh's well liked, and it could cause more trouble. Besides, he's just been married, and his wife's already pregnant—"

"Now, isn't that just like your good Irish-Catholic boy? Don't buy the bakery until you're sure there's a bun in the oven," said James, laughing again. "No, you've got to learn, Aaron, that sentiment can play no part in business. Why don't you ask Mary what she thinks? I'll wager she'd agree with me. That wife of yours is turning out to have a good head for business."

Aaron was stunned. It was the first time that his brother had ever paid Mary a compliment, but then it was the first time they'd been out of earshot of Anne. Now that he thought about it, Aaron recalled that, during the few times they'd been with the James Van Alens, Mary had used on James the same technique he'd observed with Pierce Hancock. She hadn't so much talked as listened to James, leading him with questions. It was, Aaron had always thought, an admirable way of getting around her own ignorance of any subject, and he admired Mary's use of it to get along without embarrassment in her new world. Somehow he hadn't expected it to work on James, but then James was a man, and few men could resist hearing their own thoughts echoed by a woman's pretty lips. Whether Mary would agree with James on this seemed doubtful. She might not enjoy the society of her father and brothers, but her love for them couldn't be questioned.

"Well, I just thought I'd warn you," Aaron said.

"And I just thought I'd warn *you*," James replied. "I'm going to issue orders to fire that Hugh O'Donnell in the morning. Sure you won't join us for a brandy?"

"No, thanks . . ."

Mary was already in bed when he got home but she wasn't asleep; she was nursing little Francis. It was a name—Francis O'Donnell Van Alen, her father's name—that Aaron himself had suggested to demonstrate his good will toward the O'Donnell clan. It had raised a few Van Alen eyebrows, and his mother hadn't been able to keep herself from saying, "It's the first time we've had a name like that in the family," but his father had reminded her, "You're wrong, Martha. Don't you remember Cousin Francis, Uncle Peter's son, who changed his name to Livingston and ran off to Chicago when his father sold the manor out from under him? I'm sure you do—it was he who got us involved with Mr. Lincoln." His mother didn't give in easily—"Well, there certainly wasn't any O'Donnell in it"—but no more had been said. Watching his wife and son, Aaron thought of the picture in his brother's hallway, thought how palely most art reflects life. "I just saw a madonna in—would you believe it?—James' house, his latest acquisition. But I treasure *my* madonna more," Aaron said.

Mary smiled. "Now don't you go comparing me to the Holy Mother. It's a sacrilege, and you of all people know I'm no virgin, the saints be blessed," she said. "What did James think about the strike?"

"Oh, he said it was just Irish whiskey talking . . . But he did tell me he's going to fire Hugh. I tried to argue him out of it but—"

"I think it would be the best thing that could ever happen to Hugh. He's got more charm and brains than the lot of us, but he's letting his life go to waste on this union business. As long as he works for Van Alen, he'll only think about getting even when he ought to be thinking about getting ahead like Jack."

"You really think that?" Aaron asked, and she nodded. Score one for James. "But what about the strike? Do you think James is right?"

"I just don't know. They *were* all drinking. Even if it does happen, it won't last more than a day—their women will see to that. . . . Now, take this baby to his nurse and get in with me. I like him so much that I think it's time to start making another . . .

When Aaron arrived at the Van Alen offices downtown on Monday morning, everybody was in what could be called "a state." The men had gone on strike, and James had already left for the warehouse to see what he could do. Aaron was to telephone him at once. James sounded keyed up: "Listen, Aaron, I should apologize for not paying more attention to you, but there's no time for that now. What I want you to do is get the police over here right away. And for God's sake don't let father or mother know anything about this."

"The police? Is there trouble?"

"I don't know what *you* call trouble, but I call it trouble when there are thirty or forty men sitting around here with their arms folded and nothing's moving on or off the boats."

"But has there been any violence? Any damage?" Aaron persisted.

"It's damage enough to property when every hour this goes on we're losing money."

"Calm down, James. I did talk to Mary and for the most part she does agree with you. Did you fire Hugh?"

"Yes—fired him personally. And do you know what he did? He just laughed at me. Stood there and laughed. 'When you get done dealing with the union, Mr. Van Alen, you'll find you can't just fire people for fighting for their rights,' he told me. Now you get those police."

"Listen, James, Mary's opinion is that the strike won't last more than a day. She says the women will see to that. Don't you think we should wait?"

There was a pause at the other end of the phone. Finally James said, "Perhaps you're right. But I'll tell you what to do. Round up every man and boy you can find in the offices there and bring them over here with you. *We'll* move the stuff."

Aaron's reaction was instinctive. "James, do you think *I* should . . . ?"

"Why not? When it comes to a thing like this, Aaron, either you're with us or against us. I *need* you." It was another first from James within a few hours; it was the first time his brother had ever said that he needed him, the first time, in fact, that anybody had really said that to Aaron since Tommy Wilson had recruited him for the team in Princeton. Then his brother ruined the effect by going on, "Don't forget: you can be fired too. Now get over here."

The phone went dead. Damn James, damn the whole business. Who was James to order him about? And why make this silly showing when the strike wasn't likely to last a day? Should he go? Thinking about it, he realized how he'd been accepting a good salary from Van Alen & Son for services that his brother defined as "salesman" for the benefit of any curious stockholder. He did once in a while make specific calls on certain individuals with usually satisfactory results, but it would be hard to argue that he totally earned his keep. Though James fussed at him at first, as time went by James seemed reconciled to the arrangement, even to prefer it. "Might be confusing if there were too many Van Alens giving orders around here," was one of James' offhand remarks. "Wouldn't want somebody without a real interest in the business making decisions," was another. Now James was pleading with him and threatening him at the same time. Of course James was wrought up since, in his view, everything he cared about was at stake. But could Aaron just sit back and put his rather tenuous relationship with the O'Donnells ahead of his own family? He thought he understood the frustration that moved Hugh and the other men to strike, but, well, he also had a responsibility to family, to Mary, his son Francis. No question, though, he didn't relish appearing on the other side in front of all those men from the bar who'd come to think of him as a good fellow because he could take care of himself in the ring. But he did have to go, and he took with him half a dozen Van Alen clerks and messenger boys, who were at least as reluctant as he.

All the rest of that day Aaron and his brother and other management men went grimly about their back-straining, sweat-wringing labor. The strikers, lounging against bales and boxes, jeered and hooted as the soft office workers bruised thumbs, dropped crates, tangled rigging. They couldn't get enough aboard even one boat to warrant its sailing when normally two or three would have been loaded. With the docks crowded, incoming vessels anchored out in the river, their crews drawing good wages for just sitting on the rails and watching the show. James, puffing, said, "I hate to think what this is costing us. If it lasts another day I'm going to call in the police and hire strikebreakers. There're a lot of Negroes in this town who need work."

By now Aaron knew his Irish well enough to know that that would cause real trouble, probably bloodshed, and he could only hope that Mary was right. An encouraging sign was that women did come down to the docks, and you couldn't help but hear them complaining about the loss of wages. But there was no mood of violence. The strikers, having declared themselves a holiday, retreated frequently to the nearest bar for refreshment and returned to find the fumblings of their bosses ever more amusing. At one point, however, Hugh O'Donnell confronted Aaron. "'Tis easy to see whose brother you are when the chips are down. Mary can come if she likes, but we'll not want to see your face around the house here again." Though he was earning so much in the ring these days that he'd quit stevedoring, Jack had come down to see the action, and he, too, stopped Aaron. "I'm sorry, Aaron, for you've been good to me, but I think you'd best keep your distance for a while."

When Aaron got home that night, bone-tired, he tried to spare Mary these details of his day, but, plying him with whiskey—a balm whose true use he'd never before appreciated—she pried it all out of him. "Well, if that's the way they feel, they won't be seeing me again either," she said. "They're too stupid to know which side their bread's buttered on. But don't worry, Aaron. If what you tell me about the women is true, it'll all be over by morning."

But it wasn't. When Aaron arrived at the office, before time for a change, he could hardly get through for a squadron of mounted police and a line of grinning, jostling Negroes stretching clear around into Wall Street. A clerk, sitting behind a desk just inside the door, was questioning each black man and sending those he chose out to a wagon waiting at the curb. Oh, my God! Folded under Aaron's arm was a newspaper screaming in black type about the shooting of a picket at the McCormick reaper plant in Chicago, followed by bombing and rioting in the Haymarket, where seven policemen and ten civilians were killed and many more wounded. He ran into James' office, holding the paper in front of him. "You can't do this, James. Look at what's happening in Chicago."

James no longer seemed excited, possibly calmed by his unaccustomed physical labor of the day before. "Oh, I've read all that," he said. "We're not dealing with a whole city on strike, just a little disturbance at our docks. I'm going to do all of New

York a favor by putting a stop to it right now."

"Well, you're going to do it without me," Aaron said, and turned his back and walked out. The Knickerbocker Club would be open, and the servants there were discreet enough never to inquire by so much as a glance why a gentleman would want a drink at any hour of the day.

Aaron stayed—sulked, might be a better word, he'd have to concede—at the club for most of the rest of the day. From among cronies he was able to assemble a table for time-passing, mind-numbing poker. The club's thick windows muted the newsboys' cries of "Extry!" in the street, and in any case, the doorman could be relied on to buy up their wares and stack them in the reading room for perusal by any member who might have an interest in that disordered world outside. One of these, a friend of Aaron's, thought it best, though a bit out of order, to interrupt the game by bringing a paper to the table. Aaron had only to run his eye down the descending banks of headlines to know the worst:

VIOLENCE BREAKS OUT
AT VAN ALEN & SON WAREHOUSE

Two Negroes slain, one policeman and Five pickets wounded in exchange of fire

MANAGEMENT HELD HOSTAGE

Hugh O'Donnell, leader of strikers surrounding warehouse says, "No Chicago for us. We'll hold out all summer. Let them rot in there. We'll win!"

Without even reading the story, Aaron excused himself and headed home. He was surprised to find not only his mother but his ailing father in his drawing room. "Where have you been?" both Mary and his mother wanted to know in one voice. "At the club," he said, "you could have called me." This time Mary spoke alone. "We were sure you were with James." And Aaron said, "You could have called *him*." His father spoke for the first time: "The phone lines have been cut. This is very serious, Aaron." His mother added: "Serious? Oh, Aaron, we thought *both* of you were there. You've got to do something. James could be . . . could be killed. And . . . and they've no food and . . . and no change of clothes. . . . What's the world coming to?" Aaron had never admired Mary more than at that moment when she said, "Let Aaron be. *I'll* go. I can talk to my brothers. . . ." Nor his mother, who replied, "You'll go nowhere, Mary. You're a woman with children to see to. It's hard, I know, to stay home, but it's a woman's job. I learned that in the draft riots. But, Aaron, be careful . . ."

On his way out he heard his mother saying, "Does anyone believe in praying? I do." Looking back, he saw Mary cross herself, saw his mother bow her head. His father, gray-faced and aged beyond his considerable years, simply stared into space.

What had happened to the police? The question answered itself as soon as Aaron arrived in the vicinity of the Van Alen warehouse. They were stretched in a very thin circle a couple of blocks from the building, and their function seemed to be to keep curious crowds at a distance. Aaron went up to the first policeman he could reach. "My brother and some of his men are in there. You've got to get them out—"

"No, sir, our orders is to stay back. Them strikers is armed, and one of our men's already dying in the hospital."

"But you can't let a mob seize property and imprison the owners—"

"I don't know—them's orders. We saved all the niggers, such as weren't shot, and most of the other men. Them as stayed did it on their own. . . . Hey! Where are you going?"

While the officer was talking Aaron edged around him and broke into a run toward the building. He heard the crack of a pistol; the officer was firing over his head and yelling, "Hey, come back, you!" Aaron knew then what people meant when they talked about a yellow streak in a man's back, because he could actually feel his—a cold and clammy run of sweat. He used all that speed that had served him well on the football field to reach the shelter of the warehouse where, out of breath and more than a little frightened, he came face to face with the strikers, most of whom he recognized, guarding the doors. Hugh O'Donnell was among them, and said, "Well, by the saints, if it ain't me little brother-in-law. A little late for the party, ain't you? Would have served you right if that cop had winged you."

Waiting to get his breath back, Aaron studied Hugh. He could see no evidence of a weapon, either in his hands or in the bulges of his clothes. "Hugh, I came to take my brother home," he said.

"Oh, no. He chose to stay, and by God he's going to stay until he's ready to talk to us."

"I'm not so sure he chose to stay. I'm going in and talk to him and—"

"Over my dead body . . ."

Big as he was and menacing as his words were, Hugh made no effort to detach himself from the close-packed group at the door, and Aaron said, "Look, Hugh, I can't take all of you on; but I can take you. What do you say—if you can't stop me, I go in?"

Hugh straightened his shoulders and moved forward. Aaron noticed that he was swaying a little, not swaggering but swaying. Putting him out would be simple, and evidently Hugh's friends agreed with Aaron because one of them reached out, pulled him back and said, "C'mon, Hugh. Ain't no harm I can see in him talkin' to his brother. Let 'im through."

Hugh grumbled, "Well, all right, but you go in there, and you stay too . . ."

Aaron brushed by his brother-in-law and entered an eerie world of dark silence. Evidently the gas lines had been severed along with the telephone wire. The high, cobwebbed windows were nothing but pale squares of twilight against the black walls. Somebody had found a single candle and set it on a packing crate. In its small circle of light the white faces of James and the two clerks who'd stayed with him looked like death masks. James' first words were an echo of Hugh's taunt. "You're a little late, aren't you, brother? I don't know why you came at all. There's nothing you can do."

"Oh, yes, there is. I'm going to take you out

of here."

"No, you're not. I'll be damned if I'll let a bunch of ruffians take over my property without killing me first. At least then the law will really see to them."

"Well, it's father you're going to kill—you should see his face—and maybe mother too if you don't get out of here," Aaron said. "And what about these fellows here? You fellows don't want to lay down your lives for Van Alen and Son, do you?"

The clerks were reluctant to say anything that might anger James, but their silence spoke for them. "C'mon, James, be sensible," Aaron argued. "If the law doesn't protect the property, we can sue the city, or the state. Remember the Pennsylvania Railroad got away with it back in that strike of '77 when they made Allegheny County out there in Pittsburgh pay up for the damages? You've always cited that case to me."

It was the right tactic. James was fond of finding his own wisdom remembered, and it made it easier for him to yield in front of his clerks. "You're right—I had forgotten that," he said. "Good precedent under the law. Well, for the sake of our parents—not my own, mind you—I'll go, but how? Those fellows have guns, and they're not reluctant to use them, as you'd know if you'd been here."

"I got in, and I'll get us out," Aaron said. "For once, dear brother, you might find there's some use to what you call my frivolous sporting life. You men stick close to me. As soon as we step out the door I'm going to pick a fight with Hugh. I'm sure I can take him, but the others will probably pile on me. All the better. It'll create such confusion that you can run for the police lines. Are you ready? Blow out that candle."

Aaron started for the door. James caught up and grabbed his arm. "Aaron, I can't let you do this. Those men are armed, I tell you."

"With or without you behind me, I *am* going to do it. I'm certainly not staying here. I've got another secret weapon. I flatter myself that most of those men rather like me, and the worst they'll do is rough me up, and I'm used to that. So don't, for the love of God, try to help me, James. Just run like hell . . ."

Aaron opened the door. The men stirred. Those who were sitting, among them Hugh, got to their feet. Hugh moved forward. "Stay where you are."

"I've talked to my brother, Hugh, and I'm leaving," Aaron said, and then moved with all the speed and concentration he'd learned in the ring.

He went for the solar plexus, the softest spot in a man as big as Hugh. As Aaron's right fist smashed home, Hugh collapsed with a whoosh like a popped balloon. Men were grabbing Aaron, but he was aware that James and the clerks had rushed by. Somebody yelled, "There the bastards go—get 'em!" Somebody else fired. Over the shoulder of a man trying to shove him down, Aaron saw James fall. A blaze of fear and hatred gave him strength he didn't know he had. He tossed his assailant aside and ran toward his brother. Shots from both directions, as the police opened fire too, were whistling over him. James wasn't dead—but winged and shocked. Blood was staining his pants leg below the left knee. Aaron stooped over him. "Put your arm around my shoulder and do your best to run with me. Stay low, they're still firing."

A mounted policeman clattered in to cover them, and Aaron half-dragged his wounded brother to safety behind the lines. He was conscious of an elation greater than he'd ever known when he touched a football down. A question that had always haunted him when he'd heard old Civil War veterans reminisce—could he, Aaron, make himself go through fire as they had?—had been answered.

The shooting of James Van Alen was the worst strategic error the strikers could have made. Reporters were on the scene, and within hours extras shouting *"Anarchy! Terror!"* were in the streets. An aroused business community compelled the mayor and commissioner of police to act. By dawn of the next day an overwhelming uniformed force moved in to lift the siege at the cost of only one life—that of an enraged and drunken striker—and the wounding of one officer. Half a dozen or so men found with arms were jailed, and the rest, like Hugh O'Donnell, were released. By the day after that stevedores were coming singly back to the Van Alen warehouse in hope of work. James Van Alen revealed what everybody considered a forgiving spirit by taking them on—on one condition: that they sign a paper swearing that they were not, nor ever would become, members of the American Federation of Labor. Whether Hugh O'Donnell would remain fired or not was never put to the test; he was too proud to come back. Though Aaron lost all desire to see any O'Donnells, Mary did visit infrequently, and she brought back the news that Hugh had gone to work at the union headquarters . . . .

*　　*　　*

When his father's coffin had been lowered into the grave, and Aaron could rejoin Mary again, he asked, "Why did they come?"

"For me," she said. "They didn't like it either but they thought that it was the right thing to do. Of course they wouldn't go into a Protestant church so they came here. Father wanted to come too but they thought it would be too hard for him—standing on crutches . . . You know they are . . . well, relatives . . ."

Lunch in the large, sun-flooded dining room of the late Peter Schuyler Van Alen's residence on Fifth Avenue was a trying affair. It was the first time in recent years that all of the Van Alen children and their spouses were gathered around one table. Perhaps in anticipation of some awkwardness and tension, Martha had thought to include two more-or-less "outsiders"—Cousins Sophie Van Alen and Amelia Downing. For once, Sophie in her everlasting black—some said she'd bought the dress for her own father's funeral in '63 though the skirt had been taken in to make up for the loss of hoops—and cloud of black veiling seemed perfectly in tune with a social occasion. Her voice, which had become peculiarly toneless through lack of use, also seemed suited to the stilted conversation in which everybody tried to get in a good word about the dead that wouldn't stir up any emotions, but not so some of her monosyllabic remarks, such as, "I keep thinking that my father might have still been here if it hadn't been for those Irish hooligans . . ."

On behalf of Mary to whom she'd taken what she called a "shine," Amelia, still billowy and boisterous

263

at eighty, cut into this one with a voice grown throaty from too much speaking: "Now, Sophie, that's unlikely. Cornelius was a great deal older than Peter—twelve years wasn't it?—which would make him eighty-seven today, and no Van Alen but Cousin Sally has lived that long, and she was really a Schuyler."

Apparently aroused by the sound of her name from what for her was a rare, silent funk, Sally Van Alen Hancock touched the wrong button by saying dreamily and to nobody in particular, "Oh, God, I'm going to miss him . . ."

Martha's Roosevelt-Schuyler—Van Alen backbone suddenly melted; she slumped in her chair, began dabbing with a napkin at the tears filling her eyes, then tried to apologize in a tight voice: "I'm sorry, my dears, sorry. . . . I'm going to miss him too . . . we had . . . we had . . . the perfect love . . . there was nothing he would ever deny me. . . ." Amelia, her big body heaving as if to squeeze itself out of her tight chair, said, "Yes, he was capable of the perfect love. I . . . I could see that . . ."

James, sensing disaster, got to his feet. "The last thing father would want would be for us to sit around weeping for him," he said. "In any case, we have business to attend to. Patrick has signaled me that Judge Parsons has arrived. I told him we'd meet in the men's reception room. It's . . . well, it was father's place."

There was a great deal of blowing of noses and scraping of chairs on the parquet floor. Only Sophie and Amelia, who understood that they were not expected to attend the "meeting," remained in their seats at the table. While they waited, there was coffee to come, and, if Amelia could convey the message to Patrick in a ladylike way, brandy too.

One of the reasons that Amelia liked to drop in to visit Aaron's Mary was that Mary, quick to pick up hints, served her Irish coffee, a delicious concoction with whipped cream and whiskey which Mary had no doubt learned to make in her father's bar. There was a lot to be said for being brought up in a barroom, and it amused Amelia that, when discussing Mary, the Van Alens seemed to forget that this had also been the beginning for their most distinguished relative, President Martin Van Buren, whose portrait, dominating one wall of the dining room, Amelia now saluted with a nod. If the conviviality that he learned in his father's taproom got Matty into the White House, the taste he developed there might have got him out again, Amelia reflected. She was remembering that election of 1840—that year of her passionate affair with Peter Schuyler Van Alen, whose body had just been lowered into the grave with their secret intact, as would hers, she suspected, before long—when much public sentiment had been turned away from Van Buren on the grounds that he drank fine wines rather than the hard cider that was supposed to have sustained General Harrison. What utter asses people are, Amelia thought. Her own lifelong effort to convince people that women were capable of thought had really come to nothing, and it took the utmost effort of her will not to despair. Once in a while, she'd caught a convert—and the most promising of these was Sally Schuyler Van Alen

Brewster Hancock, the once Duchess of Midstone, who was young enough and rich enough to carry on and whose bad experiences with men confirmed everything that Amelia believed about them, the deceased notably excepted. God, if you're there, let Sally keep the faith, she prayed. Feeling that the silence between her and Sophie was growing embarrassing as these thoughts bubbled to the surface, Amelia asked, "Well, do you have any idea of how Peter arranged things?"

"No. No, of course not. You know I haven't been living here these last years, and anyway Uncle Peter wasn't one to discuss such things," Sophie said. "But I do think they're in for some surprises."

"How so?"

"Well, as you know, I'm the major stockholder, Amelia, and if you could do a little arithmetic in your head, you'd realize that, as my lawyers tell me, I'm not worth much more than seven million. What with what Peter's spent on this house and that monstrosity in Newport, so as not to deny his wife, as she says, and then on that house of James' and all those divorces of Sally's and probably supporting Aaron and that barmaid, I'd doubt he had a million left."

"What about all of Cousin Sally's real estate?"

"Oh, that's in trust until . . . until Martha dies too. I know that because James is always complaining about it to me. You see, James and I . . . well, we talk these things over."

"Sophie, you surprise me. I didn't know you were so so *interested*."

"What else should I be interested in than my

266

money—the Van Alen money? No man has ever looked at me without turning away."

"Ah, Sophie, maybe you should be glad of that. Anyway, what I've never understood is why you haven't joined me. With all your resources, you could be such a help to the cause."

"Amelia, I . . . I just don't want to talk about it . . . I wonder what's happening in there."

Sophie wouldn't have to wonder long. As soon as the family assembled in the men's reception room, reeking faintly of leather, spent cigars and emptied brandy snifters, as if Peter Van Alen had just stepped out, Judge Parsons cleared his throat and said, "I'm sorry to interrupt you all at lunch—and on a day like this. But what I have to say will take only a few minutes. If you'll forgive a slightly humorous allusion to a man I admired for his own sense of proportion, Mr. Van Alen was briefer in composing his will than in a number of his public writings. Now . . ." The judge clipped a pince-nez on, pulled a very slim piece of paper from an inner pocket of the morning coat he'd worn to the funeral, and read: "I, Peter Schuyler Van Alen, being of sound mind and body, do hereby bequeath all monies, including securities and all property, real or personal, of which I am possessed at the time of my death to my beloved wife, Martha Roosevelt Schuyler Van Alen, in perfect trust that she will hereinafter deal fairly with the children and grandchildren by whom we have been blessed."

Silence, except for a little shuffling. Judge Parsons felt called upon to break it. "Well, ladies and gentlemen, that's the whole of the will," he said.

"Perfectly legal and attested to by me and two members of my staff. In view of the nature of this will, I don't feel called upon to disclose specific amounts to anyone but the beneficiary, and it was my thought that it would be more suitable to go into that on another day. Would you agree, Mrs. Van Alen?"

Martha could only nod, and the judge again tried to fill the silence. "I can assure you all," he said, "that your mother will remain in very comfortable circumstances, barring some financial disaster that is unlikely to occur as long as management of the firm remains in the capable hands of you young men here. I did feel it my duty to tell Mr. Van Alen that it was highly—uh, unusual—for a man in his circumstances to leave all his money to his wife without making specific provisions for his other descendants, but everyone who knew him, particularly in his younger years, as I did, would know his reputation for doing the unusual. I don't think that I would violate any confidence if I told you what he said to me. He said, 'Judge Parsons, I've always thought that a man and wife should be equal partners in their goods as well as in their lives. In my case, I might not have any goods to leave were it not for Mrs. Van Alen. I would probably have frittered everything away.' . . . Well, I should leave you to return to your lunch."

When the judge had left, Sally said, "Bully for father! Wasn't that just like him?" She ran over to her mother and kissed her. "You're a lucky woman, mother. Do you know that?"

"Yes, I've always known it," Martha said. "Now,

unless you're still hungry, you children run along. I think I want to lie down for a while."

Nobody was hungry.

On the way home Aaron said, "I warned you . . ."

"Well, it's better than if it had all gone to James, isn't it?" Mary said. "I think your mother's beginning to like me, or at least little Amelia. She's coming over oftener to play with her, and now that your father's dead . . . But, oh Aaron, what will we do about a bigger house? With the maids and the two children and . . . I think I'm going to have another one . . . and nanny, we don't even have a guest room."

"If what you say about mother is true, maybe we should move in with her. She's got enough rooms, God knows, and she may want company."

"Oh, Aaron, do you think we could?"

"I don't know. One thing I do know about her is that she hates to be alone. I know Sophie won't move back since she's happy at James', and mother can stand only so much of Amelia. James and Sally have their own places to look after. The thing is, could *you* stand mother? Dad spoiled her, as you've just heard, and she's had her own way for a long time. Be honest."

"To live there I could stand most *anything*," Mary said. An honest answer, as he'd requested.

That night Mary fell right to sleep, perhaps dreaming sweetly of life on the Avenue at last, but Aaron, restless and bedeviled with feelings of which he was half ashamed, stole out of bed and went down to his study to think. More than he liked to admit to himself, he'd been disappointed at the reading of the will. He had been prepared for James to get the lion's share but had really hoped that enough might come to him so that he could be independent of James, the family . . . It was little consolation that his father had been fair, so fair that he'd dodged the issue, or that James, from the look on his face, had probably been as surprised and disappointed as he. James wasn't really hurt, except in his feelings. As president of the company he drew a much larger income than Aaron and had appropriated to himself more stock; besides, he'd married into that Schermerhorn money and as a result had been given a house that alone was worth more than all that Aaron had hoped to get. Then there was Cousin Sophie. The reason James and Anne coddled her was so transparent as to be very nearly indecent. Sophie's money would surely go to James; she considered Sally so immoral that she hadn't wanted to stay under the same roof with her, and though she and Aaron had once been on the best of terms, his marriage to Mary, a daughter of the Irish whom she held responsible for her father's death and her own disfigurement, had obviously put him beyond her pale. While it was a rotten thought on a day like this, or any other, Aaron realized that his only hope of having the kind of money that would make him financially independent, as his father had been before him, as his brother was, as his brother-in-law was, now lay in his mother's death—an event that could be—and he devoutly hoped would be—twenty, thirty years away. He dismissed it from his mind.

Still, he'd held out hope to Mary that they could

live with his mother, and why had he done that when he was far from sure that Mary's hopeful reading of his mother's attentions was correct? True, after public acknowledgment and Mary's small triumph at the opera, Martha Van Alen had "kept up appearances" with reciprocal family visitations, and she did seem charmed by little Amelia, who at only two showed signs of being the most beautiful Van Alen grandchild in the lot—Anne's children having unfortunately taken after her side in looks and little Matty threatening to become a female replica of Brewster. Yet Martha's instinctive reactions like that one to the naming of Francis indicated a deep reservoir of unease about her daughter-in-law's background, a reservoir that would probably keep flowing over and making life difficult, if not impossible, between two ambitious women living in the same house. Aaron no longer had any illusions, if he'd ever had any, that he'd spirited away some docile Cinderella from her humble hearth; indeed, he had to keep reminding himself when he was put off by a display of Mary's ambition that it had been her drive and discipline, her strength in denial, that had attracted him in the first place. He had no doubt that Mary *would* put up with anything to become at least princess-in-waiting in the Van Alen palace, but would his mother, the queen?

At the moment, though, he seemed to have little reasonable choice but to suggest to his mother that they move in with her. Sitting there alone in his study, dark but for the glowing embers of a fire still dying on the hearth, Aaron realized more forcefully than ever before that he had allowed himself to be trapped by the heritage and inheritance that were his "right" by birth. It had been true, too, of the man they had buried this day. Despite the secrets he'd taken with him to the grave, his father had revealed enough in his life so that Aaron could not avoid that conclusion. Aaron would probably never understand fully that whole business that went on during the war when Van Alen & Son got into trouble for taking commissions on chartering defective ships to the government and then when his Uncle Cornelius was killed in the draft riots, but he did know that the situation forced his father, reluctantly, to give up his hopes for a political career and take over the family affairs. Over and over again in unguarded, offhand remarks his father would reveal disappointment and even bitterness about the compromises of conscience he'd found himself involved in in order to keep Van Alen & Son afloat in a rising tide of cutthroat business competition after the War.

Not least of these and one still surrounded with more mystery for Aaron than most family affairs of which he'd been little conscious as a child had to do with Cousin John Charles Smith, Jr., who'd apparently been responsible for that deceptive or stupid deal with the ships. Aaron, in fact, had always thought Cousin Charlie a rather dashing fellow and certainly an important one with all his contacts with men whose names were always in the papers like Colonel Fisk and Commodore Vanderbilt and even President Grant. But one time he'd overheard his father say, "I don't know whatever possessed me to keep Charlie on. Oh, he did bring in business as I thought he would, but at what cost. I should have listened to mother. She couldn't stand the fellow and more than once hinted that he'd tried to do something terrible to her." What could that have been? In the days before he married Mary when she used to talk to him, Cousin Sophie told Aaron, "You know your father wouldn't have all this money to throw around if *my* father had lived, or even if he'd been given a chance to express his wishes before those crazy Irish killed him. I can tell you that he'd have had Cousin Charlie running the business—they were that close. Probably would have been a good thing, too. Your father was never cut out for business. But I just know something went on between Cousin Charlie and your grandmother, and she poisoned your father's mind against him. Someday I'm going to find out what it was." As far as Aaron knew, Cousin Sophie had never found out—nor had he.

Sophie was right, though, about his father's lack of aptitude for, or at least interest in, business as he'd demonstrated by turning over responsibility as quickly as possible to James. He'd come as close to spelling out his feelings as he ever would during the troubles General Grant had back in '84. Nothing had made Aaron more appreciative of his father's heart and tact than what he did for Grant. What had happened was unfortunately all too typical of what was always happening on Wall Street.

Grant, supposedly a very wealthy man owing to his share in the brokerage firm of Ward & Grant, in which his son Ulysses, Jr., was a partner, was suddenly confronted by Ward with a demand for an additional $150,000. By then everything the general had was already in the firm. The problem, as Ward, the so-called "Napoleon of Wall Street," outlined it was that the Marine Bank in Brooklyn, of which Ward's father-in-law, a Mr. Fish, was president, would have to close its doors and default on all the Grant & Ward deposits of some $600,000 unless they could come up at once with another $400,000. Ward promised to produce $250,000 if Grant would provide $150,000. This was on a Sunday, and on Monday Grant managed to borrow the money from William Vanderbilt and gave it to Ward; by Tuesday Ward had vanished from New York, along with the $150,000, and the Grants were not only wiped out but deeply in debt. Grant turned everything he owned, including his medals, over to an embarrassed Vanderbilt, who tried secretly to return it to Mrs. Grant. She accepted only the medals in trust for the government but nothing else. By the time Peter Van Alen heard of all this, the Grants were without cash for food and household expenses, but a proud and bitter Grant would seek no more loans. It was then that Peter, too ill himself to go out, came up with a scheme and enlisted Aaron's aid. He had Aaron get a thousand dollars in cash and post it to Grant with an anonymous note saying that it came from a "grateful veteran of the Grand Army of the Republic." This, they heard later, Grant accepted with tears in his eyes. The general's valiant and successful struggle to pay off his debts and provide for his widow by writing his autobiography while dying of cancer and with Mark Twain's considerable aid was one of the things, as Aaron knew, that made his own father's problems less grievous by comparison in those last years.

But what stuck in Aaron's mind this night was what his father had said when he heard about Grant: "Something like that makes me ashamed to be part of the business community, Aaron. Oh, I suppose I could take refuge in the kind of philosophy that sustains Andy Carnegie—Darwinism, as refined by Andy's friend Herbert Spencer. You know, 'the survival of the fittest.' Jungle law, I guess you call it, and it makes a lot of sense with business as I've been seeing it these last years. Even if I could accept it as an idea, I couldn't accept it in my bones. I do believe that there's a spirit or conscience or whatever you want to call it that accounts for the 'human' in human being and that, if there is such a thing as morality, it ought to emphasize what makes us different from other animals, ought to make us care about the helpless, the less fortunate. Oh, I know that some of these fellows like Rockefeller and Andy himself are starting to give away their money, but I still wonder if that makes up for the damage they've done in getting it. You remember when we stood by Mr. Lincoln's bier, and I cried—both of us did. Something seems to have died in this republic—and maybe in me—with him that we can so give ourselves over to the worship of material values. Well, I'm in no position to preach. I've always told myself that I did it for your mother or *my* mother. If only . . . if only . . . those are about the two worst words in the language, Aaron, but in the end none of us can escape having to say them."

Was it too late for him to escape? God, he hoped

not. Maybe this will of his father's in the long run would be the best thing that ever happened to him. In a curious way his father's eccentric fairness in leaving everything in his mother's hands, that quality in his father that had made his mother almost break down at lunch in memory of his self-sacrificing love for her, might be taken as a warning. A man might be *too* good for his own good. Aaron recognized such less than noble tendencies in himself, particularly with regard to Mary. He hated to deny her anything and felt almost honor bound to live up to the image of the man she'd been persuaded to accept, the attractive, sporty scion of a wealthy family whose time and money were at her disposal. That was the easy way out, and he knew it— denying, postponing, putting aside the impulse to find for himself a real challenge, the kind of challenge that might force him to sacrifice others as well as himself. If you thought about Lincoln, who'd died a martyr, you also had to think about the Lincoln who, in life, had been called a despicable tyrant by his enemies, who had been forced to search for a general, until he found Grant, who understood that whatever logic there was to war called for the killing of as many enemies as possible and the sacrifice of comrades-in-arms along the way. Yes, he'd have to work harder than his father had against that impulse to be what everybody acknowledged at the funeral was a "nice fellow." To begin with, the fact that the will hadn't left him lazily independent meant that he'd *have* to find a way, other than being Van Alen & Son's something less than super-salesman, of establishing his own independence. Thinking about this, he recalled another of his father's rather bitter asides: "When you're a Van Alen, you're stuck with it."

It had certainly been true for Aaron so far, and he could almost envy his brother James' single-minded purpose to become more of a Van Alen than any Van Alen before him. Never, as far as Aaron could recall, had James ever so much as hinted at suffering any qualms of conscience or mind over the role he so eagerly accepted as the guardian of the Van Alen fortunes. But Aaron had never felt called to that task, and, indeed, when he'd been younger he'd sometimes thought, even hoped, that he was "adopted." Once he'd said as much to his mother, and she'd said, "Don't be ridiculous, Aaron. Just look at your father's eyes and then look at your own." So he'd settled so far with his athletics and reluctance to grub away at the business, with his romantic marriage-for-love instead of prestige, for being a different kind of Van Alen. He might have his father's eyes, might have much of his father's spirit too, but he'd have to do *more* with these attributes. The grave was the strongest reminder, he thought, of what might have been in life. He had a tremendous urge to go to his own grave as something quite different from a Van Alen, but at the moment he had no strong, distinct feeling about what it ought to be.

He poured himself a brandy to drink a solitary toast to his thought. Perhaps what he ought to do in a practical way would be to take a lesson from sports: go on playing the game he was in but be alert for the fumble, the lazy lob, the wrong tack, that opened up unimagined possibilities. He started to lift the glass to his lips and decided that he didn't need it. It was very late, and the fire had gone out, leaving him in the cool, dim light from the street lamp outside. He could go to bed now and sleep. He'd make Mary happy by moving into his mother's house, for the time being, but sometime soon, somehow he'd move out of his mother's house for good. He tossed the drink on the dead ashes of the fire. There was a sizzle and sudden burst of flame. It startled him and he laughed. And then he had a strange thought: could a shot of another kind of spirit draw flames from human ashes? He thought it had happened to him tonight. He bowed toward the fireplace and said, "That one was for you, father. And, damn it, for me too. Here's to life."

Chapter 7

MARTHA ROOSEVELT Brewster, little Matty, liked nothing better than to help her mother dress. Because she was so dark herself, she was particularly fascinated by her mother's long blonde hair, and she would beg, as she did this morning, to be allowed to brush it out before her mother pinned it up on her head; it felt finer than silk and shone like gold in the sunlight falling from the tall bedroom windows. Today it had to be brushed to a special luster because everybody in all New York would see it. She'd be proud of her mother; she always was. There wasn't a lady in the whole wide world as beautiful as her mother, not even Aunt Mary Van Alen, though a lot of people said so. And there were hardly any other ladies in the whole wide world who did the things her mother did. Sometimes it *was* a little embarrassing when the other girls at Miss Farthing's school teased her about her mother, and she had to pull Becky Belmont's hair really hard to get her to take it back when she'd said, "Your mother is crazy. My mother says so." And it *was* a little confusing that her name was Brewster, and her mother's name was Hancock, and the half-brother they went to see in England every summer was Viscount Something-or-other, but she supposed that she'd understand it all when she got a little bigger. What mattered most was that she was allowed to be with her mother a lot more than any of the other girls she knew, and they were really jealous of her, especially on a day like this.

"Would you rather be up in Newport for the Fourth, Matty?" her mother asked. "It ought to be a big celebration. This is 1890—the beginning of a new decade."

"Oh, no . . ."

"But you'll miss the Belmont party. You know they always have those wonderful angel cakes and strawberry parfait and—"

"I don't like Becky."

"You don't? I thought she was your best friend. What happened?"

"She said something bad about you."

"Oh . . . ?"

"She said you were crazy, her mother said so."

Sally Hancock laughed that throaty laugh that Matty loved to hear. "Well, I'm not surprised. Even Pierce says so."

That was another thing Matty had to deal with: Mr. Hancock wanted her to call him Pierce, since he wasn't really her father and had other children. Except when she'd bring a new friend home who'd look at her funny when she called Mr. Hancock Pierce, she rather liked it. It made her feel grown-up. Nobody ever talked about her real father, and she supposed that he was probably dead, though she did know that her mother had gotten something called a divorce, which nobody talked about either. One time her Grandmother Van Alen made a mistake and said right in front of her, "I do think the child's beginning to look like Bud," and her mother said quick as a flash, "Ssh, mother. You can't mean it." Still, why was she so dark when her mother was so blonde?

Stroke, stroke, stroke. Usually when she did this, her mother would relax, almost purr like her kitten, Tabby. Today, though, her mother seemed tense. She grabbed the brush away suddenly and began dragging it in fierce jerks through her hair. "You don't think I'm crazy, do you, Matty?"

"Oh, *no* . . ."

"Thank God," her mother said, and turned around and took her in her arms and hugged her.

Matty liked these impulsive hugs, especially when her mother had nothing on but a thin nightdress and she could feel her warm soft body and smell its musty, perfumy smell. It made her feel all cozy like she'd felt when she was really little and allowed to get into bed with her mother. This was only a short hug, because her mother said, "Now you run along and get dressed, Matty. We've got to be down at the Battery in an hour."

Watching her daughter go, Sally thought, Damn, she *is* getting to look like Bud. Well, she was only eight, and she could change a lot. But she was big for her age and had that square face and all that dark hair. Still, Bud had been handsome, and Matty could become a handsome woman like everybody said

Cousin Amelia had been before she let herself go to fat. Why in hell did a woman have to be just *pretty?* A lot of good it had done *her.* On this of all days when they were going to march right up the length of New York City and remind the world that Independence Day ought to apply to women as well as men, she ought to be glad that she had a daughter who might grow up to be handsome, even formidable, instead of just pretty. That's the kind of women the world needed, women like old Susan Anthony, who was finally getting some backhanded praise even from cynical newspapermen like the editor out in St. Louis who wrote of her, "No longer in the bloom of youth—if she ever had any bloom—hard-featured, guileless, cold as an icicle, fluent and philosophical, she wields today tenfold more influence than all the beautiful and brilliant female lecturers that ever flaunted upon the platform as preachers of social impossibilities." Unhappily, Amelia had died too soon to read that, died discouraged, died actually with that faded cartoon of her billowing self smothering a little man in her hand; died with "Men will never understand. I wanted to free them of us too." Well, Amelia would be proud if she could see her today, see her and little Matty, two women marching hand in hand through what she had no doubt would be a hail of verbal brickbats, and maybe something of harder substance?

Was she, then, crazy? Matty's reassurance was warming but not very convincing, coming as it did from an eight-year-old so obviously and gratifyingly smitten with her. Everybody else said she was, and not for the most part in a kindly, joking fashion. She didn't yet know whether Pierce would carry out his threat to leave her. It had been made the night before she left Newport and, of course, when he was drunk and without thought for anybody but himself. "My God, you'll make me the laughingstock in all my clubs!" She liked to think that her mother's concern for Matty had been genuine and stronger than her distress about the family reputation when she said, "Sally, you're *not* going to take that *child*, are you? Somebody might throw something. I really think you've lost your reason, Sally." "Aghast" would be the adjective to describe the reaction of her sisters-in-law. She might have expected better of Mary, who was a woman with a lot of spunk, but Mary was turning out to be proof of Amelia's contention that lower-class women were the most conservative of all. James, who was in the city on some sort of important business with Mr. Morgan, and Aaron, who was sailing in some New York Yacht Club race, didn't even know about what she was doing, thank God. She'd had enough in the way of discouragement from the others. It was a blessing that they'd all stayed in Newport and would be taking the air on Bellevue Avenue in their victorias and barouches and *vis-a-vis* carriages while she'd be walking up Broadway and Fifth Avenue. Now that she'd come against all advice, she was happy to be here. Hot as it was in the city, the atmosphere was more bracing than the stifling sea-wind air of Newport, where she'd recently gone out of her way at a party to congratulate Edith Wharton on one of her stories and been sickened to see the author peer nervously around at other guests and say, "Hush!

Nobody here acknowledges that I *write*." No, she wasn't crazy. They were—all those women up there in Newport riding out, as they said, for "the air" but so draped in veils for fear that the sun might rot the peach of the complexions men were supposed to admire that they could hardly breathe. She wouldn't wear any veil today, nor would Matty.

Sally was not, of course, unmindful of the fact that she was taking some small calculated risk in having Matty march with her. But at all the suffragette meetings she'd attended words had been the only weapons, and they would fly safely over the head of a small girl. If it did by any remote chance come to brickbats, Sally was ready to protect Matty with her own body. The important thing in Sally's mind was to instill in her daughter a pride in being a woman, even at her early age. She didn't want Matty to grow up feeling herself a pawn in a game played by men, as she had. If educating Matty meant introducing her to a certain amount of unpleasantness, so be it. Nothing could be uglier than what she, Sally, had encountered within all the protective walls that had been thrown up around her. Actually, even worrying about something untoward happening was silly, a sign that all her conservative relatives were getting to her with their anxieties. If her mother had anything to say about it, Matty was going to be a new kind of girl, free, and not afraid.

Battery Park, when they finally got there aboard horsecars delayed in the tangle of holiday traffic on Broadway, was a festival. Families with their picnics were spread out under the trees, and children darted in and out through the crowds like nervous fish.

Men with pushcarts, draped in patriotic bunting, were hawking ices and sodas and cotton candy; others were selling flags and red-white-and-blue balloons; a band, waiting for the march to get under way, was practicing Mr. Sousa's new "The Stars and Stripes Forever" to a continuous accompaniment of popping firecrackers. Matty was jumping up and down and saying, "Oh, mommy, this is so much more fun than Newport. Can I have some candy? Can I?"

She had to be her most motherly, just had to. There was no telling what that terrible-looking stuff would do to an excited stomach, and the walk would be long and hot with no decent water closet she could think of until they got up at least as far as the Brunswick on Madison Square. She took Matty's hand and stalled. "Just wait till we find our friends, darling."

"Friends" was a strong word. She'd no doubt recognize a few faces from seeing them at suffrage meetings, but she'd know very few, if any, names to put to them. A lot of them had good strong minds like Miss Anthony and Amelia, and they were all respectable enough. Most of them seemed to be daughters of preachers and teachers, and some of them were taking classrooms themselves since it was about the only living open to a single woman who didn't want to hang around and be somebody's kept maiden aunt. Some were married like herself, to be sure, and Sally had to wonder about their husbands as they must wonder about hers. They couldn't all be idle drunks. Indeed, occasionally a man would come to one of the meetings and speak out on his wife's behalf—rather odd fellows, most of them. One thing she could say for her friends, or fellow marchers—they were easy to spot even in a crowd like this. Not only was such a large group of unattached women unusual, but, whether or not they thought like Miss Anthony, they all managed to *look* like her, somehow severe and bony. It might be the way they dressed. Not more than two or three were in summer whites, as Sally was, and not another woman wore anything like Sally's hat, a flower-trimmed straw, trailing ribbons. They were in sombre grays and blacks and browns, as if going to church instead of a Fourth of July parade. When she saw them all together like this, Sally's enthusiasm for having Matty grow up into a militant suffragette waned some. Well, damn it, she was one of them, and it wouldn't do now to let Matty detect her reservations.

Although there were one or two other children, the women seemed quite impressed that she, of all people, had brought her daughter along. Sally was aware that the others regarded her as something of a "catch," the only one of the marching women who actually lived in one of those chateaus they'd be passing in the parade, if they got that far. She suspected that they still called her "Duchess" behind her back, but Mrs. Pierce Hancock was a name quite glittering enough to make sure of landing on the front pages of the papers—and with that darling little girl . . . Everybody knew that there was always a nurse or nanny or somebody to look after little girls like that, so Mrs. Hancock had to be making a deliberate gesture. Nothing she could have done would have been more convincing to her fellow marchers that, though her name was on the guest list at all the society balls and she was dressed for a garden party at Newport, her heart was in their cause. Everybody'd been hoping that they could get Bela Lockwood, who'd run for president in '88 on the Equal Rights ticket, to come to New York to lead the parade or at least Nelly Bly, who'd become famous early this year for her seventy-two-hour trip around the world which she'd written up in the *New York World*. Since neither of them could come, it was a blessing that they had somebody as prominent as Mrs. Hancock, so they persuaded Sally, with Matty holding her hand, to walk in front, right behind the two young women carrying the big banner that read: A NEW DECADE—A NEW DECREE—THE VOTE FOR WOMEN IN THE NINETIES.

Since nobody had asked the women to march, the idea was to fall in behind the rest of the parade—the bands, the red-jacketed firemen, the stooped old veterans in ill-fitting blue, the smart white-uniformed unit from the Brooklyn Navy Yard, the open carriages filled with top-hatted politicians. The police wouldn't dare try to make trouble for a hundred or more "respectable" women, would they? They'd have their hands full enough this day with the drunks who didn't know when to stop celebrating and the fights that would break out between the Orange and the Green over whose Independence Day it was and the toughs who'd start chasing Negroes. Let the silly women walk, they'd decide. Half of them would faint before they got as far as Fifth Avenue. When they began passing through the crowds lining Broadway, the women drew hoots, catcalls, whistles "Get back in the kitchen where you belong!" "We don't want no petticoat president!" Sally thought one comment she caught rather amusing: "With all them horses up front, mind your feet, ladies—you might slip on your own slogans . . ." Amusement soon turned into irritation when the first of the eggs caught her too-prominent hat, broke against the straw and sent a yellow trickle down over the white shoulder of her dress.

"Oh, mommy, your dress is ruined," Matty said. "Don't they like us?"

"Don't pay any attention to them, darling. Some people don't like the idea of women being independent, but it will be different when you grow up." And then to divert her daughter's attention Sally pointed to a square building with grimy, gold-lettered windows advertising a variety of goods and services—EYEGLASSES & FALSE TEETH, DR. SCHULL DENTISTRY, SHEET MUSIC FOR THE PIANO & ORGAN—and said, "Look, darling, that's where your Grandmother Van Alen used to live, where your Grandfather Van Alen was born . . ."

"Way down here? In that ugly thing?"

"Well, that isn't the house. It was taken down. Your grandfather drew a picture of it once. I'll have to show it to you. This was the most fashionable part of New York then . . ."

Out of the corner of her eye she saw a figure dart out of the crowd on the sidewalk. He was on her before she could react. At first she didn't recognize him. He was fat and unkempt, gray streaks shot through his rumpled hair and a gray stubble hazed his face. It was the eyes that were familiar—and the voice. "You're not going to make a show of *my* child like this . . ."

"*Bud* . . ."

He'd already grabbed little Matty, was picking her up. The child started to scream, and Sally, clinging to her hand, said, "Bud, let her go, get *out* of here."

A woman behind, armed with a parasol, started clubbing Bud's broad back. Bud shoved Sally so hard that, reeling backward, she caught a heel in her long skirt and fell, losing her grip on Matty. With the child in his arms, Bud ran back toward the crowd, shouting, "This is my little girl and I'm not going to let her mother make a fool of her . . ." Though Sally and some of the women around her were yelling, "Stop him, stop him!" the crowd made way for Bud. Sally thought she heard some of them cheer. By the time she got to her feet—white costume torn and brown-streaked with dust and manure—Bud had disappeared. She ran into the crowd herself, frantically pushing people aside. A woman spit on her. "Serves you right—bring a child to a thing like this." Where had they gone? They were near Wall Street. She ran down Wall—nothing. Down Broad Street—nothing. Back to Wall, up Nassau—nothing. Over Pine—nothing. Too many twisting, turning streets. She was out of breath, whipped. She *was* crazy.

Sally still had enough of a head about her to know that there was nothing more she could do alone. She needed help, but where would she find it? By now Bud could be anywhere in this whole big city, and summoning one of the policemen out there directing traffic on Broadway would be useless. It might take the whole force and then some to find them. Oh God! Please, God, don't let him hurt her. Where should she go, what should she do? Leaning against a wall and trying to catch her breath, she forced herself to think as clearly as possible. Some sort of large hunt would have to be organized, stories would have to be run in the papers, rewards would have to be offered. It could be done, would be done, but it had to be done right away—and done by men. Pierce? No, he was in Newport and probably half-seas-over already. Aaron? No way to reach him out there on the water; she'd had a glimpse from the Battery of the yachts assembling for the race and had almost envied him at the time. James? Had he said where he'd be? Something to do with Mr. Morgan whose offices were right here on Wall Street. She ran again but found the building empty, locked. Of course, it was a holiday, and the meeting would probably be in the Morgan library up on Thirty-sixth Street. She ran once more until she found a hack.

"You sure you can pay the fare, lady?"

For the first time she was conscious of what she must look like, hat askew, dress stained and ripped. She'd probably be turned away from Mr. Morgan's house, but she'd risk it. And James? It had been years since she'd come to James for anything. She hardly knew this brother of hers, but she did know him well enough to be sure that he'd be furious at what she'd done. Would he help? Well, she wouldn't think about that. He just *had* to. That he could help she had no doubt. The very fact that James was where he was demonstrated that he was one of the most powerful men in the city, in the country.

She dusted futilely at her skirts, pulled herself up and looked the hackey in the eye. "Of course I can pay. You must not recognize the address. I'm calling on my brother at Mr. Morgan's."

The man sighed, touched his hat with his whip and said, "All right, git in, lady." It was obvious that he didn't believe a word she said and probably thought her crazy. He wasn't, she thought, far from right.

Coming down on the train from Newport, James Van Alen had very mixed feelings. He'd left a furious wife behind him. This July 4, 1890, was the inaugural of the Van Alen archery tournament, and everybody who was anybody in Newport had been invited. It was considered nervy, if not cheeky, of Anne Van Alen, even though she was a Schermerhorn, to muscle in on a traditional Belmont rite, but Anne had cleverly got her invitations out first, nearly a year before, thus creating a social drama of intense interest to the little colony by the sea. Most people had accepted the Van Alen invitation, but fascinating questions remained to be answered. Who would actually come, who would go to *both* parties, who would stay? A mere appearance, especially by those lovely young things whose participation in the contest would constitute the show, could be a defeat for either Mrs. Van Alen or Mrs. Belmont. It was one time when interested gentlemen could enjoy all those peaches-and-cream complexions without peering through a veil, and the stretching of a bow worked marvelous wonders with the female form. James had been looking forward to this day with anticipation, not unmixed with trepidation, and to desert his wife when there was so much at stake was, as even he'd concede, mean. Still, it was going a little far for Anne to have said tearfully as he left, "As far as I'm concerned, you don't have to come back at all."

It was very difficult, if not impossible, to convince a woman like Anne who'd been coddled and protected and showered with everything she wanted all her life that, as James liked to put it, "money doesn't grow on trees." Her family came from those circles of old New York wealth in which the men hadn't worked for two generations. Of course, you didn't find *them* on the Avenue; they were tucked away during the winter in some comfortable enough old brownstone on a city side street and up there at Newport or down at Long Branch in the summer—that is, when they weren't traveling around Europe. Not long after the war when his securities weren't pulling as they should, Anne's father, rather than work, had simply rented his city brownstone, pulled up stakes and taken his family to Europe for a couple of years where it was so much cheaper that they could live very well indeed from the rent. James would have to admit that that experience of Anne's was turning out to be useful since, from being dragged around to all those galleries, she was a rather good judge of the art works he was beginning to acquire. James could have lived like Anne's father, too, but he was cut from old Dutch cloth and glad of it. He couldn't imagine a life without business to occupy his time and mind. He hadn't even been to Europe and didn't intend going unless, like old Commodore Vanderbilt, he could sail over in his own ocean-going yacht and be greeted by the heads of states. He was getting nearer that goal every year, and being summoned to this emergency meeting today was the surest sign of it. If only Anne could understand how big a difference there was between having a little money and making a lot of it, she'd see that he had to go today.

James wasn't sure why Morgan had called this unusual holiday meeting. He guessed, though, that it must have something to do with the Sherman Antitrust Act that had just passed the Congress. On top of the Interstate Commerce Act a few years back, this would give the government a heavy hand to mess around in the affairs of business. Such legislation could have been expected under a Democrat like Cleveland, but it was something of a shock coming from a Republican Congress with a safe Republican like Harrison in the White House. James was beginning to wonder whether the money Tom Platt had wheedled out of him was going to waste. It had been quite a bit—$10,000—and James had to admit to himself in moments of honesty that the gesture had probably been vain in every sense of the word. He could well remember that day in the early fall of '88 when Platt, a man he'd never met before, came barging into his office with a warm smile and outstretched hand, saying, "Mr. Van

Alen, I'm Tom Platt."

No more introduction was necessary since Platt's name, always followed by the phrase, "New York State Republican boss," was daily in the papers. When they'd shaken hands, Platt said, "I know you're a busy man, and I'll take only a few minutes of your time. I'm sorry to break in on you like this, but I've just been to see Mr. Morgan, and he suggested that I call on you. So since you're just around the corner . . ."

"That's quite all right, Mr. Platt. What can I do for you? I don't know much about politics, you know."

"You do know enough, Mr. Van Alen, I'm sure, to be aware that the commerce of this nation will be ruined if Cleveland has his way with tariffs. I told Mr. Morgan that we in the Republican Party think that it's time American businessmen put their money where their interests lie. He not only agreed with me, but he handed me a check for ten thousand dollars. Now I know that you were a generous supporter of Mr. Arthur, and I think it would be to your advantage to be counted among Senator Harrison's supporters. With enough money, I'm sure we can turn Cleveland out."

"I had the impression that the President was popular. He's sound enough on money, and now that he's married . . ."

Platt favored James with a slight smile. "A little like locking the barn after the horse is stolen, isn't it, Mr. Van Alen? We won't let the good people out there forget that Cleveland sired a bastard and made no bones about it, and we won't let the veterans forget that he's vetoed all those pension bills. He was elected by a fluke. If that Presbyterian preacher hadn't called the Democrats the party of rum, Romanism and rebellion, Cleveland would never have made it. I don't mean to disparage the preacher, and I know you're a good Presbyterian, Mr. Van Alen, but just between us I think you'll agree that those preacher fellows are impractical and don't realize that politics is no place for speaking the blunt truth. I'm sure from what Mr. Morgan says— he says you're one of the soundest men in the city— that I don't have to convince you that Cleveland should go. The only question is what I can put you down for."

The referral from Morgan was flattering, and it was evident that Platt's approach to other men in the business community would be to drop names and amounts. Not wishing to be thought less zealous or affluent than his banker, James said impulsively, "No need to put me down, Mr. Platt. Here . . . I'll write a check—for the same amount as Morgan's." . . .

However much it may have contributed to Harrison's election, that check had evidently impressed Morgan. The banker wasn't the sort of man to say so; indeed, he spoke rarely about anything and usually in the form of a command. But he'd begun to demonstrate his interest in James by including him in those conferences where he was trying to bring order out of the chaos in American railroading. In the process, James had come to know personally and profitably most of the railroad presidents as well as the Morgan partners, all of whom would probably be there today. It was fast company to keep, for on Wall Street Morgan and his partners were called "Jesus Christ and his twelve apostles." As if instinctively to compensate for his own face, made hideous by that bulbous red nose, Morgan surrounded himself with men so handsome that another irreverent witticism about them held that "when the angels of God took unto themselves wives among the daughters of men, the result was the Morgan partners." Whatever, the power they wielded through their ability to give or withhold loans or to float new issues of securities was awesome, and James was well aware of the privilege he enjoyed in being associated with it.

James also knew that there were a lot of Communists and labor agitators and ignorant farmers out there in the country who thought that Morgan had too much power. What they wanted was cheap money so that they could pay off their debts in devalued dollars and a lot of competition among the railroads and other businesses so that they could take advantage of rate and price wars. Even some of the young college-boy liberals like Cousin Teddy Roosevelt, who ought to know better about how you hung onto money, were being taken in by this kind of thinking. It took men of vision like Morgan and John Rockefeller to see that sound money and sensible organization were the only way to make sure of profits in business and that profits were the only way to make sure of attracting more money. Call it monopoly, if you liked, but to a man with a good business head like James' it was just common sense, particularly when it came to dictating prices and wages. What the country needed was more, not less, monopoly if the really smart businessmen were to control its destiny, as they should. Perhaps because his banking interests reached into all areas of commerce, Morgan understood this, and no man in America was too rich or too powerful to escape his discipline when he had a mind to use it.

This became clear back in '85 when Bill Vanderbilt and that little maverick Andy Carnegie were trying to break the Pennsylvania Railroad's monopoly on shipping steel from Pittsburgh to the east coast. Bill and Andy had each put up $5,000,000 and were starting to lay track for something they called the South Pennsylvania Railroad when Morgan brought them all together on his yacht *Corsair*. They said he'd held them virtually prisoners, wouldn't let them off the yacht, steaming up and down the Hudson until after sunset, and they finally saw it his way: the Pennsylvania would buy out the South Pennsylvania, but in turn would sell the West Shore to the New York Central, thus plucking thorns out of each party's side and healing wounds that threatened to bleed away Morgan investments. Although Morgan was getting things under control in the east, it was still wild in the west with men like Gould and his son, George, and this quiet little clerk of a fellow named Harriman and big Jim Hill all up to their old tricks of starting new roads just to undermine the securities of the old ones so that they could buy in. Fortunately, the money that they all needed was in the east, and Morgan was going to use it to bring them in line.

James would never forget that last meeting he'd

attended at Morgan's house a year or so ago. Like the Morgan yacht, the Morgan library with its plush red drapes, its Oriental vases, its statuary and paintings, was awe-inspiring witness to the men who gathered there that, however rich themselves, they were in the presence of at least an equal. Morgan's habit of sitting alone at a little table and playing solitaire while he let his guests bicker among themselves was a mark of his imperial disdain for lesser minds as well as, in James' view, a very clever device. When at last Morgan did drop his cards, lay aside his cigar and speak in orotund phrases, everybody listened. At that meeting he'd said, "I am authorized to say, I think, on behalf of the banking houses represented here that if an organization can be formed practically upon the basis submitted by the committee, and with an executive committee able to enforce its provisions, upon which the bankers shall be represented, they are prepared to say that they will not negotiate, and will do everything in their power to prevent the negotiation of any securities for the construction of parallel lines or the extension of lines not approved by that executive committee. I wish that distinctly understood." If that wasn't a call for solidifying existing railroad monopolies, James had never heard one. It was still up in the air, and the passage of the Sherman Act which might empower the government to expose and disrupt such secret, gentlemen's agreements seemed reason enough for calling another conference.

Because of coming down from Newport, James was a little late this day, and the library was already blue with smoke from men puffing away on their after-luncheon cigars. It was pretty much the group he'd expected—the Morgan partners; the Goulds, father and son, of Missouri Pacific; Charles Francis Adams of Union Pacific; Frank Bond of Chicago, Milwaukee and St. Paul; A. B. Stickney of Chicago, St. Paul and Kansas City; George Roberts of Pennsylvania; Chauncey Depew from New York Central; and a few other interested directors and suppliers like himself. Morgan was started on his solitaire, and the others were still feeling each other out with jokes. "I have the utmost respect for you gentlemen individually," Stickney said with a wave of his cigar, "but as railroad presidents I wouldn't trust you with my watch out of sight." That remark brought such general laughter that even the usually silent Gould was moved to tell a story. "I don't know how many of you gentlemen have ever gotten mixed up with old Dan Drew, as I did to my regret," he said, "but I will say he could show a surprising sense of humor when he had a mind to. He told me that one day he went to a Methodist revival meeting where a convert got up and started confessing to his sins of robbing men in Wall Street. Drew nudged his neighbor and asked, 'Who's he?' The man said, 'Oh, don't you know? That could only be Daniel Drew.'"

One of the smooth Morgan partners, Perkins, used the Gould story to make a transition. "Well, gentlemen," he said, "Wall Street won't again see the likes of Drew—or, I'd guess, of you either, Mr. Gould—if Washington keeps getting into our affairs with all of this restrictive legislation. Mr. Morgan regrets that he had to interrupt your holiday, but he's certain, as I am, that you can all see the threat this Sherman Act imparts to what we've been discussing. In view of this, the very least we can all do is to see that these conversations and whatever comes of them remain within these walls—"

Just then there was a knock on the door, and Morgan's butler entered. The banker, looking up from his cards, said, "I thought I instructed you that there were to be *no* interruptions. Get out of here, and be damned quick about it."

The butler stood his ground and stammered "B . . . begging your pardon, sir, but there's a very dis . . . distraught lady on the stoop, asking for a Mr. Van . . . Van Alen. She . . . she won't go away, sir."

James had never in his life suffered such acute embarrassment. He could sense that every eye in the room—particularly those shrewd, appraising eyes that glowed like little lamps in the caverns under Morgan's shaggy brows—had turned in his direction. What was going on in the minds behind those eyes? Hard to tell with a quick glance around. Gamblers all, whether at the poker table or on Wall Street, these men had trained their eyes to look rather than to tell. Most of them, Gould and himself and a few others excepted, were also men of the world; despite his high standing in Episcopal laity, Morgan was noted for seeing to it that there was discreet and agreeable feminine companionship aboard his yacht or in the hotels where he stopped on his art-buying expeditions through Europe. So those minds behind those eyes, most of them, would be suspecting that this woman at the gates—who could she *possibly* be?—was evidence of a serious mistake on the part of any successful gentleman, the mismanagement of an affair of the heart. Hot blood flushed James' face, and he couldn't trust himself even to murmur apologies as he rose and rushed, before all those eyes, to the door that the butler held open. *Who* could it be?

Very nearly the last person in all the world that James would have expected to find there at the door would have been his sister Sally—and in such a state. Being so much older and always interested in serious matters, James had paid little attention to Sally while they were growing up. She'd been, in his opinion, a rather vain and silly thing, posturing and pouting and busying herself with female trivia like clothes and such profitless "accomplishments" as playing the piano and dancing. He'd resented and never quite understood why his parents, particularly his father, had been so interested in her—and forgiving of her. From the time she'd got herself mixed up with that improvident duke until this very moment, Sally's conduct had been either outrageous or baffling, or both, and James, who'd been doing his damnedest to increase the Van Alen fortune, was bitter that Sally's "mistakes," as the charitable called them, had cost the family estate a million or so to his knowledge and no doubt more that had been slipped to her behind his back. For the sake of family unity, in which he believed only because he was aware of its high value on the exchange of public opinion, James had maintained formal contact with Sally and her various husbands—but only that. He had been deliberately cool to her, and she had, he thought, shown a perfect and gratifying understanding of his message by reciprocating. Establishing and keeping this distance had proved fortuitous for his marriage, since Anne was wary of her sister-in-law to the point, he sometimes felt, of fear. James could appreciate that. All else aside, he did have to acknowledge that his sister was possessed of natural beauty, and he did have a grudging admiration for her spirit, for the way she had held her head up like a true Van Alen no matter what had happened. In any gathering, she was formidable competition for other women. But this woman there, left standing on the stoop? She was Sally all right but scarcely recognizable. She looked like she'd been dragged through a barnyard, and there was no pride in the slumped lines of her figure or the worried, nearly hysterical expression on her face.

James stepped out and pulled the door behind him. He didn't want any Morgan servants eavesdropping on this encounter. Embarrassment had evolved into anger. "What are you doing—coming here like this? You've interrupted a very important meeting—"

"Oh, God, James, Matty's been . . . been stolen . . ."

Matty? Matty? Oh, yes, that child she had by Brewster. Children like Matty aren't just stolen, especially up in Newport where he was sure he'd seen them just yesterday. His sister must be out of her mind. Look at her. She couldn't be falling-down drunk, taking up her husband's habits, could she? He had to get her out of here before any of those men in there got curious and started looking out the window. He took her arm and headed for the

Avenue, where they could find a hack. "I just don't understand what you're saying," he said.

"He took her. Knocked me down and *took* her."

"Who? *Who* took her, for heaven's sake?"

"Bud. Bud Brewster. We were walking in the parade and—"

"*You* were walking in the parade?"

"Yes, with the suffragettes . . ."

Oh, lord. Worse and worse. It would be all over the papers within hours. No doubt those men back there would pick up extras when they left the meeting. This woman, his sister, was mad. "And you took the child with you?"

"Yes . . . how could I know? . . . I never thought I'd see him again, ever. He was supposed to be out west somewhere. . . . Oh, my God, James, he looked awful, I don't know what he'll do to her, we've got to find her . . ."

They were on the corner of the Avenue. A hack James had hailed came clattering to a stop. "Now, Sally, you get in here and go on home and get cleaned up and calmed down. There's a very important meeting back there, and when it's over I'll come on up, and we'll see what we can do—"

Sally grabbed his arms, and he winced with the pain from her grip. She literally forced him to look into her eyes, shining with tears of fear and anger. "James, you're my *brother*. Matty is your *neice*. There isn't any more important business in the world than finding her. If you don't help me *now*, I'll . . . I'll—"

"Where's Aaron? Didn't I hear he was going to be in the city?"

"For the love of God, James, Aaron's out sailing. Do you think I would have come to *you* if I could find *him?*"

"What about Pierce?"

"He's in Newport. James . . ."

James thought it over. In many ways it would be easier not to have to go back and face the inquiring glances of all those men. "All right, I'll go with you, but for the life of me I don't know what we can do about it now. You should have used your head before you got into a mess like this—"

"I *have* been thinking, and the first thing we've got to do is go to the papers . . . tell this man to take us to Herald Square."

"If all this happened in front of everybody at the parade, it'll already be in the papers."

"But we've got to offer a reward or something. From the looks of Bud, he could use the money . . ."

Well, it was something to do. She was thinking fairly straight no matter how she looked. In James' experience there were few problems that money couldn't solve. But, lord, lord, what a mess this was going to be. Everybody in the city for whom the name Van Alen spelled sound, solid and safe would discover that it also spelled silly and sordid. How could this sister of his do this to him, to their mother, to Anne and his children too? Even that Irish barmaid Aaron married was turning out to be a lady compared to his own sister. If *he* had known that Sally was going to flaunt herself, let alone her child, in that parade, he'd have found a way to stop her. James sighed, instructed the hackey to head for Herald Square and got in beside his sister. Maybe there was still some way of saving face. By their scrupulous reporting of the social comings and goings of the James Van Alens, editors around the city had shown considerable respect for his standing. If he just dropped a name or two of friends who were heavy advertisers, perhaps it could be reported that Sally and her child were just *watching* the parade, a very normal thing to do on any Fourth of July in New York. The more he thought about the possibilities of handling this deftly, the more James convinced himself that it could be a happy circumstance that she'd found him instead of Aaron.

It was Mary's idea to recruit some of her brothers when Aaron found himself in need of some muscle to man his yacht in the New York Yacht Club's Fourth of July race. "Why not?" she asked. "They may not be yachtsmen, but playing and working on the docks they've certainly been around boats all their lives. And they do have muscle." Why not, indeed? Sailing mostly out of Newport, Aaron didn't have a professional captain and crew as most of his fellow yachtsmen did. He prided himself, in fact, on being able to handle the boat himself or with the help of a few amateur friends, and he'd asked Edward Burgess specifically to design the new cutter he'd bought, after they'd sold their city house and moved in with his mother, to make this possible by leading all the running rigging except the halyards aft to the cockpit. But if he expected to get the most out of her in a race, he would need a powerful crew to manhandle the tacks and jibes and quick sail changes that the wind and course might call for. As in every sport, he wanted to do well, wanted to show them that Aaron Roberts Van Alen still had the stuff. He'd given up coaching when it became apparent that Pierce Hancock, who owned half the drag, preferred drinking to driving, and, now that he was thirty-two, he found that he couldn't keep up with younger men on the tennis court. So he was still inventing challenges.

The beginning of meeting a challenge in yachting was searching out the right boat, and Aaron was sure that he'd done that. He'd been pleased with the little sloop that Burgess, the naturalist up in Boston who'd turned to designing as a hobby, had created, and he'd been impressed when one Burgess boat after another successfully defended the America's Cup. He'd never forget that first one, *Puritan*, that sailed against Sir Richard Sutton's *Genesta* in '85. Everybody around the club had thought that the American yacht was in for a bad licking. *Genesta* was so long and narrow and deep in draft that they called her a "plank on edge," and she looked as if she could slice the water like a knife. *Puritan* was a beamy, center-boarder resembling, some said, a fat Back Bay matron. But *Puritan* won, and after that *Mayflower* and after that, in '87, *Volunteer*, all from Burgess' drawing board. Aaron's cutter was a virtual copy of *Volunteer*, scaled down to fifty feet. She had a sharp clipper bow and a long overhang astern; with her bowsprit extended and topmast in place, she could carry three headsails and a gaff topsail in addition to the main. Altogether "yar," as admiring sailors around Newport called her, and there was no reason why she shouldn't do as well as *Volunteer* on the same America's Cup course—thirty-eight miles from Owl's Head to Sandy Hook light ship to Southwest Spit buoy and back. Aaron had christened her *Cathay*, a name running through Van Alen annals for a century, from his great-grandfather's China trader to his father's private parlor car.

Getting the right crew was nearly as important as having the right vessel, but in this Aaron was at a disadvantage. Since his intention was only to race *Cathay* once to test both her and himself, it would be both a bother and heedless extravagance to sign on a professional crew for the whole summer. He did manage to recruit two college-boy sons of Newport families with some experience in racing their catboats, but he was still in need of more muscle and fussing about it when Mary came up with her suggestion. He hadn't seen the O'Donnell brothers since that day at his father's funeral, but Mary had more or less kept up with their doings through her infrequent duty visits to her father. Hugh, according to her reports, was still working for the union and just getting by on meagre wages. The A.F. of L. wasn't as yet much more successful than the Knights of Labor had been in holding men together for what seemed a hopeless fight against both their bosses and the government. Jack had given up his own ring career to become sparring partner and attendant to John L. Sullivan and had at least enjoyed a moment of reflected glory down there in Mississippi last summer when Sullivan beat Kilrain in a brutal, seventy-five-round bare-knuckled fight. Whether Jack had got much of the $20,000 gate or not, or what he was doing with himself now, Mary didn't know. But the other two, Frank, Jr., and Joe, were still stevedores and had gone back to work for Van Alen after feelings about the strike had subsided, and it was these brothers that she really had in mind. At least Aaron knew them, and it was better than searching the waterfront for strangers. Besides, since they were Van Alen employees, it was logical to give them first chance at the ten dollars he planned to pay each of them, which would amount to more than a week's wages for sacrificing one holiday. So when Aaron phoned down from Newport to the Van Alen warehouse manager to ask for space at the docks to tie up overnight on the third and fourth of July, he also left a message for two O'Donnell brothers to come aboard at dawn on the holiday, and when the manager didn't call back, he knew that he'd at least have some muscle waiting for him.

On the Fourth, Aaron was up on deck at six to study the weather, his stomach as tight as ever before a contest. He heard a hail and saw two hulks that were unmistakably O'Donnells ambling down the pier. They weren't, however, the O'Donnells he expected. As their faces became distinct in the gathering light, he recognized Hugh and Jack. His stomach tightened further. He'd never had any trouble with Jack, was rather glad to see him, in fact, but was Hugh coming to help work the boat or . . . or what? Well, too late to do anything about it, so try to get off on the right foot. Aaron climbed up the ladder to the pier and held out his hand. "Jack, Hugh, how are you? I was expecting Frank and Joe but . . ."

The brothers did shake his hand, and they did still have muscle to spare judging from their grips. "Yeah, well, you see," said Hugh, "you just said two O'Donnell brothers, so here we are. Frank says he's all worn out from slaving for the Van Alens, and Joe promised his missus and the kiddies to take them to Battery Park, and he's got no more backbone than an eel when it comes to women. And *my* missus, well, she'd rather see a ten-dollar-bill than my ugly face. And Jack here's a little down on his luck. That bastard Sullivan took him apart with what was left of his knuckles when Jack asked for a fair share of the gate, and he ain't been able to fight since."

Taking a harder look at Jack, Aaron could see the ravages of the ring—a spread ear, a crook to the nose, a gap in the teeth. He'd once been as handsome as the rest of the O'Donnells but menacing would be a better description of his looks now—menacing but for one detail: eyes like a beaten dog's. "That's tough, Jack . . ."

Jack managed a smile and a shrug. "Should have had you along to coach me, Aaron. I guess it's back to the docks for me if I can find a job. I've still got me strength."

"Good. We can use it today. Come on aboard and meet the rest of the crew. Boys, these are my brothers-in-law—Hugh O'Donnell and Jack O'Donnell."

Only their built-in manners kept the Newport boys from displaying their astonishment. Up there, the background of Mrs. Aaron Roberts Van Alen was not discussed before children. Aaron had to admire

309

the way the boys, wincing from the O'Donnell grips, said to each of them, "Pleased to meet you, sir."

Hugh laughed. "Ah, so *sir* it is from the likes of these young gentlemen? I think I may take to this ya—ah—ting."

Aaron took a slight risk. "Let me remind you, Hugh—all of you—before we get under way that this isn't yachting—it's a race, and there's only one captain on a ship."

Hugh laughed again. "Oh, there'll be no mutiny aboard this day, Aaron, if that's what's worryin' you." Then he rubbed his chin and added. "I've a good memory of your fist if nothing else—unless you've grown soft."

Aaron laughed too. "Not soft, I hope—but older, I'm afraid. Well, let me show you the ropes."

Aaron began to relax. Though Hugh couldn't keep overtones of bitterness out of his words and voice, he seemed to be in a good mood. Not only that, but he demonstrated his quick intelligence by the questions he asked as Aaron pointed out and explained the halyards for hoisting sails and topmast belayed at the foot of the mast, the sheets controlling the trim of the sails that led back to a rack of belaying pins on either side of the companionway door in the cockpit, the sliding back stays on tracks fastened to the deck outside the cockpit combing, the winches to trim the sheets. Jack kept shaking his head in bewilderment and finally said to his brother, "I told you I'd never get the hang of this." Hugh gave Jack a kind of a hug and said, "You just pull what I tell you to pull." Aaron decided to station the Newport boys forward to handle the halyards, change head sails and act as lookouts; he'd keep the brothers with him in the cockpit where he could quickly correct their mistakes. He could have used a couple more men—a navigator and somebody to spell him on the helm— but since he could sail the boat alone in extremis, he felt that *Cathay* was reasonably well-manned.

As they headed downriver they had the usual southwest breeze of summer for which Aaron was grateful, because they could get in some tacking practice. Since the wind was blessedly light this early in the morning, he was also able to set all sail and familiarize the crew with the full rig. On the first few tacks, the O'Donnell brothers bumped into each other like characters in a comedy and headsails were left flying for long minutes like laundry on a wash line. Gradually, however, a routine was worked out: Jack would fix in his mind only those few lines that controlled the backstays and main sheet and let Hugh handle the trickier head sails. By the time they were rounding the Battery, the operation was so smooth that Aaron was able to look around and enjoy the morning.

That the Republic had been born on a summer's day seemed a bit of serendipity to Aaron. It gave God a chance to smile, as he was going to do today, on this creation of man. A great brass sun was lifting itself above the dark rim of island land masses to the east and bouncing its light off the rippled waters in a sparkling shower. The Statue of Liberty, glowing the color of pink flesh in this light, most appropriately dominated the scene. It had only been in place four years, and Aaron still caught his breath at the sight of it. It was fitting that the giant lady had come as a gift from France, because, as in some strange trick of nature, the beckoning light she held aloft bounced off the heavens and shone down on all the dark places of Europe to draw westward every year more lost, unhappy souls and fulfill the prophetic promise in that poem by Emma Lazarus, now so sadly dead so young. Aaron felt a flush of patriotic fervor at being a citizen of a nation that at least tried to share its blessings with the world. He couldn't keep it to himself: "Isn't she beautiful in this light?"

Hugh brought him back to earth. "Give me your tired and poor and be damned to them," he said.

"Oh, come now, Hugh, you'd rather be here than back in Ireland, wouldn't you?"

"I don't know. I've never been there. Christ, I was born here and I'm as American as you. I just had the wrong father."

The boat was sailing well, but Aaron didn't like the tack the conversation was taking. "There are a lot of Americans who have the so-called wrong fathers, Hugh. Look at Mr. Rockefeller or Mr. Edison. Their fathers were what most people would call failures, and yet they're richer than I'll ever be."

"Oh, don't get me wrong. I ain't saying my old man's a failure. He done as well for us as he could, considering. At least he made us fighting proud of being Irish. But you got no idea how hard it is when you've got nothing for a day ahead unless you go out and break your back for whatever some Van Alen'll give you, how it feels when your stomach pains and grumbles from hunger or, worse, when you hear your kid's guts grumbling. Oh, I know you're going to say why don't I go out and get mine by hook or by crook—I got the brains for it. That's what Mary's always telling me. But I keep thinking about Frank and Joey who ain't got the brains and now Jack here who's got what brains he did have knocked out of him. Somebody's got to do something to see that they can live decent. Can't have all the brains on the other side."

It was the first time Hugh had opened up like that since Aaron had known him, and he looked at his brother-in-law with new respect. "Hugh," he said, "I know I'm on what you call the other side, almost have to be, but I do want you to believe that I wish you well. You *are* going to have to fight for what you want, but when you do I think you'll be surprised to find out how many people there are out there like me, people who at least believe in a fair fight."

"Fair? Sure and how fair can it be when you've got the law on your side? If it ain't, you people with the money buy it, and you know I'm right. And the votes—you can buy them, too. That's why I'd like to see the women vote. Maybe they wouldn't sell theirs for a free drink in a saloon—"

"Hugh, I don't think we're going to solve all the problems of the world this morning. It's a glorious day for a sail, so let's call a truce. Shake on it, brother?"

Hugh slowly reached up his hand, and Aaron took one of his own from the helm to clasp it. Again for the first time ever, they actually smiled at each other. There was more substance to Hugh's argument than Aaron liked to think about on a day like this, but he was glad to have heard it. He decided that, whatever else this day brought, it had already given him the feeling that he could come to like Hugh. The man was more than bitter; he was apparently dedicated. Aaron envied men who had a clear fight on their hands, didn't need to look for challenges . . . Well, he did have one to meet now with the race coming up . . .

"Hey now, would you have a look at that!" Jack said, pointing north. "Never realized how high it is. Man'd get dizzy up there."

The curiosity Jack was pointing out was the skeletal structure of the new World Building, rising above the dense cluster of Manhattan like a single finger from a fisted hand. The papers had been full of details—twenty-six stories, three hundred and seventy-five feet—but it was only from out here that you could really appreciate the word somebody had come up with to describe this phenomenon: "skyscraper." Looking at it, Aaron wished that his father had lived to see it rise. He was reminded of his father's prophecy that day twenty years ago when they were riding up and down the first elevator, of those entries in his father's journal that hailed every new invention. Electricity, which would power the elevators in this towering structure, *was* already changing the actual look of the world. And steel. Aaron could remember how his father would mimic his little friend Andy Carnegie's stuttering enthusiasm as he preached the gospel of steel to anyone who would listen. "I believe him, Aaron," his father would say, "and you're going to see wonders with your own eyes that men in all their history haven't even imagined." Wonders, indeed, were that skeleton with bones of steel and that bridge hung high across the East River on a web of steel that looked from here so delicate that it might have been spun by a giant spider. Aaron had no doubt that the World Building would be only the first, and soon one of the smallest, of the towers that would sprout from that strange and stony island soil on which ambitious and restless men constantly weeded and replanted their ever larger crop of buildings with every season. "The nineties will be the greatest decade in the history of America, in the history of man," some editorial writer had gushed, and at this moment Aaron could agree.

When they approached the starting line, they were surrounded by a dozen or more other yachts, some twice as large as theirs, with decks lined by uniformed crewmen and spars supporting billowing clouds of canvas. "You mean we're going to race with them?" Hugh asked.

"Yes. It's something called a handicap race. The committee gives you a time allowance based on the size of your vessel and amount of sail you carry and so on. We could come in dead last and still win, if you can believe it."

"Mother of God, it's a crazy sport, this ya—ah—ting," Hugh said.

They still had a little time, and Aaron called for practice in jibing, the most dangerous maneuver they might have to make on the course. The easy and safe way to change tacks, to bring the wind from one side of the boat to the other, was to "come about," to swing the bow of the boat through the eye of the wind at which point the sails would flutter harmlessly until the wind filled them out on the other side. For the most part, with the wind abeam or forward of the beam, coming about was the tactic of choice. But with the wind astern and the sails let out as far as possible to catch it, coming about would involve making a full circle—at the cost of too much speed and time in a race. So the trick was to jibe, swing the stern through the wind. Done wrong, a jibe would let the wind catch the sail, winged clear out on one side, and drive it over to the other with such force that it could carry away the mast. One of the stories Aaron used to make his grandmother tell and retell when he was little was about how she'd held her breath while old Cornelius Van Alen jibed his big sloop down the Hudson River. Cornelius would do it from the helm, letting the sail swing free while he steered far enough up to let the wind itself make a soft cushion for it to land on, and then square away again. They either made better boats, or better men, in those days. Aaron would never take that chance. His technique was to have the crew, in this case the O'Donnell brothers, haul the main sheet in at lightning speed as soon as he turned the stern through the wind so that the sheet would catch and control the sail's swing and then ease it out on the other side. Luckily the breeze was still light enough that a mistake would not mean disaster. The O'Donnells learned the hard way. They didn't get the sheet in fast enough to have the sail under full control, and the force of the wind driving it over knocked them down and pulled the rope through their hands with a searing burn. The next time was better, and the next nearly perfect. Aaron felt that they were ready to race.

There were only a few minutes left to go before the starting gun, and Aaron inserted *Cathay* into the grave dance of yachts, wheeling and turning back of the line as they jockeyed for a favored position. It was that time of guts-grabbing tension, that pre-action drug that Aaron had come to crave. Concentrated as he was on maneuvering *Cathay*, he was still conscious of the interest she was creating throughout the fleet. Other owners, standing useless as spectators on the after decks of their great yachts while their professional captains handled the helms, pointed, waved, saluted, doffed their caps, even yelled. "That you, Van Alen?" one of them called. "Beautiful little vessel. Looks like a trimmed down *Volunteer*. Hope you handle her as smartly." Three minutes to go. Two minutes. Aaron was where he wanted to be, to windward of all the rest. Harden up now and head for the line. He was every captain who had ever lived. "Haul in that main, Jack! . . . More, damnit, more—use that muscle! . . . That's it . . . Hugh, tighten up on that flying jib—no, not that line, the other one, the one on your port . . . your left, your left! . . . Ah, that's it!" They were over, sneaking in between a hissing hundred-footer and the committee boat so close that the blank blast from the committee boat's starting gun smudged *Cathay*'s jib.

"Jesus, Mary and Joseph!" Hugh said, crossing himself. "I thought sure we were going to be crushed. Remember, Aaron, no O'Donnell can swim."

317

Aaron laughed. "Thought sailing was a sissy sport, didn't you? Well, swimming wasn't my idea, Hugh. Can't win a race swimming. But see where we are! We've got them all covered when we tack through the Narrows. Oh, those big babies will eventually get ahead of us, but at least they can't steal our wind with all their sails."

Aaron's gamble did pay off. Though the larger yachts did pull ahead, he was able to stay clear of them, keep *Cathay* footing as fast as the wind would allow. Once they'd tacked their way through the Narrows, it was a fast reach on the port tack, with the wind almost abeam, to the light ship, an easy coming about and another fast reach on the starboard tack to the buoy. With the breeze freshening after noon and the sea turning from a chop to a gentle roll and *Cathay* flying, it was sailing at its best. They were staying well ahead of anything their size or smaller and even of some larger boats. Aaron could see that his crewmates were enjoying the experience. The O'Donnells were wallowing shamelessly in a rare bath of sea air and sun during the long reaches when their muscular services weren't needed. "They call this the sport of kings," Aaron said. "Can you see why now?"

"Aye," Hugh said. "Almost makes me wish I were rich. But, ah well, it's the easiest ten bucks I've ever earned."

"Better than fighting, Jack?" Aaron asked.

"Anything's better than fighting," Jack said.

Although they seemed to be doing very well, Aaron knew that every second still counted when the time allowances were figured, so they'd jibe

318

around the buoy and run on to the finish line with the still-building southwest wind at their back. In this breeze an error could be very costly or dangerous, but racing was taking risks. He'd just have to trust the brothers. The buoy was abeam now. "Jibe, ho," Aaron called and spun the wheel. The brothers worked like human steam engines. Over came the huge boom. Ah, lord love us, they'd caught it with the sheet. They eased it out on the other side, trimmed the jibs, and *Cathay* was running downhill toward home. "Well done," Aaron said.

"And why shouldn't it be?" Hugh asked. He held up his palms, still showing red scarring from the first jibe. "No O'Donnell gets burned twice if he can help it."

Aaron had an inspiration. "I've got to sail this boat back to Newport tomorrow. You fellows want to come along and have a visit with Mary?"

"Naw, I gotta stick by the hirin' hall," Jack said.

"I'll think about it," Hugh said.

"Well, we'll be leaving by eight to catch the tide around at Hell Gate," Aaron said.

Almost as soon as the words were out, Aaron began having second thoughts about his impulsive invitation. It was, he realized, the first time that any O'Donnell had been asked to visit any Van Alen home. When he'd brought up such a possibility without much enthusiasm early in their marriage, Mary had said, "Don't worry about it, Aaron. We're doing *them* a favor. They'd just be uncomfortable." So he'd dropped the whole matter. Why disrupt the pattern now? Just because Hugh, particularly, had turned out to be a quick and ready hand on a boat? What would they do with him in Newport or what would he do with himself? Aaron and Mary and the children were living there with his mother, as they were in New York, in the sprawling, timbered, Tudor-style "cottage" that his father had created to look like something Shakespeare might have lived in if the bard had had a million. The Van Alen place was a "must" on that daily round of social visits that took up the time of Newport's fashionable ladies. Both his mother and Mary would be furious that he'd been so thoughtless as to drag this living reminder of Mary's past in front of everybody's eyes. It would be like the time that he'd innocently suggested that Mary go to a costume ball dressed as a cancan girl and she'd burst into tears. "How could you be so cruel, Aaron?" she'd said. "You know how hard I've worked to live down that part of me." Oh, they were ladies enough that they'd try to hide their feelings, but Aaron suspected that Hugh was sensitive enough that he'd see through the pretense, and he'd certainly be uncomfortable with all of their friends. It wouldn't take much—one careless remark, perhaps—to send that chip that rested so lightly on Hugh's shoulder flying, and then there could be all hell to pay.

Under the circumstances Aaron was happy that the boat was again demanding his attention. With what was now quite a strong wind behind them, the sea was kicking up, lifting *Cathay*'s long counter and burying her nose in water. She could take it all right. She'd lift her snout and toss sheets of spray over her shoulder like a playful porpoise but wasn't it slowing her down? He still had every sail flying as did all the other boats in the fleet that he could see; the general idea going downwind was to hoist anything and everything that would catch the breeze. The yacht dead ahead, a staysail schooner half again as large as *Cathay*, had even rigged an unorthodox square sail on her foremast, but she too was wallowing badly. There must be some better way. Thinking about the problem, Aaron remembered the trick that had put *Puritan* ahead of the "plank on edge." He ordered the Newport boys to strike the gaff topsail.

With less sail, *Cathay* kept her nose in the air and was soon picking up so much speed that she overtook the schooner. When they got close enough, Aaron passed almost under the big boat's counter, stealing some of her wind in the process. The schooner's owner bawled out, "What've you got—a steam engine on that thing? It's against the rules." Hugh yelled back, "And up yours, too, mister!" Aaron laughed. "That's not quite the right expression for a gentleman's sport, Hugh, but you've expressed my feelings exactly."

The rest of the sail was a romp. When the steam yacht that served as a committee boat signaled their crossing of the finish line with a blast of its whistle, Aaron saw one of the stiff, brass-buttoned figures on its deck salute them with a wave of his white hat. "Did you see that, men?" he asked. "I'm sure that means we won, though we won't know officially until they figure the times."

"Hooray!" Hugh said. "That ought to call for a bonus, shouldn't it, captain?"

Aaron had already decided to double the figure

he'd promised them, so he said, "Yes—and something more. Here, Hugh, take the helm for a minute, and just steer for the statue."

It was safe enough since inside the Narrows the seas had slackened, and the breeze was lightening with the coming of sundown. Aaron went below, rummaged around in the locker and came on deck with a bottle of Irish whiskey in his hand. He summoned the Newport boys back to the cockpit, set out mugs and poured generous dollops. "Time for an old seagoing custom called splicing the main brace," he said, passing the drinks around, "and don't you boys tell your mothers, or they'll think I'm corrupting your morals. We all deserve it for a job well done. So here's to the *Cathay!*"

Inspired by one drink and then another, Hugh turned the helm over to Aaron again, saying, "I brought something, too, Aaron, that I didn't let you see in case you'd think I wasn't taking this ya—ah—ting seriously . . ."

Ducking down into the cabin, Hugh came up again with a small accordion in his hand. "My squeeze box," he said. "I remembered hearing that sailors always sing when they get into the doldrums, whatever that is. Now, if you'll let me wet my whistle one more time . . ."

The breeze was dying rapidly, and they were little more than drifting up the river in a golden haze of sunset. Hugh made himself comfortable with his back against the bulkhead and squeezed out a few experimental chords. "It's a new song I'll be singing from a show that just opened out in Chicago called *Robin Hood*. Fellow I know who's one of the organizers out there taught it to me. It'll be a hit sure." Then in that sweet tenor that God gave only to the Irish, Hugh began:

"Oh, promise me that someday you and I
Will take our love together to some sky . . ."

Aaron thought that he'd never heard anything so beautiful. Of course, his normal susceptibility to sentimental song was magnified by the sunset, by that sensation of well-being that followed a contest well-won, by the warmth of the whiskey. And discovering another, wholly unsuspected, facet of Hugh's personality, a talent that he envied even more than Hugh's dedication, gave him hope that a Newport visit would somehow work out too. The jaded Newport society was always looking for a new diversion, and Hugh, singing at one of their gatherings by the sea, would be a sensation. He'd have to remember to make sure that Hugh brought his squeeze box.

"Brings a tear to the eye, don't it?" Hugh said when he'd finished. "Works wonders with my missus. She thinks I'm singin' it to her, but I'm really singin' for my little Kathleen. You haven't seen her, have you? Spittin' image of Mary. How *is* Mary?"

"Fine, fine."

"You getting along good?"

"Yes. Why not?"

"Oh, just wondering. Mary was always one for having her own way—tantrums or tears. I thought maybe when the honeymoon was over—"

"It isn't over for me . . . How about another song, Hugh?"

So, serenaded by Hugh, they drifted on until, at dusk, the *Cathay* came gently to rest against the Van Alen pier. The warehouse watchman who ran down to meet them had more on his mind than taking their lines. He tossed a newspaper down to the cockpit. "You'd better read that, Mr. Van Alen." Aaron gulped down the story under the headline—$10,000 REWARD FOR VAN ALEN HEIRESS—at a glance. It took a staggering effort of his imagination to try to conjure up all that must have been going on here on land while he was having such a happy time at sea. Though it was clear enough that Brewster had snatched away his daughter, it was by no means clear why he'd had the opportunity. Why in the world had Sally brought Matty all the way down from Newport just to watch a parade and why down on lower Broadway when they could have hung out of their own windows on Fifth Avenue and seen the whole thing go by? In his haste, Aaron overlooked the sidebar story on the suffragettes in the parade which, though the presence of Sally Van Alen Brewster Hancock wasn't mentioned, might have aroused his suspicions. He tossed the paper at the others and said, "Put the boat to bed for me, will you? I don't know when I'll be back."

Aaron found his sister sitting in the almost dark of her drawing room. She hadn't bothered with light although the whole place had recently been wired for electricity, and all you had to do was flick a switch. There was a glass in her hand and a bottle of brandy beside her on a table. She looked up. "Oh, it's you, Aaron. Did you win the race?"

"Christ, Sally, what does that matter?" He put the bottle out of reach and tried to take the glass from her hand. "This won't help."

She clung to the glass, took a defiant swallow. "What else is there to do? Oh, Aaron, I've made such an awful mess of things . . ."

"Where's James? I gathered from the papers that he was with you."

Sally laughed near-hysterically. "You won't believe it—or maybe you will. He caught the last train back to Newport, said he wanted to get there for the archery party. I told him you don't shoot arrows after dark, but he said Anne was mad at him and he had to do something for her since he'd done all he could for me."

"All . . . ?"

"Well, he did try, Aaron. He did manage to keep it out of the papers that I was leading the suffragette parade."

"My God, I might have known. Sally, honey, what are we going to do with you—?"

"I don't know, I just don't know. What's important is what's *he* going to do with Matty. You know Brewster. Do you think he'd hurt her? Do you?"

"No, I don't think so," but then he'd never thought he'd rape her either. "What worries me is that I did hear from some Princeton friends that he'd been fired from his coaching job for drinking. I didn't want to tell you because—"

"Because you knew that he was as good as dead for me. He was, Aaron. I was even thinking of

325

changing Matty's name. Oh, God, Aaron, I love that child. I can't bear this. What else can we *do?*"

"Well, for one thing, we can turn some lights on here and start thinking. I suppose you've been to the police?"

"Oh, yes, James used his influence to get to the commissioner himself. He told us that, particularly with the holiday crowds, it would be like finding a needle in a haystack."

When Aaron snapped on the lights and could really see his sister, it was another blow. She hadn't bothered to change her smeared dress, and she'd evidently torn most of the pins from her hair along with her hat so that it looked like a witch's wig. Every line of her body and face sagged, as if the numbers of her age had been reversed in an afternoon from 35 to 53.

"I wish I were dead—"

"Now, come on, snap out of it. It wasn't really your fault—"

"Oh, yes, it was. Everybody, but everybody, told me I shouldn't do it, and you would have too. Do you know what Sissie Belmont thinks of me? She thinks I'm crazy. Her daughter told Matty . . . Oh, God, Aaron, Matty . . . she said *she* didn't think I was crazy, and look what I've done to her . . . If it weren't for me, she'd be up there in Newport eating ice cream and running around the lawn with sparklers and . . . oh, God, Aaron . . ."

It was hard to argue with all that. Aaron himself had never been able to get very excited about women's rights. The whole issue had been identified in his mind with Cousin Amelia's eccentricities—a rather harmless way for a disappointed maiden lady to take out her frustrations. He'd always considered Sally too normal, too interested in men to pay more than lip service to the cause. He had too much regard for Sally to go along with the others in the family—James and Mary and, he supposed, his mother and Anne too—who expressed unkind suspicions as to Sally's motives when it turned out that Amelia had willed all of her Van Alen stock to Sally. Still, he'd never suspected that she could care enough to expose herself and her child to ridicule, and, as it proved, danger. What came to him forcibly at this moment was the realization that, in recent years, he hadn't seen enough of his sister to know *what* she thought. The wariness he'd sensed between Mary and Sally had increased, at least on Mary's part, and it had been easier to keep their relations with the Hancocks on a rather formal, family basis. Neither Mary nor Sally would, of course, admit to their feelings about each other. What they did was put it all on poor old Pierce. Because of her background, Mary couldn't stand drunks, and besides, she said, Pierce made passes at her when he was drunk. Sally saw no reason to expose Pierce unnecessarily to temptation. If he had to philander, as apparently he did, let him at least keep it out of the family. Aaron, who never had been able to understand Pierce's attraction for women, thought it all pretty damn silly, but then Pierce, drunk a good part of the time now, wasn't much use to him either. So let it go. There were other things to think about and do. Now, for whatever reason, Sally had done what she'd done, and it wasn't, in fact, crazy. Hadn't he heard just today an argument for women's suffrage from a most unlikely source—Hugh O'Donnell? Hugh? My God, maybe that was it . . .

"Sally, if Bud's drinking as I've heard and looks like a bum as you've said, what we've got to do is get somebody who knows his way around the back streets and bars to look for them, to spread the word and organize his friends. I know the man—my brother-in-law Hugh. He's got all sorts of connections through his union activities and his father's saloon."

"I didn't think you got along with him. I thought he hated Van Alens—"

"He crewed for me today and . . . well . . . I saw another side of him. And I think he did of me . . . He's actually for your cause. He wouldn't think you were crazy, he'd think you were some kind of heroine. Look, I'm going to go see him right now. Anything's worth a try—"

"Yes, *anything* . . ."

Aaron picked up the bottle and waved it at her. "All right now, promise me—no more of this while I'm gone."

Sally, still holding a half-filled glass in her hand, threw it at the marble face of the fireplace, where it broke into a shattering shower.

Then she said, "I'm going to change now, I wouldn't want Matty to see me like this . . ."

Aaron nodded and left quickly. Sally Van Alen had guts. He was proud that she was his sister. He also found himself hoping that she would be able to feel the same about him.

Chapter 8

"Daisy, Daisy, give me your answer true,
I'm half crazy, all for the love of you . . ."

His voice was quicksilver, a metallic, shining flow in and around the line of song as he sang into the wind that the rush of their bicycle was creating. She didn't dare turn to look at him, expose herself to those sky-blue eyes that presumed too much about what was going on inside her. It was one thing to have thought often about this and quite another to be actually on the way. She felt suddenly scared—scared and shy—as if she were sixteen instead of thirty-eight, as if she had no clear idea of what would, or could, happen. She was glad that he was singing instead of talking. In song he was all those impossible things that she wished he, or anybody, could be, all those things she ought to have sense enough no longer to hope she'd find.

If anybody had told Sally a few years back that she'd one day find herself on the front seat of a bicycle built for two and heading toward the first deliberate sinning of her life she'd have laughed. "I'm too old for that sort of thing," she'd have said. "Bicycle riding, I mean." And if anybody had suggested that the man on the other seat would be *Hugh O'Donnell*, she'd have laughed even harder. "Really, I don't have to scrape the bottom of the barrel—yet," she'd have said. Yet here she was, aflutter with excitement and overwhelmed by that sense that her life was, as usual, unpredictable and out of control.

Sometimes now she wondered whether she hadn't fallen half in love with Hugh O'Donnell way back when he'd punched the sawdust stuffings out of Pierce Hancock at her brother Aaron's wedding reception. But of course not. Her principal emotion then had been worry over Aaron's getting mixed up with such a rough bunch. She hadn't even paid much attention to Hugh on that hot and brassy July dawn three years ago when he'd come staggering into her bedroom with Matty in his arms. The sight of her child, safe, though fussy and frightened, had eclipsed everybody and everything around her. She'd listened, out of politeness to Hugh's story, but she'd hardly been able to comprehend it.

"Big and mean he was, I'll tell you, but I guess you know that," Hugh said. "Can't believe that man was ever a preacher. Look at this shiner."

Aaron, who like her had been trying and failing to sleep in another bedroom, had come in. "Where in the world did you find them?" he asked.

"In a fleabag, way down on the East Side. Like you said, I put out the word on the saloon grapevine, and a fellow named Moriarity remembered seeing this bum with a little kid dressed like a doll in his place. Stuck out like a sore thumb, they did, because no respectable drinkin' man brings a kid with him. So we—my brothers and me—just searched the neighborhood, banging on doors until I run into this old crone who'd rented them a room and went in."

"Why didn't you get the police and arrest him?" Aaron wanted to know.

"Now where are you going to find a cop in a place like that at that time of night?"

"Well, give me the address, and I'll call them right now."

"Naw, don't do that," Hugh said. "If you think I look bad, you oughta see him. I don't think you'll have any trouble with him again. I told him—stretchin' the point a little—that I was the kid's uncle now, and the next time I'd kill him."

"But kidnapping's a crime."

"I know. I know," Hugh said. "But he is the kid's father. Before we got into the rough stuff we had a talk, and, well, the guy's about as far down on his luck as you can get. I suggested why didn't he turn her in and get the reward, but he said he wasn't interested in money. He said he was her father and just seeing her like that he sort of went out of his mind, and . . . well, I said I was taking her for her own good, and that's when he started throwing punches."

"I still think we ought to have him arrested," Aaron said.

"Forget it, Aaron, they'll never find him," Hugh said. "I guess I got to feeling sorry for him. You

331

know, I'm a father too, and . . . well, just before I left, I threw him the twenty you gave me for the race and told him to get the next train out of town. . . . Uh, I guess I'd better go now."

Matty, rocked in her mother's arms, had quieted a little and Sally asked, "Did he hurt you, darling? Did he?"

"No. He bought me a lot of that cotton candy, but he was going to take me away to . . . to someplace called Ohio and I wouldn't get to see you again, or Tabby, or Granny."

"Well, it's all right, darling. You're here now thanks to . . . to Uncle Hugh. I don't know how to thank you, Mr. O'Donnell. Oh, my God, I don't know how I can thank you. My lawyers will be in touch with you about the reward."

Hugh, already at the door, came back into the room. "None of that, Mrs. Hancock. I'll take no such thanks. We are all what you'd call family, ain't we? No, I'll take no such thanks from a Van Alen. I'm just glad you got your kid and that's an end to it. Good night."

Later, when things had calmed down a bit, she'd wanted to find a way of giving Hugh the reward, but both Mary and Aaron had argued her out of it on the grounds that Hugh was a proud man who'd be insulted. Then she came up with another idea, one she didn't even discuss with Mary and Aaron. When the next Fourth of July was approaching, the anniversary of Matty's bad time, she wrote a note to Hugh asking him to bring his family up to Newport for the day. When they heard about it Mary, and to some extent Aaron too, were upset. "I know you mean well, Sally," Mary said, "but it was really kind of thoughtless of you. Hugh's wife and children have never been out of the West Side in all their lives. I doubt that Eileen owns but one good dress—and that you wouldn't let your maid go to church in. With all the parties and things on the Fourth here, they'll be uncomfortable and embarrassed, and frankly so will I."

"Well, I won't," Sally said. "I owe that man more than I can ever pay, and Matty's been asking and asking to see her Uncle Hugh. You can have your parties. I'll keep them out of your hair."

Sally still didn't like herself too much for feeling such relief when Hugh stepped off the train alone. The official excuse for why his wife and children hadn't accompanied him was that they couldn't find anybody to care for old Frank O'Donnell, who'd been living with them since he'd been bedridden; the real reason, as Hugh later admitted, was that his wife was plain scared of meeting all those people and didn't want her children's heads turned. As for Hugh, all that business about Matty had caused him to miss his chance to sail up with Aaron and see how the rich lived off the sweat of the laboring man, and here, by God, he was.

For all that talk, Hugh was something of a revelation, even to Mary and Aaron. To help keep him out of his wife's hair, Aaron persuaded Hugh to crew for him on the day's races and that night, at just the right moment in the Van Alen archery party, prompted him to sing. Despite the fact that he'd been dressed in checks and had a tendency to mangle the language, Hugh's good looks and sweet tenor had captivated the younger set, at least. It had been Sally's satisfaction to sidle up to Mary while Hugh, surrounded by a flower garden of girls, was singing and whisper, "Well, it isn't so bad after all, is it? He's the star of the show."

Hugh had so obviously enjoyed himself and seemed so grateful that Sally, putting him on the train, said, "Let's make this a regular thing, Hugh. Come to us every Fourth and celebrate Matty's salvation."

Matty, jumping up and down beside her, said, "Do, Uncle Hugh. Please do."

"And bring your family next time," Sally added.

"No," Hugh said. "No use mixin' oil and water, but I got a bit of the both in me."

It was true. Gifted with the same kind of pride and physical attractiveness that had made Mary a Van Alen, Hugh demonstrated on subsequent visits that he could get along in Newport by putting aside for a day or two his anger at the rich and concentrating on sailing and singing and, above all, bicycling. Since, as he himself put it, Hugh "didn't know one end of a horse from the other except by the smell," it was fortunate that the bicycle craze hit Newport at about the same time as Hugh O'Donnell. The wheel seemed made for his powerful thighs, and its speed and freedom for his spirit. Like a pied piper, he'd lead Matty and the Van Alen children and any others with the nerve to follow all over the island in races and would taunt them into aping his tricks like pedaling backward or balancing with feet on the saddle and no hands. He'd also, after Sally got her bicycle built for two, pedal her sedately along

Bellevue Avenue in a show that was becoming more fashionable than riding in a carriage. Sally had worried a bit that Pierce, in his cups, might provoke some sort of confrontation with Hugh, but Hugh had averted that possibility. Sharing Pierce's fondness for whiskey but apparently possessing a greater tolerance for its effects, Hugh had joined him at the club, where his skill at poker had enriched Pierce by several thousand dollars on side bets and turned him into an O'Donnell fan. In fact, several Newport men tried to talk Hugh into dropping his union business and taking a job—"you'd made a crackerjack salesman"—but at that Hugh drew the line.

It was only with Sally that Hugh would be serious, and it was a more stimulating form of flattery than if he'd told her that she was the most beautiful woman in the world. "You know the real reason I'm here is that I admire your guts," he said early on. "You're the only one in this bloomin' lot who understands that things in this world have gotta change. Hadn't been for you marchin' in that parade, I doubt I'd have gone looking for Matty. I'd have just figured you for another spoiled woman who was gettin' her just deserts for running out on a man. But you're different, and maybe you'll come to see what I'm aiming for. I got some hope for that brother of yours, Aaron, too. You know we need some of you on our side, and the main thing in my being here is to prove to all these swells that I don't wear horns and a tail, and so I thank you for the chance." From that and similar comments, Sally came to realize that Hugh was using her gesture of gratitude very deliberately to ingratiate himself for the sake of his cause. Well, fair enough.

But whether Sally was on his side or not was a question for which she hadn't yet found an answer. Pushing for the rights of women was logical; after all, she *was* a woman. But what Hugh wanted which boiled down literally to taking money from the pockets of Van Alens and all those like them and putting it into the pockets of himself and his fellow laborers was threatening to say the least. When she accused him of being a Socialist or Communist, he said, "What the hell—I don't even know what them words mean. But I do know a man has rights in his work just like you've got rights in your property. Even Lincoln said so, if I read him right. The thing is you—all you old Dutch and English—grabbed up everything in sight before there was an America, and then you imported us to do your work for you, but you don't want to share it. Well, you're gonna have to share it."

Sally wasn't one to take that sort of talk without argument. "Look, Hugh, we were the pioneers. We were the ones who tamed this wilderness and fought off the Indians—and the British, too, for that matter. So we deserve what we've got, don't we? There's still a lot of America out there for anyone with enough guts, as you say, to go after it. Look at the settlers' rushes in Kansas and Oklahoma. Those people aren't sitting around complaining about not getting their rights."

And Hugh came back, "Oh, yeah, you ain't reading about the farmers out there—they're madder than we are. Why do you think they formed their own People's Party? I wish they'd have won. It ain't enough to have land. You've gotta have seed and plows and horses. So you've gotta borrow from these fellows right here in New York like your brother James' ugly friend Morgan. And then you've gotta ship whatever you grow on those monopolistic railroads that jack up their prices so they can buy Van Alen freight cars. You know what the farmers are sayin', don't you?—'In God we trusted, in Kansas we busted.' Oh, no, you people don't watch out and the farmers—your pioneers—will elect somebody like that young Bryan who'll give us silver and cheap money to pay off our debts, and then . . ."

But Sally wasn't through. "And then your people will lose what jobs they have. At least they're getting their dollar a day. James isn't my favorite brother, as you know, but he does know how to keep a company going and pay his workers what he thinks they're worth. If it weren't for people like James, where would any of you be? Think about that."

One of the things that she liked best about Hugh was that he said, "Well, I will think about it, seeing that it comes from you. Anybody else around here, I'd be sure they were only thinking of their own precious hides."

This summer of 1893, though, it was hard to argue with Hugh. Stocks were falling on Wall Street— New York Central from 109¼ to 92; American Tobacco from 121½ to 43; Western Union from 96¼ to 67—banks were closing, railroads were declaring bankruptcy, workers were being fired. Panic was as tangibly in the air as electricity before a heavy thunderstorm, even in Newport. James Van

Alen took the most unusual step of summoning the whole family to his marble cottage on the night of July 3, an hour after he'd come up from the city for the holiday. "I just want to assure you all," he said, "that no matter what you hear in the next few months, the Van Alen ship is a tight one and ought to be able to stay afloat. That's because I've seen to diversifying our holdings. Of course with railroads going under as they are I've thought it prudent to cut back on our production and have ordered extensive layoffs at both our factory over in Jersey and on the docks in New York. Mary, I'm afraid that's going to affect your brothers, but it can't be helped. I don't suppose Hugh will be coming up *this* year, will he, Sally?"

"Why not? He's invited."

James, whose attitude toward Hugh on his Newport visits had been cool to the point of frigid, said, "I expect you haven't been reading the city papers. He's been holding public meetings of the unemployed in the parks and talking a lot of rot about leading a march on Washington. He blames the whole thing on Cleveland's monetary policy, thinks if we had cheap money there'd be more to go around. Hugh is a real radical, make no mistake, and people up here are going to be in an unpleasant mood. This is serious business, which is why I called you all here. Phil Watson jumped under a train, the very train I was on, in the Park Avenue tunnel and killed himself, and when the news reaches here . . ."

Pierce Hancock, who'd been long at the club and was nodding through James' remarks, snapped

338

awake. "What was that? What did you say about Phil?"

"He was wiped out and took his own life. God knows how many others there will be."

"Oh, Lord, then I'm wiped out too," Pierce said.

If there was one man for whom James Van Alen had more distaste than Hugh O'Donnell, it was Pierce Hancock, who in his mind was little more than a drunken leech, sucking the blood that people like him sent coursing through Wall Street. Even so, to keep his sister out of trouble and please his mother who liked to see all Van Alens live in style, James had for years been advising Pierce on his investments. He couldn't believe what he was hearing. "You must be drunker than usual, Pierce. You forget you've got that Van Alen stock we let you buy, and I've just been telling you—"

"But I don't. Phil talked me into trading it all in for margin in the railroads. Said there was no way of losing. I even took a mortgage on the Fifth Avenue house."

"When was *this?*"

"Last year. Just this time. I remember because I was down at the club with Hugh, cleaning up on side bets on his poker hands, and Phil came up to me and said a lucky gambler like me oughtn't to be sitting tight on all those stuffy stocks. I guess I wasn't thinking too clearly so I told him to go ahead."

"I don't believe you're thinking clearly now, Pierce. Come to me in the morning when you're sober and we'll look into this thing. As for you Sally, keep Hugh out of sight if he shows up. You too

Mary. Now, please, everybody, I've had a hard day in the city and I'm tired . . ."

When the meeting broke up, Pierce bolted for the club. Martha Van Alen had her carriage waiting at the door, but Mary approached Sally. "Let's walk home together." Sally, who really wanted to be alone to absorb all this news, reluctantly agreed.

Outside, Mary asked, "What are you going to do, Sally?"

"About what? Hugh? Hugh isn't responsible for the state of the world, and I certainly wouldn't hold anyone, much less Hugh, responsible for Pierce's foolishness. Hugh will always be welcome in *my* house."

"But you've never seen him when he's all worked up. He's been so . . . so different up here, though I don't know why. But now if all the men around here are angry too . . . oh, I just can't help worrying. I just wish Aaron weren't off sailing." . . .

In the little time he spent at Newport, Aaron seemed always to be off sailing, usually alone. Something had been happening to him in these last three years since he'd been reading law in Judge Parson's office, ostensibly to fit himself for taking over the legal side of the Van Alen's operation. The very fact that he'd assumed such a chore at his age was in itself odd. The firm could afford to hire the best legal counsel in New York. Aaron's argument that the company had been wasting money on lawyers didn't make too much sense, to be honest. Still, James had apparently gone along with the idea in the hope that, armed with some knowledge, Aaron could be of more real use. Sally was more intrigued

340

with the offhand explanation Aaron had given her: "Oh, I've just invented another challenge for myself. And, good God, it *is* a challenge. Hitting the books at my age is harder than hitting a tennis ball." It was, Aaron said, to seek relief from "hitting the books" that he spent so much time aboard *Cathay*, and this year, to celebrate his admission to the bar, he was off on a solo cruise for two weeks. Though her grounds for any such suspicion were shaky, Sally nevertheless wondered if much of Aaron's sailing didn't have to do with the fact that it was a polite way of getting away from Mary, who couldn't step into a rowboat without getting seasick.

"Well, I agree with you," Sally said. "Aaron could have taken Hugh out with him. But we'll manage as long as we stay away from the archery party, and I have a feeling Pierce won't be spending much time in the club, once James gets hold of him tomorrow."

"Oh, that is terrible, Sally, isn't it? I shouldn't be thinking of my own problems when you—"

"Don't worry about me, Mary. I think I've still got my money coming, if what James says is true, and maybe this is what Pierce has needed to shake him up. He'll probably have to go to work somewhere, though God knows who'd want him. Maybe we'll both have to go to work. And maybe a good thing to stop being part of the idle rich. Don't you ever miss your dancing?"

"Never," Mary said. "It's only people like you who were born rich who can talk like that. I love every day I wake up in silk sheets. I pinch myself to make sure I'm not dreaming. All I can say is thank

God for James. He's the only one in this family who seems to know what he's doing."

"Oh, I didn't know you thought so much of James. Didn't you hear him tonight—he's fired your own brothers? Doesn't that bother you?"

"My brothers had every chance to get out that I did, and—"

"Now, Mary, they weren't the right sex. In your case, it paid to be a woman."

"Are you insinuating that I married Aaron for his money?"

"I'm sorry, Mary, I didn't mean it that way. It's just that if they were my brothers—"

"Now, look, Sally, I won't let them starve. I've been supporting dad for years, and that's what's keeping Hugh and his family going, or didn't you know? And I've set Jack up in dad's old saloon. No, I won't let them starve, but I won't let them drag me down either. That's why I don't want Hugh making trouble. You can tell him that from me."

"I surely will, Mary. Good night." Mary, Sally thought, was more of a Van Alen than she was. . . .

Hugh did arrive the next morning, and in a bad mood. All he wanted, he said, was to be alone. "Don't know why I even came up here, Sally, 'cepting I can't stand seeing Frank and Joey and their friends come around with their long faces and hearing the missus fretting. 'Course the union can't pay my pittance now that everybody's out of work."

"Well, you'll find company around here. Did you hear about Phil Watson? Killed himself. Jumped in front of a train. He was a broker, you know— Pierce's broker—and now it looks as if Pierce is wiped out too."

"Ah, 'tis a shame about Watson—a good gambling man I took him for. But Pierce too? You mean *you're* broke, Sally?"

She could have been mistaken, but Sally thought that she detected a wistful, almost hopeful, tone in Hugh's question. He'd often talked about money as a wall between them. "Ah, no, I've still got my grandmother's trust, and James says that the Van Alen ship will stay afloat—that's how he put it."

"Sure, and he keeps it that way by throwin' the crew overboard. I don't mind saying I've got little love for *that* brother of yours."

"Well, I guess the feeling's mutual. I suspect it might be a good idea if you stayed out of his way this trip—"

"I'm staying out of everybody's way. I don't know what the hell's goin' on, but you can see for yourself now the whole system's coming apart. I'm trying to decide whether to lead a march on Washington next week, and I gotta think. So if I can just borrow a bike . . ."

And off Hugh rode. Pierce, more hung over than usual with anxiety stirring up the dregs of booze in his system, went early to consult with James. Sally sent Matty to join her cousins at the Van Alen archery party—no use spoiling her Fourth, especially this year when, at going on twelve, she was old enough to compete for the first time. Then, with the house blessedly empty, Sally went out onto the veranda, plunked herself down in a rocker, kicked off her shoes, put her feet up on the rail in a very unladylike fashion and let her mind spin. She was

343

only half conscious of the sunny, bee-buzzing day (God, thank God, didn't follow the stock reports in the making of weather); of the night-blue waters of the bay gradually being starred with the little white blossoms of sail (the races went on even though, up the avenue, a black wagon was delivering the broken body of Phil Watson to his home for the last time); of the sporadic pop-poppity-pop of firecrackers, the boom of cherry bombs, the screams of excited children (the Fourth was for freedom, for fun, for letting off steam); of the discreet rattle of dishes and pans in the pantry. What Sally was trying to concentrate on this day were those inward feelings that this crisis was bringing into focus.

She wasn't particularly surprised that she had no feelings at all about Pierce's problem, however bad it turned out to be, or, if she did, that they were what everybody would consider the wrong kind of feelings—stirrings of relief and hope that at last something had come along that might end the stalemate of their marriage. Pierce had been, in his fashion, fun in those early champagne years with his preposterous play-acting at being a ship's captain or a coach driver, his zest for dancing and flirting away the nights at parties. But in these later whiskey years he'd been a problem and a damn bore. It was hard to recall when last they'd gone to bed together or exchanged what could be construed as a tender word. She knew that Pierce was crawling into every bed in which he could find a welcome, including that of one of the maids upstairs. Knowing what she did, she felt more sorry for than jealous of the other women. She wondered sometimes if it would take them as long as it had her to conclude that Pierce's failed performance wasn't their fault unless, of course, they were willing to indulge in some of the perversions he'd begun to suggest to her when liquor loosened his tongue. Impossible to imagine a woman doing such things, but from Pierce's descriptions she had to believe that some did. What she couldn't believe was that even the wildest revels of Sodom, even the most fetching twitch of the flesh at the touch of the whip, would arouse manhood where manhood didn't exist. If it hadn't been for her other shattering experiences, Sally might have walked out on Pierce. She had, however, the kind of honesty that wouldn't allow her to feel sorry for herself. She'd entered this marriage with what she thought were open eyes, and she had so far got out of it almost exactly what she might have expected—respectability, creature comfort beyond desire, some form of companionship, at least for a while. In view of her own past mistakes, was there more she could really ask? Yes, and *yes*. She was, she realized, still interested in more than waiting for death to overtake her.

Alone there on that huge porch, feet up on the rail, rocking, she made another gesture of defiance to the propriety that masked the bodies and feelings of proper Newporters, or New Yorkers for that matter; she pulled her hobbling skirts up to her knees so that the freshening breeze off the water could wash up her spread legs. Not much use, of course, since, in heat warm enough to bathe in, her legs were ridiculously encased in black stockings and white linen drawers and her hips stiffly corseted. A gesture nevertheless, and she wickedly hoped that some yachtsman out there would be scanning the shoreline with his spyglass and get a good shock from the sight of her unmentionables. Sally was quite aware that she still had the firm figure of a young woman, a body unseen and unappreciated, and a face that, despite a few life lines around the eyes and mouth, could pass for no more than thirty. Whether a gift of heritage or good living, her beauty remained, and there were many times when she thought that nature was kinder in letting women run to fat, as Cousin Amelia had, or to skeleton, like her sister-in-law Anne, and thereby letting them accept with more grace the kind of sexless existence that most of them led. Would her body be forever wasted? Despite her disappointing experiences, Sally couldn't quite get over the feeling that she'd had since she'd first been aware of being attractive—that she'd been made for some unimaginable delight. As she rocked and rocked, frustration was building in her like steam in a boiler. She almost had to hold herself into the chair, because what she wanted to do was to get up, fling all her clothes aside, dance naked to the breeze up and down that porch, and cry out, "Come, *somebody,* come and get me . . ." It would be her form of fireworks, her celebration of independence. But who in the world would answer?

The question itself edged one of those unseen realities into the front of her mind: what she really felt about Hugh O'Donnell. You'd think that, with panic in the air, she'd be worrying like he was about the world. She wasn't. Her frustrated peevishness this morning was very personal. She found that she'd been hoping more than she could have imagined that Hugh's visit would cause something interesting to happen—she didn't know what—to ease the tedium, and now he'd gone off, like some prophet, to meditate. Damn. She'd tried for years now not to admit to herself that salving her sense of gratitude had little to do with her appreciation of Hugh's visits. Though nothing that wouldn't bear putting on a Sunday School stage had passed between them, she looked forward to their discussions and arguments, which were—how Amelia would have hated *this* thought—more man-to-man than man-to-woman. She found herself fascinated—aroused, to be honest—by his passion and energy, not to mention his good looks and beautiful voice. His sometimes crude language and cruder dress and his strange thinking made him a man as surely from another place in space and time as some of the Italians and Frenchmen she'd encountered on the Riviera in her days as a duchess. And then there was that other thing about him—that thing that always worried his sister Mary: Hugh was a man who could break things, and you could feel this latent power even when he was on his best behavior, as he'd been so far in Newport. Too bad that he was married, that he was "family" by virtue of Mary; that *she* was married, that she was probably in his eyes too old and certainly too rich to have any interest in him. Too bad and no doubt too impossible. Yet there were delicious minutes of fantasy when the wall of impossibility was shaken into rubble and she—

"Now is that any way for a lady to be sitting?"

347

She hadn't heard him or seen him come around the corner, across the soft grass. He was standing there below her looking straight up into her . . . She jumped to her feet, blushing like a girl. "What do you mean sneaking up on me like that? I thought you were off somewhere—thinking. No gentleman should—"

"Ah, but I'm no gentleman. Ask any man around here. As a matter of fact, I proper enjoyed the view."

Her embarrassment, the worse for having just been thinking about him, threatened to burn her up. "That's a brazen thing to say."

"Is it now? Is it really?" He came bounding up on the porch, and it was obvious from his grin that his mood had changed. "I've never had the nerve to say it before, but I'll say it now—you *are* a beautiful woman, and I'm sure you know it, or you'd never take such a risk."

"Aren't we being a little familiar?"

"And why not? We're relatives, aren't we? You can sit any way you like for all of me. You see, with me not being a gentleman, you don't have to worry when you're with me."

She was standing now in what she hoped was a fairly haughty pose, staring out to sea, but her skirts must still be mussed, and she was conscious of being in her stocking feet. It made her feel shorter and strangely more vulnerable when he came right up close to her, so close that she was aware of the smell of him, a faint and not unpleasant aroma of sweat he'd generated in pumping his bike. He took her hand and said, "I'm here, I came back—sneaked up on you if you like—because I want you to come with

348

me and see something."

She didn't want to look at the expression on his face, into his eyes, so she kept her gaze fixed on the little boats maneuvering for the race, as if she cared about boats. His hand holding hers was not insistent; it was just there, the strength in it palpable, waiting to be used. She ought to take her own away, but it might betray her fear . . . hope? "Now what could you possibly show me around here that I haven't seen in twenty years?"

"A cove," he said, "a little sandy cove. I'm sure you've never seen it—or any of your fancy friends either. A horse couldn't get within a mile of it. Can't even make it all the way on a bike. It's so guarded by rocks you gotta walk, but when you get there it's like bein' at the end of the world . . . out of the world . . . nothin' in front of you but the sea . . . nothin' behind you but the dunes and rocks . . . nothin' around you but the gulls wheeling and screaming and dropping their shells . . ."

"My, you sound like you're trying to be a poet, Hugh. But what makes you think I'd care about a place like that? I can see all of the sea I want to right from here. What happened to all that thinking you were going to do about the system falling apart or whatever it was?"

"I've done it, done it, I tell you," he said, and now his grip was tighter, more personal. "That's why I want you to come with me. I was sittin' there looking out at the end of the world, and I decided, what the hell, everything's got to end, so I *am* going to lead that march. We're gonna walk all the way down there to Washington and tell fat Governor Cleveland that he'd better feed us—or else. But I don't know whether I'll ever come back. The police were breaking heads in Union Square when we were just talking about it, and God knows what Grover's troops will do when we try to get into the White House. Nothing scares the crap out of—sorry, but you know I'm no gentleman."

Nobody had ever used a word like that in her presence but, like his frank stare, it did remove him completely from the category of gentleman, and the thing was, she liked it, felt a contagious earthiness about him, and it relieved her from that awful burden of being a *lady*. "Don't apologize, don't stop . . ." She returned the pressure of his hand, turning to face him. This was the Hugh that aroused her, the Hugh on fire. She could feel the heat running right up her arm.

"Well, nothing scares them fat politicians like a bunch of hungry working men who ain't going to take it no more, and they'll probably shoot out of pure fright. But I'm going, and I just couldn't go without . . . well, so I came back."

"Without what? What are you trying to say?"

"You know. Neither of us is exactly a babe. I've felt it every time I came up here and been with you, but I . . . but it's taken something like this to—"

"If you're saying what I think you're trying to say, you shouldn't. I'm a married woman, and you're a married man. What you're thinking about is a sin, isn't it? You're a good Catholic and—"

"I'm not a good anything, but even if I was, all I'd have to do was confess, and I can tell you that priest of ours would get a kick out of me, Hugh O'Donnell,

350

having his way with a lady in Newport—"

"Hugh, how can you talk to me like that?" Now she was enjoying it.

"Like what? I'm just being honest, and I figured you long ago for a woman who can't be fooled, and that's why I . . . why I especially like you. One reason, anyway."

"But what about your wife?"

"This has nothing to do with me and her. I give her what I can, but I ain't been to bed with her for a year of Sundays, because every time we do we get another kid, and we can't afford any more, and she won't . . . well, you know. And don't tell me you give a damn about that Pierce. I've seen you together, and he ain't man enough for you. C'mon, Sally, come with me—*now* while all those fools are shooting arrows and won't miss us. You won't regret it, I promise."

Oh, God. No more play-acting . . . Was this what she wanted? Yes, oh, *yes*—and no, oh, *no*. He started pulling her, and she started following him, forgetting even to put on her shoes. When they came around the house she saw that he'd already got her bicycle built for two out of the barn and parked it by the path. He swung his leg over the rear seat, patted the saddle in front. "Get up." Like someone in a trance, she obeyed, and they started pedaling, and Hugh started singing.

The cove, as he'd said, was a long way from where they had to park the bike, because they could no longer make headway in the sandy loam. She got along fairly well until they reached the rocks that bit painfully into her tender feet. Hugh swung her up

351

into his arms, without gasp or strain, cradling her in strength, and carried her. When they reached a point where they could see the little beach, he stopped. "Now, ain't that fine?" he asked. It was fine—a miniature half-moon curve of soft sand that, like the bike, seemed built just for two. She nodded. And then he kissed her for the first time.

When they reached the beach, Hugh, with those powerful thighs of his, managed to ease down on the sand with her still in his arms, on his lap now. "Look around," he said. "Isn't it like I told you—not a soul, not a sight, not even the roof peak of a house to be seen. We couldn't be more alone up on the moon."

He was right. What now? Churning with a mix of fear and anticipation, she found it hard to breathe, let alone speak. It was so quiet that he must be able to hear the rattling of her heart.

Hugh, thank God, was purposeful, a man who could lead marches. "What we gotta do first is get them combs out of your hair. I want to see what it's really like. Bend over a little and I'll help . . ."

Big as his hands were, his fingers were deft, practiced. "You seem to know what you're doing," she said for lack of other words.

"And why shouldn't I? Help with my little Kathleen when the missus is busy. We've got no fancy maids, you know."

This glimpse of his domesticity should have been chilling. Instead she found it strangely warming, a frankness that kept whatever was happening now in the context of their other lives. Her hair was free, falling the length of her back. Stroking it, he said,

352

"Pure gold, it is—I might have known . . ." He turned her face to his and kissed her again, gently at first, then harder until her lips were apart and she felt his tongue searching hers and felt that melt down below that had so often been a torture, an invitation to a waltz that was never played. She was ready for him, but there was all that armor. She felt him fumbling with the buttons at her back; the corset was more than he could manage. "Stand up," he ordered, "we gotta get you out of this here chastity belt . . ."

The idea of her being chaste struck her as funny, and she laughed, and the laughter released some tension, eased the urgency. "That's better," he said. "That laugh of yours—it gives me the shivers. Here, look, I'm no good at this—you gotta help."

"Oh, you don't undress ladies every day?"

"Never. Never before, I swear. The missus . . . well, c'mon, hurry."

Quite suddenly, she who had wanted to hurry, wanted to linger. She'd gone too far to go back, wouldn't go back, but she wanted more than just to be taken, entered . . . A man who could break things could break her too. "Hugh," she said, "if we're going to do this, let's . . . well, let's do something different—"

"What do you mean?"

"Let's play a little. Do you know what I'm going to do when I get out of these clothes? I'm going to dance on the beach—the way nature made me. I've always wanted to do that ever since I was a little girl, but there was never the right place. Or time. You found that for me, Hugh."

"You're kind of crazy, you know that?"

She stripped quickly then. The rocks rimming the cove broke the breeze. The sun and sand were warm. Her body crawled with a sensation she couldn't describe; her breasts stiffened. Hugh couldn't stand it. He tried to grab her. She danced away. He lunged. She ran, and was faster than he with bare feet in sand. She ran straight into the water. It was flesh-shocking cold but she splashed out to where she could plunge in and start swimming. Usually swathed in yards of cloth when she bathed, she'd never known such tingling exhilaration, such *freedom*. Hugh was standing on the shore looking at her, shaking his head, his fist. "Come back," he yelled.

"Come get me."

"I can't, I'd get my clothes wet—"

"How romantic. Come on, coward, take them off. I did."

"I can't . . . I mean I can't swim."

"Then you are out of luck . . . it's so lovely I could stay all day—"

"You'll catch your death—"

"No, I won't. I'm used to swimming."

"All right. Damn you, I'll get you if it kills me . . ."

Idling there, paddling to stay afloat, she watched as he began to undress. For all her marriages and affairs, she'd never quite had this experience. There'd always been dressing rooms or bathrooms, nightshirts and silk robes, low lights or darkness to guard against nakedness as if it were the greater of the sins between the sexes. It was touching to see how Hugh, despite his urgency, carefully folded his shirt as he took it off, then his trousers. It reminded her that they were his good clothes, perhaps his only good clothes. She saw him shyly turn his back when he slipped off his drawers. His body was as muscled as a Greek statue in a museum—and as white. She'd never seen such white skin; it looked as if it had never been touched by light, much less sun, and, like the folding of his clothes, it spoke of that existence in the city's near slums, so different from all she knew. When he turned, she could see why he'd been shy. His member stood defiantly erect, very unlike that on any statue. He ran into the water as fast as he could, screaming from the shock, as if he'd hit fire instead of ice. As soon as he was covered to the waist, he slowed down, began wading, complaining about the cold and begging her to come in. "You've had your fun, you don't know what this has done to me . . ."

She could imagine, but she stayed tauntingly out of his depth. Finally, with water up to his chin, he tried to swim to her, flailing so that she knew he'd never swum before. His head went under; he came up gasping, spitting. She swam to him as fast as she could. "Stay still, I'll save you," she said. She crooked an arm under his jaw, dragged him the few strokes back to where they could stand. Still clutching her and choking, he said, "Jesus, you *are* killing me. If I don't drown, I'll die of the cold."

"No, you won't," she said. "Let's run."

She waded as fast as she could, then ran, kicking high and splashing toward the beach. He followed, calling, "Wait, *wait*, damn you." As soon as they reached the sand he grabbed her, held her against him, head to toe. He was shivering, but not for long. Whatever the water had done to him, her body undid, and she could feel his penis rise, hot and probing against the soft cool of her belly. He released her, went down on his knees. "God, you are beautiful. You're all gold—gold here too . . ."

He was toying with, smoothing the damp bronze tuft of hair that covered the mound between her thighs. He buried his face in the curly mass, and she could feel the tongue that had found her tongue, searching again in other yielding lips. The melt inside her was more than she could stand. Her knees gave way. He caught her, hoisted her over his shoulder and carried her to where her dress was spread out on the sand. When he stretched her out, caressing and kissing, cupping her taut nipples with his lips, her legs fell apart, her hips thrust up as she defiantly, joyously opened up to him, to the breeze, to the sun, to that incredibly blue sky. Even before he came into her, what she'd fantasized began, and then as he filled her it became an internal volcano, erupting, overwhelming . . .

She never, never wanted it to stop, and even though the flame subsided she was still a smouldering crater. He rolled off her, over onto the sand, saying over and over again, "Jesus, Mary and Joseph." It was a kind of prayer, she knew, not at all like that other prayer she'd once heard from the lips of a spent man. She felt a need for another sort of communication, but she didn't know the right words, and so she asked, "Are you still cold, Hugh?"

"No. Oh, lord, *no* . . . I've never known it could

be like this. Have . . . have you—?"

"No, I've never . . . never like this before."

"Never known a woman to either. You're some woman."

"Hugh?"

"What?"

"If it's so good . . . I mean, if we both . . . well, why don't we just do it again?"

"Sweet Jesus, don't you know what you do to a man? Look at me . . ."

She did. She propped herself up on an arm, looked at the white, muscled, marbled reach of him. Then she made herself look, really look at what had so filled her. It lay limp, lifeless. Impulse, instinct, need seized her. She rolled over, took it in her hand, slid back the soft sheath of skin, exposed the red bud. She bent and kissed it. To her astonishment it was silken, and smelling of a strange musk. And then her kiss brought it to life, and it rose, hard, sure. She vaulted over him, sucked it into her. Her mouth closed over his, and her tongue went searching. His hands, hot against the cool cheeks of her buttocks, were hard too in their urgency, pulling her down, until she was filled again. It was terrible, intolerable, she was moaning, crying, and it was wonderful, an ecstasy, and in the instant of ultimate eruption, everything went black, pure black . . .

It was she who collapsed, sprawled over him uttering little sounds, taking little gasps of air. She was spent and content, wishing she didn't have to come out of the fire-strewn dark. Gradually, though, she was aware of the warm sun on her back, of the moist joining of their bodies, of the lap of waves against the sand, of the mew of gulls, of the rise and fall of their locked ribs, of the separate beating of their hearts. "I want to stay here forever, want you to stay in me forever . . ."

"Ah, God, it don't work like that," Hugh said. And it didn't. She could feel him involuntarily leaving her, disappearing. The physical certainty that it was all over made her shiver a little, and he felt it.

"I hate to say it, luv, but it's best we get dressed and go back. Don't want them to miss us too long."

She clung to him. "*No.* I want to stay here forever. Oh, Hugh, this is such a lovely place . . ."

"I know . . . well, we can come back . . ."

"When? Another year? I can't wait. Can you? Tell me you can't wait."

"It's sure as hell I don't want to, but—"

"No 'buts,' Hugh, please no 'buts.' We'll work it out, Hugh. Won't we? Tell me we will."

"Sure, luv . . ."

That "luv" again. It was as close to an endearment as he'd uttered, but she treasured it because it had crept so naturally into his speech. As she dressed, she found sand in everything—her hair, her dress, her stockings; her girdle ground against her like a hair shirt; her skin was itchy-sticky with salt from the sea. But what would normally have been irritating discomfort was, in her present mood, a welcome, tangible reminder that she'd at last known in the flesh what had barely existed in her imagination. She even welcomed the sensation of the sharp rocks against her feet as they made their way toward the bike. Hugh wanted to carry her

358

again, but she told him, "I think I wore you out, poor man." She said it with a straight face, then smiled delightedly.

"Well, I'll admit right now I'd have a hard time going a round with a wet noodle. . . . Hey, look, what's that up there? Up by the bike."

Standing in the shade of the tree against which they'd leaned their bike was a figure as surprising to see out in this remote point of land as a fireplug in a desert. Squat, chunky, black-suited, derby-hatted, he was unmistakably a city man. "I smell cop," Hugh said. "What the hell can *he* be doing here?" As soon as they reached him, the man, without greeting or so much as tipping his hat to Sally, grabbed Hugh's hand and stuck an envelope into it. "What the hell *is* this?" Hugh asked.

"Summons—for court appearance in New York Monday the week," the man said.

"For what?"

"Trespassing, inciting to riot, striking an officer of the law. Few other charges I can't remember. Best come along with me, O'Donnell!"

Hugh had opened the envelope and was looking at the papers. "Why? All this says is that I have to be in court."

"I've another paper here," the man said, opening his coat to fish it out of an inner pocket and revealing a gun strapped under his arm. "It's a warrant for your arrest—"

"No good, I'm not in New York State. Now, if you'll excuse us, I have a lady to take home—"

"Wait a minute, buddy. I been to the judge here in town and got another warrant. Mighty mad he was

I made him miss the parade until he saw what you're charged with. He don't want any radicals around Newport. Now you come along nice like, and I won't have to use these . . ."

From another pocket, the man produced a clanking pair of handcuffs.

"Why, you . . ." Hugh said.

"Don't get yourself in more trouble, Hugh. *Please*," Sally said.

"Okay, O'Donnell," the man said, grabbing the bike. "You ride in front. I woulda kept the hack that brought me out here, but they don't pay no expense for waiting. We just got time to make the last train."

"But the lady . . ."

The man looked her up and down with street-wise eyes, and Sally could feel herself blushing. The rumpled sandy dress, the hair she'd only vaguely pinned up, the stockinged feet. She was sure he didn't miss a detail, and she was suddenly and acutely conscious of how her idyll would appear to other eyes.

"Lady, is it? Too bad about her. She can walk— teach her to consort with criminals. Now, come on. Make that train and you can have dinner in the Tombs. They say it's special on Fourth of July."

Hugh took her hand. "Jesus, Sally, I—"

She shut him off with a kiss. "Don't try to say anything, Hugh. Go. Go now. I'll be all right. And don't *you* worry. I'll get Aaron. He's a lawyer now, you know . . ."

Through the mind of Aaron Roberts Van Alen kept running the rather cheap and sentimental tune and phrases of the latest popular song: ". . . many's the heart that's broken; many's the tear will fall; many's the word unspoken, after the ball . . ." Particularly when he was alone like this out on the boat, his mind was often filled with music. Generally, though, it was of a higher order—strains from some symphony or, at the very least one of Gilbert and Sullivan's witty ditties. The workings of the mind being mysterious, Aaron never knew why any given melody seized his since so often the music seemed to have little or nothing to do with his moods or thoughts. Like the stuff of dreams, it was fragmentary, evanescent, unrelated to reality. Yet on this trip, this song was quite clearly a trite expression of the emotions with which he was trying to deal. For Aaron, the ball was over.

He was so unsettled, in fact, by what was happening, not around him, but inside him that he couldn't enjoy sailing. He'd been out of Newport a week now and had simply been lying to anchor all that time in a sheltered spot he'd found in the lee of Fisher's Island. Drained mentally and physically by preparing for the bar examiners, full of the fine points of torts and contracts, writs and warrants, motions and pleadings, he hadn't the energy to work the boat nor the desire to make decisions about where to go and when. Better just to lie here, let the days roll over him, kill time with the busy work of feeding himself, polishing the brass and holystoning the teak decks, catching an occasional flounder to freshen his diet, taking an occasional walk on the island to stretch his legs. He was so averse to focused thought that he didn't even open the books he'd brought along—a couple of novels by William Dean Howells and Henry James and Mark Twain's *Following the Equator*. He thought that he ought to find some lesson for himself in contemplating Twain's troubles. The book lying there unread in *Cathay*'s cabin had grown out of the lecture tour Twain took around the world in an effort to pay off the debts he'd been saddled with by the failure of that publishing firm he'd so successfully started with the memoirs that saved Grant's family. Good writer as he was, Twain was continually losing his shirt in one business after another, which would suggest that a man seeking fulfillment, success, happiness, or however you wanted to define what men sought, should concentrate on what he knew he could do, find whatever talent he had, and, as the parable preached, multiply it. At least part of Aaron's unsettling had to do with the fact that at thirty-five—halfway along man's allotted span—he still hadn't discovered a true talent to invest.

This business about taking up the law which his family and friends obviously considered quixotic had been, as he'd once told Sally because he thought that she might understand, mostly inventing another challenge. It had been exhilarating at first to be using his mind instead of his body, but he wasn't sure yet what else he'd hoped for. He hadn't, of course, been wholly serious in suggesting that his goal was to prepare himself to represent Van Alen interests; it had been the only practical way of keeping his salary coming in, of maintaining some sort of peace within the family while he turned his mind to study. He guessed that, given a vague and gnawing urge to do something more and different with his life, the law seemed a logical path to take. The law was the only profession, other than the ministry, with which Schuylers and Van Alens had ever been involved, and he'd probably buried in his subconscious his grandmother's reminiscences about her half-brother, the lawyer and senator, Peter Schuyler, and about her good friend, almost her adopted father, Aaron Burr. Lawyers were giants in the land back in those days, the makers of America, and perhaps it was some hope that mastering the mysteries of the law would confer on him similar stature that had motivated him. Whatever, in actual fact it had become a matter more of mastering techniques than mysteries; of learning a language, really, a language that seemed more designed to obscure than enlighten, like the Latin the priests used in church. Worse, his observation of the law as practiced in a firm like Judge Parson's, whose clients ran only to the rich and successful, convinced him that legal technique could be as conscienceless as a steel tool, shaping only what the hand that held it desired. It was common in cynical banter around the firm for somebody to quote old Commodore Vanderbilt— "What do I care about the law? Hain't I got the power?"—or brother James' friend, J. P. Morgan— "Well, I don't know as I want a lawyer to tell me what I cannot do. I hire him to tell me how to do what I want to do." James would expect this of him, but would he, could he, give it? Or should he, now that he had at last a means of making his way on his own, get out? There was no clear answer to these questions. While he'd been able to absorb the technique of the law through study, he was far from sure that law was what he was seeking.

Even more baffling was what he called in his own mind, the Mary question. It would seem on the surface that everything he'd hoped for ten years ago when he'd wooed and won her had come to pass. Physically she was still a marvel. That body she'd molded by dancing had withstood births well—four of them now—and years of relatively soft living had enhanced her by a further rounding of her hips and belly, more fullness in her breasts. Just looking at her, contemplating making love to her, could still excite him, and in this, as he knew from offhand remarks they made, other married men might call him blessed. What they wouldn't know, what he prayed nobody would ever know, was how seldom and now how meagerly the arousal she stirred in him was gratified. The grounds on which she'd eased him out of her bed were hard to fault, especially since she insisted that it had no bearing on her love for him. Basically, it had to do with her still being "a good Catholic girl" who, after what happened to little Aaron, hadn't wanted more children. The conception of Felicia had been an accident, a heedless romp after they'd both had too much champagne at the Jones wedding a year ago. Proving that her discipline hadn't deserted her, Mary had given up drinking entirely after that; he'd started drinking more.

As in the days of their courtship, arguing with Mary was usually a losing proposition. If she didn't have logic on her side, she always had religion to fall back on. How could that girl who'd been the perfect bedmate for so long, that giggling hoyden more likely than he to invite with her mischievous eyes a night of love, change so? Other women lost children more tragically when they were old enough to have personalities, and all the doctors, even the priest, had assured Mary that there was nothing she or anybody else could have done to avert Aaron's death—babies smothered in cribs every day for reasons nobody understood. But Mary had taken it as a divine sign that she shouldn't have more children. At first Aaron, grieving himself over the loss of a son bearing his name, had accepted Mary's feeling as some odd manifestation of her own grief which would subside, as grief had a way of doing. Since Mary had had little trouble delivering children, logic suggested that eventually another child would be the right way to fill the void left by baby Aaron. After an abstinence appropriate to mourning, during which Aaron thought it the decent thing to do to sleep temporarily in another room, he had finally come to Mary one night.

She had acted as if he were an invading thief, sitting up, pulling the covers tight around her. "What are you doing here, what are you doing here . . . ?"

"Well, I *am* your husband—"

"Aaron, how can you do this when . . . when you know how I feel about another baby?"

"But we don't have to have a baby—just yet. I can . . . well, take precautions."

"Oh, no, Aaron, no. That's a sin and you know it."

"Mary, Mary. Are you trying to say that we can never again . . . ?"

"Would that be so bad? We have Amelia, and we have Francis, and . . . oh, Aaron I just have this terrible feeling that if we have another, something will happen."

"But there's more to it than having babies, Mary. There's us. I mean unless you're a little deceiver, I've always thought that you—"

"Oh, I have, Aaron, honestly I have. But don't you see that it was always right—we were married, we wanted babies . . ."

"Good lord, Mary, I don't think I can stand this."

"You can always find someone who—"

"Mary, you don't mean that. I haven't looked at another woman since the day I met you. It's only you I want. I happen to love *you*."

"I love you, too, darling, you know that. But we can't always have everything the way we want . . ."

"Honey. I don't know what this thing in your head is. We *ought* to have another child. Even Father O'Brien told you so."

She began to cry. "Maybe sometime Aaron, but not now, not *now* . . ."

The urge just to take her, to assert his conjugal rights and plant a stubborn fact in her belly that would do away with her odd fancy was almost more than he could control. But then she suddenly disarmed him by throwing back the covers and inviting him in beside her. "Hold me, Aaron, hold me," she said. "Maybe I'm silly, but I'm so afraid— afraid of losing you too. Just hold me." He did, and in desperation he taught her hand what to do, and it became their inadequate and infrequent substitute for love until that one unplanned night that had left a heavy hangover having nothing to do with champagne. When she found herself pregnant she was furious with herself, with him, furious and terrified. For more than a year there hadn't been even a sad substitute for love. When Felicia was delivered, Mary turned the baby over to a nurse and nanny as if she feared that her own touch would contaminate the child. Although Felicia thrived, Mary couldn't seem to rid herself of her apprehensions, apprehensions that she shared only with Aaron.

It was a peculiarity of Mary's aberration, or whatever one wanted to call it, that it didn't seem to affect the rest of her life. Publicly she held her head high, as *the* young Mrs. Van Alen should, and whirled like a sparkler through the dinners, the dances, the appearances at the opera and Philharmonic, the morning calls and afternoon teas that used up her time. Any apprehension that Aaron had had about their living with his mother had long since evaporated as Mary had shown herself a willing pupil to the older woman in all matters having to do with the social graces. She'd won her mother-in-law so completely that one night when Aaron and Martha were sitting out a dance at a costume ball and watching Mary, expensively garbed as Marie Antoinette, waltz with a supposed King Henry VIII, Martha had said, "You know, Aaron, I was wrong about your Mary. Look at her out there—the perfect image of a queen. You'd hardly guess she was Irish," and then had squeezed his hand and added, "I should have known that you inherited your taste from me. I've never understood what went wrong with Sally . . ."

About the only thing on which the women sometimes disagreed was the rearing of the children. Indulgent with her own children, Martha was grandmotherly easy on Amelia and Francis, but Mary, as if determined that no Irish would ever show through, was coldly strict with them about everything from cleanliness, to table manners, to grammar. When it came to the children, Mary could even bend her religion; she did take them with her to mass, but she entered them in private Protestant schools with their social peers. And in the past year or so, the James Van Alens had taken to including Mary and Aaron in some of their Sunday night suppers, very nearly the highest accolade to Mary's performance as the perfect Van Alen wife. It was, Aaron had to admit, a rather astonishing achievement. As to that other business, he really ought to feel compassion for her, ought to be patient . . .

Well, he was trying, *damned* if he wasn't. Whatever he decided to do with it now, the study of the law had helped him in this; he'd been left with far less time to feel his frustration. Indeed, absenting himself from Mary's bed had given him the long hours of the night when he'd done most of his studying. At first he'd tried to borrow time by dodging all of those, to him, increasingly boring social occasions, but the effort had brought down on him such a storm from both Mary and his mother that he'd found it easier to go along. He'd been so agreeable, in fact, that any effort to work his own will was now viewed by the women as some regression in character. This sailing business, for instance. "I can't imagine what you do out there all alone on that boat, Aaron," his mother had once said. "It isn't normal. Why, the last time you came in you hadn't even shaved. I don't know why Mary puts up with it. Your father never did anything like that." Mary was closer to the truth when she said, "Sometimes I think you're just trying to get away from me, Aaron. It isn't like you." . . . Well, to hell with them; this *he* needed. God, he could be doing what so many other men in their close circle were doing—men like Pierce, escaping with booze and other women. The fact that Mary had even suggested such behavior still hurt, and the fact that he felt himself in danger of booze was worrisome. He needed somebody else at least to exchange his feelings with. He hadn't been surprised that his idle clubmates and most of his family looked on his desire to make a lawyer of himself as a touch odd in view of his already, on the surface, enviable position in life, but he'd been disappointed that Mary had been no more understanding than the rest.

The incident that brought out her feelings was a trivial one, as such incidents usually were. Early on, just after he'd started reading law in the judge's office, she'd surprised him by coming down to join him at breakfast. Except for an aging Patrick quietly fussing at the sideboard where he miraculously kept eggs and bacon, sausage and wheat cakes, coffee and tea, renewed and warmed over little spirit lamps, they could have been playing roles in one of those middle-class domestic dramas where the loving wife saw her husband off to work that Aaron knew only from the stage, and he liked the sense of belonging to the sober workaday majority of the human race that it gave him. Moreover, it was one of those days in early March when spring, ahead of its season, was softening and shining the hard, smoke-smudged facades of a city that had shut itself up against winter. Aaron had already decided to make the most of the weather by walking all the way to the office, and he knew just how Mary felt when she said, "It's such a lovely day, I just couldn't stay in bed."

"Yes, isn't it? What are you going to do with yourself?"

"Well, that's why I wanted to get up and catch you before you left. I think it would be a grand day to get the carriage out and take the children for a picnic in the park or maybe up to that wonderful place in Westchester where we went coaching. We all so need the air after this dreadful winter."

"Fine, that sounds fine. I'm sure George would be glad to get the carriage, all oiled up and ready for spring, and the horses need a real run too."

"Oh, I wasn't thinking of George. I thought you'd drive. We'd just have a family day."

"But, Mary, I have to work—"

"On a day like this? Don't be ridiculous, Aaron."

"Judge Parsons doesn't pay his law clerks for picnicking in the park—"

"Pooh. Judge Parsons works for *you*, for Van Alen, and you know it. If you can't spend a nice day like this with your family, I think you're carrying this thing too far."

"Mary, I'm serious. I'm trying to become a lawyer and—"

"Well, I just don't know why. You don't have to be a lawyer, or anything else. We have everything we want already, and when your mother dies—"

"God, Mary—"

"Oh, don't be so touchy. I'm not saying I want your mother to die. Why, she's just like my own mother now. You can see that. I'm just trying to get you to take a sensible view of things. As you yourself admit, we're going to be quite wealthy so why—"

"So why work? Why try to do something on my own? I'd think you of all people would understand that. I never saw anybody who worked like you did."

"But I *had* to. Can't you see the difference? What's the use of having everything if you can't enjoy it?"

"Ah, Mary, I was feeling so good when I saw you come in here this morning. I thought you just wanted to be with me a while before I had to go to work, the way ordinary couples do. It made me feel good, as though I . . . as though we . . . oh, forget it."

"I certainly won't . . . Let me tell you something . . . I didn't marry you to live like ordinary couples. I didn't think I was marrying a drudge. I thought I was marrying a gentleman, a sportsman. Well, go to your work, but I surely hope you get over this . . . whatever it is. . . ."

That had, so far as he could tell, pretty much remained Mary's attitude: he was afflicted with something he'd just "get over." To be fair, it was the same attitude he had about her fear of having children, except he didn't really believe the two were comparable. They settled for avoiding conflict by keeping silence on these sensitive subjects, thereby drifting apart in mind and spirit as well as body. The fact that Mary sensed in his sailing a concrete expression of that drift would seem to indicate that she might be as aware as he was of this, but neither of them were able to bring it out into the open. "After the Ball" with its maudlin sentiment was not to have been for him and Mary, who'd overcome so much in making a marriage in the first place. And yet . . . .

The Mary question. Who was Mary, *what* was she? And could he still love her? The unsettling inside him, not unlike the restless motion of the boat dancing to her anchor under him, had a lot to do with not wanting to acknowledge the answers to these questions that pressed on him. The steely purpose, the shining purity he'd found dazzling in the young Mary was proving to be cold metal. Mary quite clearly knew what *she* wanted—she wanted to be *the* Mrs. Van Alen when Martha was gone—and there was little she wouldn't sacrifice to get what she wanted. Aaron couldn't help feeling deep suspicions that the business about baby Aaron was either a conscious or unconscious ploy on Mary's part to avoid the fate of her sister-in-law Anne, who'd given James six children and who, as a result, had taken on the skeletal look of a woman drained of flesh and vitality and the harried temperament of a woman overwhelmed with the responsibility for other lives. For all her Sunday night suppers and her famous Fourth of July archery party, Anne was losing the social race to Mary. Aaron had reason to know that the men who envied him and Mary felt sorry for James: though obviously worthy and wealthy, poor Anne was turning into very nearly a hag and certainly a bore with nothing on her mind but all those children. Never close enough to James to discuss these matters, Aaron could only speculate on whether James had been in Anne's bed these last several years since the appearance of the last baby. Probably not, even though James didn't have the Catholic business to contend with. There'd never been much visible passion in that marriage which had been arranged and conducted on James' part, at least, like a successful and profitable business. Sometimes Anne in her mousy way revealed a disappointment, even a flash of anger over James' devotion to the real business of his life, making money, but in the end she'd have to acknowledge that he was faithful and the perfect model of a father, which was more than could be said for most men. Those Sunday night invitations could be looked on as Anne's acknowledgment of another bit of reality: Mary's inevitable social victory. As a result Mary and Anne were beginning to behave something like sisters, sharing child-raising and servant and decorating problems, and establishing a growing family unity that any observer would consider heart-warming. By dint of simply and persistently being nice to her, Mary had even overcome Cousin Sophie's traumatic prejudice against her Irish background; she was, in fact, achieving a minor miracle where others had failed by getting Sophie, heavily veiled, to go out with her for rides in Newport or on shopping expeditions in the city. With her usual candor, Sophie offered an explanation for this phenomenon: "Mary's so striking that nobody would even look at me when I'm with her." When Aaron wanted to know what Mary found to talk about with the old recluse, the answer was quick and simple: "The Van Alens. She knows more about your family than you could imagine. Did you know that your father hated his brother, and your mother eloped with your father, and your sister had . . . well, a premature baby. And—?" Aaron laughed. "So we're not perfect. So what?" And Mary had said, "But it's fascinating. Why didn't you tell me all these things? It makes me feel so much more comfortable being a Van Alen. Sometimes I think I may even be better than a Van Alen . . ."

A rather haunting thought, that. Better than a Van Alen? In view of what all the Van Alens had once said about her, in view of her own fears about meeting the family and her sensitive shiverings at every slight, her near-arrogance now had to be seen as a kind of miracle, wrought by his own hands as if he were a latter-day Pygmalion. His creation had, however, got clearly out of hand. She had a life of her own that had nothing to do with him. Whether she simply took his love for granted or, like the female of some animal species that instinctively eschewed the male once he'd served her, Mary had, subtly at first and openly now, exhibited more concern for the approval of the audience she was playing to than for his. The closer she approached society's glittering throne, the more she seemed to view him as little more than a necessary consort. In the context of both the family and the social circles in which they moved, Mary's behavior could be seen as completely normal, even exemplary in a woman who, passing thirty and mother to three children, had entered that matronly stage where she was expected to assume responsibility for the social success of the family and, by inference, the future of her children. And so Mary was able to wrap herself in virtue. Above and beyond her unreasoned, mystical faith in the teachings of the true church was society's sanction. When recently they'd come home from a ball and Aaron, stimulated by the dancing and probably too much brandy, had asked, damn near pleaded once more, Mary had pirouetted in front of her mirror, tossing off pieces of clothing, and said, "Poor Aaron. Can't you ever get *that* out of your head? I thought you had, and I've been so happy lately. You really ought to be proud of me— *I've* kept my figure. If you noticed, I didn't sit out a dance." Aaron had slammed out of the room, saying, "Only the most important one . . ."

Mary *was* happy, or seemed so, and he *ought* to be proud of her, not only her looks but her achievement, and he probably *should* get *that* out of his mind. There was nobody among his friends and family he dared talk to about a thing like this, but he had gone to Father O'Brien in hope that the priest might work with Mary. It was a mistake . . . "Well, my son, it will work out in God's good time," the priest had said. "She did have a child, didn't she? (Aaron hadn't mentioned the champagne.) I think you ought to admire your wife for the strength of her faith. A little self-denial is good for the soul, I can assure you." Yes, no doubt he should admire Mary. Hell, *everybody* did.

Everybody, that is, who didn't need her as he felt he needed her. Her family, for instance. Aaron had gotten closer to Hugh since he'd been coming up to Newport to visit Sally. As much as anything he'd been doing Mary a favor in keeping Hugh out of the way by taking him sailing or exhibiting his talents in the best light, but in the process he'd picked up hints from Hugh about the family's rather bitter feelings about Mary. True, she'd been playing lady bountiful to them; she'd been giving Hugh's wife a regular monthly stipend for the care of old Frank, which was sometimes all that kept them going, and she'd set Jack up in the saloon, and she'd seen to it that the other boys didn't starve if they were laid off. But when she'd blow in on a duty visit, all smelling of perfume and fluttering with flowers, she'd make it clear that the quid pro quo for her bounty was that they would keep away from her. She'd been furious when Hugh had accepted Sally's invitation but had tried to make her smiling best of it, as she'd thought that a Van Alen lady should. If the way Hugh had carried it all off had softened her a bit, it had also upset her. "I just hope he doesn't get any big ideas," she'd told Aaron. "You know Hugh as well as I do, and you know he doesn't really belong here. I don't know what's got into him, but I'm sure one of these times he'll do something to embarrass us. I'm just so nervous when he's around. . . ." And Hugh had told Aaron: "That Sally's all right. I feel great with her, but—would you believe it?—not with my own sister. I can just tell she can't wait to get me out of her sight. Oh, I admire her, I do, for the way she's wrapping all these swells around her little finger, and I ain't surprised. She had dad and me and my brothers going good too when she was little. But now, you know, I don't think she'd care if we all dropped dead." Hard words, but Aaron suspected there was more than a little truth in them. He wondered how it was going back in Newport this holiday with him away. Probably Mary would find ways to avoid her brother entirely. Well, Sally would take care of him . . .

Lying there in the cockpit idling the afternoon away in the sun and arriving at no good conclusions, Aaron glanced at his watch. About time for the races to be ending, the archery party would be in full swing. Imagining himself back there, in the heart of useless activity, muttering polite and meaningless words, Aaron was shaken by a deep, involuntary yawn. Yes, the ball was over—wouldn't that damned song *ever* go away?—and for the first time in his life Aaron suspected he could understand how it was that some men came to kill themselves. He wouldn't do that. And he wouldn't act like brother-in-law Pierce, whoring after other women, although he'd more than once been damned tempted. Who knew . . . ? Right now he only knew that tomorrow he'd go sailing, whatever the weather. He'd head east, out of the Sound, out beyond Block Island, out into the ocean where there'd be nothing in any direction but a curved horizon. He wasn't expected back in Newport for a week yet, and he had water and provisions for a longer time than that. By the time they knew he'd gone, nobody would be able to find or follow him. He should have brought more money, but no matter. The *Cathay* would somehow provide for him, if survival was in the cards for them both. Right now, he ought to lay in a supply of fresh fish.

While Aaron was bending over his lines, baiting his hooks, he heard the *Pride of the Sea* before he saw her. No special surprise, though not a pleasant one, to have a large steam yacht seek out the secure anchorage he'd found along toward sundown of a holiday like this. It was only when, studying her, he recognized the familiar shape of the Hancock boat that he was truly surprised. With Pierce generally half comatose from drink by noon every day, the *Pride of the Sea* hadn't been off her mooring all summer, and Aaron would have supposed that she was by now firmly and forever fixed to the bottom by living ropes of weed and barnacle. Yet on she came. Why here? Soon Aaron could make out two figures through the large windows of her pilot house. The little gnarled one at the wheel had to be the paid hand Pierce kept aboard to polish up the brass. The other was female, tall and blond. Though her face was masked by the binoculars she held to her eyes, he knew that it was Sally. God, something terrible must have happened in Newport, because she'd obviously come out to find him.

Churning and thumping, the *Pride of the Sea* came alongside *Cathay*. No words were exchanged as Aaron scrambled around securing the lines that Sally tossed over to him. When he handed her aboard, she hugged him. "Thank God I found you, Aaron—"

"What is it? Mother? Mary? One of the kids?"

"No, no, nothing like that. Aaron, Hugh O'Donnell's in terrible trouble."

Aaron had never before been in the Tombs, never talked to a prisoner. The dinginess of the surroundings, the bars he and Hugh had to converse through, the impersonality of Hugh's prison garb made painfully concrete the problem he had to address himself to. "You know I'm new at this, Hugh. I could get you another lawyer . . ."

"Naw, rather have you," Hugh said. "Probably isn't much you can do for me anyway. What about bail?"

"I tried, Hugh, right away, but the judge refused it. He said that radicals like you are notorious for jumping bail and disappearing. I'm afraid he wants to make some kind of object lesson out of you. So do the police, of course. To hear them talk, you'd think that by putting you away they're nipping some damned revolution in the bud . . . They aren't, are they?"

"Hell, no. You know me, Aaron. Ever heard me talk revolution? I just thought that a bunch of us ought to go down to Washington and make ourselves heard. All I've ever wanted is what a man deserves for his work."

Aaron nodded. "The only good news is that I've managed to get a jury trial. In times like these a lot of citizens have sympathy for your point of view. Now let's get at the facts. At least *I've* got to know the

379

truth. Did you hit an officer of the law?"

"Naw. At least I don't think so. I mean when they started coming in at us swinging clubs, there was a hell of a mess. All of us, including me, were just doing our damnedest to get away, and I won't deny that there was a lot of shoving and some fists flying, but—"

"Any witnesses? Any friends of yours who would speak up for you?"

"I don't know. Honest to God, I don't know who was around me, and even if I did I wouldn't want to put the finger on them. I guess they've just gotta believe me."

Not good, Aaron thought. "They're going to believe the cop unless we can shake him. Well, and I don't suppose you had a permit for a public meeting?"

"Hell, no. Union Square's a park, ain't it? Can't citizens get together in a public park and talk? What the hell's all this about freedom of speech?"

Aaron sighed. Hugh behind bars was looking more and more like a permanent picture. "I hope you didn't say anything about overthrowing the government or using force, Hugh. What exactly *did* you say?"

"Now how am I supposed to remember? I was talking right out of my head. That idea of a march just came to me. I'm sure I didn't say anything about overthrowing the government. Hell, it's the government that I want to put these miserly businessmen like your brother in their place."

"All right. But, Hugh, for God's sake, don't make any speeches in court. Just answer whatever questions that I or the prosecutor ask, and as briefly and truthfully as possible. Will you promise that?"

"Sure, sure, Aaron. I hope you know I've no money to pay your fee—"

"Don't give *that* a thought. You're family, aren't you?"

Quite a number of Van Alens, including Hugh's sister, Mary, would have cut out their tongues rather than make such a statement. Hugh's arrest, the talk of Newport and the stuff of headlines in all the New York papers, was for them an embarrassment very nearly beyond bearing. The implications that the clever and imaginative reporters inserted into their stories were horrendous. By quoting a too talkative arresting officer's description of the circumstances under which he'd found his victim, they left little doubt about a sex scandal. Worse, by juxtaposing Sally's background as a well-known promoter of suffragette causes with Hugh's alleged revolutionary activities, they raised the specter of a political plot. They were unsparing in heightening the drama by pointing out that Mrs. Hancock was sister to James Schuyler Van Alen, "one of New York's leading businessmen and churchmen and close associate of J. P. Morgan, the nation's foremost banker," and that O'Donnell was brother to the wife of Aaron Roberts Van Alen, "millionaire sportsman." One unsavory sheet went so far as to write an editorial under the damning headline: IS COMMUNISM INFILTRATING FIFTH AVENUE?

It was hardest on Mary, of course. She literally collapsed, taking to her bed with what she described as a screaming headache and refusing to talk to anybody but Aaron . . . "I knew something like this would happen. You're a lawyer now—is there any way I can publicly disown my brother?" And James went into a Rooseveltian rage, threatening personally to "see that that fellow's taken care of" if the courts failed to do their duty and letting it be known that his sister, Sally, was no longer welcome in his house. James' wife Anne busied herself with buzzing through the Newport community to make sure that everybody understood that there was no connection between *her* family and that dreadful man. Martha Schuyler Van Alen seemed more overwhelmed by sorrow than anger . . . "My own daughter, where in God's name did I go wrong?" Only Cousin Sophie took a kind of witch's joy in the affair, reminding people, "I always knew that girl was bad and would come to no good end." Pierce Hancock, bankrupt and suddenly sober, took the first train to New York, where he filed suit for divorce on grounds of his wife's adultery and claims for a monetary settlement in view of the damage she'd done his good name.

Sally Schuyler Van Alen Brewster Hancock, the former Duchess of Midstone, was an instant pariah. Nobody came calling, and people she knew found their attention riveted elsewhere if she passed them in the streets. Tradesmen waited on her politely enough—money was money—but let their eyes reveal their thoughts; strangers frankly stared, or nudged each other and whispered or giggled. She tried to shield little Matty, but the tongues of children were, as everybody knew, sharper than knives, and her daughter was being lacerated. "What did Uncle Hugh *do?* Is he really a *Red?* What *is* a Red?" Matty would ask, and add, "He's so nice to me, and such fun . . ." Fortunately, innocence or disinterest seemed to have prevented the children from grasping other implications of the affair, and financial disaster was an adequate immediate explanation for Pierce's sudden disappearance, but Matty was too bright not to tumble to everything soon. What then would her daughter think? It was the most pressing question for Sally; she could stand abuse and scorn from the others but not from her own child. Sally might well have gone a little crazy, given in to guilty remorse and self-loathing, if she hadn't been sustained by her fury at a world that would blindly condemn Hugh as a dangerous radical without trial and convict Hugh and her together of sin without knowing their feelings. She made up her mind that she'd do all she could to hit back at the hypocrites and Philistines, and to that end she prayed that she would have her brother Aaron's help.

So far, so good. It had been a kind of confirming miracle in itself that she'd found Aaron when she'd set off in *Pride of the Sea* without the slightest notion of where he might have gone and only her need for him as a compass. And she'd found Aaron in an odd mood, apparently as emotionally detached from life as his boat was from the land. It had taken hours to get him to realize the enormity of what had happened, what would happen, to Hugh, to her, to Mary, to their mother—well, to everybody . . . if Hugh could be proved innocent of the charges against him at least some of the damage could be mended; that other was only her problem, hers and

Hugh's. Aaron argued that they ought to get a good lawyer, and she counter-argued that no "good lawyer" would take the case of a man already convicted in the public mind of immorality and political heresy. "God help us, but you're probably right, sis" he'd said. "At least I don't have any career to lose. As a matter of fact, you might just have saved my life. . . ."

It was a remark that Aaron did not bother or try to explain, but he went back with her to Newport that night and on to New York the next day. He also warned her that he might find the case too much and locate another lawyer for the job. In the meantime, he suggested, there was no point in letting anybody else know his intentions. Mary and James were so wild that they actually seemed to want Hugh to be convicted and jailed, and a Van Alen appearing for the defense would only create more unwanted sensation. "It'll be hell to pay, Sally. I'll surely lose a brother and maybe a wife and God knows how mother will take it, but maybe there's another way out. I'll let you know."

There was no way out. Aaron did approach two lawyers who were known for "liberal" views and who might have had enough stature and ability to win the case. One of them squirmed; he wasn't feeling well and, besides, his case load was already too heavy. The other was blunt: "Poor fellow doesn't stand a chance. Whether he's technically guilty or not, he's got a reputation around town as a labor agitator and there are . . . well . . . other implications. I wouldn't risk my reputation on that one. Rather go to bat for a murderer any day." . . .

So, after he'd seen Hugh in the Tombs, Aaron called Sally and told her, "I'm going to take the case but only because I'm convinced that Hugh is innocent—at least in intent. Might as well let the others find out about it from the papers."

The news that Aaron would handle the O'Donnell defense was considered nearly as sensational as the arrest itself: FIFTH AVENUE LAWYER TO DEFEND LABOR RADICAL. The papers chose to ignore or play down the fact that Hugh was Aaron's brother-in-law and to play up the odd circumstances of the "great Van Alen interests" going to the support of a man accused of revolutionary agitation and known for mounting strikes "disruptive to the best interests of business and the general public."

James, nearly choleric, came down to New York at once to try to dissuade his brother. "You're more of a goddamned fool than even I imagined. I left mother in tears and your wife in shock. Why in God's name didn't you leave well enough alone?"

"Never mind God. At least don't join in that hypocrisy. I happen to be convinced he's innocent . . ."

"Even if he is, you'll never get him off. What do you know about practicing law?"

"I tried to get him more *learned* counsel. No one would take the case."

"I'm not surprised. The man's no good, never has been. Aside from everything else, he's an adulterer. If he doesn't go to prison, God knows what he and Sally will be up to. I hate to say it about our own sister, but she's no good either—"

"Listen to me, James. I don't want to hear you

385

talk that way about Sally, not *ever* again. You have no idea what she's been through."

"Whatever it is, she's brought it on herself. Sow the wind, reap the whirlwind—"

"Spare me the sermon, brother. I've heard enough of them in my time."

"Yes, and obviously they never took—not with you, or Sally. I've kept my nose clean and worked my head off to assure the good name and fortune of the Van Alens, and you've been nothing but a playboy and she's little better than a whore. Well, I'm tired of it. If you don't drop this case I'm going to issue a statement to the press that you are no longer associated in any way with Van Alen and Son."

"That's fine with me, dear brother."

"What are you going to live on? Your legal fees?"

"Regardless of what you think of my legal talents, or lack of them, I've promised to take this case and I'm going to do my damnedest. When you get back to Newport give my love to mother and Mary. I don't know when I'll get up there again."

"Love? Your mother and wife are ashamed to show their faces. Even if you have no consideration for me and the firm, at least you should have some consideration for them. What in hell is this Hugh O'Donnell to you? His own sister, your wife, told me that she thought he ought to be in jail. You're mad, Aaron, absolutely mad."

"Yes, I'm mad all right but not in the sense you mean it, James. It's clear to me that nobody wants to give O'Donnell a fair trail because, essentially, everybody, including you, is afraid of his ideas,

386

afraid that labor might some day prevail in its demand for fairer hours and wages. Frankly I've come to respect Hugh for his effort and sacrifice for his fellow workers, and I don't want to see him made a scapegoat. You call me a playboy. Well, at least I've learned from athletics about fair play, which is more than you seem to have learned from business—*or* religion. As for adultery, it has nothing whatsoever to do with the case, and as I'm sure you're aware, it's easily the favorite indoor sport in your own social circles. Look at your friend Morgan. I could indulge in a small sermon too, just to prove that religion wasn't totally lost on me: Let he who is without sin cast the first stone."

"Enough, Aaron . . . I can see that you're just not open to reason, but I tell you, you'll regret this. . . ."

When the trial got under way it quickly became apparent that the prosecution was depending almost entirely on the testimony of a police officer named Schultz. Captain Schultz told the judge and jury that he had been dispatched at the head of a force of a dozen policemen to Union Square to disperse what was held to be an unlawful gathering, in that no permit had been issued, that was infringing on the rights of others to use the park and was spilling over onto the private property of merchants in the vicinity and therefore trespassing. On his arrival at the scene, Captain Schultz heard with his own ears the voice of the accused haranguing the crowd and urging them to march against Washington, where they would "tear down the White House if need be." The captain, "being a good American"—the judge overruled Aaron's objection to this editorializing—was shocked and distressed at what he heard and fearful of rioting. Already aroused by the speaker, the crowd refused to disperse peacefully, and Captain Schultz sent for reinforcements and authorized the limited use of force—"just nightsticks, you know." As senior officer he himself undertook to arrest the apparent ringleader—"that man there, Hugh O'Donnell"—who at the top of his lungs was advising the people to resist on the grounds that they had "a right to hear free speech in a free country." When Captain Schultz worked his way up to the bench on which O'Donnell was standing, the accused jumped down, struck the officer so hard in the chest that he was thrown off balance, and made a getaway in the crowd. Once the crowd was cleared, Captain Schultz said, he returned to headquarters and swore out a warrant for O'Donnell's arrest.

The captain, red-haired and beefy and for the most part matter-of-fact, made a creditable witness. On cross-examination Aaron not only couldn't shake him but very nearly got his client into more trouble.

"How many people would you say were gathered in the square, Captain Schultz?"

"Upwards of a thousand."

"And you tried to disperse them with a dozen policemen?"

"Well, I said I sent for reinforcements. There must have been a hundred of us toward the end there."

"So you had a hundred officers and a thousand or so people milling around? The situation must have been confusing, wasn't it, captain?"

"A little . . ."

"And in all that confusion you might have been mistaken that it was, in fact, Mr. O'Donnell who, you claim, struck you?"

"No, sir. It was him all right."

"And how are you so sure?"

"It ain't the first time I've seen him. He'd been mixed up in all these strikes. I was on the line way back during the Van Alen strike when you almost got killed yourself, *sir* . . ."

"No further questions."

Schultz's testimony was corroborated by several other officers. Aaron was able to get one of them, at least, to admit that he hadn't heard anything about "tearing down the White House," and all of them agreed that they hadn't actually seen Hugh O'Donnell strike their captain. But by the time the prosecution rested, the case looked even more hopeless than Aaron had feared. Though he'd managed to hold out for a jury that could be considered Hugh's peers—mostly workingmen and small tradesmen who might be sympathetic to the complaints of the unemployed—he had no way of knowing how they'd react to the damning charge that his client was a disloyal American willing to assault the very citadel of democracy, the White House, let alone to the accusation that he'd struck an officer attempting to do what he saw as his duty. Few men, never mind their class, were without some fear of a general disruption of law and order that the prosecution suggested might result if a man like O'Donnell went free. While Aaron hoped that, with a careful handling of his client, he could raise reasonable doubts about the substance of his speech and present assurances as to his essential patriotism, the question of assault would be a matter of Schultz's word against Hugh's. Hugh had remained adamant that he knew of no witnesses to produce on his behalf except for the local parish priest, who agreed rather reluctantly to appear as a general character witness "for the sake of the wife and those little kiddies." So weak was Aaron's case that he was disappointed when the judge declared an overnight recess after the prosecution's presentation. Might as well get it over with instead of fretting through the night. Hugh seemed to feel the same way, saying as they led him away, "Christ, it's going to be a long night."

The newspapers Aaron scanned on the horsecars bearing him up to his mother's empty Fifth Avenue house had, of course, convicted Hugh. "The counselor for the defense will have to pull a very large rabbit out of his hat to take the jury's mind off the damning testimony against the radical Hugh O'Donnell," said one writer. "In view of the political ramifications of this case, it is clearly in the public interest that justice be seen to be done," opined another, "and it is therefore unfortunate that the accused is represented by an inept Johnny-come-lately attorney who has heretofore displayed competence only in such gentlemanly sports as coaching and yachting. From his performance today, it seems likely that Mr. Aaron Van Alen's first case will be his last." There was also on the business pages an announcement that Mr. Aaron Roberts

Van Alen had been relieved of his duties as vice president and director of Van Alen & Son, Inc., and an announcement from the firm's president, Mr. James Schuyler Van Alen, that Van Alen & Son had no relationship to, or interest in, the government's case against one Hugh O'Donnell. Altogether a day to forget, and he hoped to hell that Patrick had left some bottles in the pantry when he moved the establishment up to Newport.

When Aaron reached the house he was pleasantly surprised to find that he wouldn't be alone with his gloomy thoughts. Sally and Matty were there, busily yanking all the summer sheeting off the furniture. "I hate this stuff—it makes the place so . . . so spooky," Sally said. "I just couldn't stay up there in Newport waiting for news, and of course we can't go back to Pierce's house. I hope you don't mind."

"No, not at all. I'm glad you're here. I wasn't looking forward to tonight . . . The news, I'm afraid, is bad, Sally, very bad."

"Is it . . . is it over?"

"Not yet, but I suspect it might as well be. He's got all the witnesses against him and what looks like a hanging judge and what the papers call an inept attorney to defend him, and—"

"God, I'm sorry I got you into this, Aaron."

"Don't be. I wouldn't have taken it on if I didn't believe in it. I just wish there was something, some way . . ." The phone was ringing. "Now who in hell can that be?"

The voice on the other end of the line was familiar—high-pitched, jovial—though he hadn't heard it in a year or so since Teddy Roosevelt had gone to Washington as a Civil Service Commissioner. "Aaron? Teddy here. I'm out in Oyster Bay, and I see by the paper you've got a real fight on your hands at last. Bully for you! I hope you have something up your sleeve like that left jab you used to pull on me."

"Not a thing, Teddy, not a damned thing . . ."

"*That* doesn't sound like the Aaron I know. Besides, you can't afford to lose. Do you know who you're defending? Sam Gompers tells me he's one of his best organizers. A lot of tommyrot, he tells me, about threatening the government. Is that the way you see it?"

"Sure. I don't think the man's guilty of anything but speaking in the park without a permit, but we've no witnesses, and we have the pride of the police force testifying against us—"

Roosevelt nearly split his eardrums with a whinnying laugh. "Pride of the police force—that's a good one! Listen, Aaron, you know there are more crooks on the police force than in the streets. That's what I really called about. That name Schultz rings a bell. Charlie Parkhurst—you know, the minister down there at the Madison Square Presbyterian Church—has been talking to me about his crusade, and if I'm not mistaken he mentioned a Schultz. Why don't you go see him?"

That *could* be it . . . If he could put Parkhurst on and discredit Schultz, he had a chance. "Teddy, I don't know how to thank you—"

"Don't thank me. Just get *going* . . ."

When he put down the phone Aaron ran out and grabbed Sally and waltzed her around. "That was

Teddy Roosevelt. He's come up with an idea for a witness. I think maybe we've got some hope now. Pour me a drink . . . on second thought, better not. I've got to go see a minister right now. . . ."

Sally was so excited that she and Matty went with him to wait in the hack at the Reverend Parkhurst's house; she wanted to know for sure as soon as the interview was over. On the way, Sally and Aaron agreed that they, like a good many other supposedly sophisticated New Yorkers, had been taking Mr. Parkhurst's fulminations from the pulpit about corruption with a large grain of salt. The sermons received liberal press coverage because the good minister did his research personally by visiting houses of prostitution and gambling dens incognito and then preaching about the numbers of city officials and officers of the law he encountered on his rounds. It was great fodder for the public's appetite for sex and scandal but nothing much had so far come of it. At the moment, Aaron could not care less; all he prayed for was that Parkhurst had seen Schultz in some compromising position and would be willing to say so in court.

Though fortunately at home and, more fortunately, possessed of incriminating information about Schultz, Mr. Parkhurst was reluctant to use it in the interests of freeing that "Communist chap." It was only when he realized that Aaron was the brother of James Van Alen, one of the leading Presbyterian elders, that he agreed. With the minister's handshake and promise to appear in court in the morning, Aaron dismissed the hack and walked Sally and Matty over to Madison Square

Garden, where they ascended to the roof and had supper and watched a show that featured a troop of girls on bicycles wheeling in figures to the tune of "A Bicycle Built for Two."

"Oh, if you only knew what *that* song means to me," Sally said.

"Remembering details of the story on Hugh's arrest," Aaron said, "I can imagine. Well, we just may get him back for you by sundown tomorrow."

"You don't condemn me for this, do you Aaron?"

"To tell you the truth, I think I envy you. Hugh's not a bad sort at all . . . After all, I married his sister . . ." He winced a little when he said that.

"Yes, and it isn't going well, is it. Be honest. Tell me."

"No, it isn't, and from what James says, this may well put an end to it."

"I'm sorry, Aaron. You really did love her, didn't you?"

"Did? Do? Let's not talk about it. Time for me to get some sleep to do my best in court."

Mr. Parkhurst, good as his word, was in court when Aaron arrived, but Aaron did not call him at once. He opened his case with the priest who testified that he'd known the accused for years as a good family man who'd attended mass more than most. Then Aaron put Hugh on the stand and led him through a litany of "I-don't-knows," "I'm-not-sures," and "Can't remembers" to emphasize the theme of a confusion in which an honest man would acknowledge doubt. During the course of the questioning, Hugh came forth with an unexpected bit of hard information that Aaron found as exciting and gratifying as delivering an ace in tennis: he testified that the meeting in the park had not been planned at all, that he and some other unemployed men had been taking the sun in the park and talking, that the group had just gradually grown until he was asked to stand up on the bench and address them. The plan for a march on Washington just "popped into my head as I talked," Hugh said, and added that he still hadn't personally decided whether to go through with it when the meeting was broken up. So much for holding a meeting without a permit, but what about inciting to riot? Aaron decided to take a calculated risk and let Hugh talk about his ideas. "Do you recall," he asked, "saying anything about 'tearing the White House down'—or similar words?"

"Now why would I ever say a thing like that? It was Mr. Cleveland I'd be counting on to help us, and would he do it if we wrecked his house?"

"Are you then saying, Mr. O'Donnell, that you believe in the government of the United States?"

"Aye, I do. It's the government that protects our rights—or should. Without it, we'd be good and lost."

"No more questions."

A good witness, Hugh. He manged to hold his tongue and temper under cross-examination, and when he stepped down Aaron said, "The defense calls the Reverend Mr. Charles Parkhurst."

A gasp rose in the courtroom. The preacher's mere appearance was news of such significance that reporters ran for the doors and telephones to make a bulletin in the early afternoon editions. The judge and jury came to attention in their chairs. Schultz moved into an empty chair at the prosecutor's table and began whispering in his ear. Aaron moved slowly, deliberately. "Would you please tell us your name?"

"Charles H. Parkhurst."

"What is your profession, Mr. Parkhurst."

"I am a minister of the gospel."

"You are a citizen of New York City?"

"Yes, sir, I am pastor of the Madison Square Presbyterian Church."

"Now, Mr. Parkhurst, are you acquainted with Police Captain Gerhard Schultz?"

"Not acquainted, no, sir."

"But you do know who Captain Schultz is?"

"Yes, sir."

"If he's in this courtroom, would you point him out to us?"

"The man sitting at that table—the one with the red hair."

"Now, would you relate, Mr. Parkhurst, the circumstances under which you came to know who Captain Schultz is?"

"Well, I was in this bordello on West Twenty-sixth Street—"

"You were in where?"

"A bordello."

Aaron made another reactive decision like angling a volley from the net to catch an opponent off-balance. He'd risk offending the witness to amuse the jury and press, to create the impression that he, and by inference his client, were good fellows.

"A bordello? For the sake of those who may not be familiar with the latinate forms of speech, could you tell us what that means in plain English?"

The witness reddened, and the prosecutor was immediately on his feet. "Objection, your honor. This line of questioning is irrelevant. Everybody here, I'm sure, knows what a bordello is."

"I don't see that there's any harm in getting a further definition, counselor," the judge said. "Proceed, Mr. Van Alen."

"What would you call it in plain English?"

"A . . . a whorehouse."

"Yes, a whorehouse. I don't imagine you were there as a customer?"

Some jurors and spectators couldn't suppress laughter, and the judge resorted to his gavel. The witness, visibly angry, said, "No, *sir*. I was there to carry out my crusade against vice in this city."

"And it was there—in a whorehouse—that you met Captain Schultz?"

"Yes, sir."

The prosecutor was up again. "Your honor, I make a motion to dismiss this witness and expunge his testimony from the record. I don't know where this questioning is leading, but whether or not Mr. Parkhurst knows Captain Schultz is irrelevant to this case."

The judge summoned both attorneys to the bench. "Would you tell me, Mr. Van Alen, the purpose of this testimony?"

"Yes, sir. I do speak in plain English. This case has boiled down to the credibility of two witnesses— Captain Schultz and my client. I intend to cast doubt on Captain Schultz's character and, therefore, his credibility."

"Is your witness prepared to testify that Captain Schultz lied to him in the incident you are developing?" the judge asked.

"No, sir—not to my knowledge."

"Then I'm inclined to agree with the prosecution," the judge said, and, rapping with his gavel, announced, "Motion granted. The clerk will expunge this appearance from the record of this case. You are excused, Mr. Parkhurst."

When Aaron sat down, Hugh whispered, "Jesus, we've had it."

"Not necessarily, Hugh," Aaron said, and then told the court. "Your honor, the defense rests."

Aaron could detect in both the jury box and at the press table intense disappointment that he hadn't been able to continue with his witness. The prosecution had won a legal point but lost a good deal of sympathy in the process, and he knew that, however the court had ruled, the seed of doubt had been planted in everybody's mind. The prosecutor delivered an oration more to the press than the jury in which he avoided the facts in favor of flag-waving. With a license not granted to testimony under oath, he pictured the accused as a dangerous radical with a long record of instigating illegal strikes and now promoting an assault on Washington. These activities constituted a threat to business, which was "the foundation of the American way of life," and a dangerous challenge to the authority of the government of the United States. Aaron sensed the jurors were fidgeting in their seats, saw the reporters putting down their pencils. Recalling a favorite quotation of his grandmother's that "brevity is the soul of wit," Aaron took another chance. He approached the jury box with a friendly and what he hoped was a confident smile, leaned on the rail and spoke in a voice so low that the press had to strain to hear.

"Gentlemen of the jury," he said, "I'm sure you'll agree with me that the prosecutor's address might pass for a Fourth of July oration. But I'm also sure you'll agree with me that it has nothing to do with this case. Is Hugh O'Donnell guilty of the offenses with which he is charged? Captain Schultz says yes. Mr. O'Donnell says no. It's one man's word against another's since the other witnesses offered by the prosecution were not certain as to exactly what they heard or saw, as would any honest man be under such circumstances. Who's telling the truth? You've heard the good father testify as to Mr. O'Donnell's character whereas . . ." Aaron knew enough not to refer to testimony stricken from the record, so he filled a pause with an expressive shrug and said, "We are content to let the answer rest with your good judgment."

The judge in his charge to the jury paid lip service to the legal ideal that it was a jury's obligation to determine the facts without prejudice and "beyond reasonable doubt" but spent most of his effort advising them that they must treat Mr. Parkhurst's appearance as if it had not existed, advice that Aaron fervently hoped would prove counter-productive. When the jury retired, Aaron went out into the hall for a smoke. He was surprised when the reporters fell on him with congratulations: no matter what the verdict, he'd put on a good show. "I'm the fellow who said this would be your last case," one of them admitted, "but I've got to eat my words, and they don't taste so good." Aaron had scarcely finished his cigarette when it was announced that the jury was returning.

Not guilty.

Hugh hugged Aaron in Irish exuberance. "Thank you, brother. I'm really beginning to think you are my brother . . ."

"Don't thank me," Aaron said, embarrassed by an un-Van Alen show of emotion. "Thank my friend Teddy Roosevelt. He came up with the notion of the preacher."

"What the hell was the preacher going to say?" Hugh asked.

"That he saw Schultz taking money from the madam."

"Why that son-of-a-bitch."

"Not a nice fellow, I'll agree," Aaron said, "but it really did have little to do with your case. You were pretty lucky, Hugh, don't forget it. Just please be more careful next time."

"Lucky, yes . . . but because I had me a damn good lawyer. Jesus, I wish I could pay you something."

"Forget it, you're my brother, remember? . . . Now there's a lady waiting up at the house to congratulate you. If I were you I wouldn't let any grass grow under my feet."

Hugh didn't.

Chapter 9

WHAT AARON missed most was the children, particularly at this time of year when Christmas was coming on. This feeling, almost a yearning, was rather a surprise to him since he'd more or less taken the children for granted in those years when they were underfoot all the time. He'd been waiting, or at least so he told himself, until they got old enough to join him in the experiences that only he could give them, such as going sailing or playing tennis. Now they were getting to that age—let's see, it was 1897, so Amelia would be thirteen and the boy eleven and Felicia already four—and he would miss those years of companionship that he'd looked forward to. He could see them from time to time, even take one of the older ones for a weekend—Mary wasn't *that* heartless—but unfamiliarity just added to the normal strain and shyness between generations, and much of their time together was lost in feeling each other out. It would probably be easier if he could get a divorce and establish legal and regular visiting privileges, but Mary, being still "a good Catholic girl," would never consent, and he, being nominally Catholic and feeling guilty, would never ask again.

In a way, the effective loss of his children was the price he'd been obliged to pay for being a man . . . his own man . . . and for being what people called "free." Whatever else society might deny women, it gave them their children. For all her marital difficulties and star-crossed loves, Sally had her Matty, now a handsome fifteen, living with her above the art gallery she was running down there in Greenwich Village, and she had her Charlie too. Ever since he'd reached twenty-one, the Viscount Goodenough had turned the tables and come over to New York at least once a year to be with his mother Sally and half-sister Matty. Last year he'd brought a bride, and this year he was bringing a son, the first Van Alen grandchild, in time for Christmas. Aaron had been invited to join them all, and he probably would, though he'd rather have been invited to share the day with his own family in the old Van Alen mansion on Fifth Avenue. The nearest Mary had come to that was to suggest that he drop in for tea on Christmas Eve so that he could distribute his presents, and he would probably do that too. In this, he was a man who would accept crumbs. Now that he'd got himself set up in one of the bachelor apartments in the new Delmonico's just down the Avenue at Forty-fourth Street, he took his nightly walks up past the mansion—it was just about the right distance, he told himself—and would look into the lighted windows hoping to glimpse one or the other of the children. He never did. Well, he had only himself to blame. But along with the blame was a certain pride. Try not to forget the *whys* of his situation, he told himself.

Van Alens hated emotional scenes and would go to considerable lengths to avoid them. On the evening of Hugh O'Donnell's acquittal, Aaron, after sharing a bottle of champagne with his client and Sally, had discreetly left his mother's house to them and established temporary headquarters in the Windsor Hotel down the Avenue. There, on a hotel letterhead, he scrawled the most difficult composition of his life. The words came hard, so hard that it took him half an hour just to decide on the proper salutation, a salutation that would establish a certain distance without inflicting an immediate wound:

My dear Mary,

As you will have seen by the papers, I managed to raise enough doubt in the jury's mind that your brother Hugh was found not guilty on all charges. It would be hard for me to describe to you the elation I felt at the moment of that verdict. Quite apart from being able to do something for Hugh, whom I've come to like, I realized that I've at last found something both interesting and useful to do with my life. I see it as a blessing that my brother James has seen fit to cut me loose from the company as a result of my taking Hugh's case . . . it leaves me with no other alternative than to try to make my own way in the practice of law. This I plan to do, beginning tomorrow with a search for a suitable office down near the courts. It will be quite a while before I return to Newport, if ever.

I gather from what James said that my presence in Newport might not be welcome in any event. He reported that you and mother were as distressed as he over my defense of Hugh. While such an attitude may be understandable on the part of my mother, in view of Sally's involvement with Hugh, I find it strange in you since, whatever he may have done, Hugh is your brother and, as such, mine too. I'm beginning to realize that I have far more sympathy for the Hughs of this world than the Jameses, whereas your sympathies seem to be going the other way. It may be this development more than the recent stress in our personal relationships that has been causing the strain between us, which I'm sure you're as aware of as I. I think I can understand why you feel the way you do, and I hope that you can understand me, but I wonder whether at this point understanding is enough.

Much as it truly pains me, particularly with regard to the children, I'm going to propose that we live apart, at least until I'm settled in my profession. Whether I shall earn any money at all is problematical, and to ask you and the children to share in my poverty for the sake of what I'm sure you regard as a quixotic impulse on my part would be selfish, even silly, when I am sure that mother will be more than glad to see to your needs. For me to live under my mother's roof while engaging in activities that would surely distress her would not only be inappropriate but also make for unhappiness all around. As soon as I can have the papers drawn I shall also assign to you, in trust for the children, my share of the Van Alen Trust left by my grandmother so that, whatever happens to me or regardless of what my mother might do, you and they will be amply provided for. I might point out that once the papers are in your hands you can borrow against that trust as I have done in the past and as Sally is doing now. In any case you will be independent of me, though I am hoping that at some point we will be able to take up our lives together again.

If you want me to come to Newport or you want to come down and meet me here to discuss this letter, I'll be glad to go along with you. I do think, however, that, by putting it in writing I am giving us both a chance to think calmly about the matter. Give my love to mother and the children and say a few "hail Marys" for a struggling, not-so-young lawyer.

Love,

Aaron

There was no answer. No answer at all. In due course Aaron sent the papers renouncing his heritage up to Newport and heard a few weeks later through Judge Parsons' office that they had been duly executed by his wife. He had in hand a few thousand he'd drawn as severance pay from Van Alen & Son, enough to put down rent on a small office in Pine Street and a room in a seedy hotel on lower Broadway. He estimated that without a single fee he could last six or eight months if he ate in cheap restaurants and took advantage of the free food set out on bars at noon. He'd had enough clothes kept in his mother's house to last him for ten years if he didn't mind being out of style. Aaron rather looked forward to a prolonged financial struggle, partly as a test of his will but also as a conscience-satisfying punishment for having been the one to leave his marriage, never mind the provocation.

Aaron might have found those first weeks of silence from Newport and almost monastic living in his cell of a room less tolerable if he'd been alone. But he had Sally, and he spent a good deal of his time after work and on Sundays helping her and Matty search out a suitable living place so that they too could move out of the Fifth Avenue mansion before the Van Alen ladies and their entourage returned from Newport. Her only asset was her share of the Van Alen Trust, which Pierce's lawyers couldn't yet touch because it wouldn't come into her possession until her mother's death, but she was able to borrow enough against it to rent a rundown, three-story house they finally found in the Village. Only about eighteen feet wide, it was one of a solid row of similar houses called "railroad houses" because what rooms they had were strung out like cars from front to back along a side hall. There was a kitchen and pantry below street level, a parlor and dining room, served by a dumb waiter, on the first floor and two bedrooms on each of the floors above with baths at the end of the hall. There were great gaps in walls and ceiling from which patches of plaster had fallen, and the odors of half a century or more of living seemed to permeate the place. "It isn't exactly Fifth Avenue," Sally said, "but wait till you see what I do with it."

Aaron had to admire his sister's spirit. The smallest house she'd ever lived in was their old place on Twenty-second Street, which had twelve rooms, counting servants' quarters, and a marble foyer larger than a whole floor of this little structure. Not a day in her life had passed when she couldn't summon a butler or maid by pulling a bell. He doubted whether she could successfully boil an egg. Yet she actually seemed to be enjoying the challenge of making her own home as much as he was in making his own living. In a way, they were two lost sheep together and closer than ever before in their lives. The only matter on which they disagreed was his gesture in turning his inheritance over to Mary and the children.

"I agree with your leaving her, if that's what you're doing," Sally said, "but I think you're a damned fool to set her up with all that money. You *are* her husband and probably always will be with that Catholic business of hers, and you could take care of her with an allowance or whatever and still have a fair amount left over for yourself. I think you acted too fast—before you really thought it out. One swallow doesn't make a summer, and one case doesn't make a lawyer."

"You don't have much faith in me, do you, Sally?"

"Oh, sure I do, little brother, but I just hate to see that cold fish—she is a cold fish, isn't she?—walk away with everything. I have no doubt that mother, with a little help from James, will fix her up too, and the way she's playing up to Sophie practically curls my hair. You ought to have kept *something*. Sometimes I think that, now that you're Catholic too, you're making a play for beatification."

Aaron laughed. "No chance. The Lord, if he's up there, knows how selfish my motives are. For one thing, I'm salving my conscience for walking out on my family, but there's another thing I've never talked about because I was too damned ashamed of doing nothing about it. Most of that trust is in real-estate that grandmother bought over on the East Side when it was respectable and that's since been leased out under the trustees, chief of whom is James, to the Italian padrones who turn the buildings into tenements and sweatshops. Teddy Roosevelt took me through one a few years ago, and

I nearly threw up. It's bothered me ever since, so . . . well, you can see I'm not exactly a saint—more a sort of Pontius Pilate washing his hands."

"I wish you hadn't told me that," Sally said. "I'm looking forward to being rich again one day. All the Astors live off land like that and probably some of the Roosevelts too, Teddy notwithstanding. He's always been something of an ass about money, acting as if it were just *there*."

"Now that's not fair, sis. He's earned a lot from his writing, and he's always held some sort of public job—"

"All right, I don't want to criticize your friend, although I've always found him a little too . . . too overblown. It's beside the point. I'm going to get that property, if Pierce doesn't win that suit, and *then* I might do something about all that . . ."

"There—you see? You've probably got as much conscience as I do—or at least you're more practical, as women generally are. But mother's likely to live a long time yet, and there's a limit to what the banks will let you have against an undisclosed asset, so, being practical, how are you going to live?"

"I just don't know yet," Sally said. "I wasn't taught a single useful talent except possibly good taste, which I haven't much practiced. Maybe I could get a job in a stable currying horses, I used to watch the grooms often enough. By the way, did you know that Pierce has actually gone to work? Some omnibus company hired him to buy and train their teams. Well, I'll just have to think of something."

She did. Within weeks of moving into her house

Sally began to meet some of the young artists who infested the lofts and garrets of the neighborhood, and she conceived the idea of turning her first floor into a gallery in which they could display and sell their work, giving her a small commission. In such an enterprise her "good taste" was a decided asset, as were her wide contacts among people wealthy enough to buy the art. Cards went out all over the city to announce the opening of the Van Alen Gallery, and the tiny place was packed. Most visitors, including the art critics of the newspapers, went away shocked at the daring nudes and even more daring abstracts they saw hanging on the walls. But a few bought, and Sally was launched.

Seeing all this healthy activity going on helped keep Aaron's mind off the silence from Mary. Then one day in mid-September he picked up the ringing phone on his office desk and heard Mary's voice. The chill in it could have frosted his ear. "The children want to see you," she said.

"Oh? How are they?"

"They're fine, but I can't stall them any longer."

"What have you been telling them?"

"Something like the truth. That their father's busy setting up a new business and has to live down near his office. But they want to know why you couldn't at least visit."

"I haven't been invited."

"You are now. Sunday lunch. I think your mother wants to see you too, although she denies it."

"And how is she?"

"As well as could be expected with what she's had

to put up with."

"And you?"

"*I've* never felt better in my life."

Click. So that's the way it would be—cold and correct. When he arrived at the mansion on Sunday the aged Patrick was warmer in his welcome than his wife. The children partly made up for it—they were all over him. His mother, though, was nowhere to be seen until lunch was announced. When she walked into the dining room he was shocked—a little more than a month had turned her into an old woman. That straight, defiant back of hers was bent; those bright, appraising eyes were dull and watery. She was leaning, as if she couldn't stand alone, on Sophie's arm. "Sophie's moved back in with us to help take care of mother," Mary told him quietly. Aaron wondered whether to kiss his mother, decided against it and covered the awkward moment by fussing with her chair instead. She seemed confused. "I didn't know *you'd* be here," was her greeting.

"I thought I'd make it a surprise for you, mother. The children wanted to see him," Mary said.

"I should think you'd be ashamed to show your face here, Aaron, after what you've done to Mary and these lovely children and . . . and me. I just can't imagine what you're up to . . ."

"I'm practicing law, mother."

"Well, your father always hired lawyers . . . I never thought it would come to this—in the papers all the time. Judge Parsons never has his name in the papers. I just can't think where I went wrong. What did I do wrong that you behave like this?"

"Mother, you didn't do anything wrong. It's just me, something I need to do . . . By the way, Sally sends her love . . ."

"Oh, you see her? I suppose you would."

"Nearly every day. She's got an art gallery and—"

"James says it's a disgrace—nude women and pictures that look like children had made them. He's going to his lawyers to see if he can stop her from using the Van Alen name."

"Mother, you don't mean that."

"I do, and I don't blame him. That girl's done everything she can to . . . to ruin our good name. I hope she has sense enough not to come around here. She's done enough damage. She—and you too. Look at me. Look at me. The doctor thinks I may have a broken heart. He says there is such a thing. I just don't know. Your father would turn over in his grave if he knew . . ."

"Mother, I'm sorry. I guess I'd hoped you'd be a little proud of me—"

"For what? For deserting your family? For dragging our good name through the mud when you know how I've spent my whole life proving to people what the Van Alens stand for? You and Sally, birds of a feather. James is right, I did spoil both of you."

"Well, I did give you Mary," Aaron said. And thought, Talk about birds of a feather . . .

"Yes, and thank God for that. I don't know what I'd do without Mary and . . . and Sophie here. You've been a dear to me, Sophie."

Sophie reached over and patted the older woman's hand. "It's really my pleasure, Aunt Martha.

411

Nobody's ever needed me before. I'm glad Mary thought of it."

Mary got up. "Children, come with me," and, although he hadn't touched a bite, Aaron said, "I'm going too." Out in the hallway, he said to Mary, "This wasn't such a good idea, was it?"

She admitted, "No, I didn't think she was *quite* so bitter, but can you blame her?"

"No, I suppose not. You feel the same way?"

Her eyes avoided his, she didn't answer him. Instead she asked, "What's happened to Hugh?"

"Back at his job, as far as I know."

"You don't see him? I mean with Sally?"

"No, that seems to be over."

"Well, thank God for something . . ."

"When can I see the children again?"

"Anytime you want, but warn me. I might have other plans for them."

Aaron agreed with Mary about Hugh and Sally, but for very different reasons. Hugh had decided to take advantage of the publicity of his trial and run for alderman from his West Side district in the elections of '94, figuring he might do more in the long run for his cause in politics than in the stymied labor movement. In the Irish-Catholic community he wanted to serve he had at least to be seen to be a good family man, and Aaron very much wanted him to win. So did Sally. It was she, in fact, who broke off the affair ostensibly for Hugh's good . . . "It wasn't easy," she confessed to Aaron, "but I'm afraid it wasn't going to work for very long anyway. Something happened to him down here in the city, as if he were intimidated by the silk sheets in mother's house, and I'm not the girl for a whole lifetime of roughing it. I'll always love him, though, for what he taught me about myself, and fickle creature that I am, I can hardly wait for the *right* man to come along. If you know any who fit the bill, don't forget to introduce them to your big sister."

Aaron had an idea what Sally had learned about herself, but possessive, protective brother that he was, he could think of nobody who could qualify for such a gift. In the end it was Sally herself who found him, and Aaron found the man almost as fascinating as Sally did. Antonio Donatelli was a sculptor, a few years younger than Sally and handsome in a dark Italian way. He had fire in his eye and in his hand but nothing at all in his belly. He was the son of an organ-grinder who'd plied his trade at the gates of the Metropolitan Museum in the hope that art lovers would also be music lovers to the extent of tossing a few coins in his direction. Not owning a monkey, Poppa Donatelli took little Tony along to pass the hat but once in a while let the boy escape the cold or rain in the shelter of the museum, where his small eyes were wonderstruck by the giant sculptures and vivid splashes of color. "It was my cathedral," he'd say, "and if I hadn't been so little I'd probably have gone down on my knees." Since Tony had no ear for organ grinding and no use for school, a sympathetic priest got him a job with a monument-maker when his duties as monkey were passed down to a younger, more winsome brother. For years Tony patiently cut stone by day and taught himself to draw and model by copying statues in museums and public parks whenever he had an hour or so to himself. He'd become such a familiar figure at the Metropolitan that by the time he'd carved a few pieces of his own out of rejected monuments that his employer let him have, he was able to persuade the curator of sculpture to have a look at them. "That man ruined my life," Tony would say. "He told me that I was a real artist, and I've starved ever since."

Sally met Tony when he and some of his friends persuaded her, somewhat reluctantly, to take two of his pieces on consignment. They were like nothing he could have seen in any museum. Huge masses of polished granite, they were shaped only to the suggestion of the female form and called simply *Nude*. "The woman—she is everything—all power, the mother of us all," Tony rather ponderously told Sally. "This is the mass, the power, the overwhelming power of the female—you see?" Sally wasn't sure she could see all *that*, but she did think they'd look good in a Newport garden, so she put them on display. Because she had no help except when Matty was out of school, Sally would have her lunch in the gallery, and when Tony dropped in about noon one day to ask whether his pieces were stirring up any interest, she offered to share her sandwich with him. Watching him wolf it down was her first clue to how hungry he was, and she not only managed to have food around whenever he showed up after that but also began inviting him to dinner when Aaron was coming, which was several times a week. They would often talk long into the night over several bottles of wine—or rather Tony would talk while the Van Alens, brother and sister, would listen.

For a century or more Van Alens had owned

objects of art, just as they'd owned jewels and carriages and yachts, and they'd looked on them as decoration or, as in James' case, investment. No Van Alen had ever actually known an artist or been more than mildly curious about what impelled men—and, in a very few cases, women—to create the works they acquired. So these talks with Tony were nearly as stimulating to Sally and Aaron as a visit to a foreign country. The more so, because Tony and his friends, one or two of whom sometimes joined them, had scorn for the kind of art that hung on the walls and graced the fountains of Van Alens, Morgans, Vanderbilts, Carnegies, Astors, Rockefellers, Fricks, Mellons and their like. "Just decoration," they'd say. "Representational—no thought. Art should *say* something." Aaron, honing his advocate's skill, would argue, "But most of that work was done before the camera was invented, and it did serve a useful purpose to let us know what people, places and things look like." And Tony would say, "Ah, that's it, that's just it. We've had the camera for a generation or more, and now Mr. Edison is making his motion pictures. There's no more need for the artist to depict the real world. He's got to use his talents to illuminate the world of the imagination, the private vision."

Whether or not the Van Alens accepted the artists' arguments, they did find them interesting and, in view of them, Sally was more amused than anything else on the day that Tony asked her to pose for him in the nude. He seemed embarrassed. "I . . . well, you know I can't afford a model—they want fifty cents an hour and . . . well . . . you have such a striking figure . . . and are so . . . so modern in your thinking that I . . ."

Sally, having just passed forty, when women were supposed to be matronly, was flattered, but she nevertheless burst out laughing. "Why, Tony, you've been saying artists ought to work from the imagination. Why do you need a model?"

She thought that Tony blushed, as nearly as she could detect a blush on his dark skin. "Well, you see," he said, "you start with reality and abstract from it. I mean, you have to have the inspiration of reality. I mean . . . well, I *do* need a model, but I shouldn't have asked you. You're too much of a lady—"

Sally laughed again. "I don't know about that. Why don't we try it and stop worrying about my ladylike sensibilities."

It was somewhat awkward arranging the sittings. Sally refused to go to the loft that Tony shared with two fellow artists. If they were to be at her place, she didn't think it was wise to have Matty around, although she'd long since broken down and told Matty more than most would consider good for a girl of her age to know. Finally Sally hit on the stratagem of closing the gallery on Wednesdays when Matty would be in school . . . so that she could "clean up and do her books."

On the first Wednesday morning that Tony came for an appointment she had a sudden and, to her, silly attack of shyness. She'd been sensible enough to wear only a wrapper so that the act of undressing would not be awkward, but she hugged it to her as if it were protecting her from freezing to death. Tony was determinedly businesslike, saying he would first make sketches, would only take an hour of her time at any sitting, wanted her to stand in such and such a place to get the best light, and so on. While she watched, shivering a little inside her wrap, he set up his easel, set out his pencils, and said finally, "If you don't mind, would you disrobe now and stand over there where I told you?" The time had come. She did take off her wrap, but she was no longer cold . . . a blush had run the length of her body. Tony was matter-of-fact. "That's fine," he said. "Now, hold your back straight—that's better. Could you bend your left knee, as if you were about to walk? Fine. Hold it if you can."

While Tony sketched, she began to relax. What in the world had she been thinking of? This man was a serious artist going about his business, and she was ashamed almost to the point of blushing again that she'd ever had any other thoughts. Was she disappointed too? No, she told herself. Still, his dark eyes looking on every feature of her body that nobody but Hugh O'Donnell had ever really seen sent electric probes of feeling through her breasts and down through her loins. My God, she lectured herself, you're a mature woman, an experienced woman. At the end of an hour, as promised, Tony put down his pencil, started packing his papers and easel. She put her wrap back on. "Thanks," he said, "we made good progress."

"Did I . . . was I all right?"

"You were magnificent."

The next time, having experienced his professionalism, she was much more relaxed, possibly too relaxed. When in the middle of the session he suggested a pause for a cigarette, she didn't even think about putting her wrap on. He lit one and came over and handed it to her, then lit another for himself. He took a deep drag, flipped the cigarette toward the fireplace and held out his hand. "Sally, Sally," he said. "I can't stand this—can you?"

She sent her own cigarette spinning after his, put her hand in his, and said, "No."

It wasn't the same as it had been with Hugh—perhaps volcanoes erupted only once in a lifetime. But it was also better, like a comforting fire on the hearth that pops and crackles and leaves you feeling warm. Tony was tentative, and tender, a little in awe of the femaleness that inspired his art, and it was very much what she needed for her time of life when the calendar for being female was, according to accepted wisdom, running down. Tony, bless him, was as scornful of old wives' tales as he was of old artists' accomplishments. There were no more sittings on Wednesdays. For the first time in her life, Sally was totally in love, and after a few weeks she invited Tony to move in with her. She felt obliged to tell Matty the truth. "I love him, darling. He needs a place to stay, and we can't be married until my divorce comes through. Do you understand?" Matty said only, "Sure, I like Uncle Tony too."

Though Aaron would have liked to be as understanding as Matty, he was also Sally's lawyer. They'd felt obliged to contest the Hancock divorce suit because of his preposterous claims for money, in spite of the fact that Sally wanted a divorce as

418

much as Pierce. Aaron's strategy was to win against Hancock and then file for divorce on behalf of Sally. The evidence that Sally had committed adultery was circumstantial whereas they had an abundance of witnesses, including the upstairs maid in Newport, to throw at Hancock. Much as he liked Tony, Aaron felt obliged to warn: "If you take him in, Sally, it might ruin your case."

"Aaron," she said. "I don't give a damn if school keeps or not. I'm in love, really in love."

Aaron had to shrug a kind of agreement. He'd been in love once too, and he knew that reason couldn't stand up against that emotion. Well, he'd try to work something out, perhaps a settlement, on the Hancock case. Meanwhile, he hoped that Sally wasn't kidding herself. A good sign was that she'd never even claimed to be in love before, except perhaps to the Duke when she was too young really to know herself and her own emotions. Another good sign was that Tony, the first of Sally's men whom Aaron had really liked, was so obviously crazy about her. Aaron knew that most people, other than the little group of artists in the Village, would condemn Sally for openly living in sin with a man. Women were supposed to get whatever sexual satisfaction they could from whatever kind of husband they managed to catch. Moreover, they were supposed to stick by those husbands, no matter what. As he and Sally talked these things over in the light of her various predicaments, Aaron began to develop a large bump of anger at the self-evident unfairness women faced, which spread to include their anomalous position in society as virtually noncitizens. In some ways they were worse off than blacks, although they were fortunately spared the noose of the lynch mobs that were terrorizing blacks in the South. Aaron could, at last, appreciate the passion that Amelia before her, and now Sally, expended on the suffragette movement. It went deeper than desire for the vote; it was an outcry for simple justice, an assertion that a woman should have the same rights as a man over her own soul and body, that, if you liked, a woman had the same privilege to sin as a man. This was what Sally was asserting with her life, and Aaron would not condemn her—indeed, he would help her as long as she needed him.

But if he rejoiced in Sally's happiness with Tony, Aaron had to admit that it made him more miserable about himself. He had no hopes for, nor any great interest in, finding another love. If Mary would only be the Mary he thought he'd married, he'd go back to her, he realized. But he also realized that she could probably say as much of him. In fact, he had no doubt that most people would count her, not him, the injured party. All she'd done, really, was try to live up to his expectations of a wife in which he, as a Van Alen, could take pride, and he had, it seemed, condemned her for it. That she'd found fulfillment in that candy-store window of wealth and social dazzle against which she'd pressed her nose in longing as a little girl was surely both sane and natural. For her it was the American Dream, the Cinderella fable come true. She lacked as she'd warned him the education, experience and the temperament to become a doubter. She accepted the world as she saw it, and her place in it as a woman, just as she accepted her religion. In this way she was like his mother, like his sister-in-law Anne, like most women he knew, except Sally and just possibly that other Sally, his grandmother, as he guessed from the still puzzling hints and innuendos he'd come on about her life. Aaron could remember his father's praising both the practicality and the tiger-fierce concern for their own nest, their own young, that he found in women. That was Mary—it was she who would be seen by just about anybody to be marching in step. Aaron could also remember his father's wry, Van Alen-like toast that said more than he'd ever confess to: "Here's to women—you can't live with them, and you can't live without them." Unfortunately Aaron's life seemed to be confirming this.

Meanwhile he tried being a kind of Mary-watcher, but it became rather quickly clear that if he was hoping for a change in the weather, he was wasting his time. Aside from brief and icy encounters with her involving the children, he got his view of her through the papers. In spite and defiance, she threw herself more vigorously into the social life of the city than ever before. Because she remained the most photogenic of New York society matrons she was frequently pictured coming and going at balls, at the opera, on the steps of St. Patrick's, walking her charming children in the park. With his mother fading in health and spirits and Anne fading in looks, Mrs. Aaron Roberts Van Alen was at last *the* Mrs. Van Alen. She was more of a star than she'd ever have been in the theater, and in the process had become unreachable by her own family. She was not even among the mourners at the wake of Frank O'Donnell in the old saloon, but she took note of the occasion with a letter to Hugh advising him that no more money would be forthcoming. That was bad enough, but Aaron thought that she'd gone way too far when he spotted a small notice in the paper that she'd petitioned the court to change the name of their son from Francis O'Donnell Van Alen to Cornelius Van Alen III. He phoned in a rage: "Why didn't you consult me? I'm still his father. Damn it, you've no right to change the boy's name."

"He wanted it, Aaron. Since Sophie's been here she's been telling him all about her father Cornelius and her Great-Grandfather Cornelius. He wants to be more a part of the family."

"Look, if you're going to act as if I don't exist, I damn well think we ought to get a divorce."

"It's impossible and you know it. In the first place it's a sin in the eyes of the church and in the second place I *like* being Mrs. Aaron Roberts Van Alen."

"You might want to remarry."

"Never. Have you forgotten that I'm no longer interested in *that?*"

"How could I?"

"It's you who'll want to remarry, but I'm not going to give you that satisfaction. You'll have to live in sin like your sister, or don't you believe in sin?"

"We're getting nowhere as usual—"

"You should know that your son likes to be called Neil. Oh, and you might think about how much this means to your mother."

His mother . . . he couldn't seem to reach her.

She made no effort to see him when he went to visit the children, and if he sought her out she'd only talk about Mary and his children or about James and *his* children or "sweet Sophie." After his mother's initial upset and bewilderment, which he'd understood, something had taken over inside her—he and Sally hardly seemed to exist. Though she remained feeble physically, she managed to recover enough spirit to throw herself into the planning of what he was afraid would be her last great ball—in honor of James' oldest daughter Edith, who was to be presented to society in the early winter of '96.

In a way it was good to see his mother's "forgettery" that his father used to joke about function once more and allow her to hold her head as high as she was able. But, remembering their shared love of music, recalling the pride she'd once shown in his looks and charm, thinking on his own pride in her beauty and sense of grandeur, Aaron found it almost unbearable that her only way of dealing with her children whose values threatened her own was to put them out of her mind. While it was evident that he and Sally had been more profoundly influenced by their father, they owed much more than some physical characteristics to their mother. Aaron thought that his mother's "spoiling" might account for their apparent willfulness, and his mother's serene sense of superiority might account for their pride. He hadn't wanted to give his mother grief, but he also knew that she, in her time, hadn't hesitated to give *her* parents grief. She'd of course made up for it, and given time, maybe he and Sally would be able to as well.

But they were not given time. In the spring of '97, Martha Roosevelt Schuyler Van Alen, aged seventy, took to her bed with what was thought to be a cold. It turned so rapidly into a fatal pneumonia that there was no time to summon Sally and Aaron, even if anybody had thought to do so. Sally and Aaron, together and apart from the rest of the family, did attend the funeral but were not invited to the reading of the will. Instead, each of them was handed a letter from Judge Parsons. Aaron's read:

Inasmuch as your name does not appear in the most recent will drawn up by me on behalf of Mrs. Martha Schuyler Van Alen, it is felt by me, and by the family, that your presence would be unnecessary, and perhaps embarrassing, at the reading of same. A portion of her estate that might presumably have gone to you has been willed to Mrs. Mary O'Donnell Van Alen, your wife, in trust for your children, who also received small, separate bequests. Since the so-called Van Alen Trust was activated by the death of Mrs. Van Alen, it has also by your own express wishes passed to your wife, Mary O'Donnell Van Alen, in trust for your children, namely: Amelia Downing Van Alen, Cornelius Van Alen III, and Felicia Mary Van Alen. The value of a third share in the so-called Van Alen Trust, held mostly in real-estate, is estimated by the trustees at $3,000,000, yielding an annual income in the neighborhood of $300,000, which, of course, Mrs. Van Alen is free to apply to the necessary expenses of her and her children during the time of her life. If you have any questions, or wish to contest in any way the provisions of your mother's will, please contact me at my office.

Sally's letter was approximately the same except that it noted that she was now in possession of

$3,000,000 in her own right as an inheritor of a third of the trust and that her mother had included outright gifts of $10,000 each to "my grandson, the Viscount Goodenough of Midstone, England, and my granddaughter and namesake Martha Van Alen Brewster of New York City." What the lawyer had neglected to include in either letter was the amount of the estate descending from Peter Schuyler Van Alen through Martha and divided in unequal shares between James and Mary, in trust for her children. It didn't matter, because the newspapers with their usual intense interest in the affairs of the wealthy spelled it all out. Beside the Vanderbilt estates and the $77,000,000 Jay Gould had left a few years back, the Van Alen fortune was disappointing. In round figures, it was *only* $10,000,000, of which eighty percent went to "my son, James, in recognition of the great responsibility he has borne on behalf of the Van Alen family." Mary was said to have been furious, complaining, "After all, it was *I* who took care of her all these last years, and what little she leaves me she ties up." Sophie was disappointed too—she was remembered with only a few pieces of jewelry "in consideration of the ample provision made for her by her father." The amount going to James, mostly in Van Alen stock, would make him more than equal to Sophie in ownership. While Sophie had so far seen eye-to-eye with James on the business, there could come a time when she'd disagree, and she resented losing the power that she'd quietly held all these years. It had been her one justification for an otherwise unrewarding life and her hold on the family. To retain it she'd need an ally, and she saw it as a form of divine providence that Martha's illness had brought her into such close relationship with Mary. The poor girl couldn't help being Irish, but she'd certainly lived it down, and that gesture of renaming her son Cornelius had moved Sophie beyond measure. If Mary were as staunch as she seemed to be, and the boy came along as she hoped, there would be someone to leave her money to who might appreciate it more than James. No, she hadn't quite lost her power—she'd just have to be shrewder in exercising it.

With the settlement of his mother's estate, Aaron Roberts Van Alen, lawyer, was truly on his own. It would be a shock to some people, and possibly an embarrassment to him, to have to explain from time to time that he was "the other Van Alen—the poor one," but, by now he could almost imagine brother James having someday to explain that *he* was "the other Van Alen—only the rich one." Well, at least it was an attractive fantasy—and one he'd try to make real.

By that fall of 1897, Aaron's assessment of his rising prominence was quite realistic. His case load was so heavy that it kept him in court most of every day and at his desk either in the office or at his apartment half of most nights; recently he had had to take on two young men just out of Harvard to help him with researching the law. If his business brought little in the way of money, it was almost overcompensating him in notoriety. His name was always in the papers by reason of the bizarre causes he pleaded, and the reporters had coined a phrase to

426

describe him that he was rather proud of—"public defender." From the day he'd won freedom for the radical Hugh O'Donnell, men and women in seemingly hopeless entanglements with the law had sought him out. The challenges they presented surpassed any he'd ever been able to invent for himself in all those years that he now felt he'd wasted, and he would turn none of them away, regardless of presumed guilt or inability to pay. In establishing his practice, Aaron had reached into his memory for family tales about another Aaron— Aaron Burr, who in his latter days as a New York lawyer kept a box on his desk into which clients tossed whatever they could in the way of fees and out of which he often took money for clients in trouble. Aaron Van Alen did the same thing and was looked upon as something of an eccentric in the profession.

In the clubs Aaron once frequented, men bewildered by a notice that Attorney Aaron Van Alen, supposedly one of their own, had taken on the defense of yet another confessed murderer or was suing an Astor on behalf of a widow evicted for nonpayment of rent would shake their heads and say something like, "Can't imagine what the fellow's up to unless he's just playing at the law like another game." If he could have heard them, Aaron might have agreed up to a point. He had found the law, at least as contested in the courts, very much like all those games into which he'd once put so much heart. If you kept money out of it, as he was willing—even trying—to do, there was the same kind of pure testing of a man's spirit in court as in

427

sport—a matching of wits and knowledge instead of muscle. Before every case, Aaron suffered—or enjoyed—a large dose of that druglike pre-action tension that made him know in his very guts that he was fully alive. But there was more to law, much more. The stakes—the freedom, reputation, livelihood of a human being—were high enough to justify any effort, and there was that illusive ideal— justice—to be served. In the practice of law, he was finding within himself a true talent, that temperament he'd apparently inherited from his father that allowed him to keep an open mind on almost any issue. The beauty of the common law was its humanity, its acknowledgment of imperfection and error, its adaptability. Justice as seen in the courts was not dogma to be taken on faith but the best arrangement for going on with life that could be worked out under the circumstances of the moment. Like a living organism, justice was capable of evolution; each case, establishing precedent, could be seen as a changing cell within the larger body of what was called justice. Granted, seeking justice could prove as baffling and frustrating and disappointing as life itself, but where change was possible, so was hope. And true, men of the courts, lawyers and judges, were no better than the common run of men—worse often, in terms of using their knowledge and skills to subvert or manipulate the law to serve selfish ends; yet they were restrained, as on the field of sport, by rules and guidelines within which a better man had a chance to win. To Aaron the contentious, evolving law was the heart of the American experiment to create a society in which human beings of every shape and shade, of every purse and persuasion, could be free to realize their potential. Seeing society through the law, Aaron experienced a kind of revelation: America *was* an experiment, tentative and imperfect and still in the process of evolving, like man himself, and by keeping its heart pumping he, more than most, could contribute to the course and nature of that evolution. Though he'd deny it to all but the most trusted and understanding of friends, Aaron Roberts Van Alen had become a man with a mission.

One of the first to sense this, one of the few to whom he confided it, was Aaron's old college friend, Woodrow Wilson. They'd been out of touch, living in worlds apart for years, but Wilson, now a member of Princeton's faculty, conceived the idea of a banquet bringing together former football stars earlier that fall. Aaron attended with some reluctance, feeling that he'd find himself out of step with former teammates, most of whom had pursued safe and sane careers in banking or business, ministry or medicine, or, if in law, the "respectable" kind he'd learned in Judge Parsons' office. Because he had to be in court, Aaron was late getting down to Princeton, missing the pre-dinner pleasantries and coming in cold to the banquet which had been set up, appropriately, in the gymnasium. Because he'd been the star of the very first game, a chair had been left vacant for him at the head table between Wilson and a man he'd hoped never to see again in life—Bud Brewster. Aaron would have turned and left if Wilson hadn't spotted him at the door. Jumping to his feet and ringing a glass with a spoon to bring order, Wilson shouted, "Here he is—the first great tiger, Aaron Van Alen. Let's have a cheer—Tiger-tiger-siss-boom-ah!" There was nothing to do but go up, decently acknowledge the cheers and take his seat.

Could he turn his back on Brewster? Impossible in front of all those men. Brewster's hand was out; he took it. "Surprised to see me here, Aaron?" Brewster said, and without waiting for a reply, rushed on, "Not pleased either, I'll bet. Don't blame you. But I'm straightened out, Aaron, I really am. That brother-in-law of yours put more religion into me than even you once did. I was down, really in the gutter, and when I saw Matty there I went crazy, real crazy. I don't know whether you know what it's like to have a child and never . . . Well, she's better off where she is, I suppose . . . How is she?"

"Fine."

"And . . . and Sally?"

"She's having her troubles. Hancock went broke in the '93 crash and is still suing her in the courts for a divorce and part of her inheritance."

"Oh, your mother died?"

"Yes. A few months ago. Pneumonia."

"Too bad. Always liked her. How's *your* family?"

"Fine."

"Aaron, you may not believe it but I still love Sally. I was crazy then. I've learned a lot these last years. I've never married again, you know. I'm on the wagon and I've got a good coaching job and . . . well, I was wondering if she'd see me?"

"Listen, Bud, I'm glad you're on your feet, but stay away from Sally—Matty too. I mean it."

Knowing his own feelings, Aaron couldn't avoid a sympathetic twinge for this man he thought he hated. Life would be so much simpler if you could see mustache-twirling villains instead of faulted people like yourself stalking about its stage. Still, Bud could be a real problem. Aaron realized now that those crazy spells, or rages, over which Bud seemed to have no control had been a pattern since college days, and the man's continuing interest in Sally and Matty made him uneasy. Well, there was nothing more to be done about it now, so he said, "Excuse me, Bud, but I haven't had a chance for a word yet with Tommy."

Aaron turned with relief to Wilson, a man who was making his life an outstanding success. With his books and articles and speeches he was establishing himself as one of the leading thinkers of America in the fields of history and constitutional law; on campus he was one of the most popular professors in spite of his somewhat austere and patrician appearance. As Aaron had heard it, Wilson often took the side of energetic and experimental students in faculty meetings where most of his colleagues preferred to "keep things as they are." The verse for Wilson in the faculty song composed by students said it all: "Here's to Woodrow Wilson, oh/our legal adviser, don't you know./He said they can't stop us, so let her go./Here's to Woodrow Wilson, oh!" A year or so ago, Aaron would have been in awe of Wilson, or at least at a loss for what to say to him. But now he said, "Tommy, they tell me you're trying to do for the students here what I'm trying to do for the disenfranchised of New York—get them

431

a hearing."

"Yes, I've been following you in the papers, Aaron. I must say I was . . . well, surprised when you turned up on what might be called the underside of the law."

"It's a long story."

"I'm sure it is, and a good one, I'll bet," Wilson said. "Do you remember a night we stood looking up at the stars and I asked you what you wanted to do with your life?"

"I sure do, and I told you I wanted to beat Columbia. Well, I guess I still want to beat Columbia—except on a different playing field."

"No, no, it's more than that," Wilson said. "Like me, you've got a long line of Presbyterian elders standing on your shoulders, and you've finally given in under the weight."

"Actually, I'm supposed to be a Catholic now—"

Wilson laughed. "Better yet, the line's longer. I always knew you had a serious streak in you just by watching the way you played, and I wondered how long it would take you to put it to use. It's harder, I know, when you have no money. To be taken seriously, I mean . . . But you *are* serious about the law, aren't you? Some of those other lawyers sitting right out there have told me that they think you're grandstanding, and they're the same ones who said that about you on the football field. Just jealous, I'd guess. I've been watching the pattern of the cases you bring to trial, and I think I can appreciate what you're trying to do—you're trying to inch the law toward acknowledging rights that are vested in men instead of property."

432

Aaron was excited. "That's it! That's it, Tommy! I've been doing it, but I haven't been able to define it."

"Well, it's better to be able to do it than define it, just as it's better to be able to run the football than map the plays," Wilson said, and sighed. "One of these days I hope to get out into the arena. I rather envy you."

You wouldn't if you knew all the rest, Aaron thought, but he didn't want to spoil the moment with personal matters. Wilson's grasp of his intentions had put to rest the turbulent feelings Bud Brewster's presence had stirred up. When he was called on to make a few remarks at the end of the banquet, he said, "I want to tell you all that it was Tommy Wilson—that is, Woodrow here—who dragged me out onto that football field, and I'm grateful to him. I was scared to death every time I played. But I've never regretted the fright I had to overcome or the bruises. I think it was Wellington who said that the battles of Britain were won on the playing fields of Eton. I'm here to testify that whatever battles I win in court were won on the playing fields of Princeton."

When he sat down as the men around him rose to clap and cheer, Wilson whispered, "Where you belong is in politics, Aaron. You've got the making of an orator and with your money you could be independent and go a long way."

Aaron gave a negative shake of his head and smiled. There was so much Wilson didn't, couldn't know. Aaron would stick with what he was.

*　　　*　　　*

Christmas was not James Schuyler Van Alen's favorite time of the year. What with the holidays on Christmas and New Year's and the drinking that went on and the license taken in the name of "good will," too much time was lost in business. Even though his own people knew his attitudes they nevertheless managed to disappear along about noon of the day before Christmas, and so his office was nearly deserted on that day in 1897 when Senator Tom Platt walked in. Blustery and full of political good cheer, the senator strode up to James' desk and set a package, beribboned and wrapped in paper covered with bright red Santa Clauses, in front of him. By its shape, it looked very much like a bottle.

"Morgan told me I'd find you here, Mr. Van Alen," the senator boomed. "I think you and he are the only men working in the city today. Nice you let your people go, though. Morgan's are sitting around scowling at him. Well, this is just a little remembrance from the party. Merry Christmas!"

James rose, forced his Roosevelt grin and took the senator's hand. "And a merry Christmas to you, senator. What's the news about Cuba?"

"Well, President McKinley's inclined to stay out. But I don't know whether he can if Hearst here doesn't stop running those atrocity stories about Spanish concentration camps in his papers. And that fool Teddy Roosevelt down there in the Navy Department keeps wanting to rattle his battleships. Actually, that's what I wanted to talk to you about if you can spare a minute, Mr. Van Alen."

A smart businessman always had time—and

434

money, if necessary—for a senator. You never knew when you'd need them, as they had in getting that new Dingley tariff through that was giving Van Alen an edge over European competition. "Certainly, sit down, senator," James said, motioning to the chair in front of his desk.

The senator was in no hurry. He sat down, crossed his legs, took off his gloves and folded them and pulled two cigars from an inner pocket, offering one to James. Though he did enjoy an after-dinner cigar, James declined because he'd decreed that there would be no smoking in the Van Alen offices in the interests of saving time, and it wouldn't do for the one or two clerks who hadn't yet escaped to see him breaking his own rules. When the senator had lit up, he said, "I know you are somehow connected with the Roosevelts . . ."

"Yes, through my mother's side of the family. It's rather distant, though."

"Well, that's to the good," the senator said. "I'm going to be quite frank with you, Mr. Van Alen. This young Teddy Roosevelt is a menace to the party. Unfortunately, I can't do much about him since he's captured the public imagination. Strong tells me that Roosevelt damned near wrecked his administration when he was up here as police commissioner. Can you imagine trying to enforce the blue laws in New York? And that crazy business of playing Haroun-al-Raschid and running around the streets in the middle of the night, twirling his cape and frightening honest cops trying to do their duty on the beat! Better to let a few whores get away with their business than have the whole police department on your back. But of course Teddy had a newspaperman at his elbow and so across the land he's a hero of moral rectitude. Well, I'm very much afraid he's going to take a shot at the State House next year, and the only way we can head him off is with a more attractive candidate."

"I agree with you, senator, but I don't see how it concerns me."

The senator let out a puff of smoke. "I've been thinking about your brother, the lawyer—Aaron Van Alen. What is it they're calling him in the press—the public defender? Catchy, that. Since I don't know him, I thought I'd talk to you first. Is he a good Republican?"

James tried to hide his feelings. Obviously, what had been going on within the family hadn't reached the senator, and the less that was known about it, the better. "I'm really not sure, senator. He and I don't discuss politics."

"Oh, I see. Well, it doesn't really matter. The point is that some fellow who was down there at Princeton College a while back and heard him at a banquet says he has the makings of a very impressive speaker, and with his record in the courts we could build him up as more of a champion of the people than Roosevelt. Van Alen's just as good a name, and, of course, it doesn't hurt that he has a little money—I assume—to bring into a campaign. Do you think you could arrange an introduction?"

This was going too far. James had to think of some way of heading the senator off without raising too many embarrassing questions. "Frankly, senator, I don't see my brother very much now that he's left us and is so busy with the law. As I say, I don't really know his politics, but he defended that radical fellow O'Donnell back in '93, and I heard he went out speaking for him when O'Donnell was elected alderman, and O'Donnell's a Tammany man."

"O'Donnell was elected in '94, wasn't he?" the senator said. "Mr. Van Alen, in politics people have short memories. Sound your brother out, will you? . . . Well, I'm taking too much of your time. A Happy New Year to you and all the Van Alens."

The word that filled James' mind when the senator left was "preposterous." How could anyone think of Aaron, a playboy turned advocate for the devil, a home-wrecker, as a candidate for governor? Didn't morals mean *anything* in politics? James was so rattled by the discovery that some important people might think well of his brother that he decided to close the office early. He knew he couldn't concentrate on work, and he might as well get the credit the senator had already given him for being generous from those clerks who didn't have the courage to leave on their own. Preposterous! Of course James would never deliver the senator's message to Aaron, even if he ever saw him. He'd just let the matter die as it should. A good thing Aaron had pulled that ridiculous stunt of giving all of his money to Mary. He could tell from the way the senator talked that nobody'd be seriously interested in Aaron for politics once they found out he didn't have the Van Alen resources behind him. It rankled James, though, that neither Aaron nor Sally seemed to be suffering for what he considered their considerable sins. He'd been furious when his lawyers told him that he had no cause for action in removing the Van Alen name from that art gallery Sally was running. More like a whorehouse, in his opinion. He'd heard that she was living openly with some damned Italian sculptor who couldn't even carve a *likeness*. All else aside, how could a woman of her age get involved in such a thing? Anne and he had had separate bedrooms for half a dozen years now, as decent people should. He had no doubt but what Aaron was involved with some woman, but he had to hand it to Mary for not giving him a divorce. Only good thing about the Catholic Church. Aaron had probably left her because he had no self-control . . . from what Anne said Mary had refused to take any more chances after Felicia was born, which was as it should be. A good woman, that Mary, he'd certainly been wrong about her . . .

The cars going up Broadway and Fifth Avenue were so jammed with people that James could hardly squeeze in. Though none of them looked as if they had much to be merry about, they were, and the whiskey breath in the air was so strong he could hardly breathe. He finally got off at Forty-second Street across from the new library that was replacing the old Croton reservoir and decided to walk the rest of the way in the fresh air. The sight of the library triggered a thought that had been arising more and more frequently in James' head. Carnegie and Astor and Lennox and all those fellows were getting so much credit for building libraries—why, when that place of Carnegie's opened out in Pittsburgh back in '95, it got more notice in the New York press than the new Astor Hotel—it was time to organize some sort of Van Alen charity. It was good business, and it would do a lot to wipe out all the scandal Sally's and Aaron's activities had brought on the name in respectable circles. People were beginning to think of little Carnegie as some kind of a saint—only the men who were doing business with him knew better. Now that he'd pretty well got the railroads in line, James' friend Morgan was trying to make some sense out of the crazy competition in the steel industry, but Carnegie was a tough nut to crack. "You know what he's going around saying?" Morgan told James. "He's saying that Pierpont feels he can do anything because he always got the best of the Jews in Wall Street, but it takes a Yankee to beat a Jew and a Scot to beat a Yankee." Well, if he put his mind to it, a good Dutchman ought to be able to beat them all.

The time was just about ripe for James to move. With his inheritance in hand, he could spare a little. More important, what with the Dingley bill and the gold coming in from Alaska, business was booming as never before. He'd been lucky, too, to pick up quite a few orders back in '94 when that Socialist Debs closed the Pullman works out there in Chicago with a strike. He profited two ways, since Cleveland had sent the troops in there and let that fellow Debs cool his heels for a while in jail, which meant there wouldn't be any more labor trouble in the sleeping-car industry for a long, long time. Yes, the time was ripe. The question was what to do. Carnegie had a corner on the libraries, was even building them all over New York. Now that he was more or less retired, John D. Rockefeller was shoveling money into education, more than $6,000,000 just last year

to the University of Chicago, or so James had heard.
Ought to be something different. James could do
something through the church, of course, but it was
a little difficult to get your name on it. A hospital
maybe? People associated hospitals with mercy,
though as far as he could tell all they did was kill you
there. Well, he'd think about it . . .

Coming up on his mother's old place, James
decided he'd drop in and see how Mary was getting
along. Not infrequently during the past few years
Mary had been coming up to their place, ostensibly
to see Anne but actually, he suspected, to get the
kind of advice from him that only a man could give
her, such as what wines to serve at dinner, whether
he thought they ought to install a new heating
system in the old house and, lately, where she ought
to put the money she couldn't spend. It was a
pleasure to give her advice . . . she was a good
listener and had a good head on her shoulders. And
there was another thing that James tried not to
admit to himself, but he found her the best-looking
woman he'd ever seen. If anything, her beauty grew
with the years, unlike his own poor Anne's. Of
course Mary had had only three—well four,
considering that baby who died—children to Anne's
six, but there was more to it than that. There was a
look in her eye that never let you forget she was a
woman even though she was your sister-in-law. She
was still so popular at balls that James had a hard
time getting in a dance with her—a thing he liked to
tell himself was a duty in view of the fact that she no
longer had a husband as an escort. James, an elder
well-versed in scripture, knew that even entertain-

ing thoughts of Mary as a woman was a sin, worse because her relationship gave it a tinge of incest. Still, it would be unfair to her to let something like that prevent him from doing his brotherly duty, and of course being with her was perfectly proper in anyone's eyes. Thank God, Anne had come around to liking her too, or it might have been otherwise.

James was so busy with his thoughts that he ran smack into a man in the street, a man so large that James bounced backward. James started to tip his hat and apologize when he recognized the fellow— Bud Brewster. "Well, James," Brewster said, smiling, "funny running into you like this. I was just looking around the old neighborhood. Church needs a cleaning, doesn't it?"

Brewster had his hand out, but James kept his in a pocket. "Out of my way, Brewster. I've nothing to say to you. You're lucky you aren't in jail for the trouble you've caused."

Brewster did step aside, tipped his own hat and said, "And a Merry Christmas to you, too, James."

James was happy to duck into the safety of the marbled lobby of the Van Alen mansion. He'd almost gone by at the last minute and might have if it hadn't been for running into Brewster. There was one of those horseless carriages—a Duryea, he thought from the looks of it—standing at the curb. Evidently Mary had a visitor and probably not the kind he'd like to meet. He hadn't much use for the people who were buying these things—sports, mostly—and frightening the horses with their infernal racket. He agreed with Chauncey Depew who'd taken over as president of Vanderbilt's New

441

York Central and ought to know what he was talking about. At dinner a while back some fellow was asking whether he should put some money with a man named Ford around Detroit who'd built a machine to compete with Duryea, and Depew told him, "Nothing has come along to beat the horse. Keep your money. Or, if you must spend, buy a horse and you'll have enough left over to furnish it with feed for the rest of its life."

James hadn't bothered to ring, and there was nobody to greet him. While he was taking off his coat, he tried to digest the peculiar experience with Brewster. He'd really thought the man dead of drink by now, and yet there he was—healthy, well-dressed, clean-shaven, smiling even. Probably too late to press any charges against him, and in any case, in James' private opinion Sally had got about what she deserved. And look what it had led to—that disgusting episode with O'Donnell. He thought briefly of warning Sally, but quickly decided against it. He hadn't seen or spoken to her in four years, except at their mother's funeral, and had no desire to. Besides, from the look of him, Brewster was probably a more responsible citizen than Sally . . . after all, the man *had* been a minister, and a crackerjack too. James had never understood why Brewster deserted one of the most prestigious pulpits in New York to spend his life teaching boys to play games.

James followed the sound of voices, mostly the high piping of excited children, and went into the drawing room. It was festooned for Christmas—a huge tree, dripping with gold and silver ornaments, stood by the windows so that passers-by could see that Christmas was kept at the Van Alens. Under the tree the children were tearing open packages and, sitting on the floor in their midst, was Aaron. Mary was nowhere to be seen. "Oh, I didn't mean to interrupt," James said.

Aaron looked up. "Come in, come in, James. It's Christmas, you know."

"I . . . I really came to see if Mary needs any help."

"Nice of you, but I doubt it. She seems to have everything under control, wouldn't you say?"

Just to make conversation, James said, "You would never guess who I bumped into on the street, literally bumped into, right outside the door here—Bud Brewster. Can you imagine the nerve of the man, showing his face around here? Wanted to shake my hand as if we were friends—"

Aaron got quickly to his feet. "My God, did he look . . . all right?"

"Yes, well got up, smiling. Said he was just looking around the old neighborhood. Why?"

"James, I want to get down to Sally," Aaron said. "I saw the man a while back down at Princeton and he seemed to be all right, but you never know." Patting each of his children on the head, Aaron told them, "I'm sorry I have to go now. Enjoy your toys, and I'll come back the day after tomorrow and take you for that ride. I promise. James, just tell Mary I didn't have time to stay for tea."

Through the end windows overlooking the Avenue, James could see Aaron run out and jump into the horseless carriage. He might have known who would

443

have a thing like that. A governor? Preposterous. When he turned away, he saw Mary coming into the room. The children were bouncing around her, saying, "Look what daddy gave me. Look what daddy gave *me* . . ."

"Very nice . . . now you children get busy and clean up all this mess. We're having our *real* Christmas tomorrow, you know."

"Aaron couldn't stay to tea," James said, offering no more information.

"Just as well," Mary said. "I'm always nervous when he's around. But you'll stay, won't you? It's being served in the ladies' reception room."

Following her through the hall, James found his eyes on her tiny waist that curved out into hips from which her long skirts swung seductively as she walked. He remembered she'd been a dancer, and she still had a dancer's grace. Try as he would, he could not keep from thinking of what probably lay under that sheen of gray silk—snowy buttocks, round and firm, long smooth legs tapering to what he could clearly see was a dainty ankle. He was aware of a sensation, a stirring that he hadn't experienced in years since he'd made himself stop thinking about it. It was unbearable—frightening and embarrassing. He hoped it didn't show. He went to the window and made a fuss of inspecting the weather, hoping it would subside. "Looks like we'll have snow tomorrow after all," he said.

Behind him he could hear the clink of cups as Mary poured. "Oh, I hope so," she said. "It will be wonderful for the children. I'm giving them sleds—at least the older ones. I'm glad Aaron didn't think of

444

that. He doesn't realize that Amelia's too old for dolls and Neil for toy soldiers. Odd, though, they seemed to like them . . . One lump or two, James? I keep forgetting."

"Two. When did Aaron get that machine he's driving?"

"I don't know, I don't talk to him often."

"Do you miss him?"

"Sometimes . . . it's hard not having a man around . . ."

The situation had eased, and James came over to pick up his tea. "You . . . always have me, Mary. Call on me, please, anytime."

"I do—too much, I think. Anne's going to get cross."

"Oh, no, she thinks of you as her friend, her sister, as do I. Besides, families should stick together."

She blessed him with a radiant smile. "Thank you James, I've often wondered if I were a bother, but I do get lonely. Of course there's Sophie, but . . ."

"Where *is* Sophie?"

"She'll be down directly. She didn't want to see Aaron. She thinks he's a swine for leaving me . . ."

"She's not far wrong."

"Oh, I've thought about it a great deal, and I may be as much to blame as he. I sometimes think none of this would ever have happened if I'd had sense enough to shut the door earlier on my irresponsible family. What hurts me is that I tried so hard to be a . . . a Van Alen."

Impulsively James reached over and took her hand. It was the first time he'd ever touched her, other than in the correct positions of the waltz. Van Alens weren't given to impulsive, physical gestures of affection. That he'd let himself go to that extent made him realize how nearly his feelings were getting out of control. "You are," he said, "you are. I don't think I've ever told you how proud I am of you—all of us are."

She put her other hand over his and squeezed it, and the feel of her hands, warm and a little moist and so very much alive made him glad he was sitting down. My God, he'd have to get out of here . . . But she didn't let him go, kept holding him and said, "I'm glad somebody appreciates the effort." When she finally released his hand, she said, "James, I have to tell you something before Sophie comes down. Ever since your mother died, she's been getting, well, queer . . ."

"Queer*er*, you mean. Both Anne and I want to thank you for taking her off our hands. I tried to be nice to her but it was a trial. What's she up to now?"

"Well, you know she's never been really interested in anything that's happened since 1863, but now she does nothing all day but go over those old records of her father's that didn't get burned because he had them in a safe. She says Van Alen and Son isn't being run the way her father ran it, and I'm afraid she'll give you trouble at the next stockholders' meeting."

"Why, she's never been to a meeting in her life. I always consulted her out of courtesy but—"

"Don't count on it this time. She's been going out more and more lately, and I'm afraid it's thanks to me. She says that, now that *I'm* a stockholder, she'll go if I go. Poor thing, those stocks are all she cares about in life."

"Well, we'll cross that bridge when we come to it. Now, I really must go. Everybody at my house will wonder where Santa Claus is."

Mary followed him to the doorway, where he paused to say goodbye. He noticed something else about her—he was noticing too many things this day—she was as tall as he, their eyes at a level. Suddenly she leaned forward and kissed him, and something like fire shot up through his whole body and into his cheeks. "You're under the mistletoe," she laughed, "and . . . and I swear you look like a beet! Don't forget we're having open house tomorrow, and you're to bring the family."

James awkwardly left the house and somehow got on up to his own. She didn't have to do that, did she? The kiss had been sisterly enough, but the touch lingered on his lips. *Oh God, oh Lord, correct my thoughts.* He'd take the family to midnight services tonight and pray as never before. But he'd take them to Mary's tomorrow, and he was looking forward to is as never before. It was terrible, terrible that he didn't really want God to correct his thoughts, that he felt that this Christmas was giving him a gift beyond desiring. "Merry Christmas!" he shouted at a stranger on the walk, and laughed to see the man's astonishment—which scarcely matched his own at his extraordinary behavior.

Chapter 10

"I'D THOUGHT you might want Uncle James to give you away," Mary Van Alen told her daughter, Amelia, during one of their many daily discussions of the wedding plans.

"No, I want daddy to do it," Amelia insisted.

Mary didn't know whether to make an issue of it or not. God knew, James had been in many ways more of a father to the children these last years than Aaron, and he really deserved to be standing up there beside Amelia. She could probably have her way with Amelia, but there was a danger to it. For all that they were respectful to him, the children were never warm with James. In fact the older they got the more they seemed to relate to Aaron, and if she tried to work her will on this, Mary realized she risked pushing her daughter further into her father's arms out of some sort of mistaken sympathy. Perhaps it *would* be a good idea to have Aaron on hand for this, the first marriage in a new generation of Van Alens, to demonstrate to the very select company of guests that, whatever they may have *heard*, the Van Alens did the civilized thing. Where Mary would absolutely draw the line was on inviting either Sally or that wild daughter of hers, that Matty.

"All right, if your father will agree to come. Now that he's hobnobbing with Teddy Roosevelt down at the White House, he may be too busy for social events—"

"But this isn't a social event. It's my *wedding*. Actually I already told daddy I was going to ask him, and he's put it on his calendar."

"Then that's settled. I suppose you'll at least agree to have Edith as a bridesmaid and Peter as an usher . . ."

"If I *have* to."

She and James had often agreed that it would be nicer if their children liked one another better, but they'd been in a kind of competition all their lives, here in New York and up in Newport, and it was widely known that among the younger set *her* children were referred to as "the beautiful Van Alens" and James' "the rich Van Alens."

"Yes, you have to. I'd think you'd feel a little sorry for Edith . . ."

At eighteen Amelia was being married in good time, just a year after her coming out, but Edith, James' oldest daughter, had had her debut clear back in '97—a little early but then Martha had so wanted to see one of her granddaughters presented to society—and here it was already 1902, so she must be at least twenty-two. Edith was a nice enough girl, but she took after her mother in looks, poor thing, and from what James said there wasn't a beau in sight. Amelia, on the other hand, was considered the spitting image of the Gibson girl and no wonder: like almost every other girl in America her age, Amelia was forever fussing with that long, thick blonde hair she'd inherited from Aaron, imitating the Psyche knots, Bath Buns, side waves or whatever she saw in the latest Gibson drawing. Amelia insisted that her shirt-waists have that Gibson pleat that made her shoulders look broad and her waist narrow and that her skirts have that flair at the bottom that would allow her to get around the tennis court. Amelia had the face for it too—regular, squared-off features softened by lips that, as the saying went, "just asked to be kissed"—and there were those who, knowing that Mr. Gibson was sometimes a guest at the house, were convinced that she was his model. It was a satisfaction to Mary to have such a daughter since "the Gibson girl" was everybody's ideal of what a young lady should look like and be. She had only to think back at her own dreary eighteenth year when she was slopping beer in her father's saloon and perspiring in a chorus line to realize how far and how fast she'd come to be able to give the world this shining girl who'd never known a day's labor or a night's uncertainty.

Mary knew that there were some in Newport and up and down the Avenue here in the city who would say that, with all that going for her and being a Van Alen, besides, Amelia could have done better for herself than the son of one of those "Pittsburgh millionaires." But as far as Mary was concerned a millionaire was a millionaire, and John McCandless was more attractive than most. He wasn't, in fact, unlike "the Gibson man" with his blond hair parted in the middle and going back in gentle waves, his chiseled features and dimpled chin. He'd just graduated from Princeton and had some sort of sinecure in the new United States Steel Corporation, a job that seemed to allow him plenty of time to take Amelia out and try to teach her how to play golf, that new game that all the businessmen were talking up, or to drive her around in his Packard runabout. He was, Mary reflected ruefully, a great deal like the Aaron she'd married, with one important and good exception—she couldn't detect in John any of that tendency to worry about the poor working man, or to brood about the unfairness of wealth that had always seemed to keep Aaron from really enjoying himself.

Actually, this attitude was common to the whole Pittsburgh crowd, and Mary rather liked them for it. Most of them were as new to wealth as she was, and they didn't have any odd notions that it was something to feel ashamed of, for God's sake. They'd worked for it, prayed for it, and they felt that it was God's reward for doing what they'd done, and they had every right to flaunt it. When that scandal broke in the papers this past January about Charlie Schwab, U.S. Steel's president, gambling for high stakes on the roulette wheels at Monte Carlo, Alexander McCandless, John's father, told Mary, "Anybody who's ever worked for that old Scrooge Carnegie deserves a little fun. I hear Andy was so mad he cabled him to resign and wrote Morgan a letter saying he felt as if a son had disgraced the family. Well, let me tell you, Schwab sweated in the hellfires of those mills just like I sweated in the office while Carnegie was bouncing around Britain in his coaches or holed up in that windy castle of his in Scotland, and Morgan was right to ignore Andy and keep Charlie on." McCandless himself had been one of the Carnegie partners who, after living on low wages and high promises, got his million when Carnegie sold out to Morgan the previous year for $485,000,000. The first thing McCandless, like a lot of others, did was to move out of what they called "hell with the lid off" to New York, as Carnegie had done long before them. Though McCandless couldn't find a place on the Avenue, where some of the old mansions were already being sold out and torn down to build more profitable hotels and apartments— only Clay Frick who'd gouged Carnegie for some $30,000,000 by suing him for it had money enough for that—he was dickering for the Hancock place up in Newport. Mary had tipped him off to a possible bargain there, hoping to have Amelia around for the summers, because she'd heard through the grapevine that Pierce had rebought the place with that settlement he got from Sally—a settlement which proved, as Mary had known all along, that Sally and Hugh had done what everybody suspected—and was back to his old tricks, lying around drinking all day and even forgetting to pay his taxes. What McCandless wanted, as he explained to Mary, was "the best" for his children, and New York and Newport were the places to give them the right oportunities. He had a couple of daughters just about to come out, and already, in less than a year, John had found no less a bride than Amelia Downing Van Alen. Mary knew that McCandless was a little bothered about their not being one of the Protestant Van Alens, but they'd talked it all over and decided to have a wedding at home with a priest officiating, and John had agreed to sign papers allowing any children they might have to be raised in the true faith. One thing McCandless, being a religious man himself, did like about the arrangement was that, judging from Mary's own situation, there wouldn't be any divorce in his son's family.

James wasn't as happy as Mary with that Pittsburgh crowd. For once he disagreed with his friend Morgan, and privately thought that Schwab's running around Europe with a fast set—one of them was a Baron *Rothschild*—and making a show of himself at the gambling tables was a disgrace that could affect steel stock. The trouble with the nouveau riche, as most of these Pittsburgh fellows were, was that they didn't realize the value of respectability in establishing public confidence. That ass Schwab, trying to explain to Morgan, said that he didn't believe in doing anything behind closed doors, and Morgan told him, quite rightly, "That's what doors are for." Imagine what would happen if he and Mary weren't discreet? James had more than a passing interest in the Schwab affair, because Morgan had persuaded him to come in on the formation of the world's largest corporation by trading Van Alen stock for shares in the U.S. Steel. "Look, James, the day of the small company is over," Morgan had argued. "If we're building bridges and making rails, we might as well make rolling stock, and the time for you to join us is when we're putting it together and still feel generous. Remember what happened to those oil fellows who wouldn't go along with Rockefeller?" It was supposed to sound like friendly advice, but James knew a threat when he heard one. He knew, too, that there was a lot of "water" in the billion-dollar capitalization since Van Alen assets had been considerably overassessed in the trade of stocks, and any loss of confidence in the market could be a disaster. On the other hand, if the business was the success that Morgan predicted, he and all the other Van Alens would be richer than even they could have imagined. Not only richer, as far as James was concerned, but part of the truly big business that was running America and a good part of the world too, now that the flag was being flown as far away as the Philippines, and China was opened, and they were getting the European banks off their backs.

Mary knew how James felt about these things because he told her endlessly, and it was, she guessed, one of the things she most enjoyed about him. James might be chubby Dutch, but there was nothing flabby about his mind. He paid scant attention to anything but figures, because, as he said, "Figures never lie." She'd almost been persuaded by that crazy Sophie to vote her stock against the merger on what were really sentimental grounds until James sat down with her and wrote out the figures that proved how much better off they'd all be. Sophie was still muttering about bringing some kind of lawsuit, though God knew what grounds she'd have, and even of going to Aaron with it, now that he was involved in the government's suit against Northern Securities. James wasn't worried about Sophie, but that other suit got him so riled up that he could hardly speak . . . "It's all the fault of that damned cowboy in the White House, as Mark Hanna calls him, and I wish I weren't even distantly related to him. Now my own brother is in it, as if he hasn't done enough damage. Why, if they win, who's to say they won't go after U.S. Steel next and ruin us all? My God, Tom Platt's idea of putting Roosevelt on ice by getting him elected vice president certainly boomeranged. The only thing that might have been worse would have been his notion of knocking Roosevelt out with Aaron as a candidate. They're birds of a feather, believe me . . ." Mary often wondered if Teddy Roosevelt would have been like that if Alice had lived. Alice had been a real lady and she was probably turning over in her grave at the antics of little Alice, who was almost as bad as Sally's daughter, Matty Brewster, what with smoking cigarettes and drinking cocktails and running around all the time. They said her father complained, "I can either run Alice or the country, but I can't run both." Well, as James said, "Crazy Teddy was a failure at both."

Thank God, her children weren't like that. Oh, Amelia was a bit unladylike in playing all those games, probably taking after her father, but a lot of young women were doing that these days, and marriage would soon settle her down. Cornelius would be off to Yale this fall, and he was already talking to James about taking his proper place in business. Mary would have to admit that Felicia was a little too fidgety and sassy for her liking . . . she'd been spoiled by those nurses and nannies and her older brother and sister, but she was only nine and there'd be plenty of time to concentrate on straightening her out when the others were out of the house. It was probably her fault for letting the servants raise Felicia when she'd been going through that strange period after little Aaron's death, thinking that God didn't want her to have children. Now, with the others growing so fast, she was glad that she had had Felicia, and God had been good to her in making possible her love for James. When she'd still been worried about the sin of it she'd prayed for a sign, and she'd taken it as one when she'd stopped bleeding at what everybody said was an early age, only thirty-six.

James, as concerned about sin as she, had accepted her change of life as a sort of divine approval too. Otherwise they might not have had the courage. It had really been her doing, and she probably couldn't have lived with herself without that sign. She'd been sick, not very sick, but just enough to give herself the luxury of staying in bed in that early spring of '98, and James had come over to see if there was anything he could do for her. She'd fortunately taken the trouble to put up her hair and wear her best silk wrap because Michael, whom she'd hired after old Patrick's death and who wasn't quite broken in yet, had showed James right up to her bedroom door.

James stood shyly out in the hall, turning his hat in his hands. "Oh, I didn't know, I thought he was taking me up to your sitting room . . . you really ought to have a talk with him. I didn't want to disturb you, Mary, but I was just on my way home from the office and thought I'd look in to see how you're coming along. Anne would have been over but she's got a bad cold and didn't think you needed that—"

"James, come right on in. I'm not contagious," she said. "In fact, I think I'm quite well. I'm just enjoying the rest."

"Good, you deserve it," James had said, and moved tentatively into the room.

She noticed that his eyes were busy looking everywhere but at her. In a kind of celebration of independence she'd had the room redecorated right after her mother-in-law died so that she'd have a place of her own, and had let the decorator talk her into the Moorish style that was all the rage. The drapes and the canopy at the head of her bed, which was vaguely shaped like the dome of a mosque, were red velvet with long gold fringes, as were the tufted hassocks that served as chairs; a chandelier of Oriental gold filigree hung from the ceiling, and mosaics of tile in Oriental pattern framed the ceiling and fireplace. Amelia, with her taste for the out of doors and simple clothes, was so embarrassed that she'd never show friends into the room. But little Felicia loved it and would spend hours squatting on a hassock draped in veils she'd concocted from old lace curtains and pretending to be the prettiest princess in some sultan's harem.

"I forgot, you've never seen it, James. Do you like it?"

"Well, it's different . . ."

"I wanted it to be as different as possible. I'm thinking of doing the rest of the house."

"Well . . ."

"Why not? It's just that you remember the way it was, and you don't want anything to change. Isn't that right?"

"I guess so."

"I *know* so. But that's all right, James. It's what I like about you. You're the only steady member in this whole family—you and just possibly me . . . Now sit down. Please. I haven't had anyone to talk to for days."

James did sit down on a hassock far from the bed. He perched gingerly on the edge, as if the tufts were thorns. His hat was still in his hand. He didn't seem to know what to say. "Well . . . so you're well now?"

"Yes, I don't know what was wrong with me—just out of sorts, I guess."

She pulled herself up on the pillows and turned to see James better. In the movement the neck of her robe fell open, exposing the white mounds of breasts pushing above the bodice of her lacey night dress. She didn't know whether to let it alone or call more attention to the exposure by fussing with it. James' eyes were on the spot, and he shifted uneasily. "I . . . I think I'd better go now . . ."

Mary was experiencing an odd feeling, a kind of heat all over. But then that was nothing new; she'd been having a lot of this lately, including flashes that she thought would burn her skin right off. The doctor hadn't been much help: "I'd say it sounds like . . . uh, change of life, Mrs. Van Alen, but

458

you're probably too young for that. I don't usually prescribe it but some women have help from Mrs. Pinkham's remedy." Until she'd read the label and seen how much alcohol was in it, she'd been drinking the stuff every day without much effect. But she'd stopped it, because she was still afraid of alcohol after that night when she'd been out of control and let Aaron have his way with her. From the days when she'd made herself learn all those unnatural contortions at ballet school, Mary had prided herself on being always in control of her body—and almost always of her feelings. She thought that James was the same way, and she admired him for it. They were alike, they didn't let things happen to them, they *made* them happen. She could understand better than most, for example, what James and his friends were always trying to do in business: they wanted everything under their control so that they could be sure how the figures were going to come out at the bottom of the ledger. It alarmed her when her body was misbehaving as it was now. She adjusted her robe to cover her flesh and said, "Yes, I suppose so . . ."

But James surprised her. He didn't move. "Mary," he said, "I have to talk about something. It's . . . it's on my conscience. I . . . I don't think we should see each other alone again."

"Why on earth not? We're practically brother and sister, aren't we?"

She knew perfectly well why not. She'd suspected it for some time now, especially last Christmas, when he'd so overreacted under the mistletoe. At first she'd found his warming interest amusing and reassuring to her feminine vanity. Growing up admired by so many brothers, she'd learned almost unconsciously how to bring out and manipulate masculine admiration to get what she wanted, and she'd been doing that for years with James to secure her position in the Van Alen family. What could be a safer man to exercise her wiles on than this much-familied brother-in-law of such demonstrable control and respect for propriety? He was so stuffy that he'd been a real challenge, and for a long time she'd enjoyed the game. But after Anne had given up on herself and on having more children, she'd sensed that it was becoming a little dangerous.

So, yes, she knew, and yet she didn't quite want to face it. She'd really enjoyed those carefree nights with Aaron, and although she'd thought that she had enough control to switch off desire like an electric lamp, she'd find it glowing at night in occasional unbidden dreams and, more often lately, possibly owing to what was going on inside her, in idle dreams of day. If there was an image in those dreams, it was increasingly James. Not for his looks, God knew, but because of that disciplined power she felt in him, a power not unlike her own. And yet it was all so contrary to her religion, not to mention her good sense, so dangerous to the position of respectability she'd earned in society that she could hold herself in check without too much effort. Yet she'd gone on looking forward more than she knew to seeing James, to absorbing from him that confirmation she needed of her attraction as a woman, and, for certain, she didn't want it to end . . .

"Well, I . . ." He was red-faced now, almost as red as he'd been when she kissed him. "That's just it. I . . . I find I can't think of you as a sister. God help me, I've prayed over it, and now seeing you like this . . ."

"Like what?"

James waved his hand to take in the room. "In this . . . in that bed, in those clothes . . . I *must* leave."

He got up, and she noticed that he was careful where he held his hat. She might have been amused if she hadn't suddenly felt sorry for him. "James . . .?"

He'd reached the foot of her bed, paused. ". . . you don't *really* want to go, do you?"

"No, and that's why I *must* . . ."

"Then sit down again for a minute—there on the foot of the bed—and let's talk. We are mature, James, and there's no reason why we can't face this. I've needed you ever since Aaron left me, and I don't know how I can get along without you . . ."

James sat even more gingerly on the edge of the bed. "Oh, we'll see each other under suitable circumstances," he said. "I just didn't want you to think that I was avoiding you over something *you'd* done if I act differently from now on. I know it's all my problem. A good woman like you—"

She let herself laugh. "Yes, I have been a good woman, haven't I? Sometimes I tire of it . . ."

"You don't mean that, Mary."

"Yes, I do. Don't you ever tire of being a good man?"

"Not . . . not until recently. I don't know what's happening to me . . ."

461

"If it's any help to you, something's happening to me too . . ."

James gave her a new kind of look, appraising but also apprehensive. "That makes it worse, Mary. We're both in danger of . . . of something we'd regret."

"All right, so we both know the danger. Can't we deal with it without losing our friendship? Those moments with you have become precious to me, and I do need your advice on matters I don't want to share with other people, even Anne. I can control myself, can't you?"

"Once I would have said so but no more. Look at me, I think I'm shaking . . ."

He was, and his usually jovial face was a map of sheer misery. Instinctively she reached out to him. Her robe again fell open, off her shoulders and the swell of her breasts. She paid no attention to it as she took his hand. "You are, aren't you? Do you really want me that much, James?"

He looked at her, gripped her hand. "Yes, more, God help us, than anything I've ever wanted, but it's impossible, can't you see—?"

"Yes, I've told myself that too."

"It's a sin, Mary, even thinking about it . . ."

"I've told myself that too. And yet . . ."

There was a kind of hope in his voice, his hand tightening until hers hurt. "And yet what?"

"God can forgive sin if you can't help it, can't he?"

"I don't know, I just don't know."

He moved closer then, sat firmly on the side of her bed and tried to take her in his arms. "Just let me hold you, Mary, until this feeling stops—"

She came abruptly back to the reality of the situation, pushed him away. "No, not here, not now. That butler knows you're here, and I don't know when one of the children might pop in. If we're going to do this, it will have to be right . . . you'll have to make arrangements. I'm sure you're clever enough to think of something . . ."

James got up. "Of course, you're right. I forgot myself, Mary, I'm sorry, I'll go now."

As he left, she said, "But you will make arrangements?"

"I . . . I don't know, Mary. I think both of us ought to pray. We just aren't the sort of people who . . . well, you understand what I mean."

So she had prayed, and it had come to her as a sign that she could no longer have children, which was why she'd been so good for so long, wasn't it? Could the Lord be rewarding her virtue? She didn't know what answer James had had to his prayers, but the arrangement he proposed was so natural, so innocent, so easy that it had about it, too, the strange guidance of providence . . . They were all sitting about—Mary and James and Anne—talking about a spring trip to Newport to prepare for the opening of their cottages, and Anne had said, "I don't think I ought to get up there in that damp sea air. I've still got this beastly cold." With commendable casualness, James said, "Well, Mary and I could ride up together. It shouldn't take more than a day or so." Mary could not bring herself to look at James as Anne said, "That's a fine idea. You could send the children over here, Mary. They'd just be underfoot up there. Or I suppose Sophie can keep an eye on them?" . . .

On the parlor car going up, they were shy and tense with each other, talking about business, the weather, their children, anything but what was on their minds. At the station there was an enterprising hackey who'd acquired a horseless carriage. James, keyed up, said, "Let's try it. Never been in one of these things, have you?"

"Yes, Aaron's taken me for a spin."

"That's right, I'd forgotten. Well, up you go." When he'd handed her to her seat, he got up beside her and gave his own address. "Caretaker's day off—I saw to that," he said in a whisper so that the driver couldn't overhear, and asked, "Now, Mary, are you sure? I could drop you at your house."

"Yes, yes, I'm sure," she whispered back, and then she revealed her condition, her answer to her prayer, and asked him, "And did you get an answer?"

"Yes, in fact, most of all just now. If you were willing, then it was to be . . . I was wondering what we'd do about . . . I don't know anything about, about de-vices . . ."

"Oh, James, you are innocent, almost as innocent as I am. I like that, I think we're truly made for each other."

They were holding hands tightly. Impatient, James called to the driver, "Can't you make this contraption go faster?"

"I can, governor, but you'll have to stop holding hands and hold onto your hats."

They did, and soon their faces were being whipped

464

with fresh spring air, the scenery rushing by almost as fast as it did on the train. It was exhilarating. "By George, I think I'll get one of these," James shouted. "You see what you're already doing to me? Anne's afraid to ride in one, but you aren't."

"Oh, no, I love it!"

"Ah, Mary, I think we're going to have a new lease on life." . . .

Once the tension had been resolved between them, they became what they liked to think of as friends, intimate friends, not lovers in the sense of those feckless people who let passion drive them from the course of their lives. They understood each other so well, almost without explanation. He knew that she would never divorce Aaron, that it was more than religion—it was her proper revenge as well, and he never asked. And she knew that he might be unfaithful but never disloyal to Anne, who had been such a good wife and mother. Also that it was more than conscience—it would be bad for business, and she never asked.

Discretion was essential to their lives, but it added spice to their indiscretion. Thank God for the new Waldorf and Astoria, down at Thirty-fourth Street. The two hotels together had a thousand rooms, more than any other hostelry in the world, and it was so easy to get lost in the crowds. James rented a suite there for the use of business clients from out of town, and when it was empty they could safely meet within its rooms. It was often delightfully on the spur of the moment. He might call any time of any day and use their code: "Are you going shopping today?" And, yes, she was almost always "going shopping," knowing he'd be there whenever she could conveniently arrive. It had been going on for some four years now, and it just might go on for the rest of their lives. They never thought, or talked, about that. Both troubled by conscience at times, they agreed over and over again that God would not have made it so easy for them if He were displeased. Everything else they were doing was right, and this was their reward. She was *the* Mrs. Van Alen, the one with the money. They were different from other people—those who did not have the intelligence, the discipline, the means to get what they wanted, and so deserved no more than they had.

There were times, though, now that her daughter Amelia was getting married, when Mary wondered whether she was getting enough out of her relationship with James to be worth the risk; a scandal, after all, could ruin everything for Amelia, for all their futures. In making love, James was no Aaron; he was so impatient, masterful. If it left her dissatisfied in some ways, she found that, having so long been her own mistress, she enjoyed being mastered. But what especially excited her was what she had done, could do, to him. He confessed that he had never been so aroused, so out of his mind with desire; with Anne for years he'd just been doing his duty. Once when she didn't feel like it she had used the technique Aaron had taught her, and James was reduced to tears of gratitude . . . "I never imagined a woman could be so wonderful, so understanding."

By letting him master her in bed, she was turning this powerful man into a near-slave in other matters.

There was little that went on in his head that he was not eager to share with her, and she was beginning to comprehend the true extent of wealth and influence he had been building through all these years of ceaseless work and shrewd decisions. Men like Morgan, and now Frick and Mellon, listened to him and were eager to let him in on their schemes; he was pushing Carnegie and the Rockefellers off the front pages with the Van Alen Hospital and Medical Institute rising on the upper East Side, said to be the world's greatest wonder in the science of healing. It was heady to know that she could manipulate such a man, more heady still to realize that with one indiscretion she could divest him of that rather pompous respectability which had so long been his stock in trade. When her will faltered, or conscience assailed her, she would remind herself of what this liaison would mean to young Cornelius, for whom her ambition was boundless: he would replace James as *the* Mr. Van Alen. In renaming him, she'd made an ill-disguised play for Cousin Sophie's inheritance, which together with his own would have given him control of Van Alen & Son, and it was this that almost made her go along with Sophie and oppose the merger. But in arguing her out of it, James had promised a large role for Cornelius in larger enterprises, and it was a gamble she took, hedging her bet with her relationship with James. Fortunately, James' older son Peter was something of a clod, who couldn't even make it through a year of Columbia and was set to doing make-work cataloguing of his father's art collection; the younger son Arthur, at sixteen, was in scrapes that were already costing James a small fortune to hush up. And, of course, the girls didn't matter. When it came to running large affairs, it was, as Mary herself would concede, properly man's work, which was why her own ambition was focused on Cornelius. Yes, she would go on taking the risk—and quite honestly enjoying the excitement of it—until Cornelius had his opportunity. Some day he'd thank her for it, if she ever had the courage to let him know.

Meanwhile, she wanted this wedding to be perfect, not only for Amelia's sake but for the show it would make in society. Her ballroom could hold nearly as many people as that of *the* Mrs. Astor, and she was inviting most of Ward McAllister's "four hundred" to let them see with their own eyes that a Pittsburgh millionaire could be just as dashing and a lot more solvent than all these foreign aristocrats New York girls had been marrying lately, like Consuelo Vanderbilt's Duke of Marlborough and Anna Gould's Count Boni de Castellane. Lord knew, with Sally's awful experience, the Van Alens had been among the very first to learn the cost of such unions, and Martha on her death bed had made Mary promise that she would lock up her daughters in a convent before she'd let them get into something like that. Yes, it had to be a perfect wedding, and she'd have to warn James that Aaron would be there. The brothers had not exchanged a civil word in years. She thought that she could count on Aaron, who would want to make things as pleasant as possible for his daughter, but she wasn't so sure of James. He had a temper, and he was furious at Aaron's part in this anti-trust suit. Well, she always had that weapon over James' head—she could deny him her favors—and she would use it if she had to. She was, after all, a mother before she was anybody's mistress.

When in that late spring of 1902 Aaron Roberts Van Alen, attorney-at-law, received a letter on White House stationery and in the President's own hand inviting him to visit, he could not imagine what might be on the mind of his old friend, Teddy Roosevelt. It could not be purely social. When it came to that, they'd drifted apart, and he had no doubt that Teddy, almost a caricature of the great American family man with his rowdy kids tearing the White House apart as if it were their own home in Oyster Bay, disapproved of the way Aaron was leading his personal life. As far as Aaron knew, nobody could actually prove that there was anything improper going on between him and Georgia Maitland, the actress, but they *were* seen together, and he was never seen with his wife. So the letter really came out of the blue. There was no question of declining the invitation. Without good grounds a mere attorney simply couldn't refuse to honor a summons from the President; even the great Morgan had recently gone hat in hand to the White House, like the mountain going to Mohammed, and now the arrogant coal barons, grumbling all the way, were going to meet a man they wouldn't talk to on the street—United Mine Workers chief John Mitchell—in the Pennsylvania Avenue house of the President. Quite apart from any sense of duty, Aaron was very humanly curious, and he welcomed the opportunity personally to congratulate Teddy—he'd have to remember to call him "Mr. President"—for throwing the same kind of surprise punches in public life that he'd used on Aaron in the gym so long ago. Though God had given Morgan his, there were already a few more red noses in the financial capital at New York, and there'd probably be some black eyes before long.

Remembering some of his own experiences with Teddy, Aaron had been less surprised than most when Roosevelt suddenly began using government, as he himself was trying to use the courts, in an apparent effort to insure more fair play in American life. Roosevelt had always detested bullies, and in his younger years had often enough used his fists to show it. What he was doing now wasn't all that different. From what Aaron had heard, Morgan couldn't have been more shocked and hurt than when Roosevelt's attorney general, Philander Knox, a good, sound corporate lawyer from Pittsburgh himself, filed suit without notice under the Sherman Anti-trust Act against the Northern Securities Company. Accustomed to thinking of himself as the financial savior of the country, or at least that part of it that owned money, Morgan thought that he'd done it again when he created Northern Securities as a holding company to combine the railroads of the northwest and end the disastrous competition between Edward Harriman's Union Pacific and James Hill's Great Northern which had erupted in a stock war so fierce that it nearly ruined Wall Street. His thanks from an idiot President who didn't understand business, who'd never met a payroll, was to be branded a malefactor of great wealth and hailed into court for unfairly creating a monopoly that was gouging farmers and small shopkeepers along the railroads with high rates. Not only Morgan but the public was astounded since no administration had ever made use of the Sherman Act. As one paper commented, "Wall Street is paralyzed at the thought that a President of the United States would sink so low as to try to enforce the law." Roosevelt was now sinking even lower in personally trying to settle the anthracite coal strike that could leave millions cold this coming winter by bringing the operators and union together. As George Baer, representing the operators, said, "The duty of the hour is not to waste time negotiating with the fomentors of this anarchy. The rights and interests of the laboring man will be protected and cared for— not by the labor agitators, but by the Christian men to whom God in his infinite wisdom has given the control of the property interests of this country." A man like Baer was a bully just made for Roosevelt.

What did surprise and sadden Aaron was Hugh O'Donnell's attitude toward what was going on in Washington. They hadn't seen each other much since Hugh and Sally had broken up and Hugh had gone into politics. Hugh had done well and was now a councilman in the borough of Manhattan in the new consolidation that had absorbed Brooklyn and the Bronx, Queens and Richmond, and made of New York City with its three million people the second city to London in the whole world. The city was growing so fast, was so in need of everything to keep up with that growth, particularly in the way of transportation and construction, that uncounted millions were being spent with a reckless abandon; nobody knew for sure who was getting what. In putting all the street railways together into the Metropolitan Street Railway Company, Ryan and Whitney and some others of Aaron's old neighbors on Fifth Avenue had unloaded more than $200,000,-000 worth of stock so full of water that the island might one day be submerged in it; now another $56,000,000 was being raised to start digging underground for a rapid transit system.

The money was not all going up to Fifth Avenue. One of the companies cashing in on all this work was the New York Contracting and Trucking Company in which John Murphy, brother of Tammany chief Charlie Murphy, had an interest. Aaron had had to look into that company on behalf of a client and had discovered that some eighty-five of its one hundred shares were in the hands of unknown parties, perhaps Charlie himself and perhaps some of his more loyal lieutenants, such as Hugh O'Donnell. No councilman's salary could account for the fact that Hugh was now wearing Brooks Brothers clothes and, although he kept his family over in the old shabby house on the West Side to maintain his image and base of power, leasing an apartment in one of the new buildings on Park Avenue for his own convenience. He was also able to indulge what seemed to be an increasing taste for whiskey in the Waldorf bar, where as he explained, the people important to a politician hung out. Aaron who himself dropped into the bar from time to time more often saw Hugh in the company of the "Waldorf crowd"—James Keene, who'd floated the U.S. Steel issue for Morgan; Baruch; Thomas Fortune Ryan; Jacob Field—people more important to a speculator than a politician. Aaron himself had been present when somebody asked Field what he thought of Balzac, and he replied, "I dunno. I never deal in them outside stocks."

Still, Hugh was paying lip service on the hustings to the cause of the workingmen he supposedly served, and Aaron gave him credit for repeating on a larger stage his performance in Newport, where by ingratiating himself with power he might borrow some of that power to his own good ends. Lord knew Aaron wasn't one to fault Hugh for earning what he could or even for supposedly keeping a woman in the Park Avenue apartment as long as his heart was in the right place. But he learned the sad truth when one day he met Hugh in the Waldorf, standing alone for a change at the bar, and had his first opportunity in a long while for a private talk with him. Hugh was warm in his welcome, shaking his hand and calling to the bartender, "Give Mr. Van Alen what he wants on me."

Aaron could appreciate that. When their drinks came, he held his up and said, "How about a toast to my old friend, Teddy Roosevelt? He's doing in that coal strike what you've always said government should do. Even though you're a good Tammany man, you ought to appreciate it."

Hugh scratched his chin. "Well, I ain't so sure, Aaron. My friend Ryan's been telling me that if Roosevelt don't stop messing around with business, stocks'll go all to hell."

"I hardly thought you cared about Wall Street."

"I've gotta admit my friends here have been giving me a stake in the action and—"

"Hugh, it's hard to believe it's you talking."

Hugh did look a little sheepish and quickly tried to change the subject. "How's Mary?"

"I don't see her much. You probably know as much about her as I do, from reading the papers."

"Yeah, she's making a splash all right. Too bad about you and her. I guess I had a lot to do with it."

"No, it was my own doing. You just helped it along. But I'm surprised to find you aren't more excited about the progress your cause made. I wouldn't doubt that if Roosevelt has his way the miners'll finally get that eight-hour day you risked your neck for back in the Van Alen strike. What's more important is that Baer is making such an ass of himself that even the people and some of the papers are for the strikers."

"I know all that, Aaron, but . . . well, I've had my eyes opened some these last few years. I'm beginning to understand why the smart people running things don't want a lot of dumb hunkies and dagos telling them what to do. Now the Irish . . . well, an Irishman with anything on the ball can make it for himself here in New York, as you see standing right in front of you. Hell, between Murphy and me and a few others we run the place, and we'll be running the country before long . . ."

"Funny you should say that. Teddy Roosevelt said the same thing to me a long time ago when I brought Mary into the family."

"Yeah, well the man must be smart about some

things . . . uh, how's Sally?"

Hugh was signaling for another drink, but Aaron shook his head. He'd heard more than he wanted to hear. His answer to Hugh's question was cryptic and would soon be untrue: "Fine, fine." As he turned to leave, Hugh called after him, "Well, if you see her, give her my love, but tell her to stop going around trying to rile up all those women. It's getting so that a man's own wife argues with him."

God, Aaron thought as he almost ran to get out of earshot, was it for this that I turned over my own life? I could have let him rot in jail the way everybody thought I should. How could a man change so? But then, wasn't he the wrong man to be posing such a question, even to himself? He'd try, if he could, to understand Hugh the way he'd tried to understand Mary. After all, he told himself, unless you were used to it, money went to the head faster than booze. As Mary was always saying, it was only those who had it who could afford to disdain it. The irony of his own life was that, having made the gesture of rejecting it, money was now overflowing that box on his desk. He was a good lawyer, and the people he served could only thank him by paying him. It would be arrogant and hurtful for him to wound *their* pride by declining; besides, he still shoveled money out of the box to those who needed it. Well, whatever, he certainly wouldn't bother to tell Sally about his encounter with Hugh. On top of the bad news he *had* to tell her, this might crush her . . . it was clear that Hugh remained romantically in her memory as a kind of latter-day Robin Hood.

Actually, Aaron had dropped by the bar to fortify himself for taking the message to Sally that, at long last and after all these years, the Supreme Court of the United States had sent him notice of its refusal to review the case of The State of New York vs. Antonio Donatelli. Aaron had thought about it and was convinced that he'd done all he could—at least Tony would be serving a life sentence during which he might find a way to practice his art instead of being put to death—but he was far from convinced that justice had been done, and he didn't know how Sally would take it.

Aaron's personal regret was less that he'd lost the case than over the possibility that he might have prevented the awful affair in the first place . . . On that day before Christmas in '97 when he'd arrived at Sally's house, he'd found a party in full swing. Charlie and his wife and baby son had just arrived from England, and all the artists of the neighborhood had been invited in to meet them. Sally, surrounded by people who loved her, was a Christmas tree of merriment. Aaron, sipping wine and watching her and waiting to have a word with her alone, had decided to abort his mission . . . Was it necessary to spoil Sally's Christmas by telling her that James had seen Brewster on the streets of New York—way uptown at that? After all, the man did have as much right as millions of others to visit the city, and he was apparently in good shape. Forget it, or at least forget it for a day or two. Finding the joy of this reunion hard to accept in view of his own loneliness, Aaron had finished his glass and left early, and now could only rely on what came out in court.

One of the most useful weapons of trial lawyers, Aaron had discovered, was the fact that there was no such thing as absolute truth. You could arrive at an approximation of the truth through the testimony of various witnesses, of course. The process, he thought, was a little like triangulating landmarks to find your position at sea, but with a very important difference: those marks were fixed whereas witnesses kept shifting. Nowhere was it more evident that truth was in the eye of the beholder than in court where a witness, memory faded during the long wait before a case normally came to trial, tried to describe an event involving violence, emotional turbulence, shock. This being true, and Aaron himself having not been there, he was to this day not sure of what actually happened. He was only sure of the motivations involved, and in that light a justice tempered with mercy would, he felt, have exonerated Tony.

As nearly as he could get it pieced together from the stand, the bare facts of the case were this. The party at Sally's had gone on into the night with bottle after bottle of wine vanishing down the throats of the happy family members and the impoverished artists. At some time before midnight Matty had left to meet a girl friend and attend services in a nearby Catholic church. She was not a religious girl, but she liked the pageantry, the candles, the Latin chanting, the incense. Nobody else wanted to go with her; they'd make Christmas of it right there, singing carols to the accompaniment of a violin one of the artists played badly. And so it took a while for the screaming from the street that started shortly after one on Christmas morning to penetrate the party. When it did, they all rushed to the windows. Down below in the rather dim circle of light from the street lamp they saw a large man, face shadowed by the brim of his hat, holding onto Matty's arm. She was struggling to get loose, and it was her screams, punctuated by cries of "Let me go!" that they were hearing. Tony Donatelli, under a heavy load of wine, grabbed a hammer he used to drive his chisels and rushed out to help her.

Tony's most vivid memory was the size of the man—"a real bruiser, a head taller than me." Tony was glad he had his hammer. "Let her go," he ordered the man.

"Why should I? I'm her father. I won't hurt her, I just want a word with her—"

Tony moved in and, to his recollection, the man did let Matty go and struck at him with his fist. Tony wielded his hammer, it hit the man on the side of his skull, just under the brim of his hat. He went down, blood pooling the pavement under his head. Tony himself dragged the body into the first-floor gallery and tried to stanch the blood and revive the man with wet towels while one of the other guests called police. He died on the way to the hospital, and reporters on the night police beat, bored and disgruntled at missing Christmas, had the best gift any Santa Claus could hand them. With Dickens in the air as usual at that season, they turned out tales that would have been the envy of the old master himself. Refreshed by clips from the morgue about his earlier effort to abduct his daughter and bemused by his strange background, they depicted Howard E. Brewster as a man tormented by unrequited fatherly love and infused with the spirit of Christmas who was brutally slain by a drunken artist. Anyone who'd ever lost a child would weep to read those stories, which provided a sweetly melancholy counterpoint to the sometimes strained merriment of Christmas day.

Matty was the most troubled and troublesome witness. She'd been walking home from church and had just left her friend at a house a few doors down when this man stepped into the light from the street lamp and spoke to her. Before she could recognize him, she was already frightened by the fact that he knew her name and by the odd kind of strangled sound of his voice when he said, "Matty . . . ?" Then he took off his hat to her and she did clearly see his face and it was like something out of an old nightmare and she couldn't help herself, she just started screaming. She couldn't remember whether he did say anything else but he grabbed her arm in a grip like a vise and she was afraid he'd take her away and she went on screaming and yelling until Tony came out. Did she see her father try to hit Tony? No, she didn't see anything. As soon as he let her go she ran as hard as she could to the house. The prosecution was, of course quick to underscore in its summation to the jury that the unfortunate victim, according to Matty's own testimony, had said nothing threatening and that she'd seen no attempted violence on his part. Nor could any of the many witnesses looking down from the windows swear on the Bible that they'd seen Brewster make any threatening gesture; the light was dim and much of his body was hidden from their sight by Tony's back. But even more damning in Aaron's opinion was what came out in the prosecution's cross-examination of Tony:

"Now, Mr. Donatelli, the house from which you ran—Mrs. Hancock's house—was your place of residence. Isn't that right?"

"Yes, sir."

"Did you have a bedroom separate from Mrs. Hancock's?"

Aaron was instantly on his feet. "Objection, your honor. This line of questioning is irrelevant—"

The judge asked the prosecutor, "May I ask what you are trying to establish, counselor?"

"Motivation."

"Very well, proceed."

The prosecutor asked the clerk to read back the question, and Tony said, "No."

"Now when you reached the street you recognized the man?"

"Never saw him before in my life."

"But before you struck him you knew who he was?"

"Only when he said he was her father."

"*Then* you knew, of course, that he was Mr. Brewster, your—uh, Mrs. Hancock's former husband?"

"Well, only that he said so."

"And you might have been jealous, might have thought that he'd come to reclaim his former wife's affections?"

Aaron was up again: "Objection, your honor.

He's leading the witness, using pure conjecture."

"Objection sustained."

The prosecution rested. The damage had been done, the thought as firmly planted in the jury's mind as if the prosecutor had used a spade. A verdict of guilty of murder in the first degree had been returned, and to save his client's life Aaron had had to resort to the shaming plea of temporary insanity by reason of intoxication. He'd found enough questionable rulings by a prejudiced judge to ease the case up to the State Supreme Court, but the justices in Washington had now finally turned the lock on Tony and thrown away the key.

Aaron knew that he'd find Sally at midafternoon in her expanded gallery. Enriched by her inheritance, she'd bought the house next door for living and turned all three floors of the old one into showrooms. She was also able to buy works of art instead of taking them on consignment, and her generosity was said to be keeping half the Village alive. One unkind columnist said it was her way of easing her conscience "over the fact that much of her considerable income comes from rents on slum properties," but she'd discovered that she didn't actually own any properties, that in fact she owned only shares in the trust that administered them. While she could vote her shares to elect trustees, the close cooperation between the other owners, Mary and James, left her in effect without a voice. So she bought art. Her money also helped in taking Tony's case as far as it had gone, and Aaron knew that she still had hope.

"Better lock up and come over to the house," he

told her. "I'm afraid I've got some bad news—"

"No, give it to me here. The Supreme Court turned you down, didn't they?"

"Yes . . ."

She'd been standing, and she sat back against the edge of a table as if her knees had given way. "Oh, God, Aaron, it just isn't *fair.*"

She was blinking back tears. "I could cry, Aaron, but I'm not going to, at least not now. I'm going to do something else. Matty and I were afraid that this might happen and we've been talking over a way of making something come out of it. We're going to buy that house on the other side of ours and make it into a school—the Antonio Donatelli Academy of Art. Now that she's been kicked out of that damned stuffy college, Matty'll run it. She's going to try to sign up the best people from all of the museums and schools in the city to teach here parttime, and we're going to make it tuition-free, take in only poor boys—and girls too—like Tony, who didn't have the opportunity."

And then the tears came anyway.

Aaron went to his sister and hugged her. "That's the spirit, that's great. It'll make Tony as happy as anything can . . ."

Freeing herself from his embrace and blowing her nose, she said, "All right, let's not talk about it anymore. Let's talk about something else . . . Are you going to give Amelia away?"

"Yes, she tells me her mother wanted James to do it but she talked her out of it."

"Those two are thick as thieves," Sally said. "You don't suppose . . . ?"

"Sally, sometimes I think you *do* have an evil mind. No, I don't suppose, I can't even imagine it. A good Catholic girl and a Presbyterian elder? Leave me some illusions."

Sally shook her head. "Neither can I, really. Well, I'm happy for Amelia. Sometimes I wish Matty would find somebody, but the poor girl hasn't seen much to make marriage look very attractive. I only thank the Lord that she hasn't been—what is it these new doctors, these psychiatrists call it?—oh, yes, traumatized by what she's been through. I rather think her attitude may be healthy, though to some it's shocking. Do you know what she told me the other day? 'I'm never going to get married—at least walk down the aisle in white with my hymen still intact. I'm going to try it first, so I won't make the mistakes *you* made.' How would you like to hear that from *your* daughter?"

Not from Amelia, he had to admit, but it was not too surprising from Matty. Maybe it was a kind of self-protection . . . she was far from the Gibson girl that everybody said his Amelia resembled. Matty wasn't really unattractive, if you favored a large girl with rather broad shoulders and strong chin and straight brows. She smoked and drank and swore like a trooper, and she'd argue with anyone on any subject, not excluding sex, which she held any woman has as much right to enjoy as a man. Nobody was surprised when Matty was dismissed from Radcliffe for leading a troop of girls, all dressed in pants, onto the Harvard campus for a women's rights rally that ended in near riot with the Harvards drenching the girls with water from their windows and the girls responding with glass-shattering rocks. People in the family, especially Amelia, were glad then that Matty's name was Brewster. What with being involved in a murder trial and then *this*—well, what kind of a family would people think we had if they knew?

Aaron said only, "I'm sure Matty will find the right man someday. Well, I've got to be going. Teddy Roosevelt's invited me down to Washington, and I'm going to catch the night train."

"You're coming up in the world, little brother. Are you taking Georgia with you?"

"Oh, no. As I understand it I'm supposed to stay *in* the White House, and you know Teddy's a prude about things like that. I'm curious, though, I can't imagine what he has on his mind."

"If you're not taking Georgia, why not take me? He couldn't object to a sister, and I'd love to talk to him."

"I'll bet you would. Listen, I'd rather take Georgia. The last thing Teddy needs right now is a dose of women's rights."

"Why? If he's flailing around with that big stick of his, as he calls it, at the likes of Morgan and that stuffed shirt Baer, he might as well do it for us too."

"Sally, don't forget that Teddy *is* a politician. He might agree with you privately, as I do, but he doesn't like to lose fights. There's a big difference between taking on a couple of fatcats who aren't too popular with the public anyway, and half the population. No, at least let him win a few before you try to bring him into this."

Sally's bringing up Georgia reminded him that

he'd have to go up to her apartment on Park Avenue and tell her before he caught the train. She'd probably throw things at him, but it would be better in the long run than just trying to slip away. If there was anything Georgia hated, it was deceit. That's why she'd be so angry. "Damn it, if you aren't *proud* of me, stay away from me," she'd told him on that very first date when he'd suggested supper at a place other than Rector's because all of her friends and most of his would be there.

Like a traveller returning to the scenes of his youth, Aaron had started spending many of his idle evenings in the theater. When he'd seen Georgia in *A Doll's House,* he'd liked her so much that he'd gone back over and over again. She didn't seem to be acting at all—she *was* Nora, a woman of spirit so reminiscent of his grandmother and mother, of Sally, and Mary at one time too, of all the women he'd ever found truly exciting. He finally sent back his "attorney-at-law" card and was a little startled when she agreed to see him and have supper with him. But she'd made it easy for him . . . she was a kind of Nora offstage too.

Georgia wasn't beautiful, not even especially pretty in the ordinary sense of the word. She was small and too thin to aspire to the hourglass figure that remained in fashion; her nose was a bit humped and crooked, her jaw slightly jutting. But dimples softened her look when she smiled, and her deep brown intelligent eyes were the focus of her face. She was a serious person in her way and blunt as a sledgehammer. In between waving to all of her theatrical friends as they sat there at Rector's she told him, "I came out with you because I like your looks. Not only that but I've read about you, and I like what you seem to be doing. Are you married?" When he explained his situation, she said, "Good. I'm certainly not in the market for marriage. I think why I like this play so much is that I lived through it myself. I've been free as a bird since I walked out on *him,* and I intend to stay that way. I was lucky I didn't have children, lucky, I guess, that I *can't* have children. All I'm really interested in doing is going on acting, and thank God there are parts for old ladies when I get old." How old she was he couldn't tell, in her thirties somewhere, but it didn't matter. He'd taken her home that night, and she'd invited him in, telling him as soon as he'd helped her off with her wrap, "Go into the kitchen and I think you'll find a bottle of brandy and some glasses. I'll be right with you." He'd blessed her for the thought and had sneaked a good swallow while he was pouring. He was tense with nervous excitement. When he'd come back into the living room, there she'd been, sitting on a couch, dressed only in white silk pajamas, the first he'd ever seen on a woman. He'd set down the drinks and moved toward her, but she'd said, "No, I think we'd better have those. You look a little nervous, and so am I. We're going to need them because I intend to find out if you're the man for me."

Evidently he'd passed whatever test she had in mind, because it had been taken for granted from then on that they'd meet wherever and whenever they could in their respectively busy days—and usually in public places. She thought that it was

486

good for her career to see and be seen, especially with a handsome escort. He didn't mind it except once when they'd spotted Amelia in one of the mirrors that flanked the main dining room at Rector's. She was there with her John, and so concentrated on him that Aaron thought that they might just slip out, but Georgia wouldn't hear of it. "I want to meet her," she'd said, "and I'll bet she'd like to meet *me*." Georgia had been right. The fact that her father knew the star of *A Doll's House* was so exciting to Amelia that she apparently didn't grasp any other implications. Amelia, bless her, wore a very thick armor of innocence. And Georgia, bless *her*, didn't. She was not passive in love as Mary, however receptive, had been; she either knew or invented delights that he'd only heard about or read about in those unindexed books that library-wise students knew how to find in the far recesses of the Princeton stacks. "If you enjoy me, why shouldn't I enjoy you?" was how she put it. Their most uninhibited romps took place aboard *Cathay*, cut off from land and all of its depressing reminders of responsibility and rectitude, and Aaron forever blessed the intuition that made him hang onto the boat when he'd given everything else away. Not long after he met Georgia, he'd moved *Cathay* down to a berth at City Island, where they could reach her almost at will.

In the years since he'd first met her, their relationship had become almost as comfortable, and contentious, as a good marriage. The one thing Georgia would never talk about seriously was its duration. She *would* tease, "Look, the next show I'm in will probably go on the road and who knows who I might meet in Pittsburgh. I hear they're minting millionaires out there every day and a lady can always use diamonds . . ." Aaron didn't always know how to take her, and it was a fact that, his days of having an open charge account at Tiffany's long gone and his assessment of her character being what it was, he really hadn't thought about showering her with jewelry. So he'd fallen into the trap: "Well, I mean if you really want diamonds, I could hock the Duryea, and—" She'd laughed. "Aaron, Aaron, I'd much rather ride in the Duryea than have an acre of diamonds. It's *alive*." Actually, much as she liked sailing, Georgia liked traveling as well. She hadn't gone to Pittsburgh yet, but whenever she had a night or so free from the theater and the weather wasn't favorable for sailing, they'd put on their goggles and dusters and drive up to Westchester or out to Long Island and register at some inn as man and wife to avoid arguments with small-minded proprietors. They'd been managing this way for so long, it had become such a habit, that he knew she'd expect him to take her to Washington, a place she'd always wanted to see, and introduce her to the President, a man she admired, even if she had to play sick and let the understudy go on. She'd be furious at what she'd consider this squeamishness. Luckily, from his point of view, she wasn't home. He hastily scribbled a note—"Darling—invited to Washington by the President. Can't wait to say goodbye but be back day after tomorrow and tell you all about it. Love, Aaron"—and stuffed it in her mailbox and headed for the train, trying to force from his mind the howls of frustration she'd let out when she read it. . . .

Aaron had a sleepless night, kept awake less by the roll of the train and clatter of its wheels than by his feeling of excitement about the day ahead. He'd passed by the White House a number of times but had never entered it, nor ever expected to. He was neither a sightseer nor a hero worshipper, and he'd lived in houses that were, on their own, larger and more impressive. Still, being an invited guest in that establishment which stood as a symbol of great power and prestige was a rare enough privilege, even in this democratic society, to intrigue the most blasé of men. Why had this come about? What in the world could Teddy want of him? And would he be willing to go along with whatever it was? These days he was shy of honors, shy of the limelight, for both personal and professional reasons. As a private citizen, as what some called a devil's advocate, his irregular relationships with Georgia, with Sally and her Bohemian friends, were not subject to public scrutiny and criticism. Considering the cast of characters he often defended, he might even be expected to share some of their disdain of disillusion with present-day society. More important in a practical way, the hard-boiled reporters hanging around the courts whom he'd come to know and like were mostly cynical about, disenchanted with, society, and they looked on Aaron as a kind of champion of their views as well as a source of good copy. Except for his name, he was no longer a Van Alen, no longer one of *them* but one of *us*. And so the reporters, so rough on the mighty, would overlook any personal indiscretions he might be guilty of.

There were also the people he served. He kept his crowded, shabby Pine Street offices, though he could afford better, because he knew that most of them would be uncomfortable in the posh, bookish atmosphere of most law offices. They would also, he felt, be made suspicious of his sympathies by any too-visible connection with the establishment that was crushing them.

Perhaps he was too sensitive about all this, but it had led recently to an act nearly as strange in most people's eyes as renouncing his heritage. His friend Woodrow "Tommy" Wilson had written early in the year and asked him to take part in the ceremonies that would install Wilson as president of Princeton. Aaron would be granted an honorary Doctor of Laws in return for which it was hoped that he'd make a few remarks along the lines of those at the football banquet—something about the importance of sports at Princeton and Wilson's part in them. It would, Wilson suggested, be a much-reported event owing to others being honored or doing honor to him, such as Mark Twain. This Aaron could believe. Now that the old writer, with the impressive head of a white-maned lion and the tongue of a Chautauqua circuit rider, was settled in the city, he appeared at so many important dinners that they were calling him "the belle of New York." It was actually the possibility of publicity which Wilson had thought would be pleasing that prompted Aaron's response: "I regret that I feel obliged to turn down your invitation, because there's nobody more deserving of the office you are about to assume. I do hope, though, that you, who have shown such sensitivity to what I've been trying to accomplish, will appreciate that being included on the Princeton honors list could, ironically, be a problem in my work. You create an image of scholarship to achieve your ends. I try to be a man of the people to achieve mine. I hope, I think I'm succeeding. With warmest regards and congratulations." Possibly out of wounded feelings, Wilson's rather snappish reply clearly demonstrated how much of a schoolmaster he'd become at heart: "While I appreciate your motives, Aaron, I must question your judgment. Educational attainment is, or should be, universally admired and ought only to enhance your image in the mind of the meanest of men. On the other hand, I hear that you have been driving around in an automobile. To my mind, nothing has spread socialistic feelings in this country more than the use of the automobile, which presents to the countryman a picture of the arrogance of wealth, with all its independence and carelessness." Tommy Wilson had a point. Well, nobody was perfect . . .

When Aaron, taking a hack from the station, reached the White House, he found a commotion at the door. A tall and heavy-set woman of uncertain age, black-bonneted, black-gowned, black-hosed, was brandishing an umbrella and asserting her right to enter. "I must see the President and warn him. I've come all the way from Kansas. That daughter of his with her cigarettes will poison American womanhood, and nicotine will be the death of them all in this house—look at what happened to McKinley. Tell him Carry Nation's here. He'll see

491

me." Of course. Aaron should have recognized her at once from all the pictures and cartoons he'd seen of her wielding her hatchet to break up saloons. An usher, back planted against the closed wrought-iron and glass doors, was calm but firm. "I've told you, madam, that the President is engaged. Perhaps another day when you have an appointment?" Mrs. Nation tucked her umbrella under her arm and said, "Huh! I suppose you have the same motto here in the White House that they have in saloons—All the Nations Welcome Except Carry. He'll regret not seeing me." When she'd turned away, Aaron offered his card, and the usher, glancing at it, broke into a welcoming smile: "The President's expecting you, sir. Follow me."

As they stepped into the marble-floored foyer, which could only be described as homey compared to those on Fifth Avenue and in Newport, Aaron asked, "Does that sort of thing happen often?"

"All the time," the usher said, "but they're usually not as bad. I was afraid she'd pull a hatchet out from under those skirts and have at that glass door. They say the lady likes the sound of tinkling glass."

Leading him on up the staircase, the usher said over his shoulder, "You're to stay the night, sir, and the President told me to put you in the Rose Room. He really is engaged for the moment, but he thought you might want time to wash up. Luncheon is at one."

While Aaron was laying out the few things he'd brought in the small dressing room off the bedroom to which he'd been ushered and wondering what tie to wear for a White House luncheon, he heard a sound behind him and turned just in time to catch sight of a small boy hurrying for the hall door. "Come back, you scamp," he said. "What are you doing in my room?"

The boy stopped, hung his head in some embarrassment but kept studying Aaron with bright eyes. "Father says you have a lightning left, and I just wanted to see what one looks like," he said.

"Well, now, I'll just show you. Put up your dukes," Aaron said, and he was on his knees sparring with the boy when the door burst open and Teddy strode in. It wasn't exactly the way Aaron had imagined being received by the President, but it broke whatever thin ice might have formed over their relationship. Roosevelt threw back his head and whinnied with laughter, lifted Aaron to his feet with his own hand and said, "Well, Aaron, it's good to see you up to your old tricks, even if you have to pick on a child. Now, wasn't I right, Quentin? Ordinarily I'd have to scold you for bothering a guest, but . . ."

"My pleasure, Ted . . . Mr. President," Aaron said. "You look well."

"I am well. Tip-top. Why not? I've got the best job in the world, and I love it. Of course, the house they give me isn't up to your standards, but I hope you'll be comfortable."

"My standards have changed a little . . ."

"Eh? Well, well. Maybe I have something in mind that will fix that, but we'll get to it later. We have some engineers coming for lunch who are going to tell me how impossible it is to build a canal across the Isthmus of Panama, and then we have the French ambassador calling after that. He's a dreadful bore, so it being a nice day, I thought I'd kill two birds with one stone and get some exercise by taking him for a walk in Rock Creek Park. Are you up for that?"

At lunch Aaron sat in silence while Roosevelt, mustache quivering above his ever-moving lips, lectured at, rather than listened to, the gloomy engineers. Nothing was impossible in this country, in this century. Besides, he'd already acquired the Panama Canal Company for $40,000,000 of the taxpayers' money, and he wasn't going to see that go down the drain. Without the canal, America's manifest destiny to spread decency and fair trade throughout the world could not be realized. As a former naval person, he could assure them that only with a canal could America's fleet police both the Atlantic and Pacific as it was honorbound to do. No, don't talk to him about difficulties, talk about possibilities. He'd provide the money, and they'd provide the canal, and that was the end of it.

After lunch Roosevelt confessed to Aaron, "Didn't let 'em get a word in edgewise, did I? That's what you've got to do with these technical fellows— fire them up. Of course they have to listen to me because I'm President. I've found it's better getting people into the White House than into church. It's really a bully pulpit, don't you know?"

Aaron had nothing with him but a business suit, but Ambassador Jusserand was even less prepared for a walk with Roosevelt. He arrived in tails and striped trousers, tall silk hat, gray spats and lavender kid gloves. The President came down to greet him in knickerbockers, sturdy boots, rough tweed coat. He took a soft felt hat from the hand of the usher, jammed it on his head and said, "Well, gentlemen, let's not waste this nice spring sunshine." An open carriage was waiting at the door, and it took them clattering through the streets to the edge of the park. Roosevelt was busy acknowledging the greetings of passersby who recognized him and let out whoops of "Look, there's Teddy!" or "Give them trusts hell, Teddy!" When they got out of the carriage, he led them at a breath-robbing pace that he must have practiced for the scaling of San Juan Hill right through pathless brush and woods. Aaron could hear the ambassador panting, noticed that his spats and cuffs were collecting burrs; once when a branch whipped stingingly across the ambassador's face, he was sure that he heard him mutter, "merde," relying no doubt on the hope that such an American President would be deficient in languages. When they reached the creek, it was so swollen with the spring runoff that the ford Roosevelt had been heading for was under chest-high water. For a few minutes Roosevelt ranged up and down the bank looking for another sport, and the ambassador, gratefully catching his breath, said in low tones to Aaron, "I hope this means we can turn back. This is most . . . uh, extraordinary." No such luck. In his cheeriest tones the President said, "We'll just have to undress. The water may be a little cold but it tones up the skin." Aaron suspected that he was as astonished as the ambassador to see the President of the United States calmly strip to the buff, but not wanting his old friend and adversary to bluff him, he followed the leader. The wretched ambassador, looking as if he were giving his life for the sake of his country, finally began to disrobe too. Roosevelt kept eyeing the man impatiently as he carefully folded everything he took off. When he was down to nothing but his lavender gloves, he started bravely heading for the water, and Roosevelt said, "You forgot your gloves." For the first time in the ordeal, the ambassador smiled a little. "With your permission, Mr. President, I will keep them on. Otherwise it would be embarrassing if we should meet ladies on the other side." Roosevelt howled. "You're all right, Jusserand. I misjudged you." It was an admirable stroke of diplomacy, but Aaron would wonder later whether Jusserand, like he, paid for it by catching a terrible cold swimming the creek.

Fortunately, however, the cold didn't catch Aaron until days later. He was perfectly clear-headed that evening and able to enjoy the President's private company. He was the sole guest at a rare and raucous family dinner in a room built for state occasions. The only missing member was the notorious Alice, who was out at some reception or other. Then for coffee the President led him upstairs and into his own study, a comfortable book-lined room with leather furniture worn by the seats and backs of earlier Presidents, and the talk he'd always cherish began . . .

"I suppose you think I made a fool of myself out there in the park, Aaron," Roosevelt said, "but I had a reason for it. Jusserand will dine out on that story all over Washington—and Paris too. They'll realize they have a new kind of President to deal with, one who's likely to do the unexpected. . . . Well, now, I've pulled something of the same sort of stunt in that Northern Securities suit—you've heard about that . . . ?"

"I have, Te- . . . Mr. President, and I admire you for it."

"Good, that's what I brought you down here to talk about . . . And, please call me Teddy, at least here in this room tonight. Two fellows who've blacked each other's eyes as much as we have oughtn't to be formal. In any case, I've been more or less keeping track of you ever since you sprang that O'Donnell fellow, and—"

"Thanks in large part to you, Teddy."

"No, no. I just gave you a tip. You pulled it off. I can't say I approve of all the people you stand up for, but you've been a tiger in the courts and that's what I think we may need when we get up against Morgan's fellows. So I'd like you to come in with the government as a trial consultant—there'll be a suitable fee, of course. I've talked to Knox, and he agrees. Well, what about it, Aaron?"

It was perhaps the only thing the President could have asked him to do that he could accept with a clear conscience and no fear of its working against the grain of his career. He didn't hesitate. "It's not exactly in my line, but I'd be pleased to do what I can . . ."

"Bully for you! I was sure you'd be with me on this, Aaron. You know, I don't have many friends left in the financial and legal circles of New York. They think I'm a madman. But I gather you're not in

497

so good with them either."

"That's an understatement, Teddy. My own brother—he's in with Morgan on this U.S. Steel thing, you know—won't speak to me."

"Too bad, but it happens with brothers . . ."

Roosevelt suddenly paused. He took off the glittering glasses that made flashing mirrors of his eyes and daubed at them. Aaron decided he had to be thinking of his own brother Elliott, whose conviviality had led to an early alcoholic death. Aaron had always liked Elliott and now felt particularly sorry for that gangling daughter, Eleanor, that he'd left behind. He knew only too well that Amelia and her friends, in the arrogance of beauty, unkindly referred to Eleanor as the "ugly duckling." Though Roosevelt was quick to snap his glasses back on, flash his toothy smile and start talking again, that moment made Aaron feel closer to him than ever before. Teddy had known tragedy and disappointment greater than any man that had come to Aaron, but he'd handled them as he'd handled that stream this afternoon, by plunging in and wading through to the other side.

"Well, now that you mention the steel trust," Roosevelt was saying, "you come to my real problem. Your brother James and fellows like him up there don't understand me at all. When Morgan was down here trying to argue me out of suing Northern Securities, all that was on his mind was that I'd go after U.S. Steel too. I told him no—that there were good trusts and bad trusts, just like there are good and bad people, and if steel kept its nose clean, fine. I can see the advantage of organizing an

498

industry from the mines to the consumer *if* it results in better and cheaper products for the public. All I'm trying to do is get these fellows to play fair, but Morgan wouldn't believe me."

Aaron was excited by what he was hearing. "Teddy, that's all I'm trying to do in the courts—get a fair trial for those people."

"I believe it. You always were a fair fighter. It isn't easy, is it? It's much simpler to have some sort of righteous cause. I remember when I was running against Henry George up in New York and he kept harping on the single tax as a cure for all ills. People swallowed it because it was so simple, and you know, I'd have been mayor if it weren't for that. Now these fellows who've managed to corner all the money like Morgan are smart—I'll give them credit for that—and probably have done a lot to make progress possible in this country. But it goes to their heads, and they begin to think that God appointed *them* to get all they can, and the devil take the hindmost. Look at old John Rockefeller. What is it he's said?— 'God gave me my money.' He invented the trust and nothing's ever been able to shake his conviction that, even if he was ruining the railroads with kickbacks and running rivals out of business, he was God's agent. You know something else he said? 'I had our plan clearly in mind. It was right. I know it as a matter of conscience. It was right between me and my God. If I had to do it tomorrow I would do it again in the same way—do it a hundred times.' You can't really reason with men who talk like that, as I'm finding out with this fellow Baer. When you get into politics, though, you realize that there are millions of Americans who believe that God gave them some rights too, even if he didn't see fit to give them money, and my idea is that a President has to represent them too."

"Bully for you, Mr. President . . . No, that's what I'm calling you from now on."

"I couldn't have a finer compliment, Aaron. Well, we go to bed early around here so we can get up and shake the big stick vigorously in the morning," Roosevelt said with a hearty laugh. "Your bedroom's just down the hall there. Sleep well. I'll introduce you to Knox in the morning."

Men weren't supposed to be allowed into her bedroom, but Amelia made an exception for her father. When Aaron stepped in, his daughter was standing in front of a full-length mirror adjusting the bodice of her white silk dress while her cousin, Edith Van Alen, was braiding flowers into her hair at the edge of the long veil trailing down her back. Mary was sitting on the bed, appraising the operation with a cool eye and making suggestions, "A little more over to the right, Edith . . . no, down more . . ."

For greeting Aaron sang a snatch from one of his favorite operettas, *The Mikado:* "Brightly dawns the wedding day . . ."

Amelia, turning, gracefully gathering and sweeping her train behind her, gave him her best Gibson-girl smile. "Oh, daddy you're here . . . I was afraid you might be late."

"For this, never. You look good enough to eat."

"Do I? Do I really?"

"Really and truly."

If ever a girl deserved to go down the aisle in white, he was sure it was Amelia. There was a scrubbed purity to her that he'd seen only once before—at his own wedding to the woman sitting there on the bed, and he was afflicted with one of those seizures of acute sadness in the midst of happiness that was like a heart attack. He wasn't given much to praying, but he prayed now, prayed that whatever God there was would make life different for this radiant girl. Could Mary have the same feelings?

"Hello, Mary. I've been looking around down there, and you've done a splendid job with everything."

The house looked like half the florist shops in New York had been looted to turn it into bloom; one whole end of the ballroom was a wall of massed chrysanthemums, the flower of the season, behind a makeshift altar. On the bandstand a select group of musicians from the Philharmonic, to which Mary had kept up his late mother's subscription, was tuning up when Aaron looked in. Gold chairs, hundreds of them, were arranged as if for a church service. The drawing room and dining room had been thrown together for a reception and behind a bar set up at one end, right under the portrait of Martin Van Buren, a corporal's guard of bartenders were icing champagne and polishing glasses. Old "Blue Whiskey Van," as he'd been known for his drinking capacity, might well be smacking his lips. It was good that Mary had prepared for a large crowd, because surely nobody would fail to show up—rumors were going around that even the President of the United States might drop in. While most of the men who'd been invited cordially hated Teddy— "a traitor to his class"—it was the kind of hate, like that for some strange monster, that made them want to see him up close.

Mary only said, "Thank you, Aaron. Now you'd better wait outside. We've got to take that dress off and have the maid touch it up with her iron. We'll be going down at exactly three."

Before he left, Amelia asked, "Daddy, do you really think the President will come? I'm nervous enough without that."

"Now, don't worry. There isn't a nicer man . . ."

"Well, *I'm* worried," Mary said. "I'm just afraid James won't be able to keep from giving him a piece of his mind, and—"

"Mary, if you knew Teddy well enough, you'd know that he's much more likely to give James a piece of *his* mind."

At precisely three Amelia emerged from her room, Aaron gave her his arm, and they started down the stairs. Floating up to them were the strains of a wedding march—Purcell. The round notes of a well-played trumpet sent chills up his spine. Every seat in the ballroom was filled, and people were standing along the sides.

Seated on the aisle was the President, who was first to rise and face them, teeth and glasses gleaming.

"Oh, he *is* here," Amelia whispered. "My knees are wobbling."

Aaron held her arm a little tighter, "Don't worry, I'll hold you up." Aaron wondered what, if anything, Teddy knew about his real marital situation. Little or nothing, he'd guess, since Teddy was so full of his own ideas and plans that he paid scant attention to those of others, and he certainly wasn't one for gossip. Even at social gatherings Teddy would plunge into a discussion of ideas or, failing that, wander off and pluck a book from his host's shelves and stand there devouring it, a page at a glance, while the chatter rolled unheard around him. Nothing, in any case, could be more suggestive of family unity than this occasion, with a proud father giving away his daughter, an equally proud mother sitting prominently in the front row blinking away tears, cousins flanking the bride at the altar. He doubted whether in all this crowd anybody would notice that Sally wasn't there. Most, in fact, never knew or had probably forgotten that other beautiful Van Alen woman who made her debut in this very room. Yes, it was a family occasion that, because of the President's presence, would be written down in history books, and while it was probably Aaron's services to the government that prompted the presidential visit, it would be Mary and even James who would boast of it. Well, for the sake of his daughter, Aaron was happy to contribute for once to the Van Alen glitter.

After the ceremony it was the President who first kissed the bride and who offered the first toast: "To Amelia and John—may they ever be happy! To the first family of New York—the Van Alens! To that most formidable of unions—the Dutch with the Scotch!" Then, as if he realized he had invaded hostile territory or felt embarrassed about being an uninvited guest, the President left at once. Aaron regretted his going, because he'd like to have heard Teddy take on his antagonists. Having played his role, Aaron suddenly realized that he too was in hostile territory, that there was scarcely a person in these rooms abuzz with conversation animated by alcohol to whom he wanted to talk or wanted to talk to him. So he was happy when he felt somebody plucking at his sleeve and turned to see a familiar apparition in black veils, Cousin Sophie. He'd thought that Sophie was as disappointed in him as the rest of the family, but she surprised him by asking that they go off alone and talk.

He led her into his father's old reception room, where she threw back her veils and said, "I don't want you to get the notion that I approve of the way you are leading your life—deserting that lovely wife and your children—but you are the only lawyer I know, and I need legal advice."

"On what, Sophie? You know I'm a trial lawyer . . ."

"Well, that's just what I might need. I'm thinking of suing James . . ."

"Suing *James?* I thought you and he were—"

"Were. Were. You know what he's done, don't you? He's sold Van Alen and Son. It's gone, *gone.* Nothing to show for it but some stocks in some steel company. It was my father's life—and his father's before him—and, and my life . . ."

"I know, Sophie, and I'm sorry. But I presume James had the votes of a majority of the stockholders. I understand that even Mary—"

504

"Yes, I don't know what got into her. I'm more annoyed with her than you can imagine. She and James are thick as thieves, and after all *he* said about her. . . . Well, I was going to leave everything to your boy Cornelius so he could carry on the Van Alen tradition, but now I'm not sure unless I can win that suit."

"I can't imagine what grounds—"

"Grounds? I have plenty of grounds, I assure you. James isn't really a Van Alen. None of you are Van Alens, and none of you has any right to any of that stock. *I'm* the *only* Van Alen. All of it is mine by rights. Now what do you think of that?"

Aaron had gathered that lately Sophie was going queer, queerer than usual, but he'd never imagined that it had gone this far. Should he humor her or argue with her? While he was debating the question, she anticipated him.

"Oh, you think I'm crazy, don't you? The lot of you do. But I'm nct. When James started this business about selling out, I started going through all of my father's papers again, and I found this. Here's my grounds," and reaching into one of the folds of her black dress, she pulled out two yellowing sheets of paper written in ink in the same hand.

As Aaron glanced through them, his heart began skipping oddly. If they were true, the many mysteries of his life had been answered in a breathtaking flash. One sheet was an affadavit, dated 1863:

"I, Flossie Van Alen, former slave to Mrs. Sarah Schuyler Van Alen, known also as Sally, do hereby

505

swear that I was witness to a criminal connection between said Sarah Schuyler Van Alen and one Aaron Roberts, sea captain, on a Sunday morning in the spring of the year eighteen hundred and eleven in the Van Alen residence on Broadway, New York City, and that the issue of that connection, the child named Peter Schuyler Van Alen, was, in fact, the child of said Captain Roberts, for of my own knowledge there were not and had not been for many years conjugal relations between Mrs. Van Alen and her rightful husband, George Van Alen."

The document was signed with an "X (Flossie Van Alen—her mark)" and witnessed by "John Charles Smith, Jr., Esq., attorney-at-law." The second document was a note from Charles Smith of the same date addressed to Cornelius Van Alen, Esq.:

"Drew this up for Flossie in case something happens to her. Am still of the opinion that we have grounds for a suit. Peter's shares in the company were obtained fraudulently by asserting that he was a *natural* grandson of the first Cornelius Van Alen, who would have been included in said Cornelius Van Alen's will if he hadn't been born subsequent to his grandfather's demise. It would, on the basis of Flossie's testimony, appear that neither Peter nor his heirs has any rightful claim on ownership of Van Alen & Son. I have reason to believe that your mother would *never* deny under oath her relationship to Roberts, so let me know when, and if, you wish to go ahead with this. Hastily, Charlie."

After he'd read and reread the documents, Aaron

tried to compose himself so that he would not give Sophie the satisfaction that he now suspected she wanted. Very calmly he said, "Why did you show these to me, Sophie? You must know that they wouldn't hold up in court."

"Why not? My father was going to sue before he died. He told me. But I didn't know why until I found these."

"But, Sophie, look at these. They're all in Cousin Charlie Smith's handwriting. He's the only witness to them, and he's long dead. And who's going to believe the imaginings of an old illiterate slave, couched in that preposterous language he obviously dictated to her? It all smells of a plot. No, they wouldn't stand up in court, and they don't deserve to."

Aaron tore the papers in shreds, gently resisting Sophie's efforts to stop him. There was a look of fury on her face, uglier than any scars. Aaron dropped the scraps in an ashtray and lit them. While the flames danced, he said, "Much as I differ with my brother, I'm not going to let you do this to him—or Mary either. Being Van Alens is all they live for. As for me, Sophie, you picked the right fellow—you set me free. Do you hear that? Set me *free.*" Never mind that she could not understand his meaning.

Aaron left her then and started to leave the party too. He wanted to digest this amazing revelation. Whether what he'd seen was true in fact or not, it was certainly true in terms of feelings he'd had all his life. He'd never been a Van Alen, or not James' kind of Van Alen. He reached into his pocket and felt for an object he'd started carrying around with him ever since he'd left home—the only thing he'd taken because Mary had never liked it anyway.

As his fingers closed over the cool jade, he thought, "Why, grandmother, you old sly thing." He couldn't wait to tell Sally the news.

Chapter 11

JUDGE AARON Roberts Van Alen, U.S. Court of Appeals, Second District, found the letter on his desk in chambers when he came off the bench. He picked it first out of the pile, because it was addressed in handwriting, a rare item in business correspondence these days when nearly every office had a typewriter. Sally called the machine "just another male device to enslave women." She and Matty carried this women's rights business too far. He'd argued with her that the typewriter was, in fact, creating more opportunity for girls to be independent by supporting themselves under decent conditions of work; why, even around the court-house which was a known repository of political payoffs, he was seeing more and more young women whose deft fingers gave them an edge over men in typing. This handwriting was masculine, and, not recognizing it at a glance, he studied the postmark: San Francisco. He tore it open. He'd been reading the newspaper accounts of the terrible earthquake out there and its aftermath, but he wasn't aware of knowing a soul in the city. His closest personal relationship to the disaster was a sense of gratitude that Enrico Caruso, who'd been there on a concert tour, had escaped harm. In a lifetime of opera-going he'd never heard such a voice. Under an address and date of April, 1906, the letter began: "Dear Dad . . ."

My God, could it be Neil? Who *else* could it be? It was almost crushing to realize at that moment that he'd never before received a letter from his son. He saw the boy from time to time, but their meetings were usually very strained dinners followed by visits to the theater where neither of them would have to talk. Even these dates were rare and difficult to arrange because for half a dozen years the boy had been away at prep school in New England and then at Yale and up in Newport during the summers. The initiative was always on Aaron's part, and he would usually come away from seeing his son feeling that the effort had scarcely been worth it for either of them.

Aaron knew that part of the problem was his sense of guilt over being an absentee father. But he also felt that Mary and James together had managed to give the boy, whether directly or by inference, a bad picture of him. They should have left well enough alone with his name, because Neil looked more like a young Hugh O'Donnell than any Van Alen with his black, curly hair and Mary-blue eyes. Serious beyond his years, Neil wasn't much for athletics, though he had taken up golf, a game lacking, in Aaron's opinion, all those elements of risk and head-to-head competition that had made sports such an

510

attraction to him. Neil's reasons for his choice were typical Neil: "Johnnie McCandless tells me that all the young men in business are playing golf. He says you can't get anywhere without it. Why, would you believe he even has Uncle James going out on the course?" No, Aaron could hardly believe that—James taking a Saturday afternoon off. But then he had heard from some of the men he used to know around the office and ran into occasionally at the Waldorf bar that James had had a more relaxed attitude these past few years, that he was often disappearing for lunches that took the whole afternoon, and they thought that it had something to do with the merger's relieving him of sole responsibility for Van Alen & Son. James was spending a lot of time, too, on that medical complex he was building—you could see that by the papers— and on fussing around with his art collection.

Sally had a story to tell about that. James' older boy, Peter, a little delicate and effeminate as Sally described him, had come down to her gallery one day. He'd slid into her door, collar up, hat down, as if he were a spy on a secret mission. He was, as he explained to Sally, in charge of his father's collection, and he'd heard that she had somehow acquired a Saint-Gaudens and could he see it? His father so admired the statue of General Sherman up at the head of the Avenue by the park that, if he could get a Saint-Gaudens piece, it would be a real feather in his cap; he wasn't sure whether his father had any faith in his judgment, his taste. But Sally mustn't under any circumstances ever let his father know he'd been here. Could she understand that; it was embarrassing, but that's the way it had to be. Yes, she could understand that. Peter liked the piece and its price, and he worked out an elaborate arrangement for a friend to buy it and for him, in turn to buy it from the friend so that no check to the Van Alen Gallery would ever show up in his father's records. The clincher was that Peter had been sneaking back to Sally's ever since because he'd fallen in love with the modern art on her walls that James wouldn't allow in the house. He'd also talked Matty into enrolling him as the first paying pupil in the Antonio Donatelli Academy of Art. Getting to know Sally and Matty, he said, made him feel better about himself: "I never knew there were Van Alens like you . . . I thought I was the only strange one."

Peter's strangeness, Aaron thought, had a good deal to do with his own son, Neil. It was apparent that both Mary and James were grooming Neil to take over the Van Alen responsibilities. The change in name had, like an Englishman's inheriting a title, conferred on Neil a consciousness of his special rank and duty. All the boy seemed to have in mind was getting into business with his Uncle James, and this rather narrow focus accounted for the fact that he and Aaron had little to say to each other. During the time that Aaron was a conspicuous member of the legal team that won that first trust-busting suit against Northern Securities in the Supreme Court, he'd hoped that his son might have been proud of him. Instead, the boy seemed embarrassed. When prodded into talk, Neil parrotted the Jamesian line that Roosevelt with his "square deal" was a worse menace to business than Bryan with his free silver.

None of the rage for reform that was running through college campuses where young men were fired up by their hero in the White House got to Neil. He was, ironically, the son James probably wanted but didn't have; stories about his younger boy, Arthur, though he'd managed to get into Yale, were hair-raising even to Aaron.

Neil writing him now? It couldn't be because Neil thought it respectable to own up to a father who was a judge; he'd been on the bench nearly a year now without any such acknowledgment. And why had he written him here at the courthouse? He could guess with regret the reason for that. He'd long since given up a foolish pretense and moved into Georgia's Park Avenue apartment, but none of the children would visit him there, even admit that he lived there. It wasn't the sort of thing they discussed; indeed, Georgia's very existence seldom came up in his conversations with the children. Once he had ventured to Amelia, the only one who'd met her, that she'd apparently liked Georgia, and Amelia had snapped, "I never imagined that you were *living* with her then, daddy. I think it's disgusting." Unfortunately, Amelia's attitude toward him had changed since her marriage, as if in losing her purity she'd lost her charity, too. She was living the perfect "ever after" of the Gibson girl—a nice little house in New Rochelle from which her handsome husband commuted to work in the city, a chubby baby daughter named Mary, a membership in the golf club the young people of the community were forming. Aaron went out there not very often to have a look at his grandchild, but he could sense the relief his leaving always provided. Young John did not approve of Aaron's politics or personal life, and Amelia, as of course she should, approved of young John. As with Neil, conversational matter was hard to come by for more than the course of a short Sunday dinner. There were times when, seeing him after one of these visits, Georgia would say, "I really ought to get out of your life," and he'd tell her, "Without you, I wouldn't have a life."

His relationships with the children—all but Felicia, who at thirteen was still half child, half woman and capable of being delighted with, say, a trip to the zoo or ecstatic with a matinee at a musical—had become so distant and formalized that he was almost afraid to read the letter in his hands. What in hell was the boy doing way out in San Francisco? Well, on with it:

You will probably be surprised to hear from me and from so far away. I'm out here working on a crew helping to clean up the rubble and fix the buildings that fell down in the earthquake. If I wrote a whole book I couldn't begin to tell you what it's like out here. Even with all the destruction, the place is beautiful and the people are wonderful the way they're going to work, shoulder to shoulder, to make a new city. I am wheelbarrow man on the crew—can you imagine it?—and my muscles twitch so much from fatigue every night that I can hardly sleep. But the foreman says I'm better than any Chinaman he ever had, and it makes me prouder than the highest mark I ever got at Yale. I'm beginning to think that I might want to stay out here. There are all sorts of opportunities for business or anything you want, and it doesn't matter whether you are a Van Alen or not.

You may wonder how I got here, and you won't believe

that either. I 'rode the rails.' Yes, sir, jumped freights all the way across the country. I remember lying down on the supports under one of them and looking up and seeing the Van Alen stamp and laughing my head off. I don't think I would have come if it weren't for Cousin Arthur. It was his idea, and he talked me into it—shamed me into it, I guess I'd have to say. Anyway, we came together, and he's here with me, and he likes it even better than I do. The girls out here are very grateful for what we are doing, if you know what I mean, and although I haven't taken advantage of it, I'm afraid Arthur has.

Why I'm writing you, dad, is that mother doesn't know anything about this. Neither does Uncle James. They still think we're both at Yale. We even postdated letters and are having our friends mail them for us, but they'll get onto us when we don't come home for a month or so. I'm afraid it will break mother's heart when she finds out I've dropped out of Yale, and God knows what Uncle James will do. What we need is some money, because we're working now as volunteers. All we need is a hundred or so each to see us through until things are better organized here and we can get paying jobs. Arthur is afraid to write his father, so I told him I would write to you.

Whatever you do, *please* don't tell them where to find us. I know I haven't been a very good son to you, dad, but for the first time I've done something that I think you might understand.

Sincerely,
Neil

Too bad Neil had not been able to sign it "love," Aaron thought as he dropped the letter on his desk and got up to stare out the windows at the people scurrying through the streets of this city that seemed so rock-solid in comparison to devastated

San Francisco. Well, that might come later, depending on how he handled this. It took about as much effort as his imagination was capable of to visualize Neil out there pushing a wheelbarrow, aching and streaming with sweat and proud of it. With his experience in court, he should now be more aware than most that people were the most surprising creations on earth. He was, indeed, proud of the boy, but it wasn't easy not to be a Van Alen when you'd been raised in the security and anticipated assumption of power that the name implied. If Neil's unexpected enthusiasm wore off, and he came back—what then? Mary and James were not forgiving people.

Aaron could appreciate the boy's phrase—"it doesn't matter whether you're a Van Alen or not"—since he'd so often wanted to be in that position himself. Well, he was now, wasn't he?—always had been . . . He preferred to believe those strange documents that Sophie had shown him, as had Sally. They'd had quite a champagne celebration together over the news that they no longer had to think of themselves as inferior Van Alens. Yet as he'd absorbed the implications of those documents in sober thought, Aaron had come to the reluctant conclusion that being a Van Alen was mostly a state of mind and not a condition of the blood. In that sense Neil was more of a Van Alen than he'd ever been, and the effort to free himself of that state, that fate, would have to be greater, perhaps impossible. No matter what his experience, it would probably always matter to Neil that he was a Van Alen, as it had to Aaron too.

Be that as it may, the boy—or boys; he'd have to get to know this supposedly black-sheep nephew, Arthur—had picked an admirable way to exert independence. Nobody alive in America could have escaped the shocking stories coming out of San Francisco. Papers all over the country were filled with harrowing accounts of death or narrow escape, with startling pictures of smoking ruins and empty acres of rubble. No such natural disaster had ever befallen the American republic, which by that year of 1906 was like its young President flexing its muscles and asserting its power around the globe and raising its voice to preach inevitable and illimitable progress. God couldn't do a thing like that to his favored people unless, of course, it was true, as some said, that San Francisco was as wicked as she was beautiful. A number of ministers proposed this explanation, but Aaron thought that there was more insight into the probable relation between God and man in the words of a poet who, noting that one of the few buildings left standing was the Hotaling distillery, wrote:

If as some say, God spanked the town
For being over-frisky,
Why did he burn the churches down
And save Hotaling's Whiskey?

Across the country Americans responded with money, and in many cases as with the boys, their own bodies. President Teddy Roosevelt appropriated more than two million dollars for immediate relief, declining with thanks the offers of help from abroad. It was an American tragedy, and rebuilding the city would be an American triumph. With all this outpouring of emotion Aaron could just imagine how he himself at Neil's age might have been moved to go and do likewise. He'd wire the money immediately and keep the boys' secret.

It was Saturday—and spring. He'd adjourned court at noon, going along with what he thought was a sensible movement to cut the work week to five and a half days; one of the things he liked about Teddy was that he'd enforced the eight-hour day for federal employees, and it couldn't be long in coming to other workers. It was an odd coincidence that Neil's letter had arrived on this day, because he and Georgia had cooked up a rather daring plan to entertain Felicia, and they'd have to get going right away to carry it off. On the grounds that Felicia needed the discipline, Mary had put her in a convent school up in Connecticut, and their idea was to sail the *Cathay* up there this afternoon and take the girl out for a ride on Sunday. If he wrote long enough ahead, as he'd done this time, the good sisters would "parole" Felicia to him for a whole day on Sunday— after early mass, of course—but there was so little doing in the country town where the convent was located that they'd end up staring at each other in the Common Room, along with all the other parents and children, and it wasn't much of a day for a girl like Felicia compared with the fun they could have around New York.

So this would be a surprise—and something he was sure she'd like. The only calculated risk he was taking was bringing Georgia along. He had no doubt that they'd hit it off, but he didn't really know whether Felicia knew about Georgia or not; Mary was one of those mothers who believed in "protecting" her children from the truth. She'd be furious if she heard about it, but there was no reason why she should. He and Felicia had long made their little outings more exciting by keeping a pact of secrecy about certain activities between them. It started after he took her to see Anna Held in a matinee, and Mary blew up about "exposing this innocent child to that immoral woman and her off-color songs." Mary's attitude about all the musicals that were lighting up the new theaters off Broadway was a little like that of a reformed drunk about booze; because of her own youthful urges, she was afraid of their attraction for her children. As far as Aaron could tell, Felicia *was* innocent, and her delight was in the color and movement and sometimes catchy tunes they'd hum together going out. So while he did compromise by staying away from Ziegfeld shows, he would certainly take her to this season's hit, Victor Herbert's *The Red Mill,* and it would probably be reported at home as another trip to the Bronx Zoo. Aaron wouldn't go so far as to suggest that his daughter lie to her mother, but he didn't bend over backward in the other direction either. Quite often what people didn't know didn't hurt them.

As he walked out of his chambers and out of the courthouse, Aaron ran a gauntlet of lawyers, reporters, clerks, cleaning men, vendors and general hangers-on who tipped their hats to him and said, "Good night, your honor," "Have a good weekend, your honor," and the like. He would smile and nod at them, resisting manfully the urge to look over his shoulder to see what honorable person might be following him. He supposed in time he would get used to his elevation to the bench, but he still felt a little ridiculous, particularly when he'd come into the courtroom, robed in ministerial black, and everybody would rise. He could, of course, have turned Roosevelt down when he proposed the appointment, and he sometimes wondered why he hadn't. This being a day when his children were on his mind, it was probably a day on which he ought to admit to himself that his desire to look good in their eyes may have had a good deal to do with his decision. He hadn't yet been able to lure Amelia or Neil into court, but he could tell by a subtle change in their attitudes that they were at least surprised that he could attain such respectability in view of what they'd heard, or inferred, about him from Mary and James. James, he'd been told, had made no bones about his reaction, telling everybody: "Can you imagine what that idiot in the White House has done now? He's appointed my radical brother to the federal bench. As far as I know, he doesn't have any respect for law or morals." Aaron had managed to bring Felicia down to witness a short court session, and afterward she'd said, "Gosh, daddy, I didn't know you were so *important*. But isn't all that stuff you have to listen to dull?"

Yes, compared to his practice. But Teddy, persuasive as ever, had sold him on the importance of having a man like him, a man who believed in fair play, on the bench at a time when so much new legislation was coming out of Washington, and he was, of course, right. This year alone, for instance, there was the Pure Food and Drug Act, regulating for the first time a food industry that had been getting away with actual murder in the form of rotten meats and packaged stuff that was poisoned with all those colorings and preservatives, and the Hepburn Act, regulating at last the railroads and empowering the Interstate Commerce Commission to fix fair rates. Men like James were howling about "socialistic interference," and they'd be spending a lot of money on high-priced lawyers to appeal government regulations to the federal courts. When Aaron had protested to the President that this sort of thing was outside his range of legal experience, Roosevelt had said, "Nonsense, Aaron. Knox tells me you did a bang-up job on that Northern Securities case, which by the way makes it politically easy for me to reward you with this appointment. All you have to do is listen to both sides and use your common sense. There's never been a better judge than Solomon, and he didn't go to any law school I know of."

One worry Aaron hadn't been able to share with Teddy was how the appointment could affect his relationship with Georgia. They were seen so openly together that people who opposed the appointment would have no problem whipping up a scandal in the papers. As she had once in the matter of his children, Georgia had offered to break it off—she sincerely wanted him to have the job for the good he might do. He wouldn't hear of it; he'd take his chances. So far, at least, he'd been fortunate. He was still well-regarded by the working press, and the publishers who could do him most harm, Pulitzer and Hearst, were supposedly liberal and, therefore, in favor of his selection. Not only that, but he'd defended a number of the poor widows and criminals in which Hearst's *Journal*, a proclaimed "champion of the people," took great interest. He hadn't met Hearst personally; he'd only seen him at a couple of speaking events when he'd so narrowly lost the campaign for mayor last year. But Georgia knew slightly the show-girl Hearst had married and was herself said to be one of Hearst's favorite actresses. If it came to that, Aaron thought that he might find a defender in Hearst. But it probably wouldn't come to that. People were getting to be a lot more understanding about these things. When Harry Thaw shot Stanford White last year in a jealous fit over White's former attentions to his wife, Evelyn Nesbitt, you'd have thought from the public outcry that Thaw had torn down a national monument; yet everybody knew what had gone on in the architect's apartment up there on top of Madison Square Garden with girls on velvet swings or popping out of cakes. Compared to the carryings-on of a man like White, Aaron's affair was as sacred as a marriage . . .

Because he wanted to get out to the boat as soon as possible, Aaron took the subway uptown. It was, he had to admit, an enormous convenience and probably worth every penny of the graft that had been made on it. He could only imagine how excited his father would have been to see trains rolling at fifty miles an hour under the ground; as the elevator his father had so admired was making it possible for

522

the city to climb, these horizontal tubes were making it possible for it to spread. Aaron had been on the very first subway ride a few years ago when Mayor McClellan himself took the controls. He'd been invited along because of one of those odd twists that kept life from being predictable. After their disillusioning meeting in the Waldorf bar, he'd tried to give Hugh O'Donnell a wide berth, but he hadn't always succeeded. One day he'd been passing City Hall and had seen O'Donnell out on the sidewalk talking with a dapper little man whom he'd recognized as the new mayor. Aaron had started to cross the street, but Hugh had yelled, "Hey, Aaron, come over here, I want you to meet hizzoner . . ."

There was nothing for it but to go, and Hugh, introducing them, said, "My friend Aaron here went to Princeton too, so you see, George, I do know some swells."

McClellan, son of the Civil War general Lincoln had cashiered and probably a Democrat on that account, had been in Princeton long after Aaron, but he said at once, "Oh, you must be the Aaron Van Alen whose name was dragged out every football season as the hero of that first game? Well, I'm glad to meet you in the flesh. Tell you the truth, I wasn't sure you ever existed. But you look so young . . ."

"You can't see my gray hair under this hat," Aaron said.

"Well, well. Aaron Van Alen. Say, I'm going to inaugurate the subway tomorrow, and I want you to come along as my guest," McClellan said. "I'm taking a lot of the Wall Street fellows who put up the money, but it would be a pleasure to honor a great old Tiger too. What do you say?"

Out of curiosity, Aaron accepted. During the ride, he frequently wished he hadn't. That first train consisted only of open flatcars, jammed with financiers and politicians. McClellan started gingerly enough at City Hall, getting the feel of the controls, but by the time they reached Fourteenth Street he was getting the feel of the power as well, and they were racketing along at more than forty miles an hour. Everybody had to hang tight onto their hats and some, Aaron guessed, to their stomachs. When at last the train came out into the open above One Hundred and Sixteenth Street, McClellan stopped to let the group get off and pose for pictures. A number, among them Aaron, deserted to seek slower ground transport back downtown.

Aaron still preferred, when he had time, riding aboveground. There was always something to see, some old building going down or a new one rising. The ingenuity of the engineers and designers in making the most of whatever odd and expensive space was at their disposal continually amazed him, particularly in that strange, tall triangle they called the Flat-Iron Building. If the city was interesting by day, it was magic by night. Remembering as he did the soft glow of gas lamps and the dim yellow squares of candlelit windows, he still found remarkable the sight of the city springing at dusk into an instant garden of blooming lights; he felt like a child creeping down in the dark to discover the blaze of a Christmas tree. Even the plodding statistics one of the papers recently dredged up—3,000 electric signs, 100,000 lights, four times the amount of power used by London—couldn't dispel the sense of magic. He much preferred the impression Albert Bigelow Paine had caught in the title of his novel a few years back to describe Broadway—"The Great White Way." Entranced as he still was with the city, having lived there all his life, Aaron often envied those others who, coming from across the empty sea or the flat prairies of the west, beheld its stone marvels, its crush of humanity, its lights, for the first time. You could get some of their feeling from the kind of stories this fellow O'Henry was writing for the papers. New York was a wonder of the world, and Aaron, much as he liked to get away to sea from time to time to clear his head, had no wish to live anyplace else . . .

Georgia was ready when he arrived, down at the curb, in fact, packing a hamper of food and extra blankets into the new Packard touring car he'd just acquired. But she seemed worried. "It isn't that I don't want to go, Aaron, but are you sure this is the right thing to do? Felicia's very young and . . ."

Aaron put his arms around her and gave her a quick hug. "Yes, I'm sure. Get in. I want my two favorite girls to know each other."

If Felicia Van Alen had been the only "problem child" in the Convent of the Sacred Heart, she would have found the place absolute hell. The best surprise she'd had after she'd been there long enough really to talk to some of the other girls was to discover that they all were problems, or had their problems too. Oh, there were a few who were there because they had very religious parents, and a few who were there because their mothers had gone there, and a very few who were there because they were "on scholarship." For the most part, though, the other girls were there, as she was, because they weren't turning out the way their mothers—and sometimes their fathers—wanted them to, or they were in the way at home, or their parents were afraid to let them out on the street to go to the city's parochial schools, or they were just plain bad like Joannie Mitchell who although she was only fourteen actually boasted that she'd already done *it* with a boy. Everybody, of course, watched Joannie to see whether she'd swell up, and when she didn't, they began to think she was just lying to make herself important.

In a way, Felicia knew how Joannie felt, because it was very hard to feel important there in the convent. As soon as you came in, they took your clothes away and gave you uniforms—all the same, blue jumpers and white blouses and black stockings and boots. Of course, they weren't nearly as bad as those creaking black habits the sisters wore that reminded her of Cousin Sophie with all her spooky veils, but they were bad enough. No matter how wavy or long your hair was, you had to comb it up and pin it in a bun, just like all the other girls, every single morning before you came down to breakfast. So they all looked alike, even the poor scholarship girls, and the idea was, as the Mother Superior told them in chapel on that first day, to make them realize that "they were all equal in the eyes of God." Felicia knew, of course, that this was nonsense: even in those dreadful uniforms and buns some girls were prettier than others, and she was one of the prettiest of the lot, which was why she didn't really have to go around making up stories like Joannie Mitchell.

Actually, the story she did have to tell was worse, but she couldn't tell anyone ever, which was probably why she was here. Sometimes at night she'd still see it and hear it as if it were happening all over again right there in her head, and she'd end up crying herself to sleep. The nearest she ever did come to telling anybody was when one of the sisters making bedchecks, a young one who really did seem to care, found her like that and tried to get out of her what was wrong. "You're new here, Felicia, and we haven't had time to get to know each other. All the girls finally tell us what's troubling them, and it makes things ever so much easier. You know there isn't anything God can't forgive," the sister coaxed. But that was probably nonsense too, and Felicia bit her lips and stopped crying until the sister got out of the room. Even when some of the other girls would break down and tell her dreadful things like "I hate my mother" or "My father gets drunk all the time and beats me," she'd lie and tell them that she was there only because her mother thought that she ought to be in a good Catholic atmosphere since all of her cousins and friends were Protestants. It was a pretty safe lie because that's exactly what her mother had told the sisters when she brought her up there.

Of course her mother didn't know that *she* knew the real reason for her being here. What her mother said was, "I just don't know what I'm going to do with you, Felicia. Of course it's probably my fault for not paying enough attention to you when you were younger and letting you have your own way. But it could as well be your time of life. Some girls do get strange ideas when they're . . . when they're becoming women. I can't watch you every minute of the day, so I'm going to put you into this nice convent school I've heard of out in Connecticut where you'll be safe and get some discipline." That was after she'd worked up the nerve to run away from home. She hadn't worked up the nerve, though, to get really lost. She'd wandered around for quite a while until it got dark, and then she'd tried to get a friend to hide her away in her house, but when the stupid girl got caught smuggling food out of the kitchen for her, her parents found her and took her home. Maybe she should have tried to go to her father, but it was night when she thought about it, and she knew he wouldn't be down at the courthouse. For some strange reason nobody ever told her exactly where he lived; she knew it was somewhere on Park Avenue, but there were lots and lots of big apartment buildings there and how could she ever find his? Anyway, he'd probably have taken her back, because once when they were having a lot of fun together and she said she'd like to live with him always, he got that look like a judge on his face and said, "I'm afraid not, Felicia. A child's place is with its mother, or so they say . . ."

That was the whole trouble. She'd run away because she couldn't bear being with her mother after that awful day. But she didn't think she could, or should, tell even her father about it. It would be too embarrassing, and he probably wouldn't believe it, would think she was making it up. Sometimes now *she* thought she'd just made it up, but she couldn't really convince herself of that. For as long as she could remember she *had* made things up, maybe because she was so much smaller than the other children, even her youngest cousin, and had to play alone a lot with nobody but some dumb nurse or nanny to talk to. It was much more fun talking to herself, or writing down the things she'd made up. She had a whole bookful of those stories she'd never shown to anyone because they'd probably laugh at her, and one of the reasons she was sure that she hadn't made this up was that it wasn't written down in the book. Her father wasn't at all like her mother, who was always saying terrible things about him, particularly when she was with Uncle James. But if she complained to her father about how strict her mother was, he'd tell her that in spite of their differences she was a *good* woman and he was sorry but she *was* her mother and so on. So it was a question of whether he'd really believe what had happened . . .

That terrible day she'd been sent home early from Miss Farthing's school because one of the girls broke out with measles. Another thing she didn't understand about her mother was why she'd send her to this convent after insisting she go to a Protestant school like Amelia and Neil and all the Van Alen cousins so she could meet the right kind of children. If her mother only knew the kind of children she was meeting here . . . Anyway, there was nobody home but the servants when she got there unless you counted Cousin Sophie who'd gone really queer and taken to staying in her room all the time and not talking to anybody. Felicia was really happy about that, because nobody would bother her if she took her book into her mother's bedroom and wrote out a story she'd been thinking about. Ever since she'd been little that bedroom with all its red velvet and gold dangles and Moorish designs had been her favorite place for making things up, but lately her mother, who didn't understand about making things up anyway, had complained about finding her in there all the time—"You have a perfectly good room of your own, and you're old enough to understand that people need their privacy." So she never went there when her mother was in the house, and that was why when, in the middle of writing down her story, she suddenly heard her mother's laugh out in the hall, she jumped behind one of those big red drapes. It was a silly thing to do, she realized later, because nothing much would have happened but a little scolding, but her mind had been somewhere else, and she guessed that she was hoping her mother would only be in the room a little while and then she could sneak out. Anyway, there she was, and she could hear everything and see most everything if she peeked a little.

When she came into the room, her mother was kind of talking and half laughing over her shoulder, "Really, James, it's such a romantic notion. It isn't like you."

Uncle James was coming into the room after her mother and already taking his coat off. "I've wanted to, Mary, ever since that first day when we realized . . ."

Her mother was still laughing, "I think you said then it looked like a bordello."

"I didn't mean that, Mary. What I meant was that it *is* romantic, more exciting even than a hotel room. Just the thought that you sleep there every night, all those nights when we should be together . . ."

"Ssh, James. We agreed we'd enjoy what we can have and not talk about things we can't have. Come over here and give me a hand."

Her Uncle James had his coat off, his suspenders dangling. He went over and started to unbutton her mother's dress in the back. "It is safe, isn't it?" he asked.

"I don't see why not. Felicia's in school, and none of the servants saw us come in. Of course poor Sophie never leaves her room now. I can hear her in there muttering to herself, but she'll hardly talk to me. She says she'll never forgive us, you and me, for selling out. We aren't real Van Alens, she says, and she's cut us out of her will. But Neil still spends time with her when he's down from school, so I imagine it'll go to him."

"Well, that's the way you want it, isn't it, Mary?"

"Yes, I guess so. It's hardly fair to you, though. You put up with her for years."

"I'd as soon see it go to Neil. My own boys don't deserve it. . . . But, well, let's not talk about that. I love you, madam. You know that, don't you?"

"Let's not talk about *that*, James," her mother said. "It's enough that you admire my beautiful back . . ."

Her mother was all undressed, and, good lord, her

back *was* beautiful, white and smooth and tapering to a small waist and curving out again. She was getting into bed, and Uncle James started taking off his pants. Felicia closed her eyes. Her heart was beating so that she was sure they would hear it. She was coming all over funny and thought she might throw up. She wanted to gasp to get enough breath. But she couldn't, just couldn't, let them know she was there. She'd die of mortification if Uncle James didn't kill her first. He could have a terrible temper as she'd seen when one of his own children upset him. With her eyes closed, her head got so light that she felt like she'd faint. She tried opening them again—wanted to open them, which was the worst of her feelings. All she could see was the covers moving as if they were wrestling under them. All she could hear was a kind of heavy breathing, a moaning. And then her Uncle James in a strange-sounding voice said, "Ah, God, Mary, it *is* better here . . ." And her mother said, "I'm glad, James, but you'd better go now . . ."

It was then that Felicia thought that she just might be able to last. She hardly knew whether she was breathing or not. Uncle James got out of bed and started putting on his clothes. "We'll just have to come here again, Mary," he said. "It's a . . . a different feeling, as if we were more than . . . more than friends."

"Yes, it is, James. Perhaps we can work it out."

After Uncle James left, her mother, thank God, got up and put on her wrap and went into the bathroom, and Felicia ran to her own room, where she did throw up all over the rug. It was probably a good thing because it kept her busy cleaning up so that nobody would ever know while her mind, her feelings, tried to cope with the experience. She'd seen the thing, the terrible thing, that she and her girl friends sometimes talked about that people did to get babies, but she'd never imagined that they did it anyway, and she'd never, never been able to think of her mother, her beautiful mother, doing it at all. And doing it with *Uncle James,* who wasn't at all good-looking and so old and almost like her own father. Even she knew from going to mass that she'd witnessed an awful sin and that her mother and Uncle James wouldn't be able to go to heaven. But they'd seemed so *normal,* with her mother laughing and everything, that she knew they were doing it all the time. For hours she'd just wanted to die so that she'd never have to look her mother in the face again, but she couldn't die, couldn't even throw up again. The only thing worse than seeing her mother would be having her mother know, so she'd gone down to dinner and stared at old Martin Van Buren and forced herself to eat something and pretended she had to run right back up and do homework. The next day she'd run away, and the day after that her mother had brought her up here, and *she* knew that now there wouldn't be anything to keep her mother and Uncle James from doing it there anytime they wanted . . .

Felicia hated the convent, but she hated worse the thought of going home and having to try all the time to avoid her mother. Since there were so many problem girls, or girls with problems, who weren't much wanted at home, the sisters had worked out a

form of punishment that was popular with the
parents who were paying a lot of money to have their
girls away from them: any girl who wouldn't work or
broke the rules couldn't go home over holidays.
When Felicia heard about this and learned that
Joannie Mitchell didn't want to go home either
because her father knew what she'd done, or said
she'd done, and would beat her when he had too
much to drink, she cooked up a plan with Joannie.

The convent school was really just a big, old
Georgian house that had been built by some
Connecticut sea captain from the profits he'd made
privateering during the Revolutionary War. Because they believed that the girls ought to be alone
to study, or hopefully to pray and meditate, the
sisters had had the top two floors partitioned off into
tiny individual cells with nothing but a cot and
wardrobe and desk and chair. After dinner each girl
had to be in her own cell, and, after lights-out at
nine, in bed. Next to smoking cigarettes, going into
each other's rooms at night was about the worst sin
you could commit. Two girls had actually been
expelled when they were found in bed together,
though Felicia didn't know what was so bad about
that. But what she and Joannie planned was
obviously pretty risky. The thing was, they didn't
have much to lose: if they got away with it, they'd
have a little fun; if they got caught, they'd surely get
detention over the long Washington's Birthday
weekend coming up. There was always a sister on
duty in the hall who kept an eye on you even when
you went to the bathroom and kept checking the
beds until she was sure every girl was asleep. But

there was a ledge outside the windows just wide enough to walk on it if you had the nerve, and Joannie was only two cells away. So this night Felicia put her pillow and some bunched-up clothes under the covers to look like she was in bed and inched her way down the ledge, hanging onto the ivy vines, to Joannie's room. They were there, sitting cross-legged on the bed and talking, for what seemed like ages and might have got away with it all night if they hadn't had a giggling fit just as the sister was going by their door.

It worked all right—almost too well. For a while there was talk of expulsion instead of detention, but the sister who found them was the nice sister, and she insisted that they had just been sitting there and talking and with their bathrobes on and everything. Joannie and she were moved to different floors, but they were both there that long weekend and could keep each other company during the day. It was all Felicia could do to keep from telling Joannie what she'd seen, and asking Joannie what it was really like, but she'd rather have somebody think that her father beat her than know that her mother did *that*.

Thank God for her father. Nobody else ever came to see her. Amelia was too busy with her baby, and they'd been so far apart in age that they'd hardly been like sisters anyway. Neil wasn't all that far away in New Haven, but there was always something going on there like a game or a dance on weekends, and Neil hardly seemed to know she was alive even when he was home. Under the circumstances, she wasn't at all unhappy that her mother was always writing about some ball, or concert, or dinner she simply had to attend and promising she'd be up in the spring "when the winter season is over." She could just imagine how awkward it would be to sit all day with her mother in the Common Room and try to make conversation which was all there really was to do with visitors. It wasn't always easy, even with her father, but he'd promised that this time he'd come up with a surprise, and she could hardly wait.

Felicia liked to think that she looked like her father because he was so handsome, but everybody said that it was Amelia with her square face and her hair that was the color of her father's before it started going gray who looked like him. Neil looked like mother or maybe that Uncle Hugh, although she hadn't seen enough of Uncle Hugh to be sure. She often wondered why, since he seemed to be somebody important, a councilman or something, with his picture in the paper, but everybody changed the subject when she asked questions about the O'Donnells. "They're not our sort," was about as far as her mother would go in explaining. Anyway, she didn't look like an O'Donnell though she did have black wavy hair that was long enough to sit on when she didn't have to pin it up. She really didn't look like *anybody*. Though she was thirteen and supposed to be full-grown, she was a lot shorter than her mother and Amelia—what people called "delicate"; she had black eyes too, and a face shaped a little like a heart with a dimple right in the middle of her chin. For a long time when she was little and her mother kept shoving her off with those nurses and nannies, she thought from the way she looked that she was adopted. She told her father about it once, and he just laughed and said, "You're as much Van Alen as any of us. Do you know who you look like? Just like my grandmother, Sally Schuyler Van Alen. She had French blood in her, you know, and it's coming out in you." There was only one picture of her great-grandmother, a portrait done when she must have been young, and after what her father said Felicia would study and study it and was pretty sure she *was* going to look like her. She liked that part about being French, because she thought of the French as being very romantic people and about the only really good thing about the convent was that one of the sisters who'd spent a lot of time in France was teaching her the language. She was even trying to write the latest story in her book in French.

Maybe she'd show that to her father and surprise *him*. She wanted her father to think that she was something special, because he was special to her. She knew that it was strange not to have a father at home, but she'd never known anything else, and, from seeing how little attention Uncle James paid to his children when he *was* home and hearing some of the other girls here at school talk, she'd begun to think that she might be lucky. When she was with her father, they often had very good times, and he treated her as if she were almost grown up. She sometimes felt sorry for him, being all alone, but then he did have Aunt Sally, whom she'd heard a lot about but had hardly ever seen, and he was supposed to have a friend who was an actress whom she'd never met. Whenever they were together, he'd always have excuses about that—his friend was playing a matinee or out in some place like

Pittsburgh on the road. It didn't really matter because she didn't want to share her father with anybody; and she didn't want to have to think about the possibility that he might be doing *that*, like her mother. It just didn't seem believable; she'd seen him up there on the bench looking so distinguished with his gray hair and black robes, something like a kindly priest. How Uncle James, his own brother, could go around saying that her father was a "menace to society," and do the things he was doing, she simply couldn't understand.

When she let herself think about things too much, Felicia could really make herself miserable. She didn't know what she was going to do when she *had* to get out of this convent and go home, and yet she didn't know how she could go on staying here, like a prisoner in a jail. A few of the girls were actually thinking of taking orders and she'd thought of that too, had actually gone into the chapel once alone and prayed to be made a "bride of Christ." But nothing had happened; all she'd been able to think about, kneeling there, was how she'd have to cut off all that long silky hair—her "crowning glory," her mother called it. And thinking about that made her think about her mother again, and she just cried instead of prayed. She really had loved her mother, or at least thought of her as just about perfect, especially when she was all dressed up to go out somewhere, as she was almost every night, with her silk skirts rustling and her jewels twinkling and smelling like a whole garden of flowers. When she was lucky enough to be taken shopping with her mother, all the clerks would bow and scrape and

"Yes, Mrs. Van Alen" her, and often as not, when they went to church or took a walk in the park, some newspaper photographer would spot her mother and take a picture of them. When she'd made up stories about growing up, she'd wanted to be just like her mother, beautiful and rich and famous with a husband just like her father. Since her mother had always seemed happy enough about letting her father do whatever he was doing, she'd thought that that was the way it ought to be when you were grown-up enough to understand everything. But now she was beginning to understand the way it really was, and she could only cry and cry. She didn't want to be one of a thousand, or a million, brides of Christ. She wanted to be something else, and she didn't know what in the world it was. . . .

The older Aaron became the more respect he had for those broad clichés describing the human condition that people in his grandmother's time had firmly fixed in their minds. He'd learned most of the ones he knew in those last years when she'd rocked away her time and had nothing better to do than talk to a little boy playing on the floor. The one that surfaced on this occasion was "Pride goeth before a fall." It had been pride that made him decide to sail over to Oyster Bay with the thought that the President might be there for the weekend, and he could row his daughter ashore and introduce her. With his daughter along, he could get away with introducing Georgia too, as a family friend; a man couldn't be suspected of hanky-panky with a thirteen-year-old daughter along as chaperone. Both

Felicia and Georgia were excited by the possibility, and thinking and talking about it helped to ease the awkwardness of their meeting. Though both of them had been polite, Aaron had easily detected Georgia's nervous wish to be liked and accepted and Felicia's embarrassment. So his proposal about their destination turned out to have been something like an inspiration.

"Going sailing's surprise enough, daddy," Felicia said, "but meeting the *President* . . . He never spoke to me at the wedding."

"Oh, you remember him? Well, there were a lot of people, and I guess you got lost in the shuffle—"

"I can't imagine a girl as stunning as Felicia getting lost in any shuffle," Georgia said.

"She was small then," Aaron said, and smiled.

"I'm still small," Felicia said. "Was great-grandmother small?"

"Yes, and she always used to say that good things come in small packages," Aaron said. "Look at Georgia—you're almost as big as Georgia. By the way, let's not forget she's 'Miss Maitland,' an old family friend, when we meet the President."

"Really, Aaron, do you think he'd swallow that? Van Alens don't have actresses as old family friends," Georgia said.

"You don't look like an actress, and Teddy never did think much of the theater—"

"Well, I like *that*," Georgia started to say, but Felicia, bless her, interrupted.

"Oh, I love the theater. It must be so much fun to make believe. I'm always making things up."

Wanting to steer the conversation in the right

direction, Aaron said, "You do? I didn't know that."

"Nobody does. I've never told anybody before, but I have a whole book of things I made up. I brought it along because I wrote a story all in French, and I want you to see it, daddy, when you aren't so busy."

He *was* too busy to look at anything; he was sailing the boat alone. Ladies, hobbled with long skirts and crippled with heels, weren't supposed to crew on boats; he felt fortunate enough to have two along who enjoyed the ride, since ladies were supposed to have delicate stomachs, like Mary's. He'd put up only the main and working jib to make things easier, but it was enough canvas to send *Cathay* tearing across Long Island Sound with a fresh, puffy northwester almost at her back. Though the sun was bright, the wind was biting in the puffs like little claws of winter holding on, and they were all bundled up, the ladies with blankets over their knees and their hands in muffs. Because it was so early in the season, they were almost alone out there in the whole blue reach of the Sound except for an excursion steamer plodding sedately up the middle. It made them feel like hearty adventurers, and they all started singing ". . . we sail the ocean blue . . ." from *Pinafore*, partly to keep warm but partly because it was the kind of day when you just felt like singing. About the only small concern Aaron had on his mind at that moment was that with the wind in this direction they'd have to beat back, which meant that they'd have to start early because Felicia, by his solemn promise, was due by sundown—in time for vespers. Getting them away from the Roosevelts, if they were there, wouldn't be easy.

Inside Oyster Bay and at anchor, they found the wind calmer, the sun warmer. They were able to picnic in the cockpit, and Georgia had brought a bottle of wine along in the hamper. Even though he knew the girl had been given only ceremonial sips at holiday feasts Aaron poured a glass for Felicia too. The warmth wouldn't hurt her this day. She said, "That's what I like about being with you, daddy . . . you treat me as if I were grown-up." And he probably spoiled it by saying, "Well, just remember that you aren't." But she got her book out and showed him her French story, which, not being a French scholar, he could only admire for the feat itself since she wouldn't let him peek at the other entries. After lunch they all rowed ashore and walked up to Sagamore Hill, but the Roosevelts weren't in residence. By then, it didn't seem to matter because it had already been such a grand day, and Aaron put up the sails and weighed anchor and started back with the good feeling that there was plenty of time to make a relaxed sail of the return trip.

Aaron had been in and out of Oyster Bay often enough to feel fairly confident about knowing the waters without detailed consultation of the charts. The wind was still blowing out of the north with harder puffs from the west, and he was on a port tack, well heeled over and boiling along so fast that *Cathay* was tossing sparkling showers of spray into the air. By heading her up in the puffs, he was doing well on his northerly course and was sure that he had plenty of room without tacking to clear the sandy flats and bluffs of Lloyd's Neck looming on his starboard side to the east. Felicia was already feeling sad about having to go back to school, and, to keep her mind off it, Aaron prodded Georgia into telling about some of her more humorous pratfalls on stage. She was so naturally an actress that, pacing up and down there in the well of the cockpit, she was putting on a full-scale performance for an audience of two and taking all of Aaron's attention when— *Cathay* stopped dead in the water with such force that Aaron was thrown against the wheel, Felicia was pitched out of her seat, and Georgia, standing to do her act, was tumbled down the companionway stairs. By instinct, Aaron let go the sheets and, with the loose sails flapping furiously, paused long enough in the cockpit to make sure that Felicia was all right and ducked down into the cabin to help Georgia off the sole. She seemed all right too, only shaken and a little bruised, but he stretched her out on a bunk and covered her with blankets. Then he checked the bilges to see if any water were rushing in—no sign of it. He went back up on deck.

Cathay was certainly not moving at all, not even responding to the jerky chop of the wind-whipped water. There was no sign on the water's glinting surface that its depth where he was differed from where he had just been or where he was heading; yet he was surely, firmly aground. Probably on sand, he guessed, since there'd been no crack and no sign of damage below. The sails were doing no good, only rattling him with their rattling, so he took them down while he thought hard about their predicament. His first wild notion was that he'd just kedge

543

them off—take an anchor out in the dinghy and then pull *Cathay* back into deep water with its line. But he discarded the idea at once on the grounds that a forty-nine-year-old man, gone soft from sitting on the bench, and two women, both small and one of them slightly injured, could never move the mass of *Cathay* even with the aid of winches. There was little chance of getting a tow. Their joy in being alone on the water was now the worst of their problem; nobody was likely to see them until the work boats put out on Monday morning. Lloyd's Neck was close enough—too close, as he'd learned the hard way— so that they could row ashore but to what avail? When he scanned the land with his glasses, the few summer homes he spotted were still silent and shuttered. He couldn't leave *Cathay* for long in any case nor abandon the women on what looked like a wasteland. The best that could be said for their position was that they were in no possible danger of drowning. What about tide? Aaron went below again to consult his charts. It was about four in the afternoon now, and the tide had started falling at three; it would be high again shortly after three A.M. There was hope in that tide . . . an hour's difference in the rise of high tide might mean that *Cathay* would float free of her grounding at its highest flow.

When Aaron finally got around to spelling out their situation to Georgia and Felicia, the older woman was calm about it and the girl elated, "Oh, goodie," she said, "I'll miss vespers and that awful slop they have for dinner Sunday night."

"You'll miss dinner entirely, I'm afraid," Aaron said. "Georgia only packed enough for lunch. We were going to anchor in your harbor and take a train back to the city for dinner and get the boat next weekend."

"I think there's a tin of biscuits. I always leave biscuits aboard," Georgia said.

"And there's something else—there's a bottle of rum. I always leave some of that aboard for emergencies like this. We might need it to keep warm," Aaron said. "I'd light a fire, but I'm afraid when the tide goes down this boat might roll over on her side. Judging by the depth of the keel, the sandbar or whatever we're on will be high and dry by then. Don't be upset. It shouldn't hurt anything— just make it awkward to get around."

When Aaron got the bottle out, Felicia asked, "Can I have some rum, too?"

"Under the circumstances, I'd advise it—but only under these circumstances," Aaron said.

As the tide receded, *Cathay* continued to perch rather precariously on the base of her keel, and it did appear that they were on a sandbar that Aaron was relieved to discover showed on no charts; more caution wouldn't have helped him. Felicia was fascinated—"It's just like being in Noah's ark"— but Aaron explained that the ark had a broader bottom and suggested that they move, if at all, with caution, keeping to the center line of the boat. Aaron was almost holding his own breath, because now that the boat hadn't been eased down on her side by the receding water, a roll could be jarring and possibly damaging to the rigging. It was reassuring that the wind, as such winds usually did, had died at sundown, and the spring night vaulting over them was all black velvet, embossed with stars. Warmed by blankets and rum, Georgia drifted off to sleep, and Felicia whispered, "Could we go out in the cockpit, daddy? I'd like to look at the stars—and talk."

"Well, if we're careful . . ."

They crawled up the companionway stairs and sat facing each other in the well of the cockpit. Felicia said, "Daddy, I think this was . . . well, almost like God answering a prayer. I don't want to go back to that convent—ever. I want to go home with you. Take me home with you, *please*."

Aaron was embarrassed. But poised there on the thin edge of *Cathay*'s keel in a pool of darkness, he felt that he had no right to deny this child the truth. "I can't, Felicia. I have no home. I live with Georgia and—"

"But I *like* Georgia. I didn't think I would, but I do. And I think she likes me. Why couldn't I live with you and—?"

"Felicia, we'd love to have you, but it wouldn't be . . . be right. If you don't want to go back to school, I *could* take you to your mother—"

It was then that he thought that he'd let her have too much rum. "No! I don't want to go back to mother, ever, ever, *ever*. . . ."

"But, Felicia, why—"

"I shouldn't say. Don't make me say . . ."

"Felicia, I *have* to know. Your mother did tell me you were something of a discipline problem, and that's why she sent you to the convent, but—"

"*I'm* a discipline problem . . . ? It's not my fault, it's her . . . hers."

"Felicia, please. I don't know what you are talking about."

"Oh, daddy, it's too awful."

"Nothing's too awful for you to tell me, Felicia. I'm not only your father, but remember I've been in court for years, and I'm a judge and used to hearing everything."

Aaron was not, however, used to hearing what he heard then. Felicia, her tongue loosened by rum and her desire for some sort of salvation through him, broke down and, with much backing and filling, managed to get out the story of how she'd seen Mary and James "doing it"—her words that didn't need translation for Aaron. It would be a long time, if ever, before Aaron could sort out the various strands of emotions that tied themselves into a knot in his stomach as he listened to this child, his daughter, her face misted with starlit tears, fumble out this story. Among those strands, moving, twisting, knotting, were anger, jealousy, incredulity, guilt, regret, sorrow. Above all, incredulity. Mary and James. He could remember Sally's kidding about it once, and how they'd both agreed that it was impossible to imagine. Mary and James. He realized that, unconsciously, he'd been using these two immovable benchmarks to measure his waywardness or humanity, depending on how he was seeing himself. Some people simply ought to be all of a piece, solid and durable as a stone statue. Could it be that this imaginative child, desperate to get out of the convent and helped along by alcohol on an almost empty stomach, was making it up? God, he hoped so.

"Felicia, are you really sure of what you saw?"

"I can't . . . don't make me, please . . ." The child was really crying now.

"All right, but you do make things up, and you've had something you're not accustomed to—"

"Daddy, I *couldn't* make it up—my own *mother*. Oh, I shouldn't have told you. . . . I've never told anyone, not anyone . . ."

He decided he'd have to believe her, unravel one of the strands in that knot. "I'm glad you did tell me, Felicia, but you must never tell anyone else. You'll have to learn to live with it. Your great-grandmother used to say that people ought to die with secrets, and this is your first one. In time you'll understand it. Grown-up men and women need each other, thank God, or there wouldn't be any children in the world. This is one expression of their need, their love—"

"But it's a sin, daddy. The sisters are always telling us what an awful sin it is to do that unless you're married to the person."

"I won't say the sisters are wrong, but don't they tell you that we're all sinners?"

"Yes . . ."

"And that God can forgive sin?"

"Yes . . ."

"Well, if you pray, Felicia, pray that God will forgive us all. Now come over here and let me hold you. Maybe it will help to keep us both warm, and you can get some sleep. I don't know when we'll get off here."

She came eagerly into his arms. "Mother never holds me," she said. "She says I'm too big for that sort of thing."

The knot in his stomach was slipping up to become a lump in his throat. "Nobody's ever too big to be held," he told her.

"Daddy . . . ? You will take me home, won't you?"

"I'll think about it."

Soon he could feel her relax, feel her regular breathing. It was the first time he'd ever held this child in his arms, and the trusting she displayed made that lump dissolve into the first tears he'd allowed himself in years. What an unholy damn mess. From all he'd been able to judge, Mary had never quite reconciled herself to this unwanted child and had exercised with her that control and cool distance she'd proved so capable of in relation to him and her brothers. Felicia, as far as he could tell, had responded with all the fervor of unrequited love, making an idol of what she couldn't reach. In all their outings together, Felicia would innocently boast about her mother's doings and dress and demeanor as if he might share her pride in this woman because he still was her husband in name. He'd never discouraged the girl; through all of this, he'd always considered Mary to be on the side of the angels, which made her hard to live with but perhaps the best of examples to his children. He really wanted them to be complete Van Alens, happy in their heritage and not driven by doubts as he'd been. Now this. The shock this child must have suffered would be in proportion to her blind adoration of Mary. Once the eyes were opened, they could never be closed, and there remained only one screen to shield them from the unbearable brightness of truth—understanding. Maybe he could give her that. Maybe . . .

Thinking of Felicia, he thought too of that letter he'd left back on his desk. He'd almost made up his mind that it was his duty to tell Mary and James about the boys. They were, after all, still underage, and they were, after all, their responsibility. Having walked out on that responsibility, he'd finally decided he had no right to undermine its disciplines. But this night, as a result of this freak accident, his mind was changing rapidly. He still was no believer in a God who set all the surprising scenes in the human drama; he had only to glance up at all those stars, each in its way alive, to know how preposterous and demeaning to divinity it was to believe that the arranger of the universe deliberately put a sand bar in the way of a yacht out for a nice Sunday sail. He was, however, a believer in the fact that a man's response to whatever came his way mattered very much. It was a little like intercepting a pass you didn't expect in a football game. If you dropped it, you were a coward or a fool; if you froze, you were sure to be hit; if you didn't know where you were, you might run for the wrong goal. The pass he'd caught was being a father after all, and he could only try to run with it, to do his best with it.

It wouldn't be long before he'd have to move. Though he couldn't get up and look, not wanting to disturb either Felicia or the balance of the boat, he could tell from the sound of ripples against the hull that the water was rising. If they got off, what then? He wasn't going to take this girl back to that school, and, under the present circumstances, he wouldn't take her back home to Mary. Yet it would be improper and embarrassing to the girl herself, society being what it was, to have her live with him and Georgia. He could, of course, set up a separate establishment, might have to the way things were going, but that would take time. He wanted to do something to make her feel that somebody cared right now, as soon as they got off this bar. She'd have to stay with some sort of relative, and he began running through names—of course, Sally! Nothing wrong with a young girl living with her aunt, especially now that Sally was one of the leading figures in the New York art world and had taken her own kind of veil ever since Tony had gone to jail. From what he'd heard, Matty was soon going to Paris to buy for the gallery and recruit professors for the academy and Sally would be lonely. A perfect solution except for one thing. Mary would be enraged and might even bring the law on him, but he knew a bit about the law, and, painful though it might be, he'd use what Felicia had witnessed if he had to. As for Neil, he'd keep sending the boy money and keep his mouth shut; in another year the boy would be an adult and free if he chose to be. Of course, Mary and James could mess that one up too, but at least his son would know that he could trust him.

With his mind made up, Aaron could hardly endure the too-slow rising of the waters. He wished that he could feel that some God put the sandbar there and would answer his prayer to bring a tide a little over six feet. He was experiencing a surge of elation and freedom. More than what Sophie had told him, what Felicia had told him lifted that weight of guilt that he had somehow failed to become a proper Van Alen. There *were* no proper Van Alens, only fumbling, vulnerable people who could afford to buy a marble facade but no escape from their own natures. What a joy to know this for sure.

Something was moving; he could feel it right through the seat of his pants. *Cathay* was free, starting to bob a little in the ripple made by a light night breeze offshore. He shook Felicia awake, almost dumped her as he jumped to get sail on. When he got back to the helm and had *Cathay* heading away from disaster, straight out toward the Sound, Felicia, yawning and trying to orient herself, asked, "Where are you taking me, daddy? You aren't taking me back to school?"

"No," he said, "I'm going to square away for New York."

She jumped up and hugged him. He'd never known that being a father could be such a surpassing pleasure.

Chapter 12

"AUNT SALLY, do you think we ought to go through with this. I mean, do you *really* think I can become a writer?"

"I don't know much about writing, but I do like your stories, and I do know that you can become anything you want to, Felicia, as long as you don't let some man talk you into doing the dishes for him. Looking like you do, you'll have trouble with that one."

"You know I don't care about boys . . ."

"Maybe not now, but I hope you do soon. God knows, I don't think men should tell us what to do, but we can't do without them. I can't believe that Matty's really happy, though she says she is. It's so hard to tell from letters. I do miss her so, and I can only thank God that you came along . . ."

It did seem an act of providence that had brought Felicia into her life just when she needed her most, Sally thought. It wasn't a kind providence, but providence wasn't always kind. The hoopla in the press—HEIRESS KIDNAPPED BY FATHER, DISTRICT COURT JUDGE—had caused Aaron to resign from the bench and return to private practice. The custody suit filed by Mary had obliged Aaron to hire private detectives, who had been able, through a peephole in a certain suite at the Waldorf Hotel, to confirm what Felicia had witnessed and thereby make possible a quiet, out-of-court settlement of the case. It had been, as Aaron had truthfully said, "an unholy mess," but out of it was emerging, in this shy and imaginative neice of hers, a person far more interesting than she'd have been as bait for another respectable Van Alen son-in-law. There had been no "coming out" party for Felicia Mary Van Alen, though her proud father would have hired the city's biggest ballroom to stage it if she'd wanted it; instead, Felicia had asked for the money to spend a year in Paris with Matty to improve her French.

It was, in fact, the little things that Felicia inadvertently revealed about that experience, rather than anything that Matty wrote in her careful letters, that aroused Sally's suspicions about her daughter's sexuality. That poor French waif—"a shivering, skinny model"—whom Matty had adopted "out of the goodness of her heart" was pretty evidently more to her than a charity case. Felicia was fortunately still too innocent to know the implications of some of the things she reported, but Sally was not too innocent to catch them, and she knew that there would never be a "normal life" for Matty. It was why she'd stopped four or—what was it, 1912, now?—yes, five years ago pleading with Matty to come home, even though she was running herself ragged trying to supervise both the gallery and the academy. Matty was doing a good job, sending her fine things, and it was more likely that her private life would be better tolerated in Paris than in New York. Proof of that was that Matty's own cousin, James' son, Peter, was literally drinking himself to death rather than facing up to the unnatural call of his nature. Peter might have gone to Paris too, or Rome, or anywhere, and lived his own life, but James refused to give him the money on the grounds that he needed him to manage his art collection. So Peter pottered around among his father's pictures and, secretly and steadily, drank.

Given her choice, Sally would rather have produced a Matty than a Peter. She'd often reflected on the unkind fate that was bringing her again, after all these years, face to face with this thing that even she still couldn't really talk about with anybody. Fortunately, some people *were* beginning to talk about things like this; she'd gone to a lecture right here in New York by that Viennese doctor, Sigmund Freud, who was shocking everybody with his theories about infant sex fantasies and an unconscious mind. She hadn't been able to understand much of it, but she had come away with the feeling that, if the man was right, people didn't have all the control over what they were that people like her grandfather used to say they did in his sermons. The thought was both comforting and disturbing. She could think, rather than feel as she always had, that people like Matty and Peter, even the Duke, were not sinners forever damned; yet she had also to think that she had to bear much of the responsibility for the way Matty had turned out. Maybe she'd given her too much physical love to make up for a missing father and a drunken stepfather; maybe she'd innocently injured her by exposing her in that parade to that dreadful kidnapping; maybe her open relationship with Tony had disgusted Matty; maybe . . . The list of maybes was endless, and yet she still didn't see how she would have done otherwise under the circumstances of her life at any given time. What bothered her most was the feeling that Matty would never quite be happy, and yet had *she* ever been happy? What was happiness? It was a question more elusive to her now at fifty-eight than it had been at eighteen or twenty-eight or thirty-eight. The most she could say was that, except for periods of boredom, she hadn't been *un*happy, and maybe Matty wouldn't be either. If living this long had convinced her of one thing it was that there was no such thing as a "normal life"; you went on living whatever kind of life you had and trying to make the best of it.

Oh, she had regrets. She doubted that anyone she knew had more regrets. The fact that she'd allowed herself to experience a genuine ecstasy was not, however, among those regrets, as she supposed it might be for many women who lived by conventional wisdom or morality. It had saved her from what might have been bitterness in these last years when, through both age and inclination, she'd had to learn to live without it. Not without love, though. She still had Tony. Curiously, his helplessness, hopelessness, brought out in her a kind of satisfying tenderness greater than his manliness had. As often as her busy schedule would allow, she'd go up to visit him at Sing Sing. Unhappily, his kind of work in massive stone had not proved possible to arrange in prison, nor in fact did he have the heart for it. He'd been reduced to whittling, which was not his talent, but she'd take the pieces back with her and pretend that they'd sold and bring him money to buy comforts with. What really kept him alive were her stories about the students at the academy, and she'd often induce one or two of them to come up with her for a visit; then it would be almost like old times with them all sitting around and discussing art and Tony the fieriest of the bunch. How he'd managed through all this not to blame her for what had happened to him was amazing. He'd said once, but only once, "Don't ever blame yourself, Sally. I just wasn't born to get the breaks. You were the only break I ever had, and I'd do it again to save you or Matty." She'd cried all the way home from that visit, but usually she came home feeling proud to love a man who could endure so much injustice without whimpering. As long as he lived, and she could serve him, at least her life wouldn't be without meaning.

She had to admit, though, that what gave her life special interest these days was mainly Felicia. Charlie, a duke now in his own right since his father's death of a heart attack and making a name for himself in the House of Lords, was too far away, as was Matty, for the kind of involvement Sally enjoyed with Felicia. She never thought that she'd come to a day when living vicariously through another, younger person would be as important and, in some ways, as exciting to her as her own affairs, but here she was. She'd been aware of the girl's potential ever since Felicia had shyly shown her her "secret book" a few days after she came to live with her. Now she was trying to persuade her to get going, to get a start on realizing her potential before she came into all that money. It would only be a third of what was left in trust for Mary but it would be quite enough—double what she'd got because of the tradeoff with the steel stock—to turn a young girl's head. Looking back, Sally knew that it had been her own consciousness of being wealthy, along with what she was told a woman's role was supposed to be, that had disarmed her until much too late in life. She had no illusions about her supposed fame these days as a mover and shaker in the world of art: it was only her money talking, only the fact that she could afford to take chances on pieces or subsidize unknown talent; without the money, she'd be a nobody. Fortunately, Felicia, because of living so long down here in the Village in the relatively modest circumstances that Sally preferred and because of keeping her head full of make-believe, had no such consciousness of wealth—yet.

From what Aaron reported of Mary's condition, Felicia wouldn't have much time left to get her feet firmly on the ground before she would be awash in money. If Mary died, she'd get the income right away and the principle in two years. Sally knew that she ought to feel sorrier for Mary, but she simply didn't have that much charity in her soul. Bad enough the way Mary had wormed her way into her own mother's affections to become *the* Mrs. Van Alen, but worse the way she'd treated Aaron and her children. That affair with James might have made Mary—and James—seem human to Sally if they'd had the courage to own up to it. While it was her good luck, Sally despised Mary for letting her daughter go to protect her own good name; even Aaron admitted that he probably couldn't have won the case in court, because private detectives can be bought off and he would never have put Felicia on the stand. And then that business about Neil: Mary and James had had the police arrest their sons out in San Francisco and bring them back like common criminals. Aaron had been incensed, but he couldn't fight two battles at once, and Felicia's was more important, more pressing. What they'd done with Neil after they'd got him back was easy enough to follow. Sally wasn't too sure of the details, but she'd heard that Mary had finally threatened poor old Sophie with eviction if she didn't sign a will leaving her money to Neil. "They've got me in a golden trap, dad," was the way Neil explained it to his father. Now Neil and his brother-in-law were fighting it out to see who would be James' successor as head of the Van Alen division of U.S. Steel; that Arthur, who'd probably be a delightful scamp if she could get to know him, had persuaded his father to send him back out to San Francisco on the grounds that he couldn't do much damage to the family name there.

Sally sometimes wondered whether Amelia or Neil knew about their mother and James. Probably not. From what she'd gathered, they'd been cowardly enough—"sensible enough," would be the way they'd put it—to break it off as soon as they discovered that Aaron knew. Since that was all of six years ago, it gave James some sort of excuse for behaving as he was now, but not much. If he'd ever really cared for Mary, he couldn't have set off on this world cruise just after he heard about her illness. James had to be richer than God. He'd bought himself an enormous steam yacht and lined up a party of industrialists to go on a glorified selling mission to as many crowned heads of Europe and Asia as they could meet. The yacht was called the *Martha Van Alen,* and all you had to do was read the papers to follow her progress—a reception by the Kaiser in Hamburg, the Prince of Wales in Liverpool, the Tsar in St. Petersburg. Perhaps it was the truth that this had all taken a great deal of arranging and couldn't be put off for anything. Anne, for instance, couldn't go along because she had to see to the wedding of one of those younger girls, whose names Sally kept mixing up—Janet, she thought it was—and how then could he delay it for a tumor in his sister-in-law that might not amount to much. James had taken one of the secretaries he'd hired "because of the typing thing" to replace his clerks, and she'd been alongside him in a couple of the pictures and looked to be a girl who had more than clever fingers to recommend her. James, you old sinner, Sally had thought as she looked at the pictures. But James wasn't a *nice* sinner, and this business with Mary proved it.

So it was Aaron Sally really felt sorry for. She didn't quite understand why he was letting himself in for all this grief, but she had to admire him for it. They'd sat long over a bottle one night, and Aaron had really confided in her. "You know, sis, Georgia and I are great friends—lovers, whatever you want to call it," he'd said, "but sometimes I think you only fall really in love once in your life. For me, it was Mary; for you, I guess, Tony. Anyway, when she called, what could I do . . . ?" Then he'd told her the whole of it . . .

About all James *had* done for Mary was to see that she got the Van Alen suite and the best of doctors in that big medical complex he'd built. It was a room and dressing room and bath high up in a corner of the hospital wing. It was cheerful enough, with walls painted in pastel shades and hung with some of James' lesser paintings. Out of two windows you could see the East River and on a clear day the bay or a patch of the Sound, and Mary's society friends kept it so banked with flowers that it smelled to Aaron when he walked in like a mortuary, which was fitting enough in view of Mary's first words: "Aaron, I called you, because I know I'm going to die."

He couldn't believe it—then. With her color a bit high from fever, she seemed almost more beautiful than he remembered her. She'd brought along one of her maids, who slept out in the little dressing rooms and saw to it that Mary's robes and night clothes were as well tended as if she were going out to a ball, her hair in perfect order. "Nonsense, Mary," he said. "I've never seen you looking lovelier."

"That's the nicest thing you've said to me in years."

"Well, for what it's worth, it's true."

"It isn't worth much. You should see the rest of

me. They took this ugly thing, whatever it was, out yesterday, and no matter what they said I could tell from the look on the doctors' faces that it hadn't done any good. I'm scared Aaron . . ."

"Of what? No matter what else he's done, James has managed to get the best doctors in the world right here, and you ought to trust them."

"They don't know how I *feel*. I'm so weak, and . . . I don't know . . ."

Aaron felt helpless. "What can I do to help, Mary?"

She started, then, to cry. "You could hold my hand."

He pulled a chair close to the bed and took her hand. It felt fever-hot. "Have you told anyone else how you feel?"

"No. Amelia was in here, but she was so full of good cheer about what the doctors told her and she has enough on her mind with those three children."

"What about Neil?"

"Oh, he comes too, but we've never really been able to talk since that San Francisco business. I think you're closer to him than I am. And with James gone . . . and, well, I just had to have someone I could really talk to . . . I wanted at least to tell you I am sorry for the selfish way I've behaved. It's my act of contrition, I guess. Tomorrow I'm going to have the priest and make my confession." She gripped his hand, and he looked into those once mischievous eyes and saw nothing but pain, fear. "Aaron, I don't even really *believe*, or I couldn't have done what I've done. I got to thinking that nothing could touch *the* Mrs. Van

Alen. I thought I could control everything and everybody. I really did. But everything's different when you know you're dying. Aaron, I'm afraid . . ."

An efficient nurse bustled in and said, "Mrs. Van Alen's not to have visitors for more than fifteen minutes." As he got up to go, Mary still clung to his hand. "Come back again, Aaron, *please*. Remember, you're still my husband . . ."

So Aaron had gone back, many times over the last months. The strong body that Mary had molded by dancing ironically worked against the failing will in her; it wouldn't give up. Battling against the cancer, she shrank; the contours of her face turned skeletal. At one point, Aaron ordered that all the mirrors around her be removed, and she had the sensitivity never to ask for one again. Mary's social friends were the first to stop coming, and their flowers stopped coming too. Anne Van Alen, looking almost as skeletal as the patient and apparently still innocent of having been deceived, persisted in duty visits until Aaron had to ask her to stop; seeing her was too painful a reminder for Mary. Amelia and Neil came and stayed as briefly as possible never knowing what to say. Felicia, who hadn't seen her mother since the day she was put in the convent, didn't come at all, which Aaron suspected was best for them both. Aaron *was* the only person Mary could talk to except, perhaps, the priest. What she'd confessed to the priest, Aaron didn't know, but she did confess to him her passion for James, or his for her, and asked his forgiveness. "I'm certainly not in a position to forgive, Mary. It's you who should forgive me," he told her. Whatever her confession, because of her prominence the Cardinal himself came over from St. Patrick's on several occasions to give her communion. "I think maybe I do believe, I *have* to believe," she began to tell Aaron, "and I wish you could too . . ."

All this was tearing Aaron apart, Sally could tell. "The thing is, sis, she *was* so strong, which was part of the problem, I guess, and to see her going like this . . . If you understand what I'm saying, it was better to have her around to be mad at than turning saintly. . . . God, that James . . . He's written her only one letter since he's been gone, and she shared it with me. Of course, he has to be careful, or thinks he does. Anyway, he goes on and on about all the honors he's receiving and then tells her, 'My doctors report that they're giving you the best of care, and I expect you'll be quite well when I return. I do hope so, because I always like to think of you as you were. You know how I've admired your strength all these years.'"

Well, there wasn't much Sally could do for Aaron in this except to listen. So she was even happier about what she'd been able to do for him in caring for Felicia. God knew, Aaron had come to *her* rescue often enough. So what she was trying to do at the moment was give Felicia enough confidence to go up with her and meet Mr. Hearst. She'd met the publisher when he'd come into her gallery while he was windowshopping for art works—"my only relaxation," he'd told her. Well, she knew that Hearst had another relaxation: he was always in the front row at the *Ziegfeld Follies* or any other musical full of pretty girls, and that was what she was counting on. It was quite obvious from reading the *Journal* and the *American* that Hearst liked to have women writers—sob-sisters, she called them—and she was pretty sure that, once Hearst got a look at Felicia, he probably wouldn't even care whether she could write or not. Sally didn't really like doing business this way and of course wouldn't tell Felicia what she had on her mind, but with the world the way it was a woman didn't have much choice.

"Well, you'd better run along and get dressed, Felicia. Mr. Hearst is expecting us at two," Sally said.

"I'm really scared, Aunt Sally. I mean I've done some passable fiction for the college magazine, but—"

"Look everybody has to start somewhere, and surely Mr. Hearst knows that. Just keep thinking of how proud your father will be when we tell him tonight that you've got a job."

"*If* I have a job . . ."

On that fall day in 1912, Aaron Van Alen wasn't thinking about what his daughter Felicia might be up to; he would be presented with a hard decision himself. It had all started a week or more before when Hugh O'Donnell came to see him at his office. Aaron's first thought was that Hugh had somehow heard about Mary, though it didn't seem likely. One of the Van Alen medical center's services to patients who could afford it was that they were not exposed to the press, and Aaron, at Mary's express request, had not informed her brothers. "There are some things that can never be mended," was the way she put it, "and in any case I couldn't stand pity from them." Why then could she stand pity from him? And was anything really mended? He didn't know the answers to such questions. Perhaps he was for Mary a kind of only love as she was for him. A curious pride kept them from admitting such a thing to each other. What logic he could bring to bear on the situation told him that, given their different personalities and drives, it could never have been otherwise; one or the other of them would have been broken. But Mary was too busy dealing with her feelings about dying to introduce feelings of irreparable regret. So on his visits he'd mostly sit holding her hand, a clutching claw now, and let her talk about heaven and pretend to believe. "You know the real reason I sent for you, Aaron," she said to him once, "is that I had an instinct about you. You're not like the others . . . they keep smiling and telling me that I'm going to get well, except for the ones who've stopped coming because they know I'm not. You have the courage to let me die, to help me go." Nothing she'd said had touched him more, and now nothing could keep him from helping her go . . .

When Hugh walked in, Aaron started thinking of how to keep him away from Mary since he suspected that Hugh would be one of those regrets that Mary didn't need. Just seeing Hugh might be almost as much of a shock to Mary as seeing her would be to Hugh; she might not even recognize him . . . all those black-Irish good looks of his were long gone. Though still thick and curly, Hugh's hair was pure white; his face was round and puffy, whiskey-veined on the curve of his cheeks and the bulb of his nose;

his stevedore's body had softened into a large pear of fat. He still had the politician's professional heartiness, however. While he shook Aaron's hand, he punched him playfully on the shoulder and said, "I should really give you a good sock for avoiding me, brother-in-law. I saw you in the Waldorf the other day, and you didn't even look my way."

"I didn't see you, Hugh, but to tell the truth I don't think we share many interests these days—"

"But we will, we will. The governor sent me to see you . . ."

"The governor?"

"Sure and there's only one governor these days—Wilson. He's taking a few days off the campaign trail and resting down there in Princeton, and he wants you to come down and talk to him."

"Excuse me, Hugh, but how in the world do you know Wilson?"

"Oh, I know you don't think much of me, Aaron. You never did have a real head for politics or you wouldn't have walked off the bench like that. People these days don't expect you to be a saint, and they have short memories anyway. The governor's got me on his staff—to advise him on how to get out the Irish vote in New York, which he *needs*. After that, he says he'll find me a spot in Washington. What do you think of that? But listen, you will come, won't you?"

"I can't imagine what he'd want with me. We haven't been in touch for years. *You* didn't mention my name, did you?"

"Well, the governor was asking me about some people in New York who have a little class but might

567

appeal to the people—the Jews and dagos and hunkies and such—and I did think of you. Them Hearst papers have been promoting that public-defender thing, you know, and—"

"I think you'd better tell the governor that I'm awfully busy, and I have some personal problems . . ."

He wouldn't say more since Hugh obviously hadn't heard about Mary. Hugh O'Donnell in close contact with a man like Woodrow Wilson? Another of his grandmother's haunting clichés—"Politics makes strange bedfellows"—surfaced.

"I don't want you to do me no favors, Aaron—you did me enough once. But if you could have seen the governor when I mentioned your name . . . well, you know how he is—kind of frosty—but a real gentleman, a real gentleman. Anyway he breaks into this big grin and says, 'Aaron Van Alen? Jove, why didn't I think of him. He's an old friend of mine.' Then he says something kind of odd. He says, 'You give Aaron a message from me, O'Donnell. You tell him to drive down here, because I want to see his car.'"

Aaron half-smiled. That did it—that and the same kind of curiosity that took him down to see Teddy in Washington. "All right, tell him I'll come, but I'm not interested in anything but seeing him," Aaron said.

While he had shied away from politics, Aaron could not help but be wholly fascinated this election year with two old friends, or acquaintances, running for the highest office in the land and bruising each other on the stump. Teddy, unfulfilled by triumphal

568

foreign tours, by receiving the Nobel Peace Prize for his part in settling the Russian-Japanese war, by hunting big game in Africa, was back trying to unseat his own hand-picked successor, Taft, on the fairly solid grounds that his progressive program had been scuttled. He'd bolted the Republican Party when Taft was renominated and was running on the Progressive—the Bull Moose—ticket. Wilson, who'd finally jumped into the arena from his academic grandstand at Princeton to be elected governor of New Jersey, was the Democratic nominee. Already Aaron knew that he would face a difficult choice when he went into the polling booth. He'd appreciated Roosevelt's efforts at reform—the more so when he heard that Clay Frick was going around New York after the '04 election and saying, "We bought the son-of-a-bitch, but he won't stay bought"—and yet the "fair deal" Wilson was proposing seemed a sounder, more systematic program to insure some form of social justice. If there was anything that Aaron liked about the circumstances that caused his resignation from the court, it was that he wouldn't feel he owed a favor to Roosevelt when the time came actually to cast his vote. It also made it possible to go down to see Wilson with what could be called clean hands, although it didn't matter since he was determined not to get involved in anything new at this difficult point in his life.

In the end he didn't drive. He took the train because Georgia, who'd taught herself to drive and taught Felicia too, wanted the car to take a party of theatrical friends for an outing in Westchester. He thought it better not to disrupt her plans when he couldn't take her to meet Wilson, who with his three marriageable daughters was even more a proper family man than Roosevelt. It was sometimes a matter of bemused speculation to Aaron that all of the women in his life had taken to driving—even Mary and Sally had stately electrics. Not so much to head them off as to tease them, he'd quote from Dr. Bryant's warning against "high-speed diseases," which the doctor claimed from his practice were more common among ladies who because of their "more timid natures" suffered from such ailments as "wry neck, paralysis of the leg and hysteria. Nature has failed to provide them biologically so well as their brothers and husbands against wind and rain, or fit them so well for the outdoor strenuous life. The only moral to be drawn is that the human body is not fitted for high-speed automobiling." If they didn't try to be ladies, his women would probably have made an unprintable response. Actually, Aaron could appreciate the freedom driving gave them, a freedom that was really impossible in the days when going out meant harnessing up and handling a team or more of horses. He did sometimes worry a little that they'd break an arm if the crank kicked back or get bogged down in the mud holes of the terrible roads outside the city . . . but freedom always had its own risk. He himself would probably be literally risking his neck in auto races like young Al Vanderbilt if his life hadn't taken its turn away from indulging himself with the day's fashionable sport. What Aaron could hardly wait to do was to fly; when last year he'd read

570

that a fellow named Rodgers had flown a Wright plane all the way from New York to California in only eighty-two hours and then just recently that some army lieutenant had flown at more than 6,000 feet, he had come to the conclusion that flying was already where the automobile had been only a few years ago. Nothing would keep men on the ground much longer, and he wondered what Wilson thought about planes. Of course not driving to Princeton didn't matter, because he knew that Wilson's remark to Hugh was simply a way of conveying an apology for having been so pontifically short-sighted: Wilson's "countryman" was trading his horses in for Ford's Model-T as fast as he could. How his father who had honored every invention would have been excited by all this . . .

Whatever the outcome, Aaron was soon glad he'd come down to Princeton. Wilson was waiting at the door for him, dressed in his overcoat. "Good to see you, Aaron, you're just in time," he said, and took Aaron's arm. "Come along with me up to Nassau Street. Teddy's making a whistle stop—or I suppose I should call it a honking stop since he's coming over from Somerville by car—at the Nass and the boys are organizing a Parade to greet him. He doesn't know I'm in town, so I thought it would be fun just to stand on the sidelines and watch."

By the time they reached the main street, running along the front of the campus, it was filled with expectant people. The town's only policeman, known to the students as "Admiral Tinfoil," had by frantic arm wavings managed to clear the way of carriages and cars, and the Beers & Frey professional band from Trenton, surrounded by students carrying Bull Moose placards, stood in front of the balcony of the Nassau Tavern, inappropriately saluting the Harvard candidate with a Princeton march, "The Orange and the Black." Wilson and Aaron squeezed themselves against a fence across Nassau Street from the tavern to watch, along with the others, the tall windows opening on the balcony from which the candidate would emerge. After the band had stumbled through its tune three or four times, it became apparent that something was amiss. Shouts of "Where's Teddy?" and "We want Teddy!" began rising from an impatient crowd. Suddenly out from the windows stepped three or four bewhiskered, frock-coated "dignataries." Even from across the street it was apparent that the coats hung like sacks on slender bodies, the whiskers were pasted on, the figures unsteady on their feet. Wilson said, "Looks like Teddy's reception committee has been spending some time down in the senior room of the Nass."

"What's that?" Aaron asked.

"New since our day. That's where the dedicated drinkers of the senior class while away their time. Oh, oh, look at this."

The band had switched to a ragged and scarcely more appropriate rendering of "My Wild Irish Rose," and a stocky figure, also in frock coat with mustache and flashing glasses, stepped up to the rail of the balcony and raised his arms. When the music stopped he cried in a high-pitched voice, "Bully for you!"

"That's not Teddy," Wilson said. "I know that

fellow—he's a senior named Whitney. Good imitation, though."

Pounding his fist into his hand, Whitney said, "You men at Princeton lead a *strenuous* life. We Harvard men know that, especially since that first football game between us for a decade, which you won. I'm *de*lighted to be here. The symbol of our political movement is the Bull Moose, which shows power in every muscle as it crashes through the woods making more noise than sense. I have been hunting big game in Africa but I didn't find any GOP elephants, so I waited for one of their largest when I got home . . ."

By now Wilson was laughing so hard that he had to take off his pince-nez and wipe his eyes. "Oh, I should hire that young fellow," he said. "He's just killed off two big beasts in two sentences. Teddy and Taft."

The young man's impersonation was so good that Aaron could tell from looking at faces around him in the crowd that most people were too bewildered to laugh. Then suddenly Whitney stopped. The alert in the crowd, Wilson among them, called "More! More!" There was confusion on the balcony. While Whitney and his friends went in through one window, a small knot of men came out another. The real Teddy was among them. He stepped up to the rail. The band and crowd were silent. Pounding his fist into his hand, Teddy shouted, "I'm *de*lighted. You Princeton men lead *strenuous* lives. We Harvard men know that since you won that football game last fall . . ."

The duped crowd was now screaming, "Tell it to

the Marines!'' and ''More and funnier!'' Roosevelt, caught off-guard, paused but went bravely on: ''I'm glad that so many of you are here today, to join us in our great movement in reforming our political life under this great Bull Moose party . . .'' Now people were booing and shouting, ''Never!'' Wilson, nearly doubled up with laughter, took Aaron's arm again. ''Let's get out of here before he sees us,'' he said. ''I wouldn't want him to know I've witnessed this— he'd accuse me of staging it.'' . . .

Back in the quiet of his study, Wilson was still chuckling. ''You need some comic relief in politics,'' he said, ''and fortunately you get it. I have to tell you about one of the young preceptors I brought here to Princeton named Whittlesey. Well, Whittlesey's been making campaign speeches for me out in the countryside. The other day he was talking to a small group gathered in somebody's barnyard, and a heckler climbed up on a manure pile and started pestering him with questions about the Democratic platform. Whittlesey shot right back, 'I stand on our platform, sir, and I notice that you are standing on *yours*.' I'm sure he won a dozen votes for me that day.''

Wilson had to pause to laugh again and then said, ''Seriously, Aaron, I wanted to talk to you about trying your hand at that sort of thing. O'Donnell tells me that he could arrange some proper forums in the city for you—that is, of course, if you're with me. I know that Roosevelt appointed you to the bench, but—''

''Tom . . . governor, I could go along with your program, but I'm just no politician.''

"All the better. That's just what I'm looking for—support from outside the normal party channels. Listen, Aaron, politics is a lot like a game, and you're the best man at games I've known. Of course if we win I'm going to need a lot of help in Washington from old friends I can trust, like you. The Democrats haven't been in since '96, and we're going to have to clean out the stables down there."

"I can appreciate that, governor, and do appreciate your asking me, but for the sake of old times, I ought to be honest with you. I've tried to stay out of the limelight because my personal life is . . . is irregular."

"In what way, may I ask?"

"I've been separated from my wife for years."

"But you're still married?"

"Only, I fear, because she's a Catholic. And I do have a friend."

Wilson put up his hand as if he didn't want to hear more. "I see," he said, "but you did serve on the bench . . ."

"Yes, and I felt obliged to resign because of family problems. So you see—"

"I'm glad you told me this, Aaron," Wilson interrupted, "but let me tell you that I've been learning fast in government that you have to use men for the talents they possess rather than the lives they lead. I'm going to be moving a lot further than Roosevelt did into the area of controlling unbridled wealth, and your experience in that Northern Securities case as well as on the bench makes me sure that you would be a valuable ally in that program. There are many important positions that aren't, as you say, in the limelight, and I'd be willing to take a chance on you if you'll take a chance on me."

Aaron was too moved by his old friend's confidence and generosity to think about protocol. "Thanks, Tommy," he said. "I think I would like to serve with you, but it's impossible now. My wife's dying and—"

"But I thought you said you were separated."

"There are some things you can never be separated from, Tommy. She *is* my wife, and . . . well . . ."

"I'm glad you told me that too, Aaron. It makes me even more certain that I want you. You were always a fair player, and we're trying to give the American people a fair deal. I'm sorry for your personal problem, but it probably won't go on forever. I won't ask you to take part in the campaign, but if we win—a big *if,* I'm afraid, although I do have a feeling that the Bull Moose is doing more harm to the Elephant than the Donkey—please do come and see me." . . .

On the train going back to the city Aaron felt that the day had solved at least one problem for him: he'd vote for Wilson. The students' prank had exposed something he'd almost been afraid to find out about Teddy. With this Bull Moose campaign, Roosevelt was becoming something close to a comic figure; he was like one of those vaudevillians with only one line of patter, and it was wearing thin. To move on, the country needed new ideas and new people. Would he be one of them? The opportunity was clearly there, but the timing was clearly wrong.

In addition to seeing Mary through, he wanted to

see Felicia through. Though Felicia was physically with Sally, she'd become a real daughter. They were often together, either at Georgia's place or Sally's, and all through her years at Vassar she'd counted on him for advice on her studies and for the pocket money and presents a girl needed to keep up with her peers. He'd been proud of her, although he'd missed her terribly, when she chose to go abroad instead of having a coming-out affair, even though it meant doubling up on her studies to graduate with her class. Now would come the crucial years when she'd find some man, or he'd find her, when she'd have to learn to cope with all the money she'd inherit, and he wanted to be around to help her. He was honest enough to admit to himself that she probably didn't need him and that his motive was probably selfish— at fifty-five there were things that could only be lived vicariously. There was more, of course. He was fascinated by the potential he saw in the girl and quite frankly, and fatherly, in love with her.

Thinking about Felicia reminded him that Sally had insisted on his coming to see them this evening. She'd been rather coy about the reason, and Aaron decided that he'd better swing by on his way home from the station.

She'd never been so nervous. She could hardly get her fingers to behave well enough to button up the back of her dress. Aunt Sally probably wouldn't like it, but she'd picked out a very plain brown dress and hadn't put on a piece of jewelry, even the small strand of pearls Aunt Sally had given her for graduation. She'd heard that Mr. Hearst had a liking for showy showgirls, but she'd rather not be hired at all than for her looks. A man like Mr. Hearst probably didn't mix pleasure with business anyway, and she was encouraged in that thought by the pictures she'd seen of some of the women who did write for him. She wished that she had something more to show him than those things she'd made up for the college magazine, but maybe Aunt Sally was wrong about not telling her father what they were up to; he could have had some good advice. On the other hand she did like the reason Aunt Sally gave: "I think you ought to surprise him—show him you can stand on your own two feet. It isn't that your father would object, but just between us, Felicia, I detect signs in him of overcompensating for having missed so much of fatherhood, and, nice as it can be, you've got to watch that if you want to be your own person. I know I'd have been better off if my father had let me sink or swim on my own instead of buying me out of all the messes I got into." It was something to think about and perhaps accounted more for her nervousness than meeting Mr. Hearst: what if she *didn't* get a job and had to tell her father she'd failed?

Her father acted as if she were a second George Sand or something. She knew better. She'd taken literature and languages in college instead of all that history and philosophy and religion he'd studied, and she knew very well how far she was from writing anything *really* good. Her father's appreciation for literature hadn't been improved much by learning to read and write all that legal language with its long sentences and dangling clauses and qualifying words. But he always said that she took after his father, who might have been a writer if he hadn't had too much money. They'd only saved a few of her grandfather's poems and things that had appeared in the papers, and she found them so quaint—so full of "'tis'es" and "oft's" and the like—that she had a hard time deciding whether it was a compliment to be compared to him. One thing, though: she wasn't going to let whatever money she got—she didn't know how much, but everybody thought it would be a lot—be a problem. Maybe it would be useful if she turned out to have real talent and wanted to write a novel instead of, as she was beginning to suspect, just an overactive imagination and a knack with words. Whatever, she felt she first had to prove herself in something where she could use whatever talent she did have with words, and a newspaper seemed the logical place for her. So she wanted a job badly both for herself and to reward at least some of her father's faith in her.

Meeting Felicia at the door, Sally said, "Well, you certainly look like little Miss Prim. Mr. Hearst will think that I've brought my maid."

"It's the way I want to look, Aunt Sally. Anyway, there's no time to change."

"Yes, you saw to that, didn't you? Well, we'll take the electric."

"Oh, no, I want to drive. I'm so nervous it'll keep my mind off the interview—"

"And make *me* a nervous wreck the way you drive."

"I'll go slow—honestly."

Felicia's father had given her a shiny black Model-T as his graduation present. At first she'd been a little disappointed that it wasn't a fancier car, but she'd come to love it. She'd found it easy to drive with the foot pedals to shift gears, and she didn't feel as conspicuous as she did at the wheel of her father's snappy touring car. Georgia, being an actress, liked to be conspicuous, but Felicia didn't. It bothered her when men would hoot, "Ganway—watch out for the woman driver!" or make an elaborate farce out of jumping out of her way. She guessed that her father, who knew a lot about cars and evidently a lot about her too, had picked the Ford out of consideration rather than economy. Since Sally didn't know anything about this kind of car, Felicia set the throttle and choke herself and then went around front to crank it. Her father was always fussing at her to be careful about the kick of the crank, and she certainly would today. She just prayed it would start before she worked up a sweat as she sometimes did. A jerk—and nothing. Another—and just a sort of wheeze. Felicia went back to adjust the levers, and Sally said, "The electric's so much easier, let's take that." Felicia shook her head. Once more—and the flivver began to sputter and shake. Felicia ran back and jumped into the driver's seat to cut the choke and give it more throttle to keep it going, then kicked it into gear and started off. She did drive slowly, but just avoiding all the traffic and keeping her eye out for policemen at the corners helped keep her mind blessedly occupied.

It was a long drive; Mr. Hearst's offices were in his apartment in the Clarendon at Eighty-sixth Street and Riverside Drive. It was known to be the biggest apartment in New York with some thirty rooms covering the building's entire eleventh and twelfth floors and the roof garden above. When Felicia and Sally were ushered in by a doorman and directed to the special elevator that led to the publisher's office, Sally said, "From the looks of this place, I'm thinking of asking him to pay my bill."

"Aunt Sally, you wouldn't."

Sally laughed. "You don't have a sense of humor today. Well, I'm not surprised. Of course, I wouldn't, but he is a slow payer. All the dealers around town complain, but they don't dare do anything about it since he buys so much. Joe Duveen was telling me that old Mrs. Hearst—his mother who has all the money—said that 'Whenever Will feels badly he just goes out and buys something.' He ought to take a lesson from your Uncle James, who won't part with a nickel until he's sure the picture is worth twice what the dealer's asking. But then, of course, we'd all be out of business."

When the elevator stopped, they were shown into an anteroom filled with worried-looking men. Some were pacing and others sitting talking quietly together. One started arguing loudly with the rolly-polly man who'd ushered them into the room: "Listen, Thompson, you promised that the chief would see me right away. Damn it, we've got deadlines to meet . . ."

Thompson said, "There are ladies here, sir. Mr. Hearst always sees ladies first. Right this way, ladies."

The room they entered could have passed for a combination antique shop and art gallery, cluttered as it was with vases, statues, paintings, ornately carved furniture. The man who rose from behind a desk to greet them was large, jowly, soberly dressed in business black. Though he was nearing fifty, his hair was still sandy, his cheeks smooth-shaven and youthfully pink. He looked a figure to command votes, as he'd tried to do over these last years—for mayor, for governor, for president—and not at all the sinister character his opponents made him out to be. For so imposing a man, he seemed strangely shy. When he offered his hand it was limp; his smile was small and fleeting; he only mumbled a greeting. But his eyes, close-set and a light indeterminate shade of blue-gray, gave Felicia the feeling that he could see right through her. He waved them to chairs, slumped down on his own and simply stared at them.

Felicia was glad that Aunt Sally was along, because she wasn't sure she had a voice herself. Aunt Sally, however, started right out prattling about the things Mr. Hearst had bought in her gallery and complimenting him on every object she could see around her. Hearst listened for a while and then with another small, mirthless smile, said, "I hope you aren't here to sell me anything, Mrs. Hancock. My mother's complaining again that I buy too much."

"No, indeed, Mr. Hearst. I'm here to introduce you to my niece, Felicia Van Alen. She's a writer . . ."

The Hearst eyes swung to Felicia and drilled into her. The butterflies invaded her stomach. He seemed almost to be talking to himself. "Van Alen . . . Van Alen . . . Van Alen . . . oh, yes . . . I suppose you know, young lady, that our papers have been writing about how your father has been using that yacht of his over there in Europe to take a number of senators who have favored him with legislation for joyrides in the Mediterranean."

That pried her tongue loose. "But that's not my father. My father's Aaron Van Alen . . ."

"Ah, yes, the one we call 'the public defender.' Fine man, that."

Felicia had brought a copy of her college magazine. She held it up and said, "I've had some stories published in this . . ."

Hearst didn't even glance at it. He kept looking at her. "From the way you dress, you look like a sensible girl," he said, "and with a father like that . . ." Suddenly he stood up and called for Thompson. When the man appeared he said, "Take this young lady to Brisbane and tell him she's Aaron Van Alen's daughter and he should find a place for her."

The interview was over. Out in the anteroom Thompson made arrangements by phone for Felicia to see Arthur Brisbane in his newspaper office the next day. She was hired, but felt let down. On the way back downtown she said to Sally, "He only hired me because of father. He didn't even care what I can do."

"That's the way of the world," Sally said. "We all like to think we're unique, but we're all judged in relation to something or someone. Hearst himself wouldn't be where he is without his mother's money. Well, at least he didn't ask to look at your legs."

"He didn't have to. I had a feeling he could see right through my clothes."

"So did I," Sally said. "Amazing eyes. I think you might find it quite interesting working for him. By the way, I don't think there's any call to tell your father exactly what happened. He might have some silly notion of not wanting to be beholden to Mr. Hearst. The important thing is that you do have a job. The *rest* is up to you."

By the time her father came by that night, Felicia was in a new mood. She was looking forward to tomorrow as she'd never before looked forward to a tomorrow. Her excitement was greater than her fear. She was almost glad she'd been hired on the strength of her father's name, because it might mean that they'd be more patient with all the mistakes she was sure she would make. Aunt Sally had put a bottle of champagne on ice, and her father took the news in the spirit of the occasion. He hugged her and toasted her success. "Well, well, life comes full-circle," he said. "My father—our father, Sally's and mine—worked on the old *Tribune* and published his own paper. He might be a little surprised to find that it's a girl who's following in his footsteps, but not if he could see you. You really do look like your great-grandmother. Doesn't she, Sally?"

Just then the phone rang, and Sally took it. "It's for you, Aaron—Georgia."

They couldn't tell from listening to his end of the conversation—"No!" "When?" "Do they say anything else?"—just what he was hearing, but they could tell from his face that the news was bad. Whe:

he hung up he said, "The hospital called. Mary's gone into a coma. I'd better get up there—"

"For heaven's sake," Sally said, "if she's in a coma she won't know you're there, and she's got the best kind of nurses. You've had a long day down at Princeton and you haven't even had a chance to tell us about it—"

"I'm sorry, Sally, but I have to go. You can understand why. Good luck tomorrow, Felicia . . ."

She didn't know exactly what made her do it, but Felicia said, "Wait, dad, I'm going with you."

"It'll be a shock to you," he said. "You haven't seen her since—"

"I don't care, I'm *going*."

"All right," he said, "but only if you've forgiven her. I wouldn't want you there otherwise. It wouldn't be right if you—"

"I . . . I think I have . . ."

"Well, then, come on," Aaron said. "I don't like to be alone either."

When they got into a hack to go up to the hospital, her father took something out of his pocket and handed it to her. She could just barely see from the flash of street lamps they passed that it was a strange-looking animal with a green sheen to it; it felt cool in her palm. "A jade dragon," her father said. "My Grandmother Sally gave it to me when she died, and I've kept it ever since. I can't say that it has brought me luck, but it's brought me something more important—a kind of courage to face up to things . . . You're going to need that more than I, not only tonight but tomorrow . . . Well, I don't

585

know whether you *need* it, but you deserve it, because it was once a talisman of love . . ."

Felicia couldn't speak. She was too full of her feelings for her father. But clutching the little dragon that stayed so miraculously cool, she somehow knew she could get through anything . . .

Postlude

VAN ALEN watchers—and there were many in those days when the doings of the wealthy were chronicled more assiduously than those of baseball players or stars of the new motion pictures—had a busy time keeping up with their favorite characters in the latter half of the year 1915. More or less in chronological order, the stories they came upon reported:

That a young New Rochelle housewife named Amelia Van Alen McCandless became the first woman in history to shoot an 18-hole round of golf in par . . .

That an aged recluse named Sophie Vanderbilt Van Alen died, leaving an estate in excess of ten million dollars, which was no surprise in view of her combination of names, to an already wealthy cousin, Cornelius Van Alen III, identified as a vice president of United States Steel Corporation and a resident of

Greenwich, Connecticut . . .

That the marble-trimmed Van Alen mansion on Fifth Avenue, New York, where the recluse had lived, was sold by the Van Alen Trust to make way for a hotel, much to the concern of architects and historians, who deplored "this latest evidence of the passing of America's grandest residential street" . . .

That James Schuyler Van Alen, industrialist and donor of the Van Alen Hospital and Medical Institution, was quoted as warning at the institution's annual fund-raising banquet: "We are in danger of losing our greatest source of brains, not to mention business, if we do not stem the rising tide of anti-German sentiment in this country. I have personally met the Kaiser, and I can assure you, as our former Mayor McClellan has also tried to assure you, that the picture of him and his people as beasts is wrong. Some of our finest citizens are German. You in this room know more than most the contribution Germany has made to the advancement of the healing arts. We in business know that this great industrial nation should, and could, be our most lucrative trading partner." . . .

That Peter Schuyler Van Alen, curator of the James Van Alen Collection of Fine Art, died of cirrhosis of the liver in the Van Alen Hospital and Medical Institute . . .

That former judge Aaron Roberts Van Alen sailed for Europe in the company of his sister, Mrs. Sally Van Alen Brewster Hancock, the former Duchess of Midstone. In a shipboard interview, Mr. Van Alen said that his business abroad was purely personal—

to accompany his sister on a visit to her children, the Duke of Midstone, now serving as a colonel with the British forces on the French front, and Martha—also known as Matty—Van Alen Brewster, who had volunteered her services as a nurse in the French Army. Judge Van Alen declined to comment on a report out of Washington that, as a result of recent private meetings with President Wilson in the White House, he would be performing "special services" for the President while abroad. Also among the notable passengers on the same ship was Miss Georgia Maitland, who was planning to re-create in London her most celebrated New York role—that of Nora in *A Doll's House*. Asked if she weren't afraid of the U-boat menace in view of the *Lusitania*'s sinking—Judge Van Alen's sister was originally booked on that ill-fated passage—Miss Maitland said, "This is no time for fear. The people of Britain have never been more in need of the diversion the theater offers, and I am only glad I can do my part." . . .

That Arthur Schermerhorn Van Alen, son of industrialist James Schuyler Van Alen, enlisted in a new flying corps being formed in Canada . . .

That Felicia Van Alen, a star reporter for the Hearst newspapers, was granted the first exclusive interview with Edith Bolling Galt, who will become the second wife of President Woodrow Wilson in December and is, according to Miss Van Alen's account, "charming but also very able, a woman who could be president herself." In an editorial precede to this exclusive, attributed to William

Randolph Hearst himself, the publisher wrote that "we could say as much of our own Miss Van Alen, who was accorded the privilege of an interview with Mrs. Galt because she is a member of New York's first family—first in every good sense of that word . . ."

BLAZING SAGAS OF ZEBRA'S
SOUTHERN CITIES SERIES!

NATCHEZ (891, $3.50)
by Shana Clermont
Charity Bovard had fallen in love with a Yankee! And now she had to choose between pledging allegiance to her land or swearing her loyalty to her man . . .

SAVANNAH (953, $3.50)
by John T. Foster
A widow at twenty, Laurel Colton inherits her husband's ship and becomes a Confederate blockade runner—and sails straight into the arms of tawny, muscular, Yankee David Manchester!

MEMPHIS (807, $2.95)
by Shana Clermont
Yankee Blake Townsend becomes a helpless victim of Melanie's sweet southern charm. But does she truly care for him, or will she use his love for the sake of the Confederacy? . . .

VICKSBURG (789, $2.95)
by John T. Foster
Just as the nation is cleaved in two, Nora falls in love with two different men. Will she belong to proud, northern Fletcher, or give her heart to virile, southern Beau?

NEW ORLEANS (826, $3.50)
by Miriam A. Pace
Marget, Fleur, and Aurore are three rich, young Southern beauties, eager to grow up and know passion and love. When the Civil War erupts, they became three courageous women whose lives would never be the same again!

Available wherever paperbacks are sold, or order direct from the Publisher. Send cover price plus 50¢ per copy for mailing and handling to Zebra Books, 475 Park Avenue South, New York, N.Y. 10016. DO NOT SEND CASH.

HISTORICAL ROMANCE IN THE MAKING!